S
A

## CASUALTIES OF WAR

"Don't just stand there and tell me it can't be done. Find a way!"

Bristling, Rodney fired back. "What, so if I acknowledge reality, that somehow means I care about Ronon and Teyla less than you?"

"Both of you, stop it," ordered Carson with a vehemence he rarely showed. It made an impact; Rodney's mouth snapped shut. With that hard set of his jaw, his own sadness and frustration became visible at last.

The doctor finished bandaging John's forearm before speaking again, more gently. "Listen to yourself, John. What are you really hoping to find?"

"I don't know! But what's our alternative? Just let them go, forget about them?"

"Forget about them, certainly not," Carson replied, his voice solemn. "Let them go…aye, lad. I'm afraid so."

John scrubbed a hand over his jaw, fast running out of rational points to make. Hell, he was starting to run out of irrational ones. All he had—all he knew—was the fact that his teammates were out there, and it went against everything he held fundamental to leave them, whether for an hour or forever, where they lay.

Where *his* mistake had led them. He'd sent Rodney's group off unarmed, and this was the result.

"God *damn* it," he whispered.

# STARGATE · ATLANTIS™

# CASUALTIES OF WAR

## ELIZABETH CHRISTENSEN

# FANDEMONIUM BOOKS

An original publication of Fandemonium Ltd, produced under license from MGM Consumer Products.

Fandemonium Books
PO Box 795A
Surbiton
Surrey KT5 8YB
United Kingdom
Visit our website: www.stargatenovels.com

# STARGATE
## ATLĂNTIS™

METRO-GOLDWYN-MAYER Presents
STARGATE ATLANTIS™
JOE FLANIGAN   TORRI HIGGINSON   RACHEL LUTTRELL   JASON MOMOA
with PAUL McGILLION as Dr. Carson Beckett and DAVID HEWLETT as Dr. McKay
Executive Producers BRAD WRIGHT & ROBERT C. COOPER
Created by BRAD WRIGHT & ROBERT C. COOPER

WWW.MGM.COM

ISBN: 978-1-905586-06-6
Printed in the United States of America

*For David,*
*who would have gotten such a kick out of this.*

**Many thanks to:**
• Sonny Whitelaw, for introducing me to this playground and for being an incredible mentor and friend every step of the way;
• my family, for always being excited to see or even help with my work, regardless of whether or not they know what a Stargate is;
• the U.S. Air Force, for giving me both my day job (by hiring me into its Engineering Directorate) and my night job (by authorizing the Stargate series);
• and, most importantly, my husband James, for so very many things—among them, that evening up on the Boundary Waters when I said, "I'm trying to put together a plot for a new Atlantis novel," and he promptly came back with "What if there were these whips…"

# PROLOGUE

There were no letters to write.

Elizabeth Weir had sat down at her desk, turned on her computer, and opened a new document before she'd realized that the entire sequence was unnecessary. The bleak custom had become so familiar that it now felt wrong to skip it. For an odd moment, she considered writing the letters anyway, as if committing the words to paper might ease her burden in some way.

*It was my great privilege to work with your son for the past ten months...*

*Your daughter's strength of spirit shone through in everything she did...*

*This may be of little comfort, but his sacrifice saved more lives than you can imagine...*

She'd composed far too many such letters over the course of nearly three years. Each was unique and sincere, but at the core they all said the same things, and none of them fit this situation. Giving up, she closed the document and leaned her elbows on the desk, letting her head sink into her hands.

A soft knock on the doorframe forced her to pull herself upright. John Sheppard stood there, looking about as tired and beaten as she felt. She wondered briefly if maybe she should write the letters and address them to him.

"Got a minute?" he asked simply.

"Of course." Elizabeth gestured toward the chair in

front of her desk. Her military commander stepped into the office but didn't take the chair, instead standing with his hands clasped behind his back in a kind of parade-rest position. The stilted decorum of it looked strange on him, and it unnerved her.

"How are you holding up?" she asked, because it was the only thing that came to mind.

John offered a small shrug, barely detectable. "I don't know how to answer that question."

She knew the feeling. "You went to the mainland before I got back."

"I had to tell the Athosians what happened. It was… tough. They took it about like you'd expect—they're survivors. But it was tough."

His features were controlled, as always, but it was clear that he was weighing a decision. At last he exhaled sharply. "Look, there's no easy way of doing this, so I'm just going to get it over with."

Bringing his hands out from behind him, he took a step forward and laid a plain white envelope down in the center of her desk.

Elizabeth realized what it contained almost before he pulled back his hand. That recognition only amplified the ache that had long since settled into her chest. She looked at the envelope for a long moment, then glanced up at him. "You can't really believe I'll accept this."

"Half my team is dead." John's voice was toneless. "Two good people, people who followed me because they chose to, not because of a rank. They deserved better."

She couldn't dispute his statement. "Yes, they did. But that doesn't mean that you failed them. You're blaming yourself for events that were beyond your control."

For the first time since he'd entered the room, some of the tension in his frame seemed to abate, and his shoulders slumped. "Yeah, well, it's starting to look like I've let far too many things get 'beyond my control' lately."

"John, you're doing a very difficult job with a constantly changing rulebook," she said, doing her damnedest to sound unimpeachably reasonable. Though she knew—better than most—how difficult it could be to change this man's mind, she had to try. "All of us have made mistakes. Yes, these last few days have been an absolute nightmare, but do you honestly think that this expedition would be better off without you?"

He didn't respond directly, his gaze straying to the window, where the control room personnel were maintaining some semblance of business as usual. "I've never doubted my instincts like this before," he said quietly. The admission surprised her into silence. "When I've improvised or gone against recommendations in the past, it's always been because I had a clear picture of how to resolve the situation, and the benefits were worth the risks. This time...I got target-fixated. I lost sight of the big picture, and the expedition can't afford that."

"So you're just going to give up?" Elizabeth demanded, startling herself with her vehemence. "Leave us to fend for ourselves? That hardly sounds like the John Sheppard I thought I knew."

His eyes flared at her challenge, but too quickly he recognized the tactic. "There are a lot of officers better qualified for this position than I am, Elizabeth. Don't think I don't know how many times the SGC has told you that. Maybe it's time you listened to them."

"Your instincts and your experiences are exactly why

we need you here," she argued. "Do I have to remind you that, without your intervention a few weeks ago, a Wraith hive ship would have reached Earth?"

"Of course not."

"And more than that—" Rising, Elizabeth leaned forward on the desk. "We balance each other out, you and I. We approach problems differently, and that's what allows us to arrive at the best course of action for Atlantis. Everything we've been through out here has been faced together. Don't ask me to bring in some new officer with no conception of that."

They studied each other for an interminable time as she fervently hoped that she'd gotten through to him. More than anyone else, he'd been her anchor during her recent battle with the nanite infection, and she couldn't imagine taking on the unending challenges of life in the Pegasus Galaxy without his support.

Finally, John dropped his gaze. "My decision's been made. I'll continue my responsibilities here until the SGC sends a replacement. I'm sorry."

Elizabeth wasn't about to let him go quietly. Drawing in a breath, she played her ace. "There's just one thing, Colonel. As long as you wear the uniform of the U.S. Air Force, your duty station is their choice, not yours. And your commander-in-chief has been known to take my calls. This has always been a voluntary assignment, but I can make your transfer options very limited."

His eyebrow lifted. "More limited than Antarctica?"

"Much more. Remember, there are Air Force bases without aircraft."

There was no surprise in his expression; only resignation. "I had a feeling you'd say something like that."

Reaching into his pocket, he withdrew a small object and placed it on her desk beside the envelope.

Elizabeth stared at it, her resolve wilting. "John, please."

Defeat resonated through his voice. "I really am sorry, Elizabeth."

He didn't have any more words, and neither did she. Helplessly, she watched him leave her office, then reached down and traced a finger across the gleaming silver wings.

After allowing herself a few moments to mourn the end of something she couldn't quite define, Elizabeth sank back into her chair and opened a new document on the computer. Given this development, Stargate Command would need a full report on the disastrous events of the past few days as soon as possible. She might as well get started.

# CHAPTER ONE

*Six days earlier*

No matter how far from home a person drifted—and this was a fair bit farther than John Sheppard reasonably could have expected to drift—some things remained constant.

While the Ancient version of a washing machine bore little resemblance to anything Maytag had ever dreamed up, everyone agreed that it was awfully efficient. Still, there was only one room of the machines in the occupied section of Atlantis, and so laundry days often turned into a communal experience, much like in a college dorm or basic training.

In one corner, Teyla primly folded clothes and stacked them in a woven basket. Radek Zelenka had his head partially inside a dryer, muttering something that had to be a series of Czech expletives.

"Hate to break it to you, Radek," John remarked as he entered, "but there's nowhere in there for clothes to get stuck. If you're missing another sock, you'd be better off checking your quarters."

From the scientist's glower, John inferred that any further cursing would probably be directed toward him.

"Your input is most helpful, Colonel, thank you."

Teyla watched her team leader dump the contents of a large, nearly overflowing gear bag into one washer. "Do you change clothing more often than I realized?"

Her curious expression didn't fool John for a second. "Very funny. No, I stick to one uniform per day, except when something in Rodney's lab goes boom, or I have to crawl through ten thousand years of dust in the outer areas of the city, or—and I'm just picking an example at random—a recon mission turns into finger painting with six-year-olds."

"The Rianns demonstrated deep trust by allowing you to interact with their young."

"And I'm all warm and fuzzy about that, but even these spiffy Ancient washers took three cycles to get that green gunk out of my jacket." As he spoke, a pair of brightly-patterned boxers slipped out of his laundry pile and glided to the floor, proving once again that this galaxy really *was* out to get him.

Eyes glittering behind his glasses, Radek peered down at the fabric. "Are those *airplanes*?"

With reflexes that surprised all three of them, John snatched up the shorts and shoved them into the washer. "Some people have differential equations. I have airplanes. You want to put money on which one girls go for?"

Radek was still searching for a response when Teyla offered, "I am not convinced that either design would have a noticeable effect on any interpersonal situations… at least, not a positive effect."

Her sense of humor was becoming more Earth-like all the time. John flashed an approving grin at her.

Swiftly changing the subject, Radek asked, "*Daedalus* has finished off-loading supplies, has she not?"

Despite the innocence of the scientist's tone, John knew damn well what the real question was. The ship's arrival hadn't become a highly anticipated event because Hermiod's company was so enjoyable. "This morning," he confirmed. "Mail call will probably be tomorrow after dinner."

Radek broke into a wide smile, but an announcement over the citywide communication system cut off any reply he might have made.

"Unscheduled offworld activation."

Not a big shock. These days they had more unscheduled activations than scheduled ones. The emergence of the Asurans had thrown a serious wrench into Atlantis's standard operating procedure, assuming such a thing had ever existed. Having demonstrated in short order that they were not to be taken lightly, the replicator bastards had been testing the waters on a number of planets. They didn't seem interested in conquest, just information — and the occasional opportunity to put some of their revitalized, hard-wired aggression to use. And if they ran into a team from the city they were so obsessed with commandeering, well, that was just convenient, wasn't it?

John's team alone had run into them on three separate worlds and observed that their tactics had changed each time. He had a different word for the situation, and it wasn't family-friendly. On each mission, the team had hustled back home earlier than planned, often with weapons-fire singing past them all the way to the gate. He was willing to bet that Major Lorne's team had just found themselves the lucky recipients of the Asurans' attention this week. What fun.

A low rumble sounded, reverberating through the floor strongly enough for John to feel a faint tremor through his boots.

*That*, on the other hand, was not typical.

Apprehensive, he cast a glance across the room at Radek, finding him equally startled and equally concerned.

"That could not have been the jumper—could it?"

"No," John replied, his resolve drawn less from what he knew to be true than from what he *needed* to be true. Granted, they were fairly close in the relative sense to the bay that housed Atlantis's "puddle jumper" spacecraft, but for anything happening in there to be felt this far out...

The trio waited, all clearly hoping to hear a radio call that would reassure them. After a few seconds, the call came, but Lorne's ever-present calm had obviously been shaken.

"Medical team to the jumper bay!"

Everyone reacted in the same instant. Teyla was the first one through the door, but John's longer strides overtook hers halfway down the corridor. Adrenaline keeping his pace at something just below an all-out sprint, he barreled into the transporter at the end of the hall and reached for the control panel just as Teyla flung herself inside.

Instantly they found themselves outside the jumper bay. With his teammate on his heels, John burst through the hangar's double doors and immediately was suckerpunched by a rush of smoke.

Almost before he could grasp the implications of that, the haze began to clear, whisked out of the cavernous room by some kind of Ancient fire-suppression system. When he could see, he reflexively wished for the blindness back.

Jumper Five, having returned from its first mission after a long grounding for maintenance, was now grounded in the ugliest sense of the word. John was surprised that the craft had made it back at all. One of its engine pods was now a blackened gash in the jumper's side.

"*Pro boha*," murmured Radek from behind them, breathing heavily from the run.

The jumper's hatch opened with a weary shudder. "Some help here!" yelled Major Lorne from the rear compartment, seemingly trying to perform triage on three of his men at once.

Beckett would be here in seconds, no doubt, but seconds looked to be a precious commodity. John dashed up the ramp to one wounded Marine, Teyla to another. The Athosian smoothly took the field dressing out of Lorne's hand and knelt down to stanch the blood flowing from the sergeant's upper leg wound.

"They reacted so freaking fast, sir." Shaking his head, Lorne addressed his CO while turning his attention toward a corporal with a messy laceration above his right eye. "It was almost like they were anticipating us. And that hit on the engine pod—Colonel, I swear to God that we did everything we could think of."

"I don't doubt it, Major." Dropping to his knees with an inelegant *thud* against the unforgiving deck, John glanced at the remains of the jumper's first-aid kit and then at the face of the lieutenant lying beside it. Harper, he recalled. Matt Harper. Less than two years out of ROTC at Oklahoma—or was it Oklahoma State? Another mom-and-apple-pie kid, another officer who'd done everything ever asked of him and now had a hole in his chest to show for it.

John swallowed a curse and leaned in to apply pressure to the wound. Time to be The Colonel. "No lying down on duty, Harper. That's strictly a commander's privilege."

Harper blinked at him with unfocused eyes. "Sir," he managed. "Don't know...what happened."

"Doesn't matter right now," he said, forcing himself to ignore the blood welling in the young man's mouth. "Just hang in there, all right? You're gonna be fine."

Harper's response was a weak cough and an expression of growing fear. As he feebly reached out, John seized his wrist with one hand, maintaining pressure with the other. "Hey," he offered, aware that he sounded just a little desperate. "Remind me again where you went to school. Was it OU or OSU? It's almost football season back home, and I can't be mixing up my guys' loyalties when the game tapes start coming in." Even as he finished the sentence, the Marine's eyes were sliding shut. "Lieutenant! Stay with me here, damn it—"

He felt Harper's breath stutter just as Carson Beckett and his team moved in to take over. As John got to his feet and climbed down from the hatch, Teyla came to stand beside him, her features deeply saddened. They watched the medics, hearing the even-toned instructions passed back and forth as if working on nothing more than a broken finger. John suspected Teyla wasn't convinced by the calm. Having flown his share of med-evac missions half a lifetime ago, he sure as hell wasn't.

When Beckett finally sat back on his heels,

exhausted and defeated, John felt a familiar numbness creep into his bones. Turning away, he stripped off his sweatshirt and let it fall from his hand, the garment stained beyond repair with Harper's blood.

Although Rodney McKay's presence wasn't strictly required at the M1X-030 debriefing, he thought it prudent to show up anyway. For one thing, he wanted to know what had so thoroughly destroyed the jumper's engine pod. For another…well, it was an unwritten rule that no one skipped out on a debriefing after an expedition member had been killed. It would have been disrespectful, somehow, not to hear the report, even if Rodney had no desire to know the details of the lieutenant's demise.

In the briefing room, Major Lorne sat ramrod-straight in his chair with a hardened stare. Rodney took a seat next to Colonel Sheppard, who was hunched over his coffee mug, giving off don't-mess-with-me-today vibes. It was a warning the scientist rarely heeded, but this morning he decided to be magnanimous and resist pointing out that the Colonel's hair was sticking up in back in ways that couldn't possibly be intentional, even for him.

And people thought Rodney was incapable of tact.

"I've scheduled the memorial service," Elizabeth began, sliding into her own chair. "Tomorrow, shortly before our scheduled check-in with the SGC, so we can send Lieutenant Harper's body back then. We'll also need to pack up his personal effects to send back for his family."

"I'll take care of it," Sheppard said before she could turn to him, not looking up from the table. Of course he'd take care of it. He always did when they lost a Marine.

"Thank you." Elizabeth leaned her forearms on the table. "Why don't you start at the beginning, Major?"

"By now you probably know the basic story as well as I do, ma'am." Lorne delivered his after-action report dispassionately. "The Asurans apparently have assembled a network of human intel. We'd barely been in the village half a day when one of our guides started getting twitchy around us. He tried more than once to get us to split up. When we finally called him on it, he took off. We tracked him into the ruins, and that's where the Asurans got the drop on us."

"How many?" Elizabeth asked.

"Three—two with weapons and one who looked like a scientist or a doctor. That one came at Sergeant Dunleavy. I'm pretty sure he was planning to do that hand-through-the-forehead thing and drag Dunleavy's IDC out of him right then and there."

Whatever else might be said about those sons-of-robots, they were persistent. Unconsciously, Rodney slid his hand across his right forearm, where the scar from a similar interrogation had faded from everyone's sight but his. A Genii with a knife or an Asuran with a mind-probe—either way, it added up to bad guys who wanted their city, and he'd never been big on sharing.

"They pursued us." Lorne seemed aware that he wasn't being blamed for the results of the mission. Still, his voice was taut, frustration barely held in check. "Lieutenant Harper was hit about a hundred yards out from the jumper, but he made it inside. I cloaked us as soon as the jumper powered up. I guess it wasn't fast enough, because they shot something big at us and clipped the engine pod. It lost power immediately. We're lucky the pod retracted for gate transit. As soon as we got back into the jumper bay, the engine blew."

"Did you get a look at what they fired at you?" Rodney wanted to know.

Lorne shook his head. "Felt like a rocket-propelled grenade. It came from about the eight-o'clock position, so nobody saw it coming."

Irritation prickled Rodney's skin. At least with the Wraith they'd been able to procure some of the enemy's technology for study. How was he supposed to counteract whatever the replicators were throwing at them if all he had was a charred husk of an engine pod?

"You did well to get your team out of there, Major," said Elizabeth. "We'll have to reexamine our security posture before we undertake any more off-world missions. If the Asurans want Atlantis badly enough to canvass this many planets looking for our teams, we may need to find methods of being more covert."

"Perhaps my people can assist," Teyla suggested. "There are still many trade worlds that may not know the Athosians have relocated to Lantea."

"Thing is, these guys probably aren't going to quit." Sheppard pushed his mug forward and leaned on the table. "We need a better long-term strategy than ninja-Marines and Athosian stand-ins. What we need is a way to even the odds."

"A weapon," Ronon said, making Rodney jump a little in his seat. The Satedan spoke so infrequently in these meetings that Rodney tended to forget he was even in attendance.

Sheppard swung his chair around and pointed at his teammate. "Bingo."

"The scientists have spoken of such a weapon in your people's possession," said Teyla. "Can the *Daedalus* not bring one here from Earth?"

Rodney was already shaking his head before she'd finished the sentence. He'd considered that option on half a dozen occasions and rejected it as futile each time. "Based on the paltry effect our projectile weapons have had so far, it's a safe bet that the Asurans have strengthened the cohesive factors the disrupter would target. It was developed by the Asgard specifically to combat the replicators as encountered in the Milky Way Galaxy. While the Asurans may have started out their lamentable existence in that form, we have to face the fact that they have evolved significantly since the time of the Ancients—even more so than their Milky Way counterparts, which were infuriatingly adaptable in their own right. Should we be so fortunate as to surprise the Asurans with the disrupter once, their learning curve would render it obsolete immediately."

"Which is why we need to come up with something better," Sheppard countered.

"Oh, well, since you asked nicely," Rodney snapped back. "Look, we have a lot of very bright people in this city, many of them with a disturbing talent for spectacular destruction. The same goes for the researchers at Stargate Command and at Area 51, not the least of which is Colonel Carter. She's got a prototype of a new anti-replicator weapon in development. Unfortunately, these projects don't provide instant results and, for better or worse, she has next to nothing to test it on. It's not like this problem slipped anyone's mind. We've been working on it, but occasionally even I have trouble saving the day on a deadline."

"You could use a leg up?"

"A leg, a big toe—I'll take what I can get."

The Colonel swiveled back toward the head of the table. "Then I think it's time to reprioritize P7L-418."

Elizabeth's somewhat shuttered expression now closed down completely. Rodney grimaced. This was bound to be interesting, and not in a pleasant way.

A few weeks ago, the linguistics division had briefed the senior staff on a recently-translated historical record from the city database. The battle for P7L-418 had been, up until the siege of Atlantis, the largest conflict of the Ancients' war with the Wraith. The planet had housed a facility that the Ancients had seen fit to defend with the full might of their fleet. Rodney had started to doze off when the head linguist had begun listing all the assets involved, but he understood that over the course of eight days a large number of ships, on both sides, had been destroyed or damaged beyond recovery.

He'd snapped awake when the timid man had explained just what the Ancients had been protecting so fiercely.

"We've been over this," Elizabeth said, her fingers tightening around a pen. "The records implied that the facility on 418 was used primarily for weapons development. It also implied that high-risk testing was conducted there. That could mean any number of things, many of which may involve extreme hazards to our personnel or others."

"There's no way to know unless we take a look," Rodney pointed out. "If I can get my hands on a prototype weapon or even some of their notes, it might be enough to provide a jump-start on something we can use the next time any replicators come out to hassle us."

"And if the research was flawed?" Elizabeth asked quietly.

She didn't elaborate, but Rodney got the inference; it was the reason he'd agreed, however reluctantly, to steer clear of P7L-418 during the first round of this debate. A year ago they'd thought the abandoned Ancient project on Doranda would solve all their problems, and that hadn't gone too swimmingly for them. Or for the better part of a star system.

"We've learned that lesson," Sheppard replied, making an obvious effort not to glance over at Rodney as he spoke. "We'll approach anything and everything with all due caution. If it's a dead end, it's a dead end. But how could we be better off just sitting back and hoping an easier solution presents itself?"

Atlantis's leader had faced off against heads of state in two galaxies. She wasn't likely to simply cave in now. "The database is extremely vague about the aftermath of the battle. We know the Ancients drove the Wraith away from the planet, but a later record makes reference to the facility eventually being abandoned."

"Because they were losing the war and the fleet had to be recalled to defend Atlantis."

"We can't be sure that was the reason, John," Elizabeth maintained. "If the work being done there was so critical that the Ancients spent eight days and half a dozen ships protecting it, why would they then give it up?"

Rodney fielded the question. "The obvious possibilities are that they either lost interest in the research or took everything useful with them."

"Or something catastrophic happened." Elizabeth looked at him. "Did you get any details out of the database that even hinted at what they were working on?"

"Only in the most general terms. As best I can tell, the facility was a directed energy lab, which means there's a chance it met some kind of nasty radioactive end."

"Which is why the SGC keeps sending us shiny new MALPs," Sheppard insisted. "If the scan is clear, I don't see any reason why this mission should be more dangerous than any other, and there's an opportunity for a major gain. What am I missing here?"

As much as it pained him to admit it, Rodney was in complete agreement with the Colonel. "This might give us the edge we need." When Elizabeth's eyebrows climbed in surprise at their tag-team approach, he explained, "I recognize and accept your points. I accepted them the last time we discussed this, but that was before we started running into firefights on every other planet. Circumstances have made it no longer advisable to ignore the potential of this facility. If directed energy research was conducted there, it's possible I'd be able to find something that would exploit the Asurans' molecular cohesion with more success than a standard disrupter."

Sitting back in her chair, Elizabeth pinched the bridge of her nose. "I understand. I just hate the idea that this expedition seems to be turning into an arms race."

"I'm not wild about it either." Sheppard held firm, as resolute as Rodney had ever seen him in a briefing. "But I'm really tired of giving eulogies."

It all came down to that, didn't it? Rodney had a healthy sense of self-preservation, but even he could rationalize facing a potential hazard if it offered some hope of mitigating known hazards in the future. And the Asurans were a guaranteed hazard.

"I believe the journey to be worthwhile," Teyla said. Ronon gave a curt nod of assent.

"All right. P7L-418 goes to the top of the list." Elizabeth checked the calendar on her datapad. "Let's aim for the day after tomorrow. But if anything doesn't add up on that MALP scan, I'm scrubbing the mission."

The Colonel nodded, already rising from his chair. "Pre-brief and MALP deployment at 0800," he instructed his team.

Rodney followed him out when the meeting disbanded, the room's tinted wall panels rotating with graceful precision to offer them exit. "I assume you realize that we really don't have any idea what we'll find out there," he felt compelled to point out. "I mean, irrespective of the facility, we've got almost no data on the planet that houses it."

Sheppard tossed him a smirk, though the humor looked a bit artificial. "In what way would that be different from usual?"

He headed off down the corridor. Rodney sighed. "Depressing but true."

"Attention to orders!"

The military contingent of the Atlantis expedition came to attention as one, the unified clap of their boot heels reverberating through the gate-room. Lieutenant Laura Cadman stared straight ahead at the assembly of motionless gray figures, taking a kind of comfort in the formality. Atlantis was both the most intense and the most laid-back assignment she'd seen in her young career.

Every one of her teammates was a consummate professional, and no one so much as blinked when stuff hit the fan—but it had been ages since she'd last seen anyone salute.

Granted, their uniforms didn't have obvious rank insignia, so spotting senior officers in time to salute would have been a little tricky until the faces became familiar. But if Laura knew anything about the Corps, she knew that there was always a way to enforce protocol if desired. Their commanding officer just didn't seem interested in enforcing it.

Even so, a little bit of military tradition never hurt anyone. Laura was damned proud of being a Marine, and of everything that came along with that title. She knew she wasn't alone in that belief. Every so often, it felt good to remind themselves.

Colonel Sheppard seemed to get that, because he'd started calling the occasional formation. Back on Earth, government red tape was alive and well, and so the 'administrivia,' as the Colonel often labeled it, tended to take a while to reach them. When it finally did, courtesy of a *Daedalus* run, there usually were a few promotions and commendations to hand out.

"Citation to accompany the award of the Distinguished Flying Cross," Laura read aloud from the page on the podium. As she recited the description of the *Orion*'s self-sacrificing battle with the Earth-bound hive ship, the men and women who had made up the Ancient ship's last, ragtag crew filed past her to face their CO and accept their medals.

Colonel Caldwell stood in the front row, locked in at attention alongside the others. Although he was the ranking officer present, *Daedalus*'s commander wasn't presiding over the ceremony. The Atlantis detachment was Colonel Sheppard's command, and Caldwell appeared content to observe.

Laura imagined that Sheppard must have had his work cut out for him when trying to match up his people's achievements with the appropriate commendations. Outer space conflicts generally weren't covered in the awards manual. Maybe the brass back on Earth had been flexible for a change.

She moved on to the next citation, a Navy and Marine Corps Medal for a lieutenant who'd evacuated an injured Athosian hunter by jumper from a barely-accessible ridge on the mainland. After that, there were two Purple Hearts, a Bronze Star, and a Meritorious Service Medal.

Somewhere, buried in a file on Earth, there was an 'official' citation for each of these medals. Those citations didn't mention spaceships or Athosians or Wraith. They contained vaguely-worded descriptions of generic heroism at a 'forward operating location.' Anyone without clearance would see that phrase and assume Iraq or Afghanistan. It was less than honest, and it bugged all of them at one time or another, but that was life in the Pegasus Galaxy.

Turning the page, Laura came to the last medal. "Citation to accompany the award of—"

The name on the citation leapt out at her, and she halted, suddenly uncertain. She looked to Colonel Sheppard for guidance, and he responded with a small nod of encouragement.

Dutifully, she continued. "—the award of the Bronze Star to Corporal Joshua Travis."

No one spoke or even flinched, but she knew the reactions were there, hidden behind the impassive façades of her fellow Marines. The space between Laura and the Colonel remained empty as she read the citation.

It made sense, she realized partway through. The *Daedalus* had left Earth with the medals over two weeks ago. The ship must have been at the edge of the galaxy when Travis was killed. Red tape never could keep up with the fickle hand of fate.

It was a hell of a way to end a ceremony, but Travis had been a good guy and a good Marine. They owed him this much.

Lifting her gaze from the podium, she finished the well-known citation from memory and refused to change it to the past tense. "The distinctive and life-saving actions of Corporal Travis reflect great credit upon himself and the United States Marine Corps."

There was silence for a few seconds. It felt appropriate.

After the Colonel dismissed the formation, the gateroom cleared out rapidly. "Nice job today," he told Laura. "Sorry about that last one. I should have warned you it was in there."

"No sweat, sir. I'm glad he got it."

Sheppard picked up the small, flat case that held the unclaimed medal, weighing it in his hand. "Can't escape stuff like this, I guess, but damn if it doesn't drive me nuts."

Whether he was referring to the posthumous commendation or the ugliness of the overall situation with the Asurans, Laura couldn't tell. Not sure how to respond to her CO's uncharacteristically somber mood, she searched for something innocuous to say. "So…when do we get to the fun part of mail call?"

That seemed to do the trick. "Patience is a virtue, Lieutenant," Sheppard replied with a hint of a smile. "We just scheduled a new mission, so it'll probably be as soon as we get back. Unless everybody's in junk food withdrawal and can't suck it up for another day or two?"

Exaggerating her sigh, Laura grinned back. "Anything for the Corps, sir…"

"Beat it, Cadman."

"Aye, sir." She took the stairs up past the control room and headed for her quarters, hoping that the strain she'd noticed in the Colonel was a temporary condition. He was a good commander, and she wouldn't have wanted to serve under anyone else, but all the rock-and-a-hard-place decisions and steady losses had to be tough to weather.

Sometimes she was damn grateful to be a lowly lieutenant.

# CHAPTER TWO

"Rise and shine, campers." Strolling into the control room, John dropped his field vest beside the dialing computer. "It's a beautiful day in the neighborhood."

"By whose criteria?" Rodney muttered, head propped on his elbow, which in turn was propped on the database console. Elizabeth hid a sympathetic smile, knowing it would only encourage him. She'd already heard his tale of woe regarding a power fluctuation in the labs that had taken, by his probably-inflated estimation, half the night to isolate and repair. But he'd gotten the mandatory eight hours of pre-mission 'crew rest' and was bravely soldiering on. "And who put happy juice in your coffee?"

"I'm high on life," John replied amiably. "It's mission day. I'm always in a good mood until somebody starts shooting at me."

"And this time we have a chance of finding something to shoot back with." Ronon stepped into the room, one stride behind Teyla.

"That, too."

Elizabeth tried to clamp down on the twinge of unease their comments produced. She wasn't naïve; she recognized that they couldn't afford to be pacifists out here. Diplomacy was a potent tool, but it held little power when one side had considerably more to gain by taking than talking. The Stargate program on Earth had been formed chiefly to combat the reach of the Goa'uld through any and all available means. This situation was no different.

Still, she'd always told herself that the expedition had a strong moral compass. Each time they went searching for guns instead of books or tools, she felt like their needle slipped a bit further off true north.

"All right, let's get started before one of you gets the urge to do jumping jacks or something." Rodney pushed himself off the console. "First things first. We have two gate options for P7L-418."

"Two Stargates?" Teyla's forehead creased. "I have not yet encountered a world with more than one."

"We have—Earth. Until a few years ago, that is." Their chief scientist appeared to lose focus for a moment. "It was quite a trick to move a gate like that and detonate it in deep space," he recalled somewhat wistfully. "I wasn't entirely confident that we could pull it off, especially under the time constraint, but with a 747, an X-302, and the briefest hyperspace window known to—"

"How about you tell us what's behind door number one and door number two, Monty?" John broke in.

His mouth snapping shut, Rodney glared and then waved a hand at Elizabeth. She supposed the gesture was meant as an invitation, though it easily could have meant *I give up—you deal with him.*

"Yesterday morning, I helped Dr. Baker finish translating the main records relevant to P7L-418," she began, leaning over Rodney's shoulder to type a file request into the computer. The wall screen promptly came to life with a map of the star system, and she pointed to the two symbols superimposed over one planet. "There are two different gate markings. One's on the surface; the other's in orbit."

"So they had an alternate route for supplies or reinforcements." John nodded his understanding. "If the surface was overrun by the Wraith, they could escape in ships, and if there was a Wraith blockade, they could use the ground gate."

"Maybe." Rodney still sounded miffed about being yanked out of his nostalgia trip. "And if the Wraith got control of both gates?"

"Well, no plan's airtight."

"Which should we use?" Teyla asked.

"Ground gate," voted Ronon. When the others gave him odd looks, he shrugged. "The facility we're looking for is on the planet, right? Saves time."

"The database suggests that the research facility is located close to the gate, like we'd expect," Elizabeth agreed. "There's another reason to favor the ground gate, though. According to the records, the space gate was damaged. Some heavy fighting took place in its vicinity near the end of the battle, and a number of ships, both fighters and larger craft, were left derelict."

"An orbiting boneyard," John commented. "Might be worth taking a look around at some point. But as a general rule, don't use the other gate unless you're prepared to dodge space junk."

"Or end up as scattered atoms courtesy of a gate malfunction," Rodney supplied matter-of-factly. "Since a planet's gate address is determined by its location relative to various stars, both of these gates necessarily must use the same address. When Earth had two functioning gates, there was a mishap or two involving travelers being sent to the wrong gate." His fingers tapped a sharp rhythm against the console. "However, the gate with the active DHD takes priority in the system. The database specifies that the ground gate's DHD remained connected, while presumably the space gate was only engaged by a jumper's DHD when required. Given the reported damage to the space gate, we're going to the ground gate whether we like it or not."

Teyla's gaze shifted from the screen to Elizabeth. "Did the records suggest that the planet was inhabited?"

"At the time of the battle, the facility employed hundreds of people," Elizabeth answered, "both Ancient researchers and human assistants. It's not clear whether or not everyone left when the facility was abandoned."

"In our experience, the Ancients have never been all that big on taking the hired help with them when they bail out of a place," John reminded them.

"True enough." Rodney stretched his arms up over his head. "Are we ready to send the MALP planet-side, then?"

"I'd say so." Elizabeth stood back from the dialing computer as he entered the address. In the room below, points of light chased each other around the immense ring, and the event horizon flooded into being.

The MALP operator, a young engineer, had gotten this particular assignment after three different people had approached Elizabeth with tales of his skill at the video games in the rec room. He manipulated the remote-controlled probe with ease, sending it through the puddle and rotating it in the tightest circle its bulk would allow as soon as the video feed appeared on the control room monitor.

"Pretty nondescript." John peered at the image, which appeared to show an open field. In the middle distance, off to the left of the gate, a stand of tall, arrow-straight trees rose into a gray sky. The ground was rocky, covered in places by scrub grasses. "Anybody home?"

"No sign of it so far," Rodney reported from just behind the engineer's shoulder, where he appeared to be backseat-driving the probe. "Take it twenty meters southwest. No, southwest relative to the MALP. Look, just—turn right and bring it around the side of the gate."

The image on the screen bounced as the MALP trundled along, eventually reaching the edge of a long, descending slope. Judging by the view, the gate appeared to be located on a rise. Partway down, a building was tucked in against the hill. Due to the distance and angle, the camera wasn't able to bring it completely into focus. Rodney straightened and glanced over at the rest of his team. "Well, there's a structure there, at least, but no energy readings. I'm loath to move much further in that direction, because the current perspective suggests uneven terrain. I'd rather not flip the MALP."

"Easy enough for us to check out, though," Ronon said. "Looks like a short hike."

Rodney spun toward him. "Now that you've brought it up, we need to discuss your definition of a 'short hike.' Last time—"

John cut him off. "Rodney."

"I'm just saying, I get blisters."

Elizabeth watched the camera pan back across the unremarkable landscape and wished for some of her lost optimism back. Once, she had approached each new mission with a sense of eager anticipation, thinking of the knowledge they might uncover. Now, as often as not, her thoughts were dominated by the hazards they might face.

The International Oversight Authority had made it clear, after a hive ship had learned the location of Earth, that her decisions were being scrutinized—always after the fact, and from a galaxy away, but scrutinized. While job security was hardly her first priority, she understood that the risks taken by the expedition had to be carefully managed. They took enough necessary risks out here that they couldn't afford to entertain any unnecessary ones.

But John was right. They couldn't simply cross their fingers and hope for a defense against their adversaries to fall into their laps.

"How's the atmosphere on the planet?" she asked Rodney.

"Breathable. Nothing in the way of toxins, radiation, et cetera. Temperature is a comfortable nineteen—"

"Sixty-six," John corrected under his breath.

"*Must* you do that?"

"Gentlemen." There were days, Elizabeth reflected, when working with her top advisors felt a lot like herding cats.

"And, last but certainly not least," Rodney continued as if he hadn't heard, "there's a DHD."

"All right." She looked at each team member in turn. "Does anyone foresee any other areas of concern for this mission?"

Ronon and Teyla shook their heads. Rodney pulled his pack onto his shoulder, while John crossed the room to retrieve his vest and P-90. "Elizabeth, I think the biggest concern we should have right now is the chance that we'll come up empty."

No excuses, then. "In that case, I guess you have a

go." She caught her military commander's gaze and held it. "Be safe."

Teyla exited the gate with her weapon raised, visually sweeping the area. She often found that the small camera on the probe did not effectively convey to her a real sense of the planets they visited. Perhaps it was because she had lived most of her life without such pictures, but she did not find the same diversionary value in movies and television that the Earth team did. Colonel Sheppard and the Marines seemed enthralled whenever they received new recordings of sporting events, but she found their informal games on Atlantis far more entertaining, because their determination, their enthusiasm, was genuine and palpable. When watching a flat image on a screen, there was very little to feel.

Here, she had expected to find more depth of color than the MALP screen had shown. In this case, however, the picture had been accurate. She could see that the forest surrounded two-thirds of the perimeter of the elevated plain, the ground sloping down to meet the trees. The remainder was open to a range of sizable mountains in the north, many miles away. To her left sat the gate's dialing pedestal, blending in with the muted grays and greens of the landscape.

Before long, Rodney had stowed his weapon in favor of a handheld scanner from his pack. "You're a trusting soul," John remarked, his P-90 still held at the ready.

"Not really," the scientist replied absently, focused on calibrating the scanner. "I figure I have the worst reflexes on the team, so if anything unpleasant pops up, any one of you is far more likely to take care of it before I can even aim."

He didn't see John's answering grin, but Teyla shared it. Trust came in many forms, after all.

"Keep your eyes open," John told them. "I'm gonna send the MALP home."

By unspoken agreement, she and Ronon took up positions on either side of the pedestal, watching the forest for any movement, as their team leader pressed the symbols of Atlantis's address.

John tapped his radio as soon as the wormhole was established. "Control, this is Sheppard. So far, so good. Go ahead and recall the MALP."

In response, the machine obligingly rolled toward the gate and vanished into a ripple of blue.

"MALP received," Elizabeth reported. "Good luck. Radio check in eight hours."

"Understood." John closed the connection and turned to Rodney. "Anything yet?"

"Maybe." Rodney checked his watch and then squinted at the readout. "I'm getting what looks like a hit for electromagnetic energy, but something's squirrelly."

"Squirrelly?" Even the other Earth native on the team looked bemused by his choice of words.

Waving a dismissive hand, Rodney clarified, "As in odd, bizarre, downright wrong. Look at your watch."

John obeyed. "0912 Atlantis time."

"And it's still ticking, right? If these readings were correct, the second hand would have stopped dead as soon as we stepped out of the gate. The EM level's that high. Supposedly."

"Could your equipment be broken?" Ronon asked.

Rodney fixed him with a patronizing look. "Gosh, it

never occurred to me to check *that* before leaving on a vital mission. Why don't you check your gun, too, just in case?"

"Settle down," John advised. "Is there any reason to think what you're reading could be dangerous?"

"No. Even if it were a legitimate result, it wouldn't hurt us, and most Ancient equipment is shielded from EM interference." Lifting his head, Rodney pointed toward the trees behind the gate, where the ground sloped away from them. "Unsurprisingly, the readings are coming from the direction of the structure located by the MALP, so we might as well head that way."

Continuing to keep watch as they walked south, Teyla raised her eyes to the slate-colored sky. As she glanced behind them, a sudden trail of light over the mountains drew her focus. "A starfall," she commented.

Turning, John followed the direction of her outstretched hand just before the light winked out. "On Earth, they say you're supposed to make a wish when you see a shooting star."

"Only mutant crickets say that," Rodney grumbled from the front of the group. Teyla didn't bother asking for an explanation of the peculiar statement.

John shook his head. "I bet you traumatized a lot of babysitters as a kid, Rodney."

"Only one. I was ten, and she couldn't figure out my trig workbook. I merely pointed out to her that *I* might have been better equipped to supervise *her* than vice versa." When Rodney finally deigned to glance up at the sky, he frowned. "Huh. You know, that might not have been a meteorite."

He swung his pack to the ground and hunted inside.

"So-called falling stars are usually nothing more than chunks of rock, heated to the point of glowing as they fall through a planet's atmosphere," he explained, finally coming up with a pair of binoculars.

"I have seen a starfall before, Rodney." On occasion Teyla had to remind the scientist that she did not lack for knowledge simply because she had not gained it on his world.

"Not like this, I suspect." Rodney put the binoculars to his eyes. "The database suggested a fair amount of space junk remained in orbit after the battle."

Having already lifted his own viewing device, John gave a low whistle. "You're saying you think those are *ships*?"

"What's left of them. It's impossible to tell at this level of magnification, but it's likely." Rodney passed his binoculars to Teyla. She attempted to focus on a tiny dot high above them and could only make out an indistinct shape that might indeed have been a spacecraft.

"Might the second gate be among those ships?" she asked.

With a shake of his head, Rodney took his equipment back. "According to the database, the gate's in a geosynchronous orbit. From the ground it would appear to stay stationary over a specific point, one that happens to be a considerable distance away from here."

Ronon accepted John's binoculars and studied the sky for himself. "Guess they weren't kidding about this being a major battlefield."

"If those *are* ships, they're not going to come down on our heads in a fireball or anything, are they?" John asked warily.

"I think they're in too high an orbit. If we didn't have the highest-powered binoculars that taxpayer money can buy, we wouldn't even have been able to see them. What you saw falling earlier was probably a Dart." Rodney repacked the binoculars and slung the bag back onto his shoulder. "They've been up there for ten thousand years—they'll probably last another few hours. Besides, most of the mass would burn up and disperse in the atmosphere."

"Okay." John didn't sound entirely convinced, but he resumed walking. "Back to tracking some squirrelly EM readings."

Although the team remained on alert, the brief walk was rather pleasant. A cool breeze rippled the tree branches, and birds chattered musically overhead. Coarse grass brushed against Teyla's ankles as she moved across the ground.

Finding himself at the edge of the slope, Rodney glanced downward and stopped abruptly. "If that turns out to be what we came for, this'll be a bit anticlimactic."

Teyla looked below them to where the forest met the rising terrain and saw a building nestled against the foot of the ridge. Its architecture might have been Ancient, but it was small, hardly the size of Atlantis's gate-room.

"Maybe there were more buildings, and this is the only one left." John started down the hill.

"Hold up!" Rodney suddenly ordered.

Startled, John halted and pivoted to face him.

Bent over his scanner again, the scientist frowned. "Now this is just getting creepy."

"Want to explain?" asked Ronon.

"If I could, it wouldn't be creepy." Rodney scrubbed a hand through his short hair, clearly frustrated. "Something's messing with the scan. For a second there, it was showing a group of life signs set back in the forest, but only for a second. It's like the equivalent of getting a noisy signal, or static, or…something."

"Is the effect more pronounced now that we are closer to the building?" Teyla suggested.

"Hard to tell, but I think so. In any case, there's an easy way to find out." He motioned for the group to continue.

Teyla noticed that Ronon watched the forest more carefully while they made their way down the slope.

As they neared, the true state of the building became clear. The single-level structure was intact, but clearly damaged. Great gashes had been torn in the roof, and scorch marks marred the material that made up the walls. Teyla recognized the burn patterns; this was the work of Wraith Darts.

Making a circuit around the building, John reached out to touch a charred section of wall. "Feels like the same stuff we have on Atlantis," he said. "If this is the research facility…"

Ronon finished the thought. "The Wraith must have come back after it was abandoned."

"Question is, was that ten thousand years ago or ten days ago?" John bent to examine an errant piece of roof lying near the entrance, where the door was oddly undamaged. "I'm betting it was closer to the first option, but it'd be nice to know for sure."

A row of delicate flowers growing against one wall captured Teyla's attention. She looked closer and found them surrounded by freshly tilled soil. "Someone has been here recently," she called to the others. "Look at the ground."

"I doubt the Wraith are taking up gardening as a hobby," Rodney said.

"No, she's right." John adjusted his grip on his weapon ever so slightly. "If this area had been left alone for even a few years, it would be completely overgrown with plants by now. And we've see a few *thousand* years turn a hive ship into a mountain. Somebody's keeping this place up."

"Maybe they should have started by fixing the roof instead."

A soft click caused all of them to turn toward the door, which Ronon had opened. "Oh, great!" Rodney's eyes bulged. "Thank you for carefully considering the possibility of a booby-trap before going full speed ahead."

"Who would set a trap in a ruin?" Ronon retorted.

"I don't know—maybe the same type of person who does landscaping on ruins?"

"Well, it's open now, and we're still here," John said reasonably. "And we didn't come all this way just to take pictures for Better Homes and Gardens."

"I'll stand guard." Ronon took up a post by the door. As always, Teyla appreciated his instincts. The fleeting life signs Rodney had noted earlier had not strayed far from her mind.

Activating the flashlight on his P-90, John eased forward, Rodney close behind. Teyla entered the building last, her vision adjusting gradually. Some sunlight filtered through the damaged roof, but Rodney switched on a flashlight to improve matters.

As the light beams played over the room, Teyla felt

a pang of disappointment. If there had been anything of value in this place, surely it was beyond recovery now.

Laboratory equipment and computers similar to the ones found in Atlantis were strewn across the floor in pieces. Long countertops had been ripped from the walls and splintered. One corner held a number of warped, sagging cabinets which must have been consumed by a fire.

John let out a long breath. "Damn," he said quietly. "I guess it was a long shot, but—"

"Don't start moping just yet." Rodney was still taking readings. "If this place is dead, why is my scanner going six kinds of crazy right now?" He crossed the room, stumbling only once over the rubble while continuing to track the elusive signals. "Aha—what do we have here?"

The back wall, which appeared to Teyla to be flush against the hill behind the structure, nevertheless contained two more doors: one with a standard handle, and one with no handle and a familiar-looking panel mounted beside it.

"At the risk of opening myself up to more Monty Hall jokes, there's something behind this door." A trace of excitement crept into Rodney's voice as he edged closer to the panel door. "I should have known. Why build a critically important facility out in the open if you don't have to?"

"You're saying there are more labs built into the hill?" asked John, his dejection fading.

"Significantly more, I suspect. Come here," Rodney told their team leader, jerking his head with an air of impatience. "Make yourself useful and give me some light. I only have two hands."

John rolled his eyes and acquiesced, each step crushing

shards of glass under his boots. He took Rodney's flashlight and held it in one hand, directing the beam from his P-90 with the other. "I gotta say, nothing makes a guy appreciate his position on the Atlantis food chain like being ordered to hold a flashlight."

"Many people with more postgraduate degrees than you have gotten me coffee, Colonel Uppity." Rodney reached for the panel next to the first door. Before he could attempt to pry it open, the panel responded to his touch, sliding back to reveal an illuminated map.

"It still has power," John noted, turning off the flashlight and stuffing it back into Rodney's pack as the scientist studied the map. He reached for the handle of the other door and found it locked. "What do you suppose is behind this one?"

"A closet." Rodney dismissed the idea, focused on the panel. "Nothing technological. This one, on the other hand…"

"Is it possible this facility houses a ZPM?" Teyla wondered. Even though they had come in search of weapons technology, a ZPM would be a truly fortunate find.

"Not according to the scanner, but at this point I don't completely trust the scanner." Rodney's face split into a satisfied smile. "The extent of this place is incredible. There must be ten times more lab space concealed in the hill. If the structure was built into the hill purposely, rather than having ten millennia of dirt accumulated on top of it, the labs very well may have escaped the Wraith attack unscathed."

"That map looks like it belongs in a transporter." John leaned closer to inspect it and received an elbow to the ribs.

"Don't crowd me. I think that's precisely what this doorway is. It's just designed differently than the ones on Atlantis. Apparently here you have to choose your destination before you get in." Rodney considered his options carefully before touching his fingers to a location on the map.

Teyla waited for the door to open.

It did not.

"Perhaps it sustained damage," she suggested.

"It was working well enough to open the map for me." Rodney sounded mildly put out as he turned to John. "You try—see if it likes your blueblood gene any better."

With a half-shrug, John tapped the same area of the map Rodney had pressed, then another, and another. There was still no response. "Maybe putting the map outside the transporter instead of inside was a security feature. It'll only let you in if you're on the cleared list."

"That's…not an altogether ridiculous theory. In that case…" Fumbling in his pockets, Rodney retrieved a multifunction tool and ran his fingers down the wall below the map. He must have located an access point, because the tool slipped into a groove, and a neatly-organized rack of crystals and wires slid out toward him.

Cautious, Teyla watched from a few steps away as he reached toward the rack without hesitation. "Are you confident in your knowledge of such systems?" At his indignant stare, she explained, "You did say that this transporter is designed differently than those on Atlantis."

"The underlying principles are identical. Relax, Teyla. I'm fully confident."

"So what else is new?" muttered John, only to adopt an

expression of innocence when Rodney spun toward him.

"Everyone's a comedian. Get that light down here."

Evidently choosing to withhold any further comment for the time being, John trained his weapon's light on the rack as Rodney reached into a mass of wires at the rear.

"It's really not brain surgery," Rodney commented as he worked. "Disconnect the power supply, remove the crystal that controls the security protocol, reconnect the power supply."

"And we know which crystal controls the security protocol?" John inquired.

"In fact we do." Rodney tugged a bundle of thick wires loose from its housing. The map immediately went dark. "Our transporters back home don't have this security feature, and I've memorized its crystal set. This set is identical—except there's an additional one here." With surprising dexterity, he rotated the dissimilar crystal and slid it free. Slipping it into a pocket on his vest, he then replaced the wire bundle, and the map lit up again. "There. What did I tell you?"

His faint smugness was lost on Teyla as she stared at the map panel with increasing concern. Seeing her reaction, John glanced down. "Uh, Rodney…that thing was glowing *blue* before, wasn't it?"

"Of course it—" Rodney paled as he took in the map, now blazing red. "Crap."

An incandescent flash assaulted her, and then there was only darkness.

# CHAPTER THREE

Well, he wasn't dead, so that was a start.

The bright streaks in Rodney's field of vision required some time to identify. At last he recognized them as the holes in the roof of the Ancient research facility. Some kind of power surge had knocked him flat, and whatever illumination the transporter map had provided was now gone.

A few meters away, a focused beam of light rose from the cluttered floor, as Teyla came up out of a crouch with her P-90 raised. "John, Rodney, are you injured?"

"Ow," answered a muffled voice from somewhere nearby. Rodney took a moment to assess his physical state. He'd landed on his back amid some rather uncomfortable rubble, but aside from the painful bruises—

The door banged open, adding more light to the scene. Ronon barreled in, weapon at the ready. "You guys all right?" he demanded when it became clear that no immediate threat existed. "Where's Sheppard?"

Under Rodney's shoulder, the rubble shifted, and he scrambled to his feet. "Sorry!" he stammered upon realizing that his team leader had been pinned underneath him. "Sorry, very sorry."

Rolling over with a wheezing groan, Sheppard glared up at him. "What the hell do you have in that pack of yours? Did Radek stow away in there, or what?"

Rodney met the glower with one of his own but offered the Colonel a hand up, which was accepted. "You could have said something."

"I said 'ow'."

"Something more descriptive."

"I didn't have the lung capacity." Upright once again, Sheppard picked a few shards of glass out of his sleeve.

"What happened?" Ronon wanted to know.

Rodney wasn't entirely sure, but he wasn't about to say so. "The power requirements of this transporter must be handled differently than what we've seen on Atlantis."

"That, or disabling the security feature triggered *another* security feature," Sheppard guessed.

Their Satedan teammate didn't smile often. When he did, Rodney considered it an alarming display. "McKay, you didn't 'carefully consider the possibility of a booby-trap'?"

Just what Rodney needed: someone else on his case. "Discover the wonders of irony some other time. This was a power surge, not a failsafe trigger."

"How can you be certain?" asked Teyla.

"Because if the Ancients had intended to seriously dis-courage trespassers by that method, they'd have built it to do more than just knock us over." He bent down to reexamine the slightly singed access panel. "Somebody want to give me some light again?"

With a grumble that sounded like 'I must be nuts,' Sheppard stepped up next to him and reactivated his light. "Maybe it's just well and truly broken, then."

"If it has a viable power source—and all indications up until two minutes ago suggested that it does—there's no level of 'broken' that I can't fix. It might require a call home for some specialized tools, but I'm hardly going to let a *door* hold us back for long."

The scanner had fallen to the floor a while earlier. Rodney retrieved it and aimed it into the open access port. The handheld device was an Ancient gadget he'd appropriated during an early exploratory trek through Atlantis's labs, and as such was shielded from the effects of electromagnetic interference. It detected the presence of EM just fine, however, and right now it was blinking like mad. The field strength was off the charts—and yet the readings didn't make sense.

"Something behind this door is emitting an energy pattern I've never seen before," he reported to the group. "It registers as an electromagnetic field, but it's not interfering with our Earth-made equipment the way an EM field should."

A short burst of static issued from their radios; Sheppard had keyed his microphone experimentally. "On the kid world, M7G-677, we couldn't even use these while we were under the EM shield," he recalled. "How is this different?"

"I don't know yet. It's as if there's a positive intermodulation effect, although I'd be surprised if it could be predicted by a standard Taylor series…" Behind him, Rodney could almost hear his teammates' eyes glazing over. Too bad for them—he did some of his best thinking aloud, and they could just deal with it. "In any case, the energy running through this thing is amplified somehow. When I removed that crystal, I may have altered the conductive paths through the rack, and the circuit couldn't handle the load when the power was reconnected."

"You're saying we blew a fuse?" Sheppard summarized.

Still facing the panel, Rodney rolled his eyes. "Yes,

that's precisely what I'm saying, except my version wasn't painfully simplistic and utterly superfluous to the point."

"So what is the point?" Ronon seemed to be in a low-tolerance mood.

"That this transporter is—or was—drawing power from something nearby. And while that something is not a ZPM, it has the equivalent energy output of one. It's likely that whatever development occurred in this facility was focused on that energy source." What had begun as a faint nudge of theoretical interest blossomed into genuine excitement. Standing up, Rodney turned toward the others. "We might get more than a weapon out of this. We might be able to, if not end, at least cut back our dependence on ZPMs."

Sheppard gave a low whistle. "You really think that's possible?"

"Possible, yes. Probable, not so much, or we'd have seen the technology in wider use elsewhere in the galaxy. But I won't be able to learn anything more until we can get into that lab and see the extent of the research."

Teyla adjusted her vest. "What do you require?"

Good question. Rodney had no idea how this energy source operated; it might have any number of unstable characteristics. He needed the transporter working, but not at the risk of causing another, perhaps larger, overload.

"A naquadah generator," he replied. "Just a small one, to provide power to the transporter when I bypass its primary power system. And a couple of other odds and ends. If we start back to the gate now, I can have the equipment here in two hours and a functioning transporter in four."

"All right, I guess we're headed back the way we came." Sheppard picked his way through the debris toward the entrance, climbing over a fallen countertop in his path.

Once outside, where he didn't have to concentrate on trying not to trip, Rodney allowed himself to mentally skip ahead a few steps. Any power source capable of sustaining itself throughout the Ancients' ten-thousand-year absence clearly had longevity comparable to a ZPM. Could it have a similar capacity? If it did, what was the tradeoff? Why weren't there wonder batteries like this all over Atlantis?

None of the answers his brain supplied to the latter questions filled him with confidence. Doranda, among other missions, had given him plenty of reasons to be wary of Ancient experimentation. Although their intentions may have been noble, the devil was in the details, and they were unequivocally lousy at cleaning up their messes. Some days he found it hard to believe that the word 'hubris' hadn't been coined specifically for them. Other days he was thoroughly convinced that it *had*.

Still, they'd come up with some damned impressive gadgets in their time, he had to admit. And if any of their technology would help him stave off the mortal peril that seemed to lurk around every metaphorical corner in this galaxy, then he'd do his best not to appear ungrateful.

The team started up the incline that led to the gate. Teyla walked with Sheppard, listening to his muddled description of a movie he hoped the *Daedalus* had brought to add to the city's DVD library. Ronon hung back beside Rodney and said, unsurprisingly, nothing.

It didn't occur to Rodney to wonder why his teammate looked so watchful until a commanding voice from behind them shouted, "Go no further!"

Then he remembered the brief glitch of a life sign he'd spotted amid the trees upon their arrival. Not such a glitch after all, apparently.

The foursome spun around, weapons at the ready, only to be met by twice as many angry locals and twice as many weapons.

So much for that whole 'not dead' thing.

Ronon studied the newcomers over the barrel of his gun. A squad of eight men and women had fanned out to surround the team, all dressed in fitted tunics of coarse-looking fabric. Each brandished a coil of unfamiliar material in a manner that identified the object as a weapon. Long and thin, it gave the appearance of metal, but he'd never before seen metal move like a snake.

"Hi there," Sheppard greeted, his pleasant tone belied by his grip on his P-90. Ronon could see the tension in his leader's stance even from the corner of his eye. "We're—"

"Do you have no respect?" spat one of the men, slightly built with close-cropped salt-and-pepper hair. "Does the Hall mean so little to your kind that you would defile it this way?"

"Our kind?" Ronon repeated, standing as tall as was possible in a shooting stance. He had a size advantage over all these people, and if he had any chance of intimidating them, he was willing to give it his best effort.

"Hang on a minute." Sheppard took a step forward. His motion prompted a flurry of activity from the guards, or whatever they were. They released their metal coils, each now holding the weapon only by a rigid handle at the end, poised to strike.

Lifting one hand in a conciliatory gesture, the Colonel tried again. "Listen, I don't know who you think we are, but it's a good bet that we're not them."

Another guard, a willowy female, examined McKay from head to toe. The scientist squirmed a little under her probing gaze. "They do not resemble Nistra, Kellec," she said finally. "No raider I have ever encountered has worn clothing of this type."

"How does that matter, Merise?" The one called Kellec kept his gaze trained on Sheppard as he spoke to his comrade. "They are raiders, Nistra or not." Addressing the team, he demanded, "Where is your ship?"

"We didn't bring one," Sheppard replied evenly. "We came through that big ring up the hill."

Kellec's eyes narrowed as he considered that piece of information. Before he could offer any judgment of its truthfulness, McKay became emboldened. Studying the weapon in the woman's hand, he raised his eyebrows. "What are those, whips?" A trace of a superior smile appeared on his face. "People, I hate to break up your fun little threat-fest, but if you really want us to capitulate, you'll have to do better than—"

His haughty statement ended there. The woman, Merise, moved before Ronon could react, her whip flying out to snatch the scanner from McKay's hand and fling it to the ground.

McKay gaped at it, yet he still managed to summon a bit of outrage. "Excuse me, that's delicate—"

The end of the whip struck his wrist with a stinging slap and wrapped itself into a succession of tight loops around his sleeve. Throughout the display, Merise barely moved.

McKay's gaze darted back and forth between his ensnared wrist and the less-than-amused whip wielder. "You know what?" he offered weakly. "Forget I said anything."

That felt like provocation enough to Ronon. He took a menacing stride toward the nearest guard.

"Worthless scavengers," the man sneered, brandishing his whip.

"Hey!" Sheppard's voice carried over the group. "Let's calm the hell down." He cast a warning glance in Ronon's direction. "*Everyone*."

The two apparent leaders regarded each other for a long moment. There were no further acts of aggression, but neither were there any signs of resolution. The standoff was beginning to grate on Ronon's nerves.

"Please." Teyla spoke in calm, measured tones. "We are not familiar with your people and customs. Tell us what offense we have caused, and we will atone for it."

With a short bark of disbelieving laughter, Kellec echoed, "What offense? You disgrace the Hall of Tribute with your weapons, you plunder its riches—"

"*Riches*?" Now it was McKay's turn to be incredulous. "The place is…" Realizing that Sheppard was giving him a very dangerous look, he wisely chose to shut his mouth.

"—and you have the audacity to ask what offense you have caused?" Kellec demanded.

"We did not recognize what your Hall of Tribute was, and we have taken nothing from inside." Placating, Teyla moved her P-90 to one side, dropping her aim. "To prove it, we will show you everything we carry. But you will need to release this man's arm." She tipped her head to indicate McKay.

After a brief hesitation, Kellec nodded to Merise. The woman's cool expression did not waver as she flicked her hand to remove her whip from McKay's wrist.

Wincing, McKay flexed his hand a few times before lowering his pack to the ground. "Fine, take a good look. But try not to touch anything unless it's absolutely necessary."

Ronon watched him take each item out of the bag but kept most of his attention on the guards. Two of them hovered behind the scientist, alert for any glimpse of a trinket from their beloved ruins among his possessions.

"We heard a great noise from inside the Hall," Kellec said, less accusing and more cautious than before.

McKay paused in his task, and there actually might have been a trace of embarrassment in his reply. "Yes, about that—we were only trying to operate the transporter. For informational purposes. We didn't do anything that can't be, uh, repaired."

Strangely, the guard leader didn't seem upset that they might have caused damage. Instead, he was looking with fascination at some of the equipment McKay had spread out on the ground. "Like that which the Hall contains, but not the same," he said, half to himself. He raised his eyes to Sheppard. "You have the ability to use the tools of the Ancestors?"

In answer, Sheppard took his life sign detector out of his vest pocket and turned it toward Kellec, displaying the lighted screen. "Not all of us, but some do."

The guards' cool response to his demonstration was

unexpected, yet not unwelcome. Ronon had gotten used to witnessing extreme reactions from strangers to the news that the Earth team carried Ancestor blood; everything from near-worship to outright hostility. These people, by contrast, seemed mostly intrigued.

"Then they cannot be Nistra," Merise said quietly to her leader.

"Indeed not. Rather, they are our kindred."

Kindred? Ronon shot Sheppard a questioning glance, which was returned.

Kellec stepped closer to them, but his bearing suggested no threat. "You truly came through the Stargate?"

"That's right," said the Colonel.

They must have done something right, because the whips were put away at last, affixed to the guards' woven belts.

"I am Kellec, chief warrior of the Falnori."

Relaxing a little, Sheppard lowered his weapon, and Ronon followed suit. "Lieutenant Colonel John Sheppard. My team—Teyla Emmagan, Ronon Dex, and the one freaking out about his gear is Dr. Rodney McKay."

"A pleasure," McKay muttered, refusing to be distracted from gathering his equipment.

"We're explorers," Sheppard continued, "and we're interested in learning about the work that went on here back when the Ancients were around. That's all we wanted—we didn't come to steal anything from you."

A half-truth, Ronon thought; if they hadn't come upon a native populace, they gladly would have taken anything they found of use.

Kellec, however, was preoccupied with something

else. "Your trespass in the Hall can be forgiven. But you entered while carrying weapons, and that is a more difficult matter."

"Wonder what the over-under is on how many shrines we mistakenly desecrate this month?" McKay hauled his pack onto his shoulder again.

"I'm not the city bookie," Sheppard replied tightly. Turning to Kellec, he said, "We really apologize for intruding on the Hall. We didn't know it was sacred to your people."

"It is not sacred, at least not in the way you may believe," the chief warrior explained. "The Hall holds great historical significance for us. It is the place where we remember the sacrifices of the Ancestors, made to defend this world against the Wraith so long ago. We do not worship the Hall, but we honor it. One way we do so is by entering only with pure intentions. Weapons of any kind are strictly forbidden on its grounds."

That declaration triggered an understanding for Ronon. "You heard us earlier, but you waited until we came outside to confront us."

With a single nod, Kellec said, "To take any sooner action would have required that we too enter the Hall while armed. Such an endeavor would have been a grave dishonor to each of us and to our houses. Even to prevent the scourge of a raid."

"These raids happen often?" asked Teyla.

Merise's features darkened, and the other warriors adopted expressions that appeared to be carved in stone.

"Too often of late," admitted Kellec. "You must come to the capital. Cestan will no doubt have questions for you, and he will be able to tell you better of the menace wrought by the Nistra."

It hadn't been presented as an ultimatum, but they were still in some trouble for the weapons gaffe, so a refusal seemed like a bad idea. Besides, if they were going to have any chance at getting back inside the ruined laboratory, they'd have to, as the Earth natives often said, work and play well with others.

Sheppard appeared to have come to the same conclusion. "Sounds like a plan," he agreed. "I take it Cestan is your leader?"

"We are citizens of Falnor, and Cestan is our governor." Kellec held out a hand, motioning in the direction of the forest. "It is not a long journey. We will arrive before the sun begins to leave its peak."

A skyward glance told Ronon that the sun was nearly overhead already.

The group set off toward the woods and soon came across a reasonably well-traveled path, the Atlantis team bracketed at the front and rear by the Falnori warriors. The canopy of trees soon swallowed most of the sunlight, giving the trek a desolate feel. Ronon's senses remained sharp, primed to detect any unexpected sound or motion. The warriors might have decided to trust them, but only up to a point. He saw no reason to do any differently.

"So there's a native populace around here," Sheppard began conversationally, keeping his voice low and his expression placid. None of the Falnori paid him any additional attention. "That would've been good to know."

"Don't look at me," McKay said, instantly defensive. "The scanner has a limited range, and I told you multiple times that it was acting up. The energy source in the facility registers oddly on what I'd call standard Ancient equipment—it must have interfered with life-sign detection. Whatever work went on here, it must have been a pretty highly regarded project. Usually the first requirement for new technology is for it to be compatible with everything that already exists."

"These people recognized the significance of the gene," Teyla observed, "and called you 'kindred'. Might they have the blood of the Ancestors as well?"

"If they're descendants of the facility's workers, I don't see why not. At one time there were a large number of both Ancient researchers and human aides living here. It's possible that this society's incidence of the gene is comparable to that of Earth." McKay's lips curved in a wry smirk. "Dating one's lab assistant, apparently, is a universal practice."

"And these Nistra they hate so much?" Ronon asked.

Sheppard shrugged. "Don't know, but I'm thinking they don't sound like folks we want to invite over for dinner."

"How would you estimate our chances of getting this Cestan guy to let us take another look around the ruins?" McKay wanted to know, his strides lengthening to keep up with his teammates.

"Once again, Rodney: I'm not your bookie. But we're sure as hell going to do our best to sell him on the idea." The Colonel scanned the trees around them, a subtle visual sweep that likely went unnoticed by everyone except Ronon.

"It is possible that the Falnori have set the transporter to respond only to them," said Teyla.

McKay shook his head. "Not likely, even assuming that some of them do have the gene. If their level of technological sophistication was that high, wouldn't they have devised something with a little more kick than those whips?"

Watching the Falnori ahead of him, moving with assurance and vigilance, Ronon said, "Maybe they have, and we just haven't seen it yet."

The idea seemed to set McKay back a step. "I'm honestly not sure whether I should be fascinated or frightened by that concept."

"There's got to be something worth a second look around here. Otherwise there'd be no reason for anyone to stage raids." Abruptly, a faint smile passed across Sheppard's face.

McKay frowned, suspicious. "What was that about?"

Sheppard's eyes glinted with amusement. "I was just thinking… So far on this mission, we've got raiders and we've got whips. All I need now is a fedora."

"Oh, good God." After giving the Colonel his most long-suffering look, McKay walked ahead. "The fact that I'm expected to obey the leadership of an overgrown teenager with a rank is perpetually mind-boggling to me."

"It's a rough life, isn't it, Rodney?" Sheppard turned in the scientist's direction as he spoke, but Ronon could tell he was sweeping the area again. For all his jokes and casual demeanor, the man's tactical instincts were well-honed. Ronon's military service on his home world had been cut short, but he'd been a soldier long enough to recognize both good commanders and bad ones. He appreciated following someone whose abilities in the field he'd never had cause to doubt.

So far everyone seemed to be relatively calm and content on this walk, but he was fully aware of how quickly that could change. They knew very little about these Falnori yet, and often the unknown turned out to be the most formidable enemy of all.

# CHAPTER FOUR

As it turned out, they didn't have to walk the whole way. Good thing, because the capital wasn't exactly right around the corner. Once they'd hiked for the better part of an hour, the forest thinned out, giving way to gently rolling hills covered in some kind of grain. There was no city yet in sight, even after John fished out his binoculars again.

When Rodney emerged from the trees and arrived at the same conclusion, he visibly deflated. "We really need to come to a consensus on what does and does not constitute a 'long journey,'" he grumbled.

Before John could think of a polite way to ask Kellec how they expected to reach this supposed capital by midday, they came upon a well-built wooden carriage, easily big enough for the entire group. Like an old Conestoga wagon, but without a canvas top, it was harnessed to an animal that resembled an oversized Clydesdale horse—if horses ever sat upright on their haunches. John was pretty sure they didn't.

"They are swift and obedient, but many of them do not like the woods," Kellec explained, running his fingers down the animal's flank. "This one is quick to startle, so it was easier to complete the forest trail on foot."

Quieter, too, John thought, which had probably factored into the decision.

Upon seeing the wagon, Rodney's displeasure grew, at least in volume. "Oh, this'll be comfortable."

"You want to keep walking, Rodney, be my guest." John grasped the side rail and swung himself up into the wagon. Taking a seat on one of the long benches that lined the interior, he twisted around to offer Teyla a hand, only to find that she'd already climbed aboard, with far more grace than he'd shown.

Ronon boosted Rodney up and then hauled himself over the side. The warriors seemed awfully agile, clambering into the wagon like circus gymnasts and taking positions along the benches. One went to the front and gathered up the reins, giving them a decisive tug.

The animal promptly plopped its forelegs down on the ground and took off at a rapid pace. Immediately John abandoned any effort to compare the beast to a horse. Its gait was more like that of a rabbit, bounding forward on both forelegs at once and then moving both its massive hind legs to catch up. It was fast, but a little on the bouncy side.

"Just for the record, my spine is being traumatized," Rodney informed his teammates in a low but distinctly unhappy voice.

Sympathizing with his scientist was even lower on John's to-do list than usual. "Try serving as the crash mat for one of your teammates and see how your spine likes *that*."

"I said I was sorry, didn't I?"

The scenery flew past, the fields of wild grain soon replaced by rows of green plants that might have been vegetables. It was clear that these areas had been deliberately planted. Civilization couldn't be too far away.

John grimaced when the wagon hit a particularly unforgiving bump and looked over at Merise, sitting across from him. "Your people do a lot of farming?"

"Crops fare well here," she replied, pushing wind-blown strands of coffee-colored hair back from her face. "We grow what we need for ourselves and for trade."

"Do you trade with neighboring peoples," Teyla inquired, "or with other worlds?"

"We have a long-standing trade agreement with the Nistra."

Huh. Something about *that* didn't add up.

The skepticism in Ronon's voice was obvious. "The people who raid your place of honor? You trade with them?"

The Falnori woman's expression was hard to decipher. John spotted frustration, for a start, but also resignation. "Our history is complex. Governor Cestan will be able to explain."

Before long, a cluster of structures rose out of the fields on the horizon. As the wagon drew closer, John tried to gauge the city's size. It wasn't a New York or Los Angeles, but it wasn't a one-stoplight town, either. More like a decent-sized suburb, maybe. Most of the buildings looked to be only one or two stories high, though one dominated the settlement, covering an area the size of an Earth city block and looming three or four stories above the others. The capital, he guessed.

Everything appeared to be built out of wood with the occasional piece of stone. Probably not all that recently, either. The construction was antiquated by Earth standards; most likely there weren't any power tools stashed away in anyone's sheds around here. Still, it all looked sturdy, and almost graceful. When they neared one of the perimeter buildings, John could see a fairly elaborate design carved into the slats that formed its roof. He'd never been much of a student of architecture, but the amount of time such a purely aesthetic detail must have taken to complete suggested that these people took their craftsmanship seriously.

The wagon slowed as it entered the city, and the packed dirt of the main street instantly felt more forgiving under the wheels than the rougher rural path had. A few other, smaller wagons traveled the street, and people milled around, going about their business with hardly a glance toward the group of warriors and visitors. Most of the foot traffic came and went from a series of small, connected buildings that might have been a marketplace. A little girl skipped happily along a stone sidewalk and was helped up by a tolerant adult when she stumbled.

Wardrobes were mostly simple, tunics and robes and the like. Some townspeople were livelier than others, but no one seemed too poor or undernourished. If the ATA gene was present and recognized here, were these the 'haves' or the 'have-nots'? Or did they draw no distinction between the two?

Set in the city center, the capital didn't look all that different from the surrounding structures, size notwithstanding. The same perfectly aligned beams—just a lot more of them. Their clean, elegant lines reminded John of a long-ago assignment in the Far East.

After the wagon came to a halt beside the sprawling capital, the warriors disembarked, and the Atlantis team followed their lead. John reached out to grab the back of Rodney's vest when the scientist performed a less than flawless dismount.

"I will inform Cestan of your presence," said Kellec,

with a slight bow of his head. "In the meantime, Merise will show you to the training field. Our warrior apprentices are working on an exercise which you may find interesting."

The chief warrior vanished into the capital through a set of double doors, leaving John and his team to look to Merise for direction. The earlier drama at the Hall of Tribute came to mind. They weren't going to just waltz into the seat of leadership without so much as a question about their weapons, were they?

She made no attempt to disarm them, though. Instead, offering only a "follow me," she led them up a stone walkway to another entrance. Once inside, John was again impressed by the level of detail in the décor, from the carved patterns along the walls to the woven mats on the floors. As they walked, some of the warriors left the group, until only two remained to share guide duty with Merise.

"Kellec mentioned the training field," Ronon said. "Is this place the headquarters of your military as well as your government?"

Judging by her expression, Merise didn't quite understand the question. "Governor Cestan is here, and the warriors serve the governor. What use would we be were we elsewhere?"

"So you all live and train here, in this capital building?" John asked.

He received a nod in reply. "Is it different for your people?"

Come to think of it, it wasn't, at least not on Atlantis.

Two flights of stairs and another door led them onto a long balcony overlooking an open courtyard in the middle of the complex. On a neatly-trimmed grass field that could have stood in for any parade ground John had ever seen, about two dozen men and women worked with whips. They completed a prescribed set of motions in perfect sync, similar to the way Teyla began her staff-fighting classes.

"How very lion-tamer Zen," Rodney observed, already sounding impatient. "How long is your governor likely to be? Because we—"

"Cool it, Rodney," John cut him off, giving Merise an apologetic look. "I take it these are new recruits?"

The Falnori showed no reaction to either John's attempt at tact or Rodney's lack thereof. "They are soldiers who have proven their ability and loyalty, and therefore have been selected to become warriors. Few are chosen for such a high honor."

So the whip-wielders they'd met were the elite troops. John wondered what kinds of weapons the rank and file carried.

"Ah." The first glimmer of a smile graced Merise's features as she looked over the railing. "They are about to begin."

In the courtyard, the apprentices had started setting up a row of body-sized bolts of cloth. Training dummies, probably. As the others watched, one apprentice stepped up to face a dummy, holding his whip out to his side, away from his body. All of a sudden, he seemed more focused—and more apprehensive. John leaned forward on the railing, his curiosity tweaked.

In a blur of motion, the whip blazed through the air, striking the dummy with a sharp *crack*—and the cloth was consumed by a blinding flash.

"Holy—" John jerked back in shock. Below, the apprentices whistled and clapped their comrade on the back. Only a pile of loose ash remained where the dummy had stood.

Rodney's mouth opened and closed twice before any actual sound came out. "How the *hell* did that happen?" he finally managed.

Either John was imagining things, or Merise looked just a bit smug. "It is a difficult skill to master," she commented. "You can understand why we would not entrust it to all of our soldiers."

For once, Ronon looked well and truly impressed. "The end of the whip can be lit."

"No." Rodney was using his surrounded-by-idiots voice again. Combined with his obvious astonishment at what he'd just witnessed, it made for an odd tone. "Simply flicking a lighter couldn't do *that*. It didn't burn conventionally at all. It's like the dummy was instantly incinerated."

"An electric charge?" John suggested.

"Better, but still woefully inadequate. No electric charge strong enough to put out that kind of heat could be packaged that way. The whip is so small, and there would have to be some method of controlling it..." Rodney's eyes fell to the whip at Merise's belt, and he paled. "God—you could have taken my hand off with that thing earlier!"

Now the warrior's expression was downright cunning. "If I had so chosen, I could have done much more."

A little late, John got the picture. They hadn't been brought up here just to kill time. This was a demonstration, and a none-too-subtle message.

Swallowing convulsively, Rodney said, "Okay, good to know. Thanks for, ah, restraining yourself."

Another apprentice faced the next dummy squarely, fingers alternately flexing and curling around the handle of her whip. Her thumb flicked against the handle, creating a barely-detectable hum in the air, just before she lashed out. Again, the dummy went up in smoke. Triumphant, the apprentice released the apparent on-off switch before returning the whip to her belt.

"Some kind of superheating effect," Rodney mumbled to himself, watching with equal parts awe and alarm. "The power requirements alone—"

"I see you have been fully introduced to our warriors."

The voice was resonant and originated from somewhere behind them. Everyone turned, the warriors bowing low.

"Governor," Merise murmured, her gaze downcast.

Cestan was, strangely enough, more powerfully built than most of his warriors. His black hair, graying at the temples, almost reached his shoulders, and he stood a couple of inches taller than John. Not as tall as Ronon, though, which was somehow reassuring.

"I welcome you to Falnor," the governor greeted as the warriors rose and moved to flank him. "Kellec tells me that you have come through the Stargate."

"We have." John went through the introductions again, and Cestan acknowledged each team member with a nod. "We got off to a bad start, what with the trespassing in the Hall and everything, so we'd like to formally apologize for that."

"I believe your error can be forgiven." Fixing John

with a probing gaze, Cestan clasped his hands in front of him, placidly ignoring the surprise displayed by his warriors. "If you did not knowingly cause offense."

"We did not," Teyla hurried to assure him. "We had no knowledge of your people's existence, let alone your customs. We intended to explore the facility in search of technology we believe may be present inside."

"Specifically, an energy source," Rodney jumped in. At least he hadn't mentioned weapons right off the bat. "You know the one. You're already using it."

John blinked, not sure what had prompted that leap of logic.

"It's a reasonable conclusion," Rodney insisted when the rest of the group stared at him. "Those whips are powered by something I don't recognize, something that's messing with my scans the same way the transport in the Hall did."

Only then did John notice that the scanner hanging unobtrusively at the scientist's side was active. When he put his mind to it, Rodney could be pretty damned sneaky.

Fortunately, their host didn't appear insulted. "You speak of the adarite," he said simply.

"Adarite?" Ronon repeated.

"An ore found in the mountains. To our knowledge, it is unique to this world." Cestan glanced from the crazily flashing scanner to Rodney's face and back again. "Kellec did say that you were children of the Ancestors, as we are," he mused. "I admit that I did not fully believe it until now."

"We live in one of their cities." John didn't see any need to tell him which one. "We have access to a fair amount of their technology."

"If that is true, could you not have overpowered the warriors and taken what you needed?"

Maybe. Probably, especially if they'd sent for Marine reinforcements. But that was a judgment made in hindsight, and besides… In any case, Cestan's frank appraisal of them was starting to make John twitchy. "That's not the way we do things," he replied.

That seemed to confirm something for the governor. After a moment, he turned toward the door, his dark blue robe swinging out behind him. "Come. I suspect there is much we can discuss."

As the team moved to comply, John got the feeling they'd just passed some sort of test.

The corridors didn't look any different the second time through, although they took a few extra turns on this pass. "You have the use of an Ancestors' city and everything it contains," Cestan remarked, setting a decisive pace. "What need do you have for more?"

Teyla lengthened her stride to keep up. "There is a race of beings which even the Ancestors could not defeat."

"The Wraith." Cestan's tone was grim. "We know all too well. Our people were fortunate that their last culling was brief."

"Well, there's them, too, but we're talking about someone else," John said. "Someone who wants our home, preferably without us in it. They're coming after us, and we were hoping to find something in the Hall of Tribute that might help us defend ourselves against them."

"We are open to many types of trade," Teyla added. "If we might be allowed to visit the Hall—"

"Perhaps we each may learn something here first."

Before Cestan reached the nearest door, a warrior hurried ahead to open it for him. John stepped through behind them and found himself in the training field they had been observing previously. The apprentices had finished their exercise and taken off, leaving a couple of dummies behind.

"As you suspected, Dr. McKay, the whips are powered by adarite." The governor held out his hand, palm up, to Merise, who placed her whip in it. "Our history tells us that many uses for the ore were once known. However, much of our knowledge of the Ancestors' work has faded from memory over the generations. Many of the machines left to us have fallen into disrepair. Mostly we are able to make adarite lamps, and of course the whips."

Leaning in, John examined the weapon. The flexible portion looked like a braid of several very thin strands of metal. One brighter strand stood out from the other, more tarnished ones. The handle had been fashioned from the same metal as the unique strand—adarite, no doubt—and was encircled by row after row of tiny etchings. "A lot prettier than any weapon I've ever carried," he admitted.

Cestan smiled. "Our craftsmen take great pride in their work. Many weeks of labor are devoted to a single whip."

"Yes, nice work," said Rodney brusquely, reaching for it. "May I?"

Merise opened her mouth—probably to tell Rodney where to stick his outstretched hand—but Cestan passed the whip to him. "I have hope that, in studying the adarite with the insight of the Ancestors, you may be able to tell us more about its other uses which have been lost to time.

It may be of some assistance to you as well."

"Governor," Merise said urgently, her eyes never leaving her whip.

"Do you have so little faith in your brethren, Merise?" Cestan arched one eyebrow and inclined his head toward his other two bodyguards. "If the visitor, who has no experience with your weapon, were to challenge two expert warriors, who would you expect to win?"

Only partially mollified, if her sharp sigh was anything to go on, Merise reluctantly stood aside.

"I can only do so much here, with limited diagnostic capability," Rodney warned, holding the whip handle up to eye level. "And I'll have to rely on our own equipment, since this adarite seems to give garbage readings to Ancient scans. Listen, I saw them turning these things on and off—?"

"Find the widest engraved band on the handle and squeeze it," Cestan instructed. "Take care to hold it away from yourself and others."

As if suddenly remembering that these things were dangerous, Rodney shoved the whip into John's hand. "Go ahead. Power it up," he directed, reaching into his pack for a gadget, presumably something Earth-made.

With a shrug, John closed his fingers around the handle and squeezed. Instantly he felt a slight tingle in his arm, and the metal strand within the whip began to glow. "Kind of tickles," he commented.

"There is a constant, minimal level of power in the handle. Pressure discharges a much greater amount of energy." Merise was obviously itching to get her weapon back, so he released the power band and handed it back to her.

"Could you give us another demonstration?" Rodney had retrieved something like a beefed-up voltmeter from his pack. "For analytical purposes."

"Gladly." The warrior stepped clear of the group and raised her whip over her head. With a spin worthy of a dancer, she attacked. The whip stood out straight and struck the nearby dummy from the side, reducing it to a brief flare and then smoke.

John had known it was coming, and it still dazzled him.

"Incredible," Rodney breathed, his head buried in his equipment. "It's an electrothermal release on the order of..."

No way was John letting *that* detail slip by. "So I wasn't far off with the electric charge theory after all?"

"Try not to let it go to your head. The generation mechanism has to be much more efficient, though." When Rodney finally looked up, he had that manic gleam in his eye that usually signaled a Nobel Prize fantasy. "This could be huge."

"We believe the adarite was the reason for the Ancestors' interest in this world," Cestan informed them.

"No, I mean *huge*. For *us*." Catching himself, Rodney amended, "That is to say, I'm sure we can help the Falnori understand the ore's properties and explore other applications as well."

Ronon folded his arms. "As well as what?"

"The discharge from that relatively small weapon is strong enough to incinerate organic material. I suspect it would also have the effect of superheating the water in a human body, the results of which would be both spectacular and gruesome." Rodney glanced at the warriors, whose expressions confirmed his assumption. "It breaks down the structure of whatever it touches. Just imagine what kind of damage it—or, better yet, a scaled-up version—could do to nanotechnology."

He'd had John's attention before, but the word 'nanotechnology' provided a jolt of its own. "You think it would work against the Asurans?"

"It would undoubtedly have a disruptive effect on their molecular cohesion, and the discharge frequency varies enough that adapting to counter it would not be a trivial task. As an added bonus, it probably wouldn't do too badly against a Wraith, either." Like usual, Rodney was already about five steps ahead of the others. "We'd need to investigate better delivery methods, specifically something that wouldn't require such close proximity to the target. The potential applications are virtually unlimited. If we explore the Ancient research facility, I'm confident we'll find data to jumpstart our efforts."

This was what they needed, what they'd come for—a fighting chance.

"You are interested in learning more, I take it," Cestan remarked, a trace of amusement in his voice.

John stared at the whip in Merise's hand and felt a flicker of guilt for his excitement. No matter how many jokes certain teammates cracked about Pavlovian responses, he didn't harbor any deep and abiding love for weapons. Weapons broke stuff and killed people. He knew that at least as well as anyone; he accepted it as an ugly yet fundamental aspect of his profession. Nowhere in the oath did it say he had to like it.

But others had weapons, too, and he sure as hell didn't

like sending folded flags and empty explanations back to grieving families. He couldn't stop the Asurans from coming for Atlantis any more than he could stop the Wraith from needing to feed, but he could defend his people with everything he had. If that meant appearing a little too fascinated by firepower on occasion, he'd live with it.

"Yes," he told Cestan, his gaze still resting on the whip. "It's safe to say that we're interested."

Teyla had frequently heard her Atlantis colleagues refer to a man named Murphy. Experience had taught her that the law named for him was often valid. However, she preferred a different Earth maxim: if something appeared too good to be true, it often was.

For that reason, she remained more cautious about this new development than her teammates. Moreover, she found their reactions noteworthy. It had come as little surprise that Rodney had kept up a constant, one-sided conversation ever since taking his readings of the weapon. She had not, however, expected Ronon's rapt attention, and John… John's demeanor suggested a sense of hope, something she hadn't seen from him in quite some time.

"How readily available is this adarite?" asked Rodney, breaking out of his academic fugue at last. "We'd need a sizable amount just for study, to say nothing of actual development and fabrication of armament hardware."

"We'd be happy to work with you on a beneficial trade agreement," John told Cestan. "Either for services—like you said, we may be able to develop other applications for adarite—or for tools or raw materials. There are a number of ways we could help your people."

"Regrettably, our supply of adarite is quite limited. That is another subject we must discuss." The governor's grim expression lent weight to Teyla's concern. Nothing worth having was ever easily won. "The mines are located deep in the mountains. For generations, access has been controlled solely by the Nistra."

That name again—so intertwined with everything they'd learned about these people. "Would you tell us of the Nistra?" Teyla asked. "How have they become both a trading partner and an adversary?"

"A question that has been asked by all of us at one time or another," Cestan replied, his resignation evident. "We were one people, long ago. When the Ancestors departed to battle the Wraith elsewhere, they left many heirs among the populace. Some of these heirs had the ability to operate the devices that remained, and thus they held positions of importance. Those who were purely of this world began to believe that the heirs, both able and not, were favored over them. Only a few generations passed before the Wraith returned."

His sorrow appeared fresh, though his tale was born of events long past. "The culling that followed was as brutal as any described in our history. Our people tried to protect themselves by fleeing into the Hall of Tribute and other shelters. But many could not reach a place of safety in time, and the city was ravaged. Those who survived soon became bitterly divided. The able heirs were accused of protecting their brethren at the expense of the pure natives."

Recalling what Merise had said earlier—that someone with the gene could not be Nistra—Teyla said, "So the heirs of the Ancestors became the Falnori, and the others became the Nistra."

"Yes."

"Were the accusations true?" Ronon asked. "Was preference given to the heirs?"

Teyla tensed at the blunt query. Cestan's features tightened, but his response was measured. "Never. Not then, and not now."

"You're sure about that?" John pressed. "No offense, but all this started thousands of years ago."

"I will demonstrate. Kellec mentioned an Ancestor device you carry?" He lifted his hand in a wordless request.

John pulled out his life sign detector and gave it to the Falnori leader. The screen did not light. When Cestan passed it to Merise, however, it awakened.

"You rose to power without having the gene—the ability," Ronon said.

"We do not trouble ourselves with who was born to whom, nor does it matter to us who does and does not possess the ability. To borrow your phrase, it is 'not the way we do things.'" Cestan was emphatic on that point. "By now, after generations of damage and disrepair, we have so little left of the Ancestors' work that the ability is all but meaningless. Yet the rift has been torn, and it cannot be mended."

"The Nistra settled new territory, near the mines?" John guessed.

"At first they claimed merely to desire their own land. Our forebears and theirs agreed to declare the Hall and the Stargate neutral territory, to be used for trade and remembrance. For centuries we lived apart and in peace. Because they were nearer the mines and our lands produced better crops, we offered them a portion of our harvest each year in exchange for a quantity of adarite. Beyond that our two peoples rarely met.

"As our population grew," Cestan continued, "more adarite was required. Just over one hundred years ago, the Nistra moved their villages closer to the mining territory in order to increase production, and they began to act as though the mines belonged solely to them. It was then that the trade agreement began to sour. At last the Nistra seized the mines and threatened any Falnori who dared approach."

Rodney frowned, his scanners forgotten for the moment. "And you're still giving them food every year?"

Spreading his hands wide, Cestan answered, "We have little choice. By honoring what remains of the agreement, we receive a small amount of adarite. Were we to break it, we would receive none. Adarite power is long-lived, but not limitless, and the release of that power quickly damages the other materials contained in the whips. They do not last long. Although we also need the ore for the few tools of the Ancestors we still possess, it is mostly needed for the whips, which provide our best defense against the Wraith…and others."

Teyla was under no illusions about the meaning of 'others' in this context. "Your warriors spoke of raids on the Hall," she prompted.

Cestan's mild frustration quickly transformed into fury. "An outrage that defies comparison," he spat, stalking across the field. "It has occurred only within the past few seasons, though it has been more frequent of late. The Nistra had always honored the Hall until now. Suddenly they have no respect for its meaning and come in groups to ransack it for trinkets. It has become so intolerable that, for the first time in generations, we have considered denying this harvest's trade. They have even attempted an incursion here in the city, but they seem much more interested in the Hall. As if we have nothing of value to them."

"And the no-weapons rule prevents you from placing guards," said John.

"As does the fact that it is not our land to guard. Instead we send daily patrols into the forest, like the one you encountered."

"Is it possible that only a small number of the Nistra are involved?" Teyla asked. "Have you not tried to discuss the matter with their leadership?"

"Overtures have been made and rejected. Confrontations end in violence and sometimes bloodshed. I fear all paths may end in full conflict."

The governor turned back toward his guests and laid out his entreaty. "We are building a stronger army, but proven warriors are few. You have the might of the Ancestors. If you could provide us the means to properly defend ourselves against the Nistra threat"—here his gaze swept over their P-90s—"we could spare some of the adarite from our meager stores for your use."

Now the terms had been made plain. The Falnori were less interested in any scientific advancement than in better weaponry to defeat their enemies. *Is your goal any nobler than theirs?* Teyla reminded herself.

Still, they couldn't simply hand over a cache of guns and explosives.

John cocked his head. "What did you have in mind?"

Satisfied that his visitors hadn't immediately refused his offer, Cestan explained, "Something that can reach further than our whips, and that does not depend on adarite. For this we would give an amount of ore proportional to the number of Falnori you are prepared to equip. In time, if fortune is kind, perhaps the adarite will be more available."

"We may be able to make a deal."

At the Colonel's words, Teyla spun toward him, startled. This was hardly their usual method.

Apparently having similar thoughts, Rodney leaned in and spoke in a low, falsely polite voice. "Colonel, you know how it drives Elizabeth nuts when we come home as arms dealers."

"I'm just exploring options, Rodney, so chill." John addressed Cestan again. "How big is your army compared to theirs?"

The direction of this conversation unnerved Teyla. Given a choice between waiting to see where it led and taking action, she preferred the latter. Stepping forward, she asked, "Governor, may we take a moment to confer? There are details of your proposal that our group should discuss."

She could feel her team leader's piercing stare, but he said nothing. "Of course," Cestan replied. "Such matters should never be treated with haste."

Giving a slight bow of courtesy, he drifted to the far end of the field, his trio of warriors trailing behind. The team walked in the opposite direction until they were assured of being outside hearing range.

John pivoted toward Teyla, making only a token attempt to mask his irritation. "Since when do we cut in on each other like that?"

"You were preparing to supply arms for a dispute in which we have no part," she reminded him, unmoved.

"I was considering all potential trade avenues for a commodity we could really use. That's a long way from arming everyone." John set his hands on his hips. "How trigger-happy do you think I am?"

"Not 'trigger-happy,'" Teyla said quietly. She had no wish to accuse her friend. "Focused on your people's needs."

He looked at her without speaking for a few seconds, acknowledging her point. "We *do* need it. A weapon that breaks nanite bonds might be the difference that saves our expedition."

"Then we will do all we can to procure some of this ore. But we must remember how little we truly know of these people. We have only their word that this conflict exists as they describe. Our initial impressions of a society have been proven wrong before."

She did not need to elaborate. The memories of Genii betrayal and Daleran upheaval spoke loudly enough.

"I get it. And I wasn't about to give away the store." Rolling his shoulders as if to dispel the noticeable tension there, John sighed. "Okay. We need to know if these guys are for real, and we're generally opposed to starting wars. What if we propose to mediate a new treaty between the Falnori and the Nistra? Cestan's interest, or lack of it, will give us a good idea of how sincere he is. And if they make nice for a while, the adarite will no longer be used as leverage, so we'll have a better chance at getting some of it."

Eyebrows climbing, Rodney raised a finger to signal

an objection. "I suspect it also drives Elizabeth nuts when you offer her up as a mediator without asking."

John wheeled on him, and the irritation returned. "Would it be so hard for you to cut me a break for ten damn minutes?"

"Just stating an issue. Overall it's a better plan than giving them rocket launchers."

"Thanks for that ringing endorsement." John silently sought his other teammates' approval, which Teyla was now more than willing to grant. Ronon gave a nod as well, and they walked back toward the field's center, where Cestan waited expectantly.

"We have a counter-offer," John began. "The leader of our expedition is an experienced diplomat. We would like to open a dialogue between your people and the Nistra. With a impartial third party to guide the negotiations, maybe some misunderstandings can be cleared up and a new agreement reached."

Teyla watched the governor carefully, alert for any sign of duplicity. When Cestan responded after a pause, his answer seemed considered, not contrived. "I am not confident about the chances for success at such a venture," he admitted. "It has been tried before, though never with an outside mediator." He lifted an unwavering gaze to meet John's. "But what would we be if we did not try?"

The Colonel smiled. "We hoped you'd see it that way. We can provide security for the talks. Somewhere neutral, probably close to the Hall, would be best."

"I agree. Perhaps we can avoid some of the acrimony of past encounters. What would you ask in return for your efforts?"

Rodney plunged ahead before anyone else could

speak. "A small amount of adarite and a whip for us to start our research."

Without blinking, Cestan turned to Merise. "Find Vanil and ask him to bring a fist of adarite from the vault. Then go to the armory and fetch a whip."

The warrior immediately moved to obey, disappearing through the doorway. Rodney wasn't finished, though. "And an opportunity to study the Hall. You can send your people along to baby-sit if you want, and I won't take so much as a pocketknife with me for defense, but I have to get in there."

At first Teyla worried that the scientist's demand might stall the pact. Then Cestan replied, "In the morning, I will send a messenger to the border under a flag of conference. If Galven, the Nistra leader, agrees, you will be granted entrance to the Hall when negotiations begin."

"Sounds fair," said John, glancing at his watch. The sun was already sinking toward the horizon. "We have to check in at home pretty soon. Can we send someone back tomorrow to wait for Galven's response?"

"I will send an escort to the gate to await your return. Until then, please accept the other elements of our accord as a gesture of friendship."

Merise soon reappeared with an additional whip, followed by a shorter man carrying a canteen-sized box. Smiling in what appeared to be genuine goodwill, Cestan placed the whip in John's hands and the box in Rodney's. "I thank you for your willingness to seek peace for our world. It is possible that you may be the ones to finally bring it within our reach."

Having opened the box to peer inside, Rodney answered dismissively while examining his prize. "Believe me, the pleasure is ours."

# CHAPTER FIVE

The off-world team trooped in for the debriefing in characteristic fashion. Teyla took her seat with poise, John slouched back in his, and Ronon all but hurled himself into a chair. Rodney brought up the rear, still working through a litany of complaints he'd begun seemingly before emerging from the gate.

"…is it too much to ask that they cushion the benches in their deplorable excuse for public transportation?"

Amused, Elizabeth let him wind down on his own. Tirade notwithstanding, her chief of science looked invigorated. As did her military advisor, come to think of it.

"Should I infer that the research facility showed some promise?" she inquired.

"You could say that." With a flourish, Rodney set a medium-sized box on the table in front of him. "Allow me to introduce you to adarite, an ore mined on P7L-418. It appears to have a few things in common with naquadah, but its energetic properties are pressure-dependent and far simpler to harness. Not to mention stronger. A simple whip infused with this material can release the electrothermal equivalent of a lightning bolt."

Next to him, John helpfully held up an innocuous-looking whip as a visual aid.

"I'll know more once we analyze the sample, but I'm convinced that this could be developed into a weapon to disrupt nanite cohesion." Satisfied, Rodney sat back in his chair, presumably anticipating a congratulatory word.

It *was* good news, so Elizabeth decided to play along. "That's excellent, Rodney," she said warmly. "So you found raw materials rather than research data?"

"We haven't been inside the actual facility yet," John told her.

"But we will," Rodney jumped in.

"We ran into some locals first." John elaborated on the Falnori and their disagreement with the Nistra. As she often did, Elizabeth found herself fascinated by the apparent evolution of the society. These people had once lived and worked alongside the Ancients, and their off-spring had maintained some of the equipment for as long as possible. Without the full knowledge and capabilities of their predecessors, though, and hindered by periodic Wraith cullings, the Falnori had been unable to advance significantly in a technological sense.

She wondered fleetingly if maybe they were better off that way. There were times, many of them defined by the Asuran threat, when technological sophistication didn't seem like all it was cracked up to be.

"It's worth keeping in mind that we haven't heard the Nistra side of the story yet," John concluded, stealing a sideways glance at Teyla as he spoke. "Best guess is that they'll claim ethnic persecution or something along those lines. If what Cestan said is accurate, the Nistra probably believe the Falnori don't view them as equals. Of course, the Falnori deny that, which is why we need a diplomat."

"And we believe the Nistra will accept me as a mediator, in spite of the fact that the Falnori met us first?"

"They have to." Judging by Rodney's expression, he thought he was stating the obvious. "If they don't, they all stay mad at each other, and I don't get into that lab."

Elizabeth took that to mean 'we're crossing our fingers and hoping for the best.' She tucked her hair back and leaned over her datapad to make a note. "What about the accusations that the Nistra have been raiding this Hall of Tribute? How would they benefit from such an act?"

"Beats me," John replied. "It's not like they can use anything in there. Most of what we saw in the outer building was broken, and they don't have the gene to operate anything further in."

"They could be doing it just to provoke the Falnori," Ronon said. "If they want a war, that might be the quickest way of getting one."

Something about that idea didn't feel right to Elizabeth, but she didn't have nearly enough information about the state of affairs to hazard another guess. "So now we just need a response from this Galven," she said.

"Ronon and I will travel back to the planet in the morning to await word," Teyla offered.

"In the meantime, I have a major analysis project to begin and a Czech to drag away from his futile study of jumper propulsion optimization," Rodney said, fingers drumming on his prized box. "So if we're done here—?"

"Go," Elizabeth told him, shooing him with her hand. "Keep me posted on what you and Radek learn. And let's finally take care of the mail call tomorrow. Everybody's about to start climbing the walls."

"I'll get with Lorne and make up a roster for security shifts at the peace talks." John aimed a thumb over his shoulder as he stood up from the table. As the group dispersed, Elizabeth heard him say under his breath to

Rodney, "And you were sure she'd be pissed about me volunteering her services."

She smiled to herself, closing the file on her datapad. In truth, she was intrigued by the opportunity. The challenges of running the city were absorbing on their own merits, but she was a trained negotiator, and rarely did she get the chance to use those skills.

Having swiped her own mail out of the delivery pile yesterday—there were a few perks to being in charge—she'd read her university's alumni magazine last night before bed. So many of her colleagues were spearheading talks that would guide the years to come on their world: Africa, North Korea, the Middle East. They were doing truly noble work, the work to which she'd once dedicated her life; and she was a galaxy away, working without a net, occasionally signing off on tactics that her younger self would have protested at the top of her lungs.

Had she been on Earth, she probably would have had to fight the urge to knock various dignitaries' heads together. Squabbling over ideologies seemed so petty and useless now that she knew what other, more fundamental enemies existed.

If they were lucky—and God knew they were due for a streak of luck—the expedition would benefit from the upcoming talks just as much as the Falnori and Nistra. For that reason, among others, she couldn't find it within herself to long for home. There was a job to be done here, and she fully intended to see it through.

Looking over the landscape, unchanged since their visit the day before, Ronon heard the familiar sound of the gate disengaging behind him. "We were supposed to meet our escort here?"

"That was Governor Cestan's instruction," Teyla answered. "I will confess that the idea of another ride to town does not excite me."

"I know what you mean." For once, McKay's complaining had been justified. Ronon might have said more, but the sight of two figures climbing the hillside forestalled him.

"Day's greetings," Kellec called to them as he and Merise approached.

"To you as well," said Teyla. "Are you meant to bring us to the capital?"

"The governor bids us to wait here, with you, for the messenger's return." Merise swung a cloth sack off her shoulder and set it on the ground. "It should not be long. In any case, we have food and drink."

She took a seat in the grass, and Kellec joined her. Ronon exchanged a glance with Teyla. Maybe they should have brought something to occupy themselves. One of those number puzzles of which the scientists, and occasionally Sheppard, seemed so enamored… Or maybe not.

"We're out in the open here," Ronon had to point out. "If the Nistra don't like what the messenger has to say, or if they decide to mount a raid today, wouldn't it be better to have a larger group?"

"If warriors are needed, they will come." Kellec inclined his head toward the forest behind them. "When flying a flag of conference, it is prudent to show fewer arms than you care to use, but possess more."

It made sense, or at least enough sense for Ronon to

accept. Someone was watching their backs; that was all he needed to know.

Teyla sat down, tucking her legs up beneath her. "Will the talks be held in this area as well, since it is considered neutral?"

"In his message to Galven, Governor Cestan requested that the Hall be used, as it has been in the past." Merise set about unlacing the straps from her right shoe.

"Not a very comfortable place to hold a long negotiation," Ronon commented. "You'd have to move all the damaged equipment."

Kellec frowned. "I believe you misunderstand. Should Galven agree, the talks will be held in the main Hall, not the entryway. There is more than sufficient room inside, and it was left untouched by any attacks."

Ronon didn't want to be the one to tell these people that McKay had broken the door mechanism, even if the scientist could most likely fix it or find a way around it within hours. Except the transporter hadn't unlocked for him or Sheppard, both of whom had the gene. Which meant he'd just obtained some new information.

"You are able to enter the main Hall?" Teyla asked. "You know how to operate the security on the door?"

A perplexed look came over the chief warrior's face. "Security has never been a concern. We make use of the stairwell into the Hall, not the door with the lighted panel, which appears to have no exit."

There was a stairwell. Of course. The transporter probably led somewhere further inside the facility, either for convenience or for additional protection. Ronon smirked, thinking of the trouble McKay might have saved himself if he'd focused on the second door instead of the first.

After that, an awkward silence fell. It stretched for a few minutes, magnifying the wait, until Teyla broke it by turning to Merise with an inquisitive smile. "Do you choose to become warriors, or is the path chosen for you?"

Her shoe now adjusted to her satisfaction, the Falnori woman reached into her bag and withdrew a loaf of soft bread. Tearing off a piece, she offered the loaf to Teyla. "The choice to become soldiers is our own. Becoming a warrior requires something greater than a mere choice."

"It is a simpler road for some than for others," Kellec asserted, accepting the bread when Teyla passed it to him. "Merise, for instance, was nearly born with a whip in her hand."

"You exaggerate, Kellec." Merise shook her head, but tolerated the remark. "My father was one of the city's finest craftsmen," she explained. "From an early age he schooled me in both the art of creating the whip and the skill of controlling it."

The bread made its way to Ronon. He found it sweet and surprisingly delicate. "Much effort is devoted to the creation of a whip, is it not?" Teyla asked.

Unhooking her whip from her belt, Merise moved to show the visitors its attributes. "The most difficult aspect is the fall." She indicated the long, flexible part. "A thin strand of adarite runs from the top of the handle down the length of the fall. It must be a continuous strand of a certain width, or the weapon will not discharge sufficient power. Adarite can be worked with heat, but it is fragile. It takes years of apprenticeship to fashion a quality whip. Few who take up the trade have the focus to master it."

Teyla examined the whip's construction, skimming her

fingers along the braided fall. "Would you teach me some of your handling skills?" she requested. "It would occupy our time, and I am curious to learn."

Merise looked to Kellec for permission. The chief warrior responded by handing his own whip to Teyla. Once she had secured her dark hair away from her face, Merise dropped into a familiar combat stance: one foot slightly behind the other, toes turned out. The whip hung loosely at her side. Teyla copied the position.

"Guess you have to be careful not to accidentally turn the thing on," Ronon said.

A rueful smile curled the corner of Kellec's mouth. "A key reason why only the finest of our soldiers are selected for the warrior order."

The two women went through a series of basic motions, which Teyla picked up quickly. In the forward jabs, sideways sweeps, and spins, there were notable similarities to her usual fighting style, although the whip had a much longer reach than her staffs. It appeared almost like a dance: fluid, yet with a percussive force provided by the occasional *snap* of the weapon. Ronon was impressed by Merise's control. Despite the length and pliancy of the whip, she was able to put her strikes exactly where she wanted them, near or far. He found it difficult to predict her moves.

At the warrior's silent invitation, Ronon took her whip—careful to avoid the power band on the handle—and tried to mimic Teyla's movements. His fighting skills ran toward guns or hand-to-hand, so he wasn't nearly as coordinated at first, and he found that he had to work harder than he'd expected just to maintain the pace and keep the whip from touching anything it shouldn't.

Still, he could see how such a weapon could have its advantages, even if the spinning moves made him a little unsteady.

After a few minutes, Teyla returned Kellec's whip to him. "Thank you," she told him, brushing damp hair back from her forehead. "It is a demanding style."

She looked tired, more so than Ronon would have expected for such a short period of activity. As he handed Merise her whip, something in the distance caught the attention of the group.

A rider approached, sitting astride one of the beasts that Sheppard had dubbed 'Energizer Bunnies on steroids.' A scarlet and gold banner, presumably a flag of conference, billowed out behind him. The messenger, Ronon identified. That hadn't taken as long as he'd feared.

As the rider drew nearer, he slowed the animal to a walking pace and then dismounted, keeping hold of the reins. "Day's greetings, Chief Warrior," he called.

"Day's greetings," replied Kellec. "Have you the Nistra's answer?"

"I have, sir. Minister Galven accepts the governor's invitation. He will come to the Hall at the appointed time with only his personal guards. However, he cautions that if he does not find the guards provided by the mediator to be satisfactory, his acceptance is forfeit."

"That won't be a problem," Ronon said.

Kellec smiled. "I am gratified. Please go and tell your people that the talks are set. We will take the good news to the governor."

Something more than anticipation lingered in the man's eyes, though. Ronon glanced at Merise and found the same expression. Caution, maybe, or suspicion. From the looks of it, no one was all that confident about the prospects for a positive outcome from these talks. He found himself hoping that if these two groups really were primed to do battle, they would at least let him and his team get out of the way first.

"At last," Rodney said theatrically, plunking himself down on a nearby chair. "For a while I thought we were going to have to wait until the *Daedalus* came by *again* to get our damn mail."

"Relax, Rodney. I'm sure your bulk order of Twinkies is safe." John grinned at the immediate spluttering his comment produced.

"I do not hoard Twinkies. It was only that first supply run, because it had been so long since we'd had anything resembling actual food. And would you keep your voice down? The last thing I need is Marines with stealth skills and scientists with rewiring skills trying to break into my quarters in search of a junk-food stockpile."

The mess hall was one of the largest spaces in the occupied section of Atlantis, and it was rapidly filling with people, all eager for a taste of home in whatever form it might take. For John, who'd pretty much been military from birth, home tended to be wherever he was currently assigned, but he could admit to some interest in the latest movies and sports DVDs Stargate Command graciously provided with each supply run. And Frosted Flakes. God, he hated it when the mess ran out of Frosted Flakes.

They still had a few minutes until the official start of mail call, so he perched on the edge of Rodney's table. "How are you guys coming along on your analysis of the adarite?"

Next to Rodney, Radek Zelenka shrugged. "We have a good sense of its molecular structure. Similar to naquadah, as Rodney theorized—"

"More precisely, similar to naquadria." Rodney ran over his research partner's explanation without hesitating, oblivious to Radek's exasperated gaze. "In the sense that it's highly energetic and only stable in certain forms. It makes one wonder if the ore formed naturally on the planet or if it was a byproduct of the Ancients' charming pastime of terraforming."

Yeah, John had felt charmed by their all-too-recent terraforming adventure, all right. He figured he should probably take note of that comment about stability, but Rodney and Radek were on the job, so he wasn't overly concerned.

"However, the crystalline structure is brittle," Radek continued. "Manipulating it will not be as simple as standard metalworking. And we do not yet have a method for directing the discharged energy once it leaves the ore, which will be necessary before we can develop any sort of distance weapon."

"You'll make it work," John said, realizing a half-second too late that his tone had sounded more like a command than an expression of faith.

Rodney tossed him a long-suffering scowl. "If for no other reason than it would be vexing to break my streak of day-saving, yes, of course I'll make it work. But I'll need some time."

"How much time do you think we *have*, Rodney?" John retorted. "How long do you think it'll take the Asurans to build another cityship and point it toward us?"

Now Rodney was looking at him strangely. "You want to dial back the paranoia for a minute? That's supposed to be my role. As soon as I get into the facility on 418, things will go faster."

As tough as it was to admit, Rodney was right. John needed to step back and let them do their jobs. A little embarrassed, he pushed himself up from the table. "Well, good luck with it. Anyway, I think it's time to get this show on the road."

He headed for the front of the room, where Elizabeth was standing next to two large pallets stacked with boxes and four containers of envelopes. Her eyes twinkled. "Colonel, would you like to do the honors?"

The enthusiasm of the room was contagious. "As you wish, Doctor." John climbed up on the table and whistled sharply to get everyone's attention. "Okay, you all know the drill. No opening anything or making trade offers until all mail has been distributed, just to keep the noise level down. After that, you're on your own. Now, the first item goes to…" Elizabeth handed him a package. "Sergeant Ruiz." Cheers and clapping accompanied the beaming sergeant up to the front.

The event lasted nearly an hour, and John decided he was glad he'd come after all. It wasn't every day he got to see the expedition so uniformly happy. Carson lit up when he received an oversized box marked *Perishable*. "Mum's scones," he exclaimed blissfully, and the offers for bartering escalated so quickly that John had to whistle again to quiet the room down. Radek's stack of letters was an astounding four inches thick, but when Rodney and others demanded to know who'd sent them, he responded with only a closed-mouthed smile and a few hushed words in Czech.

One of the newer scientists had been worried for weeks about a brother in the Army who'd been deployed to the desert. John had heard about it through the rumor mill, so he especially enjoyed handing her an envelope postmarked Balad, Iraq. The young woman almost bowled him over in her joy. It was easily the highlight of his day.

When every package had found an eager owner, John jumped down from the table and wandered over to see what his colleagues were up to. Carson's scones had turned out to be the hot commodity this time around. His mother must have baked for a solid week, because his box was packed to the brim with dozens of the biscuit-looking things, frozen for the long trip. A crowd had formed around him, but he steadfastly refused to entertain any trades.

"Oh, I don't *believe* this!" Rodney fumed. Before John could ask what might be so offensive about scones, the chief scientist shoved a magazine in his face. "A typo. Have I somehow angered the gods of physics, or am I just surrounded by morons at every turn? I fight through three levels of Air Force bureaucracy to get this paper cleared for publication, and they introduce a typo!"

John squinted at the dense text and tried not to be too impressed by the alphabet soup of degrees following the name *M. Rodney McKay*. Rodney really didn't need the ego boost. And what was that 'M' for? "I don't see it," he offered.

"I wouldn't expect you to. That insufferable Matthias Palmer at MIT, however, will spot it immediately, and criticism from lesser minds is high on my list of things that are intolerable."

"Okay, but he's on Earth and you're here, so how much crap can he really give you?"

Rodney paused. "You make an excellent point."

On that positive note, John elected to leave the controlled chaos of the mess hall behind. He headed for his quarters, wondering what movie would get the popular vote for tonight's rec-room viewing. Actually, they'd probably show a World Cup game or two. Soccer wasn't one of his favorite sports, but it had been a while since football season, so he'd take what he could get.

He waved his hand in front of the wall sensor, and his door obligingly slid open. Before he could enter, Elizabeth's voice called out, "John."

Turning in the doorway, he watched her take long strides to catch up to him. "I thought you were reading your mail with everyone else."

"I swiped mine earlier." Atlantis's leader gave him a conspiratorial smile, but he could sense the inquiry behind it. "I'm glad you were there," she said quietly. "You don't always participate."

"Yeah, well." John knew how perceptive Elizabeth was, and he was pretty sure she'd realized at some point how little mail he received. Truth be told, part of the reason he often volunteered to play postman was to distract people from noticing that fact. It didn't bother him—after all, he was used to it. He just didn't want to be fodder for the liveliest gossip mill ever spawned.

"I didn't really want to give you this in front of everyone, though, so…" Elizabeth held an envelope out to him, clearly watching for his reaction.

Puzzled, John took it from her and examined the postmark. Some tiny crumb of memory told him that he should recognize that address—

Then he got it, and his chest tightened painfully. Looking up at Elizabeth, he found sympathy in her expressive eyes. That was just about the last thing he wanted, so he forced a smile. "I appreciate it."

For once, she seemed hesitant in her response. "John, I'm sure she's still hurting. If she lashes out at you in that letter, just because you're the only one she knows how to blame...don't listen."

*Easier said than done.* What he said aloud, however, was a simple "Thanks."

Elizabeth touched his arm briefly, and left. John stepped into his quarters and sat down hard on the bed, feeling like he'd been blindsided. The door swished shut behind him.

He stared at the neat, feminine handwriting on the envelope, addressed to Lieutenant Colonel John Sheppard at Peterson Air Force Base, Colorado. Surely Lara Ford had known when she wrote out the envelope that its final destination wouldn't be Peterson, even if that base had been the last official duty station of her cousin Aiden. She'd shown a surprising level of comprehension and poise last year when John had visited her to break the news of Aiden's disappearance. What she hadn't shown was forgiveness. John respected that, because he hadn't wanted any.

Lieutenant Aiden Ford belonged to a terrible cadre that seemed to be growing by the day: people who had been lost under John's command, people who had followed his orders and hadn't come home.

Back on Earth the Air Force ran a class intended to teach unit commanders how to lead. John kept getting the class registration notices from the SGC and kept ignoring them, because there was no way he was leaving Atlantis long enough to attend, but also because no classroom course could tell him how to deal with what he saw and did out here.

His Marines looked at him like he had all the answers. Lack of alternatives, he guessed. There wasn't anyone else for them to look to.

He was a realist, and logically he knew that there was no way to completely avoid losing people. He wasn't arrogant enough to believe he could control everything that happened to the expedition. But the questions were always there, lingering in the back of his mind—what could have been different, what right turn should have been a left—and they just kept piling up.

After a long moment spent contemplating the envelope, he stood up and went over to his desk. Trying not to picture Aiden Ford's too-young face, he opened the bottom drawer, put the still-sealed letter inside, and shoved the drawer shut.

*I'm sorry, Ford. I swear I am. But I've got Harper and Travis and four other guys hanging over my head right now, and there are only so many ghosts I can handle at once.*

# CHAPTER SIX

The Marines fanned out, directed by Major Lorne to take up sentry positions around the gate area. Cestan had demonstrated how far out from the Hall the no-weapon boundary lay, and they would follow it strictly. Elizabeth zipped her jacket higher against a cool breeze and watched the arrival of the two leaders and their parties.

On her right, John leaned in and commented, "Does it say something disturbing about me that I feel naked without my gun?"

"I'm more disturbed by your use of the words 'gun' and 'naked' in the same sentence," she returned under her breath. "Now be good."

"Yes, ma'am."

From the woods emerged a tall, navy-robed man who must have been Governor Cestan, flanked by four guards. One carried a banner attached to a pole: the flag of conference, she presumed.

A similar quintet approached from the direction of the mountains, alighting from an animal-drawn cart. Elizabeth was mildly startled by the appearance of the Nistra delegation. The older man—Minister Galven, no doubt—had the grooming and deportment of a leader, but his guards didn't look nearly as strong and fit as the Falnori. They were lean from ill health rather than conditioning. Already, it seemed, there was more to the situation than she'd known.

The delegations stopped a few yards apart and regarded each other without speaking. Elizabeth took that as her cue. "Gentlemen, thank you for agreeing to these discussions," she greeted. "My name is Doctor Elizabeth Weir. My team and I are visitors to your world, and we have not come to tell you how to lead your people. Rather, it's my hope that by acting as a third party mediator, with no alliance to either side, I can help you to reach an arrangement that will be equitable to all and promote understanding between your two societies."

Neither side made any overt response to the introduction. Undaunted, she continued, "Shall we move to the Hall of Tribute so we may begin?"

Stepping forward, two of Cestan's guards detached their whips from their belts and handed the coils of ore and leather to their comrades. Apparently both sides planned to leave personnel at the gate, because two of Galven's guards did likewise. Trust, obviously, was in short supply here. Ronon, who had shocked no one on his team by choosing to stay outside with the Marines, took custody of his teammates' relinquished P-90s.

"Give a yell if anyone approaches the perimeter," John instructed, tapping the radio affixed to his vest. "From any direction. And keep an eye on your new pals."

"Will do," said Ronon.

The motley crew started toward the damaged outer building. Cestan and Galven both kept their gazes focused directly ahead, neither acknowledging the other during the walk. John, Lorne, and Teyla stayed between the two parties, maintaining a subtle separation, just in case. Elizabeth could see Rodney practically humming with anticipation beside her. He had brought two of the city's power specialists along to dig into whatever technological treasures lay within the Ancient facility, and he obviously didn't care to waste any more time.

The interior of the structure was every bit as demolished as its exterior suggested. Flashlight in hand, Lorne helped Elizabeth climb over a splintered table as they followed the Nistra guards into a back corner. Behind a fallen section of roof lay two doors. The guards approached the second door and manipulated its handle this way and that. Eventually the door opened to reveal a nondescript stairwell.

When he caught sight of it, Rodney's cheer dimmed, and he grumbled a complaint about information that would have been helpful earlier.

The stairs led them down about two stories, depositing them in a room that caught Elizabeth off-guard. No evidence of any attack was visible here. At one end of the expansive room sat a V-shaped table and easily enough chairs for the proceedings. The rest of the space was lined with Ancient equipment, leading to a hallway at the far end that must have continued into the rest of the facility. All of it was clean, orderly—and lit.

Her surprise must have shown, because Cestan spoke for the first time. "Our scholars are permitted to study and reflect here. A group visited earlier and prepared the Hall for our use."

Already bouncing from console to console, trying to determine the optimal starting point, Rodney managed to quash his curiosity long enough to ask, "May I infer that we're free to look around?"

The governor cast a pointed gaze at Galven, as if challenging him to disagree.

"I have no objection to the furtherance of knowledge," the minister replied calmly.

"Excellent. Good luck with the treaty and all that. We'll check in." Rodney made an impatient come-here gesture at John, who fixed him with a withering look before crossing the room to join him.

"Not the warrior," Galven said sharply.

John paused in mid-stride. "I'm sorry?"

The Nistra leader studied him with a glacial expression. "You are a warrior, not a scholar. As such you are not granted access to the works of the Ancestors. You will remain here."

A humorless chuckle came from Cestan. "Do you make this claim honestly? After your raiders have stolen so much from within these walls?"

"My people have done nothing of the sort," Galven snarled. "Does *your* hypocrisy know no limits?"

"Gentlemen, please." Elizabeth could feel the tension building, and they hadn't even begun negotiations yet. "For the moment, let's concentrate on the issue at hand."

"Which is absurd," Rodney declared, making little effort to defuse the situation. "Colonel Sheppard's not a—well, he is, but isn't that oversimplifying things? I mean, in his defense, he can calculate pi to twenty significant figures before you can say—"

"I watched you relinquish your weapon earlier," Galven said to John, who still stood uncertainly in the center of the room.

Rodney frowned. "Of course you did. You saw me do the same thing. *I'm* certainly not a warrior."

"No, you are not." Galven kept his eyes on John as he answered. "But a weapon does not make a warrior."

A message of some sort seemed to pass between the older minister and the younger colonel, making Elizabeth wonder if Galven had once been a warrior himself.

After a moment, John dropped his gaze and turned back to Rodney with a half-shrug of acceptance. "He's right about me. Kinda tough to deny it."

"And that would be one of the reasons why I'd rather have you with us," Rodney persisted, his voice almost too low to be heard. "Can't we work something out?"

In truth, Elizabeth wasn't wild about the idea of letting anyone wander off unescorted, either. She deferred to her military advisor, however, and said nothing.

John shook his head. "We can't afford to jeopardize this. And these guys have been poking around in here for thousands of years. You'll live. Go find cool stuff."

With a huff of irritation, Rodney acquiesced. "Like I said, we'll check in." The trio of scientists headed for the corridor.

Taking the initiative, Elizabeth walked over to stand at the head of the table. "Governor, Minister, if you please."

The leaders moved to opposite sides of the table without argument, the other representatives of the three groups filling in around them. There was a refreshing lack of formal ceremony. Elizabeth wasn't naïve enough to believe that the full proceedings would be nearly as civil and sensible.

"I'd like to begin by hearing the terms of the current agreement from each of you, in order to ensure that there is no ambiguity or misinterpretation," she announced. "And I'll have to ask, out of respect for all involved, that each side be allowed to present a complete statement without interruption. There are no time limits here; no one will be denied an opportunity to be heard on any topic." She folded her hands atop the table. "Minister Galven, since some of my people have spoken previously to Governor Cestan, I suggest that you speak first."

"Very well." Galven's close-cropped hair was snow white, but his piercing blue eyes gave the impression of someone much younger. "The accord has changed many times. The most recent version was struck seven generations ago. It calls for a trade meeting each year, after the harvest, held outside this Hall. The Nistra contribute one carriage of ore for every three carriages of grain and fruit provided by the Falnori."

Elizabeth turned to Cestan. "Do you dispute that explanation?"

"I do not," the governor acknowledged. "However, it is incomplete. The total amount of goods to be exchanged is determined at a conference held three days before the trade. Each year for the past ten, the Nistra have offered smaller and smaller amounts of adarite. It has gotten to the point where we must ration our use of lamps."

"Enduring the darkness is less difficult than starving." Galven's tone was laden with scorn. "My people would gladly offer more adarite if we could. But many are in poor health and unable to work in the mines as well as before. Even so, we honor the accord to the best of our ability—something the Falnori apparently no longer feel honor-bound to do."

Cestan's eyes narrowed. "In what way have *we* supposedly broken the accord?"

"By your repeated incursions into our mining territory, and your egregious theft of large quantities of adarite."

"That is untrue!" Cestan came out of his chair, clearly incensed. "You had no legitimate claim to the mountains in the first place, and yet we refused to contest your misappropriation in the name of peace."

"In the name of peace, or of cultural purity?" Galven sneered.

"Gentlemen!" Elizabeth raised her voice. She hadn't expected her no-interruptions rule to hold for long. Still, they were already dragging up ancient history only ten minutes into the talks. "As I understand it, the division of lands occurred generations ago. I don't believe we can resolve any questions surrounding the legitimacy of that process here. Let's instead focus on the current situation. Governor, you deny the minister's assertion that your people have stolen adarite from the Nistra?"

"I deny it in the strongest possible terms." Regaining his composure, Cestan sat down again. "The Falnori hold their honor paramount. We are *not* thieves. The audacity of such a statement is only compounded by the recent behavior of the minister's own people. Or is it considered acceptable if the raid is perpetrated on a neutral site—for instance, this Hall?"

This time it was Galven who sprang to his feet. "Ludicrous and insulting," he spat. "And a blatant diversion from the heart of the matter."

As the volume in the room escalated, Elizabeth shared a glance with John, then with Teyla and Lorne. None of them appeared any more hopeful than she felt. This was shaping up to be a long day.

"You have *got* to see this."

"Obviously. Not at this particular instant, however."

"But it—"

"Kendall, it's been here for ten thousand years. Nothing in this facility is going to blink out of existence in the next ten minutes." Sitting on a low storage cabinet—had the researchers taken all the chairs with them when they left, or what?—Rodney jabbed at a few more buttons on the nearby console. Every so often he came upon an Ancient lab that used a different computer protocol than Atlantis did. He was starting to think they'd done it intentionally to challenge him.

"Like switching from Mac to Windows to Unix," he muttered to himself before raising his voice. "Look, peace talks don't come together in an hour or two. We may have days to explore this place. Let's just get a basic idea from the database about what's here, and then go room-to-room later."

When he glanced up from the screen, though, he found Kendall and Wen crouched on the floor beside an unidentifiable piece of equipment. They'd apparently pried open a panel on the side and detached some sort of battery for examination.

"Oh, congratulations on that headfirst dive into the shallow end of the pool!" Rearing up from his makeshift seat, Rodney glared fiercely at them. "Did it occur to you at any point that removing that power supply might have affected other equipment in the room—like, say, the computer I'm working on?"

Wen raised his head. "Did you lose power?"

He hadn't, but… "*So* not the point!"

The two electrical engineers looked only faintly chastised. Kendall shrugged. "No harm, then. This one wasn't active, anyway."

Some people, Rodney decided, didn't have enough sense to know when they were being told off. Gritting his teeth, he went back to his console. "Fine. Fill me in on what your blind flailing has accomplished so far while I work on a more prudent plan."

"This appears to be an adarite power cell," said Wen. "We know that the ore produces energy when subjected to pressure. Here, a casing tightens around the adarite when activated by a mechanical linkage in the machine. The contact between the adarite and the casing completes the circuit, as it were."

Briefly, Rodney wondered if he'd tripped such a linkage when he'd first attempted to get the transporter in the ruins working. Traditional Ancient design, but adarite-powered...a Franken-transporter. Lovely.

"It's remarkably simple," Kendall put in. "The efficiency losses are very low, too. I guess, if you could run your whole facility with this stuff, you wouldn't be too worried about gadgets powered by traditional Ancient sources being unusable. And even after sitting dormant all this time, it cranked up immediately."

Rodney didn't have to watch them to know that they'd reconnected the power supply and were monitoring its output. He was more interested in the readout in front of him. "Give me a file directory, you overgrown abacus," he threatened the Ancient computer, typing every obscure list prompt the expedition's programming team had divined, one after another. At last the recalcitrant terminal gave up the goods. "Aha—victory is mine."

Within seconds, Kendall was at his shoulder,

peering over at the screen. "Is that a map of the labs here?"

"Complete with descriptions of the projects to which each lab was devoted." Rodney aimed a finger at the hallway diagram glowing on the screen and grimaced as his back complained. Sitting sideways on a damned cabinet was in no way an ergonomically sound practice. "Clearly the Ancients had big plans for adarite before the war with the Wraith monopolized their time and resources. They were trying to apply it to everything from toasters to trains."

"Think of what this planet could have been if they had completed their work," Wen wondered.

A surprisingly insightful observation. What would this civilization's history have been? The Wraith still would have shown up off and on, but the Falnori and Nistra might have had more of a chance to develop as a society between cullings. For all anyone knew, the populace might never have split down the middle.

There was nothing useful to be found at the end of that little rumination, though. "Well, since Colonel Sheppard is likely to revoke my dessert privileges if I don't come back with something that goes kaboom, let's narrow our focus to the weapons lab."

As Rodney examined the readout, a spatial orientation issue occurred to him. If they were located where he thought they were on the map, the facility extended further than he'd realized—conceivably further than even the locals realized. The area designated for weapons research was on the extreme edge of the map, not far from what appeared to be—

"There's a second entrance to this place," he said

suddenly.

Kendall's forehead wrinkled. "Are you sure that's what that symbol means? Nothing was visible from outside."

"Which might very well have been intentional. Much of the work being done here would have been under heavy security; no doubt that was the reason for the facility being built under a hill like this. It's possible the Falnori and Nistra don't even know the alternate entry point exists. Perfectly logical, though. Having only one way in or out would be against any fire code ever written."

"So let's go check it out."

The urge to roll his eyes was strong enough that Rodney didn't bother to fight it. "You don't get off-world much, do you, Kendall?"

"What?" the engineer said, getting defensive.

"You want to do everything and you want to do it all right now. These things require some consideration, some flexibility. A soft touch—"

Kendall's disbelieving laugh cut him off. "Have you *met* yourself?"

Rodney barely blinked. "Yes, respond to constructive criticism with personal insults. Very helpful."

"Are we going or are we not?" Wen had reattached the panel and stood up. "Your squabbling gives me a headache."

It galled Rodney to have to acknowledge Kendall's viewpoint, but he could be the bigger man. "The weapons lab is reasonably close to the alternate entry point. Probably because the weapons researchers would have been the ones most likely to need a rapid escape route if something went wrong with their projects. In any case, we might as well head in that direction."

The trek turned out to be longer than it had looked on the innocuous little screen. Rodney's near-eidetic memory—he'd always believed true photographic memory to be a myth—kept them on the correct route, even after he bypassed the locking mechanisms on two sets of doors and all signs of recent activity disappeared. He was willing to bet that the transporter they'd found earlier led to this higher-security area, which might be a possibility worth investigating later, because the endless walking wasted a lot of potential research time.

Clearly none of the locals had been this far into their vaunted Hall, or they would have tidied up. Past a certain point, many of the lamps that lined the walls were inoperable, their transparent sheaths smashed on the floor.

"Could these areas have been damaged in the Wraith attack?" Wen asked, switching on his flashlight. "We must be closer to the surface than before."

Rodney had noted the slight incline of the corridor, but it wasn't a steep enough gradient to have brought them anywhere near the crest of the hill. He'd lost any sense of where they were in relation to the gate ages ago. "If the alternate entrance is located on the side of the hill, maybe." Which was possible. The entrance they'd used had been on what he considered to be the back of the rise, nearest the Falnori forest and opposite the land leading to the Nistra mountains. Neither group would have had any reason to go looking for a hidden entrance in their version of a demilitarized zone.

Slowing his pace, Rodney aimed his flashlight into a lab along the way. The room did bear some resemblance to the ruined building on the surface, with equipment strewn across the floor. Something about it all didn't quite fit, though.

"The walls and ceiling are completely intact," he said, mostly to himself. "Nothing in here shows any fire damage. I don't think the Wraith did this."

"Someone else came in here and trashed the place?" Kendall didn't appear too pleased by that concept.

"Well, Cestan did seem rather ticked off about some alleged Nistra break-ins. Maybe he was telling the truth."

The trio moved with a little more caution after that. Rodney told himself that the odds of anyone else poking around in here at this particular moment were so low as to be negligible. For one thing, a half-dozen Marines and a really intimidating Satedan were patrolling the gate area. Granted, the alternate entrance was, in all likelihood, some distance away from the gate area... Oh, hell, was that a noise?

He whipped around to look at Wen and Kendall, whose alarmed expressions confirmed his suspicions. And just when had he ended up in *front* of them?

Flattening himself against the wall, he shut off his light and listened intently. Voices could now be heard reflecting off the smooth walls, weak reverberations making the words indistinguishable.

Rodney inched forward, trying to view the situation objectively. If they needed to contact anyone for help, using the alternate entrance would be more practical than going back the way they'd come. It was closer, and it might enable them to use their radios, which didn't transmit well through so much rock and reinforced structure.

That, of course, presumed they could *get* to the alternate entrance. When he summoned his courage to peek around the next corner, he spotted faint light emanating from two sources: the doorway to another lab, and an opening at the far end of the corridor. The opening had to be the alternate entrance; it appeared to be a large hatch set high in an inward-angled wall, positioned at the top of a three-meter ladder. The people who had left it ajar were almost certainly the owners of the voices he heard coming from the illuminated lab.

Crouching low, Rodney risked a quick glance into the room. He counted at least five people ransacking its contents, holding up items for inspection and stuffing some of them into oversized packs. Every so often someone would offer an opinion on a device's value, occasionally prompting an argument. Judging by their well-made clothes and the pistol-style guns at their belts, they had some experience in this arena.

Rodney turned to instruct Kendall and Wen and found them well within his personal space. *Deliver me from amateurs.* A decisive shoving motion conveyed his irritation, and they shuffled backward. The military had hand signals for these things. Unfortunately, the military wasn't *here*. Damn it, why had they picked today to cave in to unreasonable native rules when the natives themselves weren't playing fair?

*If* these pirate rejects were natives, a fact of which Rodney wasn't at all certain. He hadn't seen clothes or weapons like that on any of the Falnori or Nistra representatives, to be sure, but it would be the height of naïveté to presume that he'd seen every charming facet of this planet. And how likely was it that someone had gotten through the gate without alerting the guards? Of course, these people could have arrived days ago, for all anyone knew. Reports of the scavenging gang once led by Colonel Maybourne came to mind.

In any case, he had precious little time to wonder about it. Feeling ridiculous, Rodney pointed at the hatch, mimed a running action with two fingers, and jammed one of those fingers against his lips to emphasize the need for silence. His companions nodded vigorously, wide-eyed.

It wasn't so hard. All they had to do was get past the doorway without being seen and then up the ladder without being heard. The Marines could take it from there.

Rodney ineffectually willed his pulse to quit racing and waited until the raiders got themselves embroiled in another argument. As the dispute grew louder, he bent as low as his knees would allow and hustled across the doorway. Wen and Kendall weren't far behind.

No one seemed to have noticed, if the ongoing insults inside the lab were any indication. Exhaling a long-held breath, Rodney grabbed hold of the ladder and climbed toward the hatch. For all their faults, the Ancients built things to last, even ladders. His ascent was accompanied by not a single squeak. Two more rungs and—

The barrel of a gun greeted him almost as quickly as the daylight. Behind it, a raider eyed him, looking amused.

In his head, Rodney cursed his lack of foresight. What self-respecting bunch of thugs wouldn't leave a guard outside to stand watch?

"Crap!" hissed Kendall below him. "Sergeant, we're close by and we need help—"

The attempted radio call was aborted when the raider hauled Rodney through the hatch, tossed him aside, and aimed at Kendall instead.

That settled it. Local customs be damned. From now on, assuming he survived the day, Rodney wasn't going as far as the *bathroom* without a sidearm.

# CHAPTER SEVEN

In many circumstances, Teyla enjoyed negotiating trea-
ties. She found well-reasoned debate to be stimulating,
and there was always much to learn about new societies
and potential allies.

However, such talks could also be singularly frustrating. This one was already falling into the latter category.

No one had initiated any physical attacks, but the argu-
ments so far had been heated. Neither ruler seemed willing to believe any statements made by the other. Teyla
admired Elizabeth's patience. Atlantis's leader had not
reacted to any of the inflammatory claims put forth except
to press for more information. She gave no indication of
leaning toward either side.

Of course, John and Major Lorne appeared unbiased
as well. They looked as though they wanted nothing more
than for the proceedings to end.

"Minister Galven, you spoke of many Nistra being in
poor health," Elizabeth commented. "Could you elaborate?"

Galven's tone now sounded more despondent than
accusatory. "Our winters are harsh, and we have less to
sustain us than we once did. The hunting clans provide
what they can, but every person who hunts is another
person unavailable for the mines. And mining is arduous
work which cannot be done by all."

"Your people are threatened by hunger, then?"

The minister hesitated slightly, as if the description was

not quite accurate. "We are weakened, more susceptible to disease. For many the weakness first manifests itself in the mind."

A short burst of static issued from the Atlantis team's radios, interrupting the discussion. Frowning, John twisted the dial on his receiver. "Say again," he transmitted back, only to hear more static. "One of the problems with being underground."

Another burst sounded; then, "—need to check it out."

The voice had been Ronon's. After trading a look with Teyla, John said, "I'm sorry to disrupt everything, but we'd better see what's going on outside."

He started to rise from his chair, halting when two frosty glares settled on him.

"You are Dr. Weir's chief warrior, are you not?" Cestan asked.

Clearly uncomfortable with the scrutiny, John replied, "We have a different name for it, but yes."

"Surely your subordinates are capable of performing their duties while you remain at your post."

Remembering Kellec, seated at Cestan's right, Teyla began to understand. These leaders would not have attended a crucial conference without their chief warriors. If John left, Elizabeth's standing might be lessened.

"Colonel Sheppard serves all of our people equally, not just me," Elizabeth stated. "If he believes it necessary to be elsewhere for a while—"

"No." John sat back in his seat. "Far be it from me to upset any kind of balance here. Teyla?"

Teyla had been considering the same option, so she was prepared for the request. "I will go." She rose and offered a small bow to the other participants.

"Be back here in fifteen minutes flat, or I'm going to assume we've got a problem."

"Understood." John had requisitioned her a watch from Earth, many supply runs ago. Although it did not perfectly represent the Lantean day cycle, it often proved useful. As she climbed the stairs back to the surface, she set the timer to alert her in ten minutes.

When she emerged from the ruins, blinking against the suddenly increased light, she saw no sign of Ronon or the Marines on the hillcrest. Her first instinct was to move in that direction, in case they had regrouped by the gate. Then her radio signaled, and she heard Rodney say, "Look, we don't really care what you steal. Just let us go, and everybody can walk away."

Teyla tensed. The scientist's radio must have been set to 'vox,' transmitting whatever he said over the frequency. Obviously the conversation was not a pleasant one.

"We won't even tell anyone about the side entrance," Rodney continued, his voice growing slightly more desperate.

Side entrance? Immediately Teyla set off to circle the hill rather than scale it. For all his self-absorbed tendencies, Rodney McKay was indeed a highly intelligent man. Without his comment, she might have lost much-needed time in locating them.

"Haven't seen weapons like those before," said an unfamiliar voice, perhaps one of Rodney's captors. "This isn't your world."

"No, it's not," answered one of the Marines. "And those aren't your gadgets."

"Forget about the gadgets and concentrate on the guns, Sergeant." Rodney spoke rapidly, as he often did when stressed. "They have six and you have six. They also have *us*. Somehow I don't think attempting to intimidate them is going to work."

Six guns. Five Marines and Ronon, plus the three unarmed scientists, against six adversaries. The raiders Cestan had described, perhaps. Teyla had only a small knife in her boot as a weapon. Reinforcements could be called, but the area was open enough that a gate activation would likely be heard by all and might further complicate matters.

She crept slowly, leaning into the incline to disguise her silhouette as much as possible. Before long the voices could be heard through the air, and she shut off her radio to ensure that it would not give away her position.

"You're going to have a hard time taking us out without getting your friends hurt," said one of the captors. "Put your weapons down, and we'll let them go once we're safely aboard our ship."

"I don't think so." That was Ronon.

*Ship?* Kellec had mentioned a ship in their first encounter, when suspicions had been high. The mention of guns seemed notable as well. Most likely the notorious raiders were off-worlders, then. On occasion, she'd encountered their type while trading: people who appropriated whatever material goods a society had to offer, then escaped without sign through the Stargate. A low form of life, to be sure.

Teyla pushed herself flat against the steep hillside and edged closer until she could survey the situation. Rodney and his two companions were kneeling on the ground, a gun trained on each by armed men standing behind them. The other three raiders were locked into a standoff with Ronon, the Marines, and the Falnori and Nistra guards.

None of the raiders was facing exactly in her direction, so she risked raising her head to scout the area more thoroughly. About thirty paces behind the captives sat a small ship, similar to a puddle jumper, though not an Ancestor design. Surely it hadn't originated on this world, given what they knew of the Falnori and Nistra.

Teyla's priority, though, was a strategy to remove the guns currently pointed at her teammates. Although the raiders were outnumbered, they showed no sign of yielding, and they could easily kill the scientists before anyone could stop them. She considered her options. Create a distraction? With no way to communicate her intentions before acting, the danger for all of them would be great. Another tactic, then.

"Greetings," she called, stepping into view. Many heads and not a few weapons swung toward her. "Perhaps I can offer you a more worthy trade."

Rodney's expression plainly questioned her sanity, but one of the raiders spoke up. "And what do you have that might interest us?" His eyes swept over her, assessing her with something beyond a business interest.

She was taking a calculated risk. In her experience, raiders were concerned with profit above all else. Selling their ill-gotten wares held far more importance than any violent act. She simply had to convince them that she had something of higher value to them than three lives.

They liked the technology of the Ancestors, it appeared. Teyla glanced at her watch—this would require careful timing, as well as luck—and stripped it off her wrist. "Have you ever traded with the Tanesians? They have been known to offer their finest jewels for a device such as this. It alerts the wearer to an enemy's approach."

"Does it, now?" The apparent leader of the raiders moved closer to her, seemingly unconvinced yet still curious. "How's that?"

"It will sound an alarm, allowing the wearer time to duck low and prepare for attack." Trusting Ronon to comprehend, Teyla sent a meaningful look toward Rodney, hoping he would decipher her intent. His eyes flared wide for a brief moment, and he gave a barely perceptible nod.

The raider frowned and held out his hand. "Let me see," he demanded.

"Gladly." A quick glance told her that she had three seconds. Rather than step forward and hand the watch to him, she instead tossed it in an underhand lob. It landed in his palm, half a second before the alarm erupted with a shrill beeping sound.

Rodney threw himself face-first into the dirt, yanking his comrades down with him. Ronon and the Marines wasted no time in opening fire.

The startled raiders reacted more quickly than Teyla would have liked, returning fire as they spread out. She dropped into a crouch and caught the sidearm pitched to her by Sergeant Ellis. One Falnori guard was hit and collapsed to the ground; before long, the other was struck while attempting to aid his comrade. Seeing that their wounds were mortal, Teyla felt a pang of sorrow. They had been young and severely overmatched, but they had not fled.

"The raiders are falling back to their ship," Ellis reported, raising his voice over the report of his P-90.

"I vote we let them go!" Rodney yelled, staying down to avoid the crossfire.

"They are responsible for the turmoil on this world!" Teyla shouted back. "They will make for the gate. We can attempt to cut them off."

Ronon fired one final blast at the retreating raiders, watching it deflect off the hull of their craft, and turned to sprint up the hillside. Teyla and the Marines followed in close pursuit, the scientists and Nistra guards lagging behind.

The incline was long, and Teyla's lungs began to burn as she pushed onward. However, the raiders must have required some time to power up their ship. The Stargate was already coming into view at the top of the hill by the time she heard the whine of engines overhead. The ship swept past and swung around in a wide arc to face the gate, which soon whirred to life.

"They have an…onboard dialer," Rodney panted from somewhere behind her, sounding impressed and winded. "Where the hell…'d they get that?"

Through illicit means, no doubt. More significant in Teyla's mind was the fact that the ship itself did not appear to be armed. Quite a fortunate state of affairs. Waiting until a familiar rush of noise accompanied the engagement of the gate, she dashed out between the craft and its destination, pointed her borrowed handgun at one engine, and fired multiple shots.

No effect from the small weapon was noticeable. The Nistra guards swung their whips in vain, unable to reach their target. The ship remained airborne, flying directly over their heads toward the event horizon only a few paces away. As it did so, one of the raiders opened a hatch and threw something out onto the ground.

The ship vanished through the gate, just as she heard a horrified shout from John. "Teyla—*get out of there!*"

She had no time to wonder where he had come from, because Ronon slammed into her from the side without warning. A great explosion lifted her off her feet, and then she knew nothing more.


John had acted against instinct when he'd sent Teyla to investigate the fragmented radio call rather than go himself. While he trusted her implicitly and in no way believed her incapable, the responsibility was his. He'd let the political niceties of the situation sway his judgment, though, worried that offending their hosts might risk their access to the technology and materials on this planet.

He regretted the decision almost exactly ten minutes later, when another brief radio transmission broke through: static peppered with the unmistakable sounds of gunfire.

Out of his chair in a split-second, he waved Lorne back when the Major moved with him. "Stick to Dr. Weir no matter what," he ordered in a low voice. "She might need a bodyguard after all."

"Understood, sir."

Throwing Elizabeth an apologetic look over his shoulder, John headed for the stairs. "Everybody stay down here, out of sight."

Demands and accusations flared up in his wake. He ignored the raised voices, taking the steps two at a time and mentally kicking his own ass the entire way. *What*

*kind of idiot lets himself be out of contact with his team on
a planet two steps away from declaring war?*

As soon as he reached the surface, he was confronted
by a chaotic mass of noise. Most of the sounds he could
isolate and identify: P-90s on automatic, along with a
9-mil and Ronon's blaster. And something else. Not a
jumper, but close. All of it seemed to be coming from the
gate area.

Hustling up the slope, he keyed his radio. "Somebody
want to give me a sit-rep?"

Surprisingly, it was a wheezing Rodney, not one of the
Marines, who answered. "Had a visit…from some raiders."

Okay, that was well and truly confusing. "Why aren't
you still in the labs?"

"Second entrance. Tell you later. Get *up* here."

For once, John had no objection to being told what to
do. He picked up his pace, finally arriving at the gate in
time to see a ship screaming toward the event horizon.
Teyla, Ronon, and the Marines fired volley after volley at
the craft as it passed, with no luck.

A small, round object fell to the ground just before the
ship was swallowed up by the puddle, rolling to a stop
only a few yards from where Teyla and the Nistra guards
stood.

Recognition, immediate and awful, stopped John cold.
"Teyla!" he yelled. "Get out of there!"

Ronon must have realized what it was at almost the
same moment, because he raced toward her. Before he
could shove her out of the way, the grenade detonated.

The shock wave was strong enough that it knocked
John flat from thirty yards away. By the time he was able

to push himself upright, the ringing in his ears slowly sub-siding, he saw that the wormhole had snapped shut, almost as if cut off by the blast itself. A rough circle of grass in front of the gate had been blackened, and on its perimeter lay the scorched, broken bodies of the two Nistra guards, clearly beyond help.

There was no sign of Teyla or Ronon.

"What the hell just happened?" he demanded.

A couple of the Marines had been caught in the periphery of the blast as well. Thankfully, they were in better health than the Nistra and their clothing had offered them more protection. Sergeant Ellis went to assist Corporal Adams with his leg wound, while Rodney and two shell-shocked engineers stood nearby, staring at the now-silent gate.

"Rodney!" John strode forward and grabbed his friend's arm. "What *happened*?"

After a pause, Rodney blinked and turned to him with stunned eyes. "The explosion," he said dully. "It pro-pelled them through the event horizon just before the gate shut down."

John wasn't sure how close Ronon and Teyla had been to the grenade. There was a chance they might not be too badly injured—wherever they were. "Did you see what address the raiders used?"

"Yes, but—"

"But nothing. If we know the address, we can go after them. You memorized it, didn't you?"

The subtle challenge brought Rodney swiftly back to his usual form. "Of course I did," he snapped. "I also observed that the grenade had a surprisingly strong con-cussive effect on the wormhole, and there's really nothing good that can come of such effects." He hurried over to the DHD, fumbling in his pocket for a scanner. "I need to check the transit data against some historical files back on Atlantis before we go charging off on a rescue."

"Fine. As long as we make it quick. We don't know how much time they've got." *If any*, he refused to say aloud. He'd be damned if he was going to write off half his team.

"Colonel, report." Elizabeth's voice came through the radio.

So much for her staying put in the underground facility. "I thought I said—"

"We're in the ruins, which still qualifies as 'out of sight.' I think you can understand why I needed to use the radio. What's going on?"

John couldn't blame her for wanting answers. "There was a raider attack," he said curtly. "They escaped in a ship through the gate. Ronon and Teyla accidentally ended up going through with them."

"Damn," she said quietly.

"It gets worse. The Falnori and Nistra guards that were left at the gate are dead. All of them."

He heard her intake of breath and the outraged reactions of Cestan and Galven in the background. "What's your plan?"

Good question. Scanning the remains of the Atlantis group, John replied, "McKay, Wen, and Kendall are with us—apparently there's another way out of the facility, and the raiders were using it. I'm going to take them and head home. Rodney's got the gate address the raiders used so we can go after our people. A couple of my guys are a little banged up, so we'll take them back with us and send you some reinforcements. Assuming you want to continue the talks."

"I think I have to try. Especially now that there have been fatalities…this is going to make things substantially harder."

"Yeah, I'll bet." Afraid to waste too much time, he added, "We'd better get going. We'll check in as soon as we know something."

"All right. Good luck."

Hurrying over to the injured Marines, John bent down and slung Corporal Pratt's arm across his shoulders. "Help Adams," he told the engineers, jarring them into action at last. "Rodney, dial the gate."

By the time he stepped into the gate-room, John felt about ready to crawl out of his skin. Adrenaline, primed for a potential rescue mission, battled with a gnawing fear he wasn't ready to acknowledge. "A little help, please," he called to the security team on duty. In response, two Marines moved to take the wounded corporal off his hands just as Carson and a medical team arrived.

John immediately bounded up the stairs to the control room, aware that Rodney was right on his heels. "So what's the problem with a concussive effect on an open wormhole?" he wanted to know.

Rodney's expression as he sat down at the dialing computer was grim. "Believe it or not, a large enough force applied at exactly the wrong moment can shift the wormhole's matter stream. Some years ago, SG-1 was in transit when an active gate was struck during an attack. Half the team was bounced accidentally to Earth's second gate in Antarctica, before anyone even knew the second gate existed."

"So Ronon and Teyla might have ended up at another destination altogether?" That didn't sound like an impossible obstacle. "Then they can just dial back here."

"Not necessarily. Not if they didn't make it very far to begin with." Rodney uploaded the data from his scanner, wholly focused on the console in front of him. "On first glance, the data I grabbed from the DHD on 418 seems to suggest that, when the wormhole's stability was disrupted, it almost folded back in on itself."

"Almost? We know they weren't bounced back to through the planet's gate."

"Physically impossible, since the matter stream only flows one way." Rodney's tone grew subdued. "What's the next closest gate?"

Suddenly the fear pulled ahead of the adrenaline. His stomach in freefall, John asked, "You think—?"

A defiant glower cut him off. "I don't want to *think* anything until I *know*."

The control room personnel had backed off to give them space. John spotted Wen and figured he must have explained the situation. A painful silence settled over the room for a few drawn-out seconds. At last, Rodney lifted his head, looking utterly defeated.

"It's confirmed," he said quietly. "The data says the matter stream was reflected back to P7L-418. The shock wave must have bounced them to orbital gate."

*No.*

Shutting his eyes against a rush of emotion he couldn't afford, John forced himself to think. This wasn't over, damn it. He spun toward the gate tech hovering nearby. "Call upstairs and have Jumper One preflighted ASAP."

"Yes, sir," the tech answered automatically.

The command shook Rodney out of his daze. "What do you expect to accomplish with that?"

"Do whatever you have to do to make sure the wormhole connects to 418's space gate." John headed for the stairway to the jumper bay. "I'm not abandoning our people."

"Abandon—Colonel, did you forget how this works? If we dial 418 right now, whatever we send through will go to the ground gate. I can't override the planet's dialing system without expending a lot of time and complex effort. I certainly can't replicate the original shock wave with any degree of precision. We'd have to fly up to orbit and locate the space gate by jumper, and I think you know as well as I do how long that would take."

Too long for two people exposed to the vacuum of space to survive. John stopped on the third stair. He had to face facts; it had been too long already.

But if the Pegasus Galaxy had taught him anything, it was that exceptions and unexpected outcomes were a way of life.

Carson chose that moment to enter the control room, setting his medkit on a chair. "Adams and Pratt will be fine," he reported. "Would someone care to tell me how they acquired burns and shrapnel wounds?"

"Teyla and Ronon are dead," Rodney answered bluntly. "The same explosion that injured the Marines knocked them through the gate to 418's orbital address. They're floating around the planet like so much space junk, and yet Sheppard seems to think we can magically rescue them."

"I didn't say that." John stepped back into the room

and turned away from the doctor's obvious shock, trying to get a handle on just what he was really trying to do. "I said we don't leave people behind."

"Not when we can help it, no. Unfortunately, there are some rules even you can't break. The best result we can hope to achieve now is recovering the bodies." Rodney stood up from the computer and folded his arms. "Carson, care to help me out here?"

Clearly still coming to grips with the awful truth, Carson took a hesitant step forward. "Colonel, maybe you'd better let me have a look at that arm."

Not comprehending, John glanced down. A five-inch-long hole had been scorched into his left sleeve, a patch of skin blistering underneath. It stung, now that he noticed it, but not badly. Not anywhere near badly enough to distract him from this.

He shrugged out of his jacket to let Carson work and continued to argue his point. "We haven't even checked to make sure the city database was accurate."

"Accurate?" Rodney repeated. "When has the database ever had a typo?"

"It doesn't always have complete information," John insisted, hearing the weakness of his argument all too clearly. "This gate might be set up differently, or—"

"Just what do you think we're going to find out there? Candy Land? The records were very detailed on what happened during the battle for P7L-418. There's enough debris in orbit that you'll have to be extremely cautious about our approach to avoid crashing into a derelict ship." Rodney's hand flew up as if to block John's imminent protest. "And before you say we could utilize the jumper's shield, understand that you'll need to deactivate said shield while recovering the bodies, which may be a difficult proposition amid the wreckage. Keep in mind also that you'll have to do some sensor sweeps to figure out exactly where in orbit the gate *is*."

Rubbing tired eyes, Rodney concluded, "I've been working through the various scenarios ever since I realized the situation, Colonel. Believe me, I've already grasped at every straw within reach. This isn't something we can resolve simply by thinking harder, and it certainly can't be resolved by rushing in blindly. Everything I just described will take time to plan and set up. No matter which way we approach it, this is a recovery mission, not a rescue."

How could he accept that? John got in Rodney's face, yanking his half-bandaged arm out of Carson's grip in the process. "Don't just stand there and tell me it can't be done. Find a way!"

Bristling, Rodney fired back. "What, so if I acknowledge reality, that somehow means I care about Ronon and Teyla less than you?"

"Both of you, stop it," ordered Carson with a vehemence he rarely showed. It made an impact; Rodney's mouth snapped shut. With that hard set of his jaw, his own sadness and frustration became visible at last.

The doctor finished bandaging John's forearm before speaking again, more gently. "Listen to yourself, John. What are you really hoping to find?"

"I don't know! But what's our alternative? Just let them go, forget about them?"

"Forget about them, certainly not," Carson replied, his voice solemn. "Let them go…aye, lad. I'm afraid so."

John scrubbed a hand over his jaw, fast running out of

rational points to make. Hell, he was starting to run out of irrational ones. All he had—all he knew—was the fact that his teammates were out there, and it went against everything he held fundamental to leave them, whether for an hour or forever, where they lay.

Where *his* mistake had led them. He'd sent Rodney's group off unarmed, and this was the result.

"God *damn* it," he whispered.

The control room seemed frozen in place. Finally, the tech ventured, "Sir, Jumper One is preflighted and ready for deployment."

Only Carson and Rodney dared to watch him for a reaction. Rodney's chin jutted out in challenge, while Carson's eyes reflected concern and sorrow.

In his entire life, John had never been so helpless.

"Cancel that," he said, hardening his voice. "Assemble another security team to send back to the planet. Rodney, take whoever and whatever you need to set up the recovery mission. I…" What could he do now? "I'll take Jumper One to the mainland."

He'd already started toward the stairs to the jumper bay once more when Rodney reminded him, "You're in charge here while Elizabeth's off-world."

"Then I guess that means *you're* in charge for a while. I have to break the news to the Athosians that Teyla's not coming back."

"Someone has to," said Carson. "It doesn't have to be you, not right this moment."

John didn't stop. If he stopped moving, he'd start feeling, and that would be the ballgame. "Yes, it does." It was the last thing he would be able to do for her. He was determined to do it right.

# CHAPTER EIGHT

"Unconscionable," bellowed Cestan, his face reddened in fury. "This vile act shows the true colors of the Nistra. To not only dishonor the Hall, but murder our warriors and strike out at those who have come to help us work toward peace—"

"How unexpected for you to immediately accuse us." Galven's tone made it clear that sarcasm was in no way a foreign concept on this planet. "Do you forget that we suffered losses as well? What evidence have you to suggest that the raiders were Nistra?"

"This was merely the latest and most brazen in a long line of raids." The Falnori governor paced behind the table.

"I would agree," Galven responded coldly. "Dr. Weir, perhaps you will now concede that I speak the truth about the adarite being stolen from my people?"

Elizabeth held up both hands to quiet the room, feeling like a junior high school teacher. A substitute teacher, even, given how much heed the two men were paying her. "I am drawing *no* conclusions about the identities of the perpetrators at this time," she told them, her voice level. "For one thing, the raiders escaped in a ship. Do either of your peoples have access to that kind of technology?"

"With the meager amount of adarite we receive from the Nistra?" Cestan scoffed.

Galven's fists slammed down with a *thunk* as he leaned dangerously across the table. "We can hardly make whips from what remains after your gluttonous thefts."

Same song, different key. Elizabeth massaged her temples with her fingers. For a few minutes, she'd thought she had a chance of breaking through the leaders' intractable viewpoints. Then they'd heard the shots over the radio, and it had all come apart.

A subdued "Ma'am?" from the stairwell drew her attention to Sergeant Markovich, one of the security team leaders. John must have sent him from Atlantis to augment the Marines already in place. The sergeant hovered only two steps inside the room, his features carefully expressionless.

"Excuse me," she said, leaving the table and the battle behind. "Sergeant?"

"We've secured the area, ma'am. All of it this time. The second entrance was well-hidden—a hatch with the best camouflage surface I've ever seen, in terms of both color and texture. Whoever opened it must have previously found it from the inside. Otherwise no one would have known it was there."

"What's the status back home?"

The sergeant held her gaze through a brief pause, and Elizabeth felt some of the warmth leach from her skin.

"Ma'am, Dr. McKay confirmed that Teyla and Ronon accidentally traveled to the planet's space gate."

He didn't elaborate. She neither needed nor wanted him to. She closed her eyes, suddenly tired beyond measure.

"All right," she said softly. "Thank you." *God, now what?*

On numb legs, she walked back to the table. Cestan and Galven might have noticed her absence; it was impossible to tell.

"The Falnori lands lie closer to the Hall," Galven was saying. "It would not have been difficult for your kind to stage this 'raid' to disrupt this accord and further your own cause."

Cestan laughed, a caustic sound without a trace of humor. "You clutch at smoke. It was I who first agreed to take part in these talks."

Steeling herself to head back into the fray, Elizabeth raised her voice. "Minister, Governor, I think you've lost sight of a critical point. The raiders had a ship. That fact suggests that they were not Falnori or Nistra, but uninvited guests from elsewhere."

Galven didn't miss a beat with his reply. "Possibly *not* uninvited. A convenient arrangement for someone who wishes to conceal his involvement."

"That claim could just as easily be applied to you!" Cestan fired back.

Elizabeth bit down on the inside of her lip to keep from screaming out her frustration. Were these men serious? Each blaming all the ills of the world on the other? "Gentlemen, please," she said wearily. "How much contact do either of you have with travelers through the Stargate? Do you have trading partners on other planets who could be responsible for something like this?"

"Not many, and none steady," answered Cestan.

A nod signaled Galven's agreement. "Of late there has been little to trade."

"So you say. Yet you have shown no evidence of these supposed raids into your territory." Cestan's demeanor grew thoughtful. "Just as Dr. Weir's people found mine, other off-worlders could have found you. Have the Nistra struck a new accord with someone else? Is that where your adarite goes?"

"You speak of evidence?" Suddenly Galven looked slightly paranoid and rather dangerous, his eyes darting back and forth between the governor and Elizabeth. "*These* off-worlders 'found' you, and we have only their word as to what happened here today. How can I be sure of *their* honesty?"

That did it. Elizabeth faced the Nistra leader squarely, skewering him with her gaze. In the iciest tone she could summon, she said, "Minister, my people came here in good faith, and two of them are now dead. If you think this is an appropriate time to question our intent, let me state in the plainest possible terms that you are *mistaken*."

It was a minor victory of sorts. Both men briefly fell silent, taken aback. After a moment, a subdued Galven spoke up. "Please accept my apologies, Doctor. I was not aware of your losses."

"Nor was I," Cestan added immediately. "Today we all mourn. A line has been crossed. These raids cannot continue. If the boundaries of the Hall are not respected, it may be time to consider enforcing them with guards."

"Falnori guards?"

"Stop." Elizabeth held up a hand, keeping a tenuous grip on her confidence. True, the first round of negotiations had deteriorated into wild conspiracy theories, but there might still be something left to salvage.

There had to be. She refused to accept the possibility that Ronon and Teyla had died for a petty territorial squabble.

"I don't believe we're accomplishing anything of value

right now. I propose a day-long recess for all of us to care-fully consider what our goals for these talks should be." She put every ounce of authority she possessed into her next statement. "I suggest that all parties either come back with open minds, or don't come back at all."

Turning on her heel, she strode toward the stairs. Cestan made an aborted attempt to head her off, but his protest died when Lorne blocked his path. She heard the Major move to follow her as she took the steps without so much as a glance behind.

After releasing Corporals Adams and Pratt to their quarters, Carson was relieved to find the infirmary empty of patients. He wasn't sure he'd completely grasped the fact that Teyla and Ronon were gone, and he suspected that when the reality of it finally hit him, he'd be useless for a good while.

Most likely there would be those among the expedi-tion who didn't feel the loss of two aliens as keenly as they would for one of their own. It had been a long time, though, since Carson had even thought the word 'alien' in that context. Kind Teyla, graceful in every sense of the word, and loyal Ronon, who'd defended this city and its inhabitants as if he'd been born to it.

On second thought, maybe keeping busy would serve him for a bit longer. Carson had no desire to conjure up an image of his friends' bodies floating abandoned in space, nor did he need to recall the look in Colonel Sheppard's eyes when he'd at last conceded defeat.

Surely there were some supplies around here some-where that were due for an inventory.

Seven shelves of medical tape and rubber gloves later,

Carson heard the main doors to the infirmary slide open. Stepping out of the supply room, he found two science team members looking around with uncertainty and some trepidation. "How can I help you gentlemen?"

Radek Zelenka rubbed the back of his neck, ruffling unkempt hair as he hesitated. "My head aches," he finally admitted.

For a moment, Carson was oddly grateful to have someone to help, someone within his reach now that two others were beyond it. Instantly he shut down that line of thought. "When did you first notice the pain?"

"About a day."

"And the severity?"

Radek's shrug was muted, as if the motion might exacerbate his discomfort. All he said, though, was, "So far it has been manageable without aspirin."

A bit odd, that. Radek wasn't the squeaky-wheel type, but neither was he overly stoic. "At the risk of treating you like Rodney," asked Carson, "if it's manageable, what's got you concerned enough to come here?"

The Czech aimed a pointed glance at his companion—Dr. Wen, Carson recalled.

"I have noticed a slight headache ever since returning from P7L-418," said Wen.

"And you think there's a connection? Radek, I didn't realize you'd gone off-world with the team."

"I did not." Radek's demeanor was grave. "However, of anyone in the city, Wen and I have spent the most time in contact with the ore."

*That* was quite a wrinkle. "I see." Having no other response, Carson produced a penlight. Comprehending, Radek took off his glasses to submit to a cursory examination. "Pupils are a bit dilated, but not to an alarming degree," Carson noted. "I trust you've locked up the adarite sample?"

"It is in an airlock chamber in the energy lab," Wen assured him.

"Good. I'll want to run some tests of my own on it. Realize, of course, that two people are not enough to be considered much of a pattern." With a reassuring smile, he clapped a hand on Radek's shoulder. "This might be a simple coincidence."

"It might." Radek didn't look at all comforted. "But what was I doing three hours ago?"

"I couldn't begin to guess. Was it something significant?"

"I would not know. I cannot remember."

Carson felt the smile bleed away from his face. If Radek was serious—and he certainly looked serious—this had just escalated from a minor issue to a substantial concern. "Short-term memory loss in addition to the headache. Any other symptoms?" Radek shook his head miserably, and Carson turned to Wen. "And you?"

The engineer shifted from foot to foot. "My memory is intact, I think, but parts of the mission are…fuzzy. One would expect a hostage situation to have some clarity in hindsight."

"All right. Over here." Carson steered Radek over to the Ancient-designed full-body scanner and gestured for him to hop up on the bed. Once the scientist was settled, the machine began mapping him from head to toe. It wasn't long before Carson had enough data to be troubled.

He reached for his earpiece to call the control room.

"As soon as all three of them are available, please have Dr. Weir, Colonel Sheppard, and Dr. McKay meet me in the infirmary. There's a potential new development they need to be aware of."

The image that greeted Rodney upon entering the infirmary was one of Radek and Wen, sitting on neighboring beds and being attended with far more solicitousness than Carson normally showed Rodney. "I'm afraid I'll need to keep you under observation for a while longer," the doctor was telling them. "Anything I can get you to help pass the time?"

With a wounded-puppy look—*oh, give me a break*, Rodney resisted saying—Radek asked, "Perhaps one of your mother's scones?"

Carson's gaze sharpened. "Don't push your luck."

"What's going on?" Rodney demanded. "Is something wrong with them? And where'd you two hide the adarite?"

Radek rolled his eyes. "Stop. Your heartwarming concern may cause me to weep."

"Well, you're evidently not dying, so excuse me for showing a little pragmatism." A beat later, Rodney glanced at Carson. Couldn't hurt to confirm it, considering the situation. "They're not, right?"

"No, Rodney, I'm fairly sure they'll be fine." Carson paused as the doors opened to admit Elizabeth and, a few strides behind, Sheppard. Both looked like the weight on their shoulders was getting to them. Rodney avoided the Colonel's gaze. Their discussion in the control room still bothered him, for reasons he didn't care to examine.

"What do you need to show us, Carson?" Elizabeth

asked, her professional demeanor firmly in place.

"Nothing good, I'm afraid. It appears there may be some side effects caused by exposure to adarite."

"Side effects?" Sheppard's eyebrows climbed. "From a rock?"

"An exceptionally energetic rock," Rodney clarified, already occupied with a cursory self-exam. He'd had contact with the adarite sample. His breathing seemed all right; pulse was a little elevated—

"Relax, Rodney." Carson had noticed his surreptitious checks, or at least his understandable anxiety. "If you feel all right, you *are* all right. We believe the symptoms are temporary after such a short exposure."

"I'll consider relaxing after you tell me what kind of symptoms you're referring to," Rodney snapped.

"Neurological. Specifically, cognitive deficits." Carson crossed the room to a wall-mounted screen, which displayed a multicolored cross-section of a human brain. "The scanner works a bit like a magnetic resonance machine would on Earth. Among other things, it measures the blood flow and electrical activity in various regions of the brain. These are the hippocampus regions, which control the storage of memories." He pointed to the sides of the image, indicating two groups of bright red and orange splotches. "Here you see a typical level of activity. Neural pathways are being formed, creating memories. Now contrast that with this scan of Radek from this afternoon."

Another image appeared on the screen next to the first. The corresponding areas on the second image were darker, the warm colors replaced by a scattering of blue and green. The sight worried the hell out of Rodney. "I thought you said they were going to be *fine*! That looks like incremental brain death!"

"It's already beginning to resolve itself," replied Carson, unperturbed.

"Yes," Radek interjected. "For instance, I recall being denied baked goods a few minutes ago."

Elizabeth's forehead wrinkled in confusion.

"Not to worry—that's a perfectly rational statement." Carson sent Radek an exasperated look before continuing. "I've yet to isolate the specific cause, but it appears that some property of adarite inhibits the transition of information from short-term to long-term memory. I'm no manner of neurologist, so I'll need to read up on a few issues. The effects, though, remind me of some older case studies from medical school on electroconvulsive therapy."

"Shock treatment?" Sheppard asked. "That screwed with memory?"

"I've been told that ECT patients often lost a fair amount of time surrounding their sessions. In this case, the adarite may be emitting the equivalent of an electric charge. Not anywhere near as strong as an ECT treatment, I wouldn't think."

Remembering the not-quite-electromagnetic interference he'd detected on the planet, Rodney wasn't so sure. "It's a different type of energy, so comparisons aren't worth much. For all we know, it may spike when the adarite is pressurized," he suggested. "Such as when a whip is powered up. Damn it, there's *always* a catch, isn't there?"

"Carson, you said earlier that you thought a brief exposure wouldn't produce any lasting effects," said

Elizabeth. "What about longer exposures?"

The doctor shook his head. "I can't say without any experience. Some studies of extended ECT usage reported cases of permanent cognitive deficits."

In two minutes, all Rodney's ideas for harnessing adarite power had gone up in smoke. He stood there, feeling like the rug had been yanked out from under him. Again. This galaxy had an infuriating habit of behaving like Lucy Van Pelt, taunting Charlie Brown with the football.

Elizabeth, however, appeared to have something different on her mind. "Minister Galven mentioned many of the Nistra being in poor health. They're the ones who mine the adarite. For the last few generations, they've been trying to increase production, only to see their situation worsen. Is it possible the adarite is responsible?"

"Although I'd need to examine one of them to confirm it, I think that's very likely," said Carson. "The last few generations, you say?"

"That's right. The Nistra even moved their villages closer to the mining territory."

"Which must have increased their exposure levels," Rodney realized. "Small wonder that their society is starting to disintegrate."

Elizabeth pressed her lips together, considering the new development. "This will change the negotiations markedly," she said at last. "One of the main points of contention is the procurement of adarite. When both parties learn that they're fighting over something so harmful…I can't begin to predict how they'll react."

To say nothing of the fact that Atlantis no longer had much of an incentive to help out with these people's dispute. Rodney stole a glance across the room, more concerned about the Colonel's reaction than those of the Falnori or Nistra. Sheppard had been counting on finding a weapon to use against the Asurans—more than Rodney deemed healthy, if the truth were told—and it had just been snatched out of his grasp.

Sheppard's expression was still as determined as ever. "So how do we get around this?" he wanted to know.

Carson blinked. "Get around it? I'm not sure I understand."

"We need this stuff, Carson. There has to be a way to counteract whatever effect it has on the brain."

As usual, Rodney was a few steps ahead of him. "Not without altering the energetic properties of the ore, I suspect. We'd lose most of the power we set out to utilize. And any shielding robust enough to block EM-type transmissions of that strength would be impossible to work within." He heaved a sigh. "Believe me, I'm as disappointed as you are."

Normally, he would have labeled Sheppard as a pretty perceptive guy. Today the officer didn't seem to be taking the hint. "Then we limit exposure," he maintained, absently scratching his bandaged forearm. "Work in shifts, maybe. We can't just give up on the research."

Carson hesitated. "I'm not sure that's wise—"

"I'm very sure that's *not* wise," Rodney declared emphatically. "Did you miss the detail about unknown long-term effects to potentially include amnesia and cognitive impairment? What part of 'I need all my brain cells intact' is unclear to you?"

Immediately he found himself under the searing stare of an indomitable colonel. "*Nothing* about this is unclear to me, Rodney," Sheppard said in a low voice. "What do you suggest we throw at the Asurans when they show up to take Atlantis? This is our best shot at finding a way to stop them. You said yourself that we've got nothing else."

"I never said that I wouldn't keep looking, though! There has to be another approach. One that doesn't involve putting ourselves at risk."

"Sometimes risks have to be taken when tailor-made solutions don't exist."

"Do you honestly think you're the only one worried about our chances against the replicators from hell?" In an unusual flash of insight, Rodney realized he was angry at Sheppard—and why. "You don't even realize that you're running off the rails, do you? You're obsessed with this semi-mythical weapon that's going to solve all our problems, and it's wrecking your judgment."

"*You're* going to lecture me about being obsessed?" Sheppard fired back. "After Doranda?"

The remark sliced deep, all the more so because it was accurate. Rodney's hubris over Project Arcturus had been forgiven, he'd thought, but obviously not forgotten. "I'm in a unique position to recognize the signs, I think," he responded tightly. "You're so desperate to have an answer for the Asuran threat that you sent us into an unfamiliar location unarmed, and look how that turned out."

He knew he'd struck a nerve when Sheppard's ever-present veneer of calm cracked and he turned sharply away.

"Don't do this, either of you," Elizabeth said softly. "You're a team."

"We're all that's *left* of a team." Sheppard stalked

across the infirmary bay, radiating fury on an unprece-
dented level. The odd thing was, it didn't appear to be
directed at Rodney or anyone else. It was real enough,
though; Sheppard was nearly shaking with it. For a man
who seemed to pride himself on keeping his cool, he
looked dangerously close to letting control slip away.

"You do what you think you have to do," he told
Rodney, tension holding his frame taut. "But don't tell
me how to do my job. You're not the one responsible for
defending this city, and you're sure as *hell* not the one
answering to the families of the Marines we keep ship-
ping home in body bags."

"And none of that alters the fact that some things in the
universe are fixed constants, no matter how much righ-
teous anger you summon!" Damn it, Rodney missed his
teammates too, but he knew beyond all doubt that neither
of them would have wanted this. "What do you want us
to do here, Colonel? Tell me. Do you really want to try to
build a weapon from something that will destroy our ability to remember why we *need* a weapon?"

"Maybe I do! What if it's the best option we have? I
don't know!" Sheppard yelled.

There was a long silence, in which his wild-eyed frustration fell away, leaving only agonized helplessness in
its wake. Rodney had never seen such emotion from
Sheppard before, and it shook him. A new possibility
arose: maybe the Colonel's anger had been aimed more at
himself than anyone else.

"I just don't know," Sheppard repeated quietly.

Rodney knew, because he felt it as well, and he could
see that the realization was going to hit Sheppard sooner
rather than later. What they wanted, as impossible as it

might be, was for Ronon and Teyla to have died for something.

Defeated, Sheppard pivoted on his heel and left the infirmary, punctuating his exit by slamming his open hand into the wall.

The surreal silence hung in the air after he'd gone. Elizabeth stared at the door, clearly at a loss. She looked back at Rodney with a plea in her eyes. "Rodney, there has to be something more we can do to study the adarite before we give up on it."

A few minutes ago, Rodney would have rejected the concept just on principle. Now, after seeing his team leader come close to unraveling in front of him, his perspective had shifted. "I...yes. There are a few tests we can still run with the sample contained in the shielded chamber."

"Aye. I'll help," Carson murmured.

In all likelihood, they'd end up in exactly the same place after those tests as before, but they'd run them anyway. After everything the expedition had weathered, it couldn't be pulled apart by something like this. Rodney was almost sure of it.

John had been walking for ten minutes before it occurred to him to wonder where he was going. The biting wind that assaulted him as soon as he stepped out onto the lower southwest pier was fitting. He needed to confront and be confronted.

"What the hell do you expect me to do?" he shouted into the rolling waves. He didn't rationally anticipate an answer, but then again there *had* been an Ancient lurking around in their city systems not too long ago. Angels in the architecture. He snorted in contempt. An angel would have *helped* them, rather than stood idly by as those apathetic Ascended always did. Sometimes he was almost ashamed of his genetic inheritance.

Or maybe he was just ashamed, period. What had he done today? What had he tried to do? Rodney was right about the disaster on 418. The safety of the off-world team had been his responsibility, and he'd let it slide because he'd just had to know what was in that facility. He'd dropped his guard, and Ronon and Teyla had paid for it.

Then he'd been so determined to give their sacrifices meaning that he'd all but ordered the science team to fry their own brains. God, what was *wrong* with him?

His teammates had died for nothing more than a failed mission. Two people whom he'd brought to the team, who'd stayed because they trusted him. Every week another Marine came back hurt or worse—from the Asurans, from the Wraith, from skittish natives with damned spears. No matter what he did, it kept happening, in the same old ways, and in new and terrible ways. Maybe it was unavoidable.

Or maybe his fitness to command really was eroding one casualty at a time.

He didn't know what he was doing out here. He never had. Leadership had fallen to him because of rank at first, and he'd kept it solely because no one else had any further or better experience than he did. The more he thought about it, the more he realized that such flimsy reasons weren't nearly good enough. Not when so many lives depended on making the right choices.

A wave crashed against the pier, sending saltwater

spray high into the air. John turned and went back inside. The chill followed him through the corridors and into his quarters.

*"Target fixation, my man,"* he could hear Captain Holland saying in that Midwestern drawl. One more ghost from one more choice that had failed. *"Happens to the best of 'em. You just gotta step back and figure out what's best for the mission."*

Sitting down at his desk, he opened the drawer and noticed the envelope still waiting inside, marked with Ford's cousin's name. He hesitated for a moment, but found that it only solidified his resolve.

Holland. Sumner. Ford. Ronon. Teyla. They were at the top, but the list went on and on.

John refused to add any more names to it.

He reached past the envelope for a pad of paper and a pen. Somehow a computer word-processing program didn't have the appropriate gravity for a letter of resignation.

# CHAPTER NINE

She heard the birdsong first, a low-pitched, melodic chatter not unlike that of the canyon gulls on Athos. Gradually she became aware of other sensations: a cool breeze across her face, a trace of moisture in the air, and pain.

Teyla stirred minutely, halting when the motion roused an insistent ache at her temple. A hand closed around her shoulder, and she forced her eyes open. Once her sight became focused, she found a concerned Satedan looming over her.

"You okay?" he asked.

"I—believe so." Aside from the vicious pounding in her head, a few cuts and scrapes appeared to be her only injuries. She began to push herself up to a sitting position, soon aided by Ronon's arm at her back. "And you?"

He shrugged. "Coat protected me from most of the flame." Crouching next to her, he pulled at his hair and examined a couple of dreadlocks that looked slightly singed at the ends. In spite of his indifferent response, she could see a patch of reddened skin on the side of his neck. "And like Sheppard keeps telling me, I have a thick skull."

It occurred to Teyla that she had no idea where they were. A rocky forest of some type, unfamiliar to her. "What happened?"

"You remember the raiders?"

Unfortunately, she did. "We were firing at their ship as

it went through the gate."

"They left us a present—an explosive. Probably trying to keep us from following them. I tried to get you out of the way before it blew." Ronon's expression was rueful. "Wasn't fast enough."

"Obviously you were, since I am alive. Thank you."

He deflected her gratitude by continuing. "The blast must have knocked us through the gate just behind the raiders. Don't know if they made a mistake when they dialed, or if this was a halfway stop for them, or what, but there doesn't seem to be much of anything around. I never even saw the ship again after we got here."

Teyla scanned the area. She observed a number of massive boulders interspersed with evergreen trees, and little else. "I do not see a gate."

"It's a few paces away, on the other side of these rocks. I figured we should get out of sight in case anyone came back. It hasn't been long, but there's been no gate activity yet." He stood and stretched, his spine cracking. "Your radio got lost somewhere, and mine's broken."

"You thought it better to stay here than return to Atlantis?"

Ronon grimaced. "You're not going to like this part."

It would have served no purpose to ask what aspect of this mission she *was* meant to like, based on events so far. Rather than explain, he held out his canteen and a packet from the small medical kit in her vest. She swallowed the pain tablet and permitted him to pull her to her feet. "Show me."

The walk was brief, as promised, and served to clear her head somewhat. The air had a crisp, clean scent, and the continuing birdsong accompanied them. She caught sight of one of the birds at last, a blue-gray animal much more diminutive than its voice suggested.

Rounding the side of the rock face, which towered at least ten times as tall as Ronon, she drew up short in surprise.

Debris littered the ground in a wide swath that extended as far as she could see. Most of it appeared to be metal, the remnants of a great structure of some type. Unlike the Ancient facility on P7L-418, the destruction here was total. She could identify large beams among the vast spread of smaller fragments. Under a thick layer of forest growth that obscured many details, the pieces were badly warped. Clearly it had been many years since the building had collapsed.

Amid the rubble, wedged in a ravine that split the rock face, stood the Stargate. Teyla amended her mental description immediately, for 'stood' was hardly an appropriate word. Despite having traveled to countless worlds, this was a circumstance she had never before witnessed. The huge gate was overgrown with so much vegetation that it was barely recognizable. She could see that it was cocked at an odd angle, tipped precariously forward—about twenty degrees off vertical, Rodney would have said. Little wonder that their arrival had been less than comfortable; the orientation of the gate must have caused the wormhole to pitch them onto the ground.

"The gate does not look like it was intentionally placed in this position," she said, choosing her footsteps with caution as she made her way through the wreckage.

"More like thrown," Ronon agreed. "I think all this junk used to be a building that housed the gate. A large one, maybe ten floors high. The gate could have fallen when it the building was destroyed and ended up like this."

With only the sides of the ravine to support the ring's considerable weight, she worried about the likelihood of somehow dislodging it. "It may not be stable."

"It's fine. I checked."

Teyla did not care to know how he had performed such a check.

"Besides, it looks like the building came down a long time ago. If the gate's stayed in place this long, it's stable."

What might this facility have been? A laboratory like the one on 418? Had it succumbed to a Wraith attack as so many others had?

There was a more immediate issue to address, Teyla realized. "Where is the dialing device?"

"Can't find one."

Her head snapped toward him, perhaps an ill-advised motion given her headache.

"I haven't covered the whole area yet." Ronon adopted a defensive tone. "I needed to make sure you were okay first."

Teyla softened her gaze. "I understand. I did not mean to question your actions." Still, the fact remained. They needed a dialer to get home, and none was apparent. "The raiders were able to dial the gate from within their ship."

"Yeah." He didn't say what he surely must have been thinking: since the structure was little more than a ruin now, there was no guarantee that a working dialer still existed. "Let's start our search over here."

They paced off a rough grid in order to ensure that they wouldn't overlook any areas. Nearby trees donated medium-sized branches to the cause; after a section of debris-strewn ground had been thoroughly searched, the pair stabbed a branch into the dirt in each of the section's four corners to mark its boundaries.

Hours passed while they combed through the wreckage, clearing tangled vines and mosses away from any surface that did not look naturally formed. Ronon took charge of moving the largest pieces, but both felt the strain. On occasion a smooth, curved piece of metal would snare their attention, only to raise false hopes.

With each branch placed, Teyla's dread became more acute. Often, out of increasing desperation more than anything else, they would err in their measurements and allow the sections to overlap so that they searched some areas more than once. All of it was to no avail.

The sun inched closer to the mountains. Ronon sat down hard, wiping sweat from his brow onto his sleeve. Resigned, he shook his head. "If there ever was a dialer in that building," he said, "there's nothing left of it now."

Teyla closed her eyes, unable to ward off the despair any longer. Without a device to dial the gate, and with no way to even identify their location, they were stranded.

"I appreciate you finally gracing us with your presence."

"Keep your shirt on, Rodney. Janczyk's on his way with the scanner." Carson glanced around the laboratory as he entered. He rarely had cause to visit many of the areas Rodney's team had devoted to Ancient technology research; his skills were required chiefly when someone touched something they shouldn't have. The directed energy lab was more austere than most. Other science sub-teams had personalized their respective labs with posters and photos from home. No such individual touches were visible in this room—only intimidating machinery separated by bulky metal and polymer shields, along with a neatly hand-lettered sign that read 'Don't screw up.'

Charming.

"You've got the sample in the airlock chamber?" Carson asked.

With an impatient gaze cast toward the ceiling, Rodney answered, "Yes, although the airlock feature itself is not of great use to us, since energy of this form can be transmitted through many types of solid boundaries. It's a wave, put plainly, not altogether different from a sound wave. Though I'd rather blast hip-hop music through my skull at top volume than hang around this stuff too long. Our somewhat optimistic theory is that the chamber's protective shielding will block enough of it to allow us to take some measurements before we start to forget why we're here."

"Are all physicists as naturally cheerful as you are, Rodney?"

Focused on initializing a machine that resembled an oscilloscope, Rodney frowned distractedly. "What?"

"Forget it." Carson turned as the lab door opened and Janczyk wheeled in a diagnostic imaging scanner, Earth-made because of the interference adarite induced in Ancient technology. "Jan, there's room for that over here."

As Janczyk wheeled the scanner past him, Rodney paused, and Carson could almost see the wheels turning in the scientist's head. Rodney never seemed to know how to act around Janczyk. He might have been one of the more socially awkward members of the expedition, but in this particular case he was hardly alone.

Before becoming one of Carson's more diligent research assistants, Karl Jancyzk had been a lance corporal in Atlantis's Marine detachment. He'd been in the city about a year when an off-world encounter with a Wraith had accelerated his twenty-two-year-old body to the physical age of almost seventy. The quick actions of his teammates had allowed him to become one of the few people to survive a feeding.

With only the barest notion of how the Wraith feeding process worked, Carson had despised the fact that he could do nothing to give the man back his stolen youth, so he'd listened when Jan confessed his dread of returning to Earth. The military had planned to give him a new identity to match his apparent age, and security concerns would have prevented him from reuniting with his family. Instead, Carson had suggested that he be retrained and allowed to stay in Atlantis. Colonel Sheppard had pulled up Jan's personnel file and noted his high test scores in the biological sciences, and Jan readily accepted Carson's offer of a research post.

The Marines, to their credit, still counted him as one of their own, and everyone had seen far stranger things in their time with the Stargate program. Even so, it couldn't be easy for a man not long out of high school to look and feel twenty years older than anyone else in the city, to say nothing of the mortality questions that must have blindsided him. One of Pegasus's everyday injustices.

The equipment was readied, and immediately a faint vibration could be detected on the pseudo-oscilloscope.

"Does that frequency happen to ring a bell?" Rodney asked. "No pun intended."

"Funny." Carson studied the readout. "It's in a harmonic range that could certainly be disruptive to neurological function. Neurons fire in specific patterns; in the hippocampus they fire almost in circular chains. If the adarite emits a wave that's on exactly the right frequency—or, rather, the wrong one—it's possible that it could un-sync that pattern and prevent the transmission of signals to other parts of the brain."

"And what a lovely thought that is." Rodney reached for the airlock chamber control pad. "I'm going to increase the pressure in the chamber to confirm whether or not this frequency is related to the energy discharge."

"Don't take it up too far," Carson warned. "This material is incredibly powerful."

"Thank you, Sherlock. I thought I'd just kick it up to three atmospheres and see if our brains short-circuited." Glaring derisively, Rodney tapped out a command on the keypad. "Increasing to 1.2 atmospheres."

Almost instantly, a spark lit the chamber, and the readings on the screen spiked. Rodney swore under his breath and brought the pressure back to one standard atmosphere. "Well, that was conclusive. The release of energy is correlated with the output of this frequency."

"So if we found a way to dampen the frequency, the adarite would no longer produce any power."

"Infuriatingly, yes."

A mild clatter sounded behind them. Carson turned to see Janczyk backed up against a shelving unit, holding his head in his hands. "Jan?"

It took two more calls before his assistant glanced up,

confusion clouding his eyes. "Sorry, Dr. Beckett. I just, uh, got this wicked headache all of a sudden."

"Did it coincide with the energy spike?" At Jan's blank expression, Carson traded a look of alarm with Rodney. "Jan, do you remember seeing Rodney increase the chamber pressure a minute ago?"

The ensuing silence spurred Rodney into action. "The chamber's shielding isn't effective," he deduced, slamming a thick metal cover down on the transparent lid of the chamber. "We just smacked ourselves with a level of brain-scrambling energy that was magnitudes higher than what Radek and Wen received."

"Infirmary. Now." Carson grabbed Jan's arm and steered him out into the corridor. Following close on their heels, Rodney locked the lab door behind them.

As soon as the trio arrived in the infirmary, Carson directed Jan onto the scanner bed, trying not to get ahead of himself. He didn't feel any different than he had earlier. Maybe there was more at work here than they yet realized.

Rodney paced the room, clenching and unclenching his fists at his sides. "I can't believe I was shortsighted enough to subject myself to that risk," he fretted. "What if I just destroyed my memories of my entire postdoctoral year? The loss to quantum mechanics research alone——"

Already Carson had had his fill of the scientist's brand of hypochondria. "Are you experiencing a headache and disorientation?" he asked, matter-of-fact.

The query only marginally slowed Rodney down. "Well, not yet, but my brain's always worked on a different level from those of other people, so who knows…"

"Short-term memory, Rodney. It disrupts the formation of new neural pathways, not existing ones. If you can remember the reason why you think you're screwed right now, you're not in fact screwed."

Occasionally logic had its perks. Rodney closed his mouth while he considered the theory.

"It's because I'm old, isn't it?"

Caught off-guard, Carson brought his gaze down from the dimmed neurological areas displayed on the screen to Jan's wizened, worried face. "That's why the adarite affected me first, or most, or whatever," continued the young man—Carson insisted on thinking of him according to his actual age, not the fragile husk the Wraith had left him. "I'm halfway to Alzheimer's anyway, and this just pushed it even further along."

"There's no reason to think that." Carson kept his voice firm. "The scan isn't showing any greater effect than Radek's and Wen's did earlier. You just happened to get your exposure in a shorter, heavier dose."

A moment later, it hit him. Both he and Rodney felt fine, while Jan's scan looked just like the results from Radek and Wen. What did Carson have in common with Rodney that the other three men did not?

"Rodney, your turn," he said suddenly, patting the diagnostic bed. Rodney blanched, evidently interpreting the order as a cause for concern. Carson threw up his hands. "I just got through telling you not to worry, didn't I? If it'll make you feel better, I'll have someone run the scan on me as well. Later. Right now I just need your results to act as a baseline for comparison against those who have shown symptoms."

"Oh. Say so next time, will you?" Rodney scooted onto the bed and lay down.

With an anxious Jan at his shoulder, Carson watched as a new neurological map was drawn on the screen. The activation in the hippocampal regions was diminished ever so slightly relative to a normal brain, but the effect was almost negligible compared to the scans of the other adarite-exposed scientists. He stood back, his suspicions confirmed.

As soon as he was free of the scanner, Rodney sat up, drumming his fingers on the bed in a staccato rhythm. "Well?"

"It's the gene," Carson replied simply. "It has to be."

For all his arrogance, Rodney really was every bit as intelligent as he claimed. The light in his eyes suggested that he was already working through the implications. "Of course. Why else would the Ancients have developed adarite technology? They were unaffected."

"And perhaps that's the reason for their eventual abandonment of the research. Their lab assistants would have had difficulties when exposed."

"It's so hard to find good help these days," Rodney said dryly. "Elizabeth needs to know about this. Turns out there's a more direct reason why the Nistra are worse off than the Falnori."

"Aye." Carson glanced at Jan. "How are you feeling, lad?"

"Relieved, Doc." Jan pushed a hand through steel-colored hair and pointed over his shoulder at the door. "I'm gonna get back to work. On something else."

"Go right ahead." After a moment, Carson turned back to Rodney. "Does this change anything for us? If your scan is representative, and it should be, there's still an effect on those with the ATA gene. It's minor, but it's there. Over time—"

"It could be harmful. We have no way of knowing, and I'm certainly not volunteering myself or anyone else as a guinea pig. Not to mention the fact that we'd have to keep the adarite somewhere remote, who knows how far from anyone not in possession of the gene." Rodney's face had reverted to its earlier grim state. "Sheppard's going to be pissed. Although that would hardly constitute a change from the status quo."

Carson considered telling Rodney about the rumor going around, the one where Atlantis's military commander had walked into Elizabeth's office and handed her his resignation. He decided against it. Rumors could be quite wild in the city. It was usually best to ignore them—even the troubling ones.

Instead, he said, "The Colonel's not had an easy time of it lately, Rodney, and he's as human as the rest of us."

"Speak for yourself." The remark fell flat, and Rodney stared at the floor for a beat or two. "The memorial service is going to be on the mainland. Elizabeth convinced the Athosians to wait until she wrapped up the debacle on 418 so she could participate."

With a nod, Carson started toward the door. "If she's headed back to the planet tomorrow, we'd better go explain this new development."

Many hours had passed since either Ronon or Teyla had last spoken. They had chosen to make camp near the gate ruins in the hope that Atlantis had some knowledge of their location and would be sending assistance. Ronon had taken the first watch and had dutifully woken her at regular intervals, as Dr. Beckett had instructed them to do when dealing with a possible head injury.

In spite of their meager supplies—two canteens and a few meal bars—it was not a difficult night. Both were accustomed to a somewhat nomadic existence, and, if Teyla was truthful with herself, she often missed the wind when sleeping in the sterile, re-circulated air of Atlantis.

When morning came without word from their teammates, however, her outlook grew less optimistic. Her head no longer ached, but they would run out of provisions before long, and the immediate area did not seem likely to offer any food or water.

The low rumble of Ronon's voice broke the stillness, echoing her thoughts. "We can't stay here forever." He'd been perched atop a rock nearly his own height, and now jumped down to ground level.

"I agree." Teyla rose from the cool ground and slipped back into the jacket she had used as a pillow. "Have you seen any sign of life—either animals to hunt or a settlement?"

He shrugged. "There are some faint tracks over there." Facing away from the gate, he pointed toward a stand of trees. "Looks like pretty small game, but I'll take what I can get."

Although she knew it would be prudent—necessary, even—to search for food and assistance, she found herself reluctant to stray too far. "We will need to take care to mark our path. This area is secluded, and we must not lose our way back to the gate."

The look of disbelief Ronon gave her in response was almost comical. Belatedly she recalled that for seven years his life had depended on being able to fall back to a planet's gate without delay. "I meant no offense."

"Didn't take any." He adjusted his holster, and she spared a moment to be grateful that they at least were armed. Wandering through the nearby debris, he gathered up an armful of small rocks and chunks of metal. "Remember how Sheppard signaled us when he was stuck in that time portal?"

She did. When they'd stuck Rodney's camera into the time dilation field so many months ago, they'd discovered a large arrow on the cave floor, fashioned from rocks and pointing in the direction John had gone. "We can leave a similar sign by the gate for the Atlantis team to find. It will confirm our presence on this world." She kept the next thought to herself. *If Atlantis has any idea where we are.* She trusted Rodney's resourcefulness and John's resolve, but such traits were not always enough. "Good idea."

"Took me half the night to come up with it." The admission was offered freely, which Teyla thought admirable. Nothing ever seemed to embarrass Ronon. He trusted his friends to accept him as he was, and he remained unconcerned about what anyone who was not a friend thought of him.

With a small smile, she moved to assist. Together they cleared debris from a three-meter square section of ground and then assembled the collected pieces into large, rough letters: 'R' and 'T'.

"They can't miss that," Ronon asserted. "Let's go."

He chose an exploratory route that wound through the trees. Teyla allowed him to lead, keeping a sharp eye on their surroundings. As they walked, she noticed a gradual incline to the forest floor. It was difficult to judge distances while the trees obscured her view, but there were mountains not far off, and they were approaching the foothills.

Bending low, Ronon examined a scuff mark in the dirt. "More animal tracks," he said quietly. "Pretty recent."

After nearly an hour of hiking, the forest thinned, and the terrain dipped to form a cave of sorts in the side of a hill. Before Teyla could take more than a cursory look, she heard a soft noise, as if branches had brushed together. She lengthened her stride and signaled for Ronon to listen, causing him to halt in mid-stride.

The noise repeated, and she caught a tiny blur of motion off to her right. Both she and Ronon dropped into a crouch to avoid giving away their presence. A creature ducked around the hill and sniffed at the moss on the trunk of a nearby tree. It appeared similar to a game animal her people had hunted on Athos—but smaller, standing only as high as her waist. She considered it a blessing; if luck had deserted them completely, they might have found this planet barren of any food sources.

Ronon advanced into the clearing without a sound, drawing his blaster from its holster. He took careful aim and—

"Stop! Name yourselves."

Instinctively the Satedan brought his weapon to bear as he whirled toward the voice. Teyla extended a calming hand. A local populace could be an even greater blessing to them. "We are lost travelers," she called into the woods.

To her surprise, a group of eight men and women materialized out of the trees, emerging from behind boulders and climbing down from branches. She identified them as hunters upon seeing the spears and bows they carried.

Ronon looked impressed that the group had escaped his detection, though not impressed enough to lower his blaster. Fixing him with a pointed stare, Teyla laid her hand on his arm until he relented. "We mean your people no harm. Rather, we ask your assistance," she continued in a measured tone.

The hunters' response was to raise their bows. "How simple-minded do you believe us to be?" sneered the leader. "Your kind is well known among us, marauder. We refuse to be deceived."

*Marauder?* Sharing a glance with Ronon, Teyla began to get a sense of what her Earth-born teammates called déjà vu.

# CHAPTER TEN

As soon as the hunting party aimed their weapons, Ronon had his trained as well. Sure, they could use these people's help, but not if the price was to be an arrow in his chest. Hadn't they just had this same experience on P7L-418?

"You have been visited by raiders as well?" Teyla seemed to be considering the probability of such a coincidence. Not likely, to Ronon's way of thinking. Maybe the raiders on 418 hadn't dialed this place by mistake after all. "We do not belong to their number. In fact, we were attempting to stop them on another world when we were accidentally transported here."

"A convenient tale." The lead hunter sized them up, pale eyes sharp with distrust. Her dark hair was captured in a tight knot at the nape of her neck, giving her face an angular, severe look. She looked skittish. The whole group did, come to think of it.

"An honest tale," Teyla returned. "We carry only what you see. We have little food and no means of transport. How can we be a threat to you?"

"That question has been answered in painful fashion before."

One of the hunters stepped forward—an adolescent, younger than any member of the Atlantis expedition. "Dantir, keep your place!" hissed the leader.

The teen ignored the warning, openly studying Ronon. "I've never seen anyone as big as you," he observed.

"It's not so rare where I come from." Ronon noted that all the hunters were relatively slight, some bordering on malnourished. None of them stood even as high as his shoulder. They wore boots that appeared to be nothing more than thick soles bound to their feet and laced up over the ankle. Their clothes were sturdy and plain, made from rough fabrics and animal hides. Not uniforms, at least not intentionally, but they might as well have been for the lack of variety.

"Where do you come from?" the boy, Dantir, wanted to know.

"Somewhere a long way from here." It occurred to Ronon that he wasn't sure if he meant his home world or his adopted city. At the moment, it didn't much matter. "We don't mean to cause any trouble. We just want to go home."

"Do your people use the Stargate?" Teyla asked. Receiving only blank stares in response, she tried again. "The Ring of the Ancestors?"

"The big metal circle in that direction." Ronon gestured with his gun. "It's wedged between some rocks in what remains of an old building. You must have seen it."

The leader replied cautiously. "We have seen the ruins, but they are of little use to us. How should we use this ring you speak of?"

"For transport. It connects many worlds. Although it still functions, it is missing a key piece…" Even as Teyla attempted to explain, Ronon could tell she wouldn't make much progress. These people obviously had no idea what a Stargate was, much less a dialing device.

"Is that how you arrive to rob from our village?" another hunter demanded. "Does your ship travel through this magical ring?"

"We don't *have* a ship." Ronon tried to rein in his frustration. "If we did, we wouldn't stand here and argue with you—we'd use it."

When Dantir took another step forward, Ronon was forced to lower his aim. He really didn't want to shoot a curious kid. "All we want is to find a way home," he insisted, more quietly. "If we can't…we still don't need to be your enemy."

Not all the hunters appeared convinced of the visitors' honesty. Dantir, however, continued to watch Ronon with rapt fascination. "You travel to other worlds," he said, awed. "Like the tales of the Ancestors?"

"Yes, indeed. The ring was their creation." Clearly heartened by the comment, Teyla glanced from him to the leader. "You know of the Ancestors, then?"

"Only that they once defended our world but were at last chased away by the Wraith," said the woman, sounding impatient. "They do not help us now. Dantir, step *back*."

"You taught me that we do not turn people away from our circle without reason, Mother," the boy answered, his eyes never leaving Ronon. "They have not given us reason to doubt them."

Ronon had no idea why the kid was so focused on him. He knew that a big man with a weapon didn't make the most trustworthy picture. Somehow, though, the kid was willing to vouch for him. He'd take what he could get. "And we won't," he vowed, holstering his gun.

The leader acknowledged her son's claim by lowering her bow. Grudgingly, the others did likewise. "Your words carry wisdom, if not respect," she told him with a glare of rebuke. Turning to the visitors, she continued, her features softening slightly. "Dantir is correct. Unfounded suspicion is not noble, and I apologize for mine. My name is Ilar. You may join our hunting circle."

"Thank you." Teyla relaxed a bit, hope still evident in her gaze. "Might there be someone among your people with knowledge of the ring, or of the building that contained it? A village historian, perhaps?"

Ilar hesitated. "There were many storytellers among us, once," she allowed. "Or so I have been told. It is becoming a lost art. I fear we may have little knowledge to offer."

The light in Teyla's eyes dimmed, but her smile did not falter. Ronon chose to pay more attention to the immediate situation. They'd found a native society, one that might at least provide them food for a time. The problem of getting off this planet could be faced later.

"We will hunt for the remainder of this day and the next before returning to our village," said Ilar. "You may travel with us if you wish."

Ronon glanced at his teammate, leaving the choice to her. He knew Teyla had been reluctant to leave the gate for fear a rescue team from Atlantis would fail to find them. All the members of the off-world teams had recently had transmitters placed under their skin so that they could be easily located, but as yet no one was certain of the devices' range. If a rescue was as improbable as he suspected, however, their best chance—as slim as it might be—lay with these people.

After a moment, Teyla gave a slight nod. "I am Teyla Emmagan," she replied. "My companion is Ronon Dex. We would be honored to join your hunt."

Dantir beamed and fell into step beside Ronon as the group moved out. "Are you properly called Ronon or Dex?"

With a shrug, Ronon said, "Ronon's fine."

"Very well. We are tracking the paledon, Ronon," Dantir explained. "Winter comes, and the village will need to store much meat."

"Paledon." Ronon watched the trees for movement. "Is that the small four-legged creature we saw before we ran into you?"

"It is," the boy confirmed. "We will pick up its herd trail, and I will show you how we hunt."

A muted laugh came from one of the older hunters. "You are on your first hunt yourself, and you mean to show the off-worlders how it is done?"

"My aim is truer than yours, Temal," Dantir shot back.

Ronon grinned to himself. This kid had guts. Then he spotted a flash of fur disappearing behind a rock, and he halted. The instincts of the hunters were well honed, because they immediately noticed and followed his lead.

Before long, a paledon stuck its head out from behind the rock, and after another moment it emerged fully. Ilar silently fell to one knee and drew her bow, but something startled the animal, and it began to scamper away.

Without a second thought, Ronon leveled his gun. The energy bolt sizzled through the air and dropped the paledon instantly to the ground.

"Ronon!" Teyla's voice was appalled. A beat late, he wondered if he might have offended their hosts: some cultures that hunted for sport placed specific rules on such pursuits. But these people needed the food. They couldn't get too angry about his method.

Risking a look at the hunters, he found their expressions shocked and impressed. Dantir's eyes were huge as he smiled widely.

Ilar found her voice. "Perhaps," she said, "this arrangement will benefit us all."

From her elevated vantage point on the walkway outside her office, Elizabeth watched the security team form up in the gate-room. To be sure, her second journey to P7L-418 would be undertaken more solemnly than the first. There would be no idealized optimism this time. Atlantis had nothing to gain from the proceedings; she was returning solely to help the Falnori and Nistra find a way to coexist. She could only hope that both groups' leaders would take her at her word.

John stepped out of the control room to join her. "Jumper Three's starting its second orbit," he reported neutrally.

Without knowing just what debris might be lurking right on the other side of 418's space gate, it had seemed more prudent to send a jumper through the ground gate and fly it up to orbit to scan for both the gate and Teyla and Ronon's transmitters. The recovery team had departed about an hour ago, and John hadn't left the command level since.

"Anything yet?" Elizabeth asked, knowing she'd already have heard if the answer was positive.

He shook his head. "There's a lot of space out there. It might take a while, but we'll find them." Glancing over at her, he asked, "What about you? Sure you want to do this?"

She raised her eyebrows. Maybe she'd let him off the hook in their previous discussion, but time had renewed her resolve, and in her view the subject of his resignation was far from closed. "Are you asking if I'm sure about going back to 418, or about leaving you in charge?"

Subconsciously, maybe, she'd hoped to produce a flinch with that comment. He didn't oblige. "I recommended Rodney."

"Yes, you did. But you also agreed to remain at your post until the SGC could send a replacement on the *Daedalus*, and if I hand the reins over to the chief science officer instead of the chief military officer, people are going to start asking questions that I don't think you'll want to answer just yet."

With a slight tilt of his head, John conceded her point. "I *was* asking about going back to 418. There's not much we can accomplish there."

"If we can do anything to keep the leaders from coming to blows, I'll consider the trip a success." Elizabeth leaned one elbow on the railing, facing him. "We jumpstarted this fight. Granted, it may only have been a matter of time before it escalated to this point on its own, but we brought the two sides face to face. Now six people are dead, and two societies are moving toward a pointless conflict. We can't walk away from that. Sometimes we have to do the right thing for all concerned, not just the expedient thing for us."

"I understand. I'm just not sure how far we should be willing to go to protect these people from their own outrage."

She didn't have a ready answer for him. Objectively she knew that they'd have to draw a line sometime; if tensions came to a head, she couldn't put Atlantis's Marines between advancing armies. Still, she had to believe peace was possible, and she had always believed that the carnage of needless battle was the purest form of tragedy.

Too many of her principles had been shaken by this galaxy already. She needed to cling fiercely to those that remained.

"These people shouldn't be at odds," she said at last. "They don't have incompatible values or beliefs. All I have to do is convince them of that."

"While also giving them a surprise about the ore that drives their respective economies. Better you than me." John sighed, rolling the strain out of his shoulders. "You think they'll listen this time around, or just step up the rhetoric? Or worse?"

She shrugged, choosing not to muzzle a brief burst of fatalism. "War is the continuation of politics by other means, I've heard."

The rueful twist of John's lips resembled a smirk, but it was entirely humorless. "Somehow I think Clausewitz would've had more to say if he'd met this galaxy."

At that point they were joined on the walkway by Carson, shouldering into a tactical vest as he walked. "I must say I have my doubts about whether the governor and minister will understand a warning about the hazards of adarite any better coming from me than they would from you," he remarked.

Not long ago Elizabeth might have believed his comment to be rooted in anxiety about going off-world. Carson Beckett had not been the most eager member of the Atlantis expedition at first, at least when it came to anything outside his infirmary. Now, of course, she knew better. If a task had to be completed for the greater good, whether it involved the weapons chair or an off-world mission, he wouldn't hesitate.

He might not sleep all that well afterward, she reflected, recalling with a twinge their utter failure with Michael, but he would act.

"I don't want to run the risk of being unclear and making the situation worse," she told him. "This way you can back me up if my Cliffs Notes version of the neurological effects goes astray."

"This may sound paranoid," said John, "but are you prepared to trust both those guys? As unlikely as it may be, there's still a chance that one of them is in league with the raiders."

In spite of the circumstances, Elizabeth felt encouraged by his caution. The Colonel may have been willing—too willing—to give up his title, but its associated responsibilities came more naturally to him than he may have realized.

"We can't eliminate the risk completely," she replied. "All we can do is assess it and mitigate whatever elements are within our control."

John made a face. "Why am I getting creepy flashbacks to the Air Force's Operational Risk Management course?"

"Because I once oversaw an Air Force installation, and civilians aren't exempt from taking that training." She zipped up her jacket. "Try to keep the archeology team from executing a hostile takeover of Rodney's unidentified Ancient gadget locker while I'm gone, would you please?"

"Never happen. They're too afraid he'll booby-trap

something vital in their quarters." A hint of a smile finally reached his eyes, forced though it might have been. "Be safe," he said, echoing the request Elizabeth so often made when their positions were reversed.

"Will do. We'll check in as scheduled."

She headed for the stairway, Carson following. No sooner had their boots hit the gate-room floor than Major Lorne fell into step beside her. "Dial it up!" he called to the control room.

After the event horizon materialized, she cast a glance up at John, standing at the railing. She raised one hand in a tentative wave and turned to step through the gate, wondering if, when she saw her teams off from that post, she looked quite as alone as he did now.

The Marines secured the whole of the gate area as soon as they emerged from the wormhole. Leaving nothing to chance, Lieutenant Cadman began to sweep the perimeter with a scanner appropriated from Rodney. If one alternate entrance to the Ancient facility existed, the possibility of *two* alternate entrances was very real.

Elizabeth noted a shift in the general atmosphere as she approached the Hall. For their first meeting, Governor Cestan and Minister Galven had brought four guard-assistants apiece. Today each man had eight. Hardly a promising start. The wind was stronger today than it had been before, and the calculating stares being traded across the open expanse brought to mind images of a gunslinger duel at dawn.

"Minister, Governor," she greeted them formally. "I'm pleased to see that both of you deemed our discussion to be worth continuing."

"I am here over the objections of my advisors," Cestan informed her. "The most recent incident has convinced many among my people that the Nistra are uninterested in securing a meaningful accord."

"I am here as well, Governor," Galven pointed out archly. "Our commitment to peace is not for your people to judge. And, might I add, it has been only shaken by these reprehensible raids and by the insistence of the Falnori on using this latest one as an excuse to vilify us."

Before the same tired accusations could be dragged out again, Elizabeth broke in. "It's commendable that both sides are present, and the issue of the raids will certainly be part of our discussion. First, though, I would like you to hear from my chief of medicine on a topic that concerns all of us."

The unexpected request seemed to jar both men out of their indignation, at least temporarily. She considered it a moral victory when the group entered the Hall with no further comment, and she tried not to dwell on the fact that a full four guards from each faction remained outside to stand watch this time. Lorne spoke quietly into his radio, alerting his Marines to keep an eye on the augmented security detail.

Once the delegations had taken their seats around the table, Elizabeth wasted no time. "Gentlemen, I'd like to introduce Dr. Carson Beckett. He's highly experienced in the field of medical research, and he's discovered a characteristic of adarite that may affect our negotiations."

Though his discomfort would be apparent to anyone who knew him well, Carson spoke with calm patience. "I've studied the sample we were given and found that the energetic properties of the ore damage the mind.

Difficulty with short-term memory is the first symptom, as evidenced by some of our people after only a brief exposure. I believe the long-range impact to be quite serious." He faced Galven. "Minister, you told Dr. Weir that many Nistra suffer from poor health. Are your miners commonly among those afflicted?"

Gray brows knitted as the older man considered the question. "It is possible," he allowed. "But they ail because they are hungry, not because they are forgetful."

"I'm afraid it may be a bit more complicated than that, sir," said Carson, his bedside manner on display. "Memory is only the most significant area of influence we've identified; our people also have reported headaches and difficulty thinking clearly. A memory deficit could potentially cause a kind of ripple effect, impacting higher-level function in addition to simple tasks, like eating or washing, that could lead to health concerns."

"If this were so, we would have realized it." The Nistra leader was understandably skeptical. "We have been mining the adarite for generations."

"The damage may be partial or limited, and it's likely your people have unconsciously adapted their behavior to compensate over the years. They may also have become inured to the discomfort our people felt upon first exposure. The current generations of your people have spent almost all their lives in the mining territory or near adarite in some manner—they don't know what it would feel like to be free of the effects. You had no way of making the connection. We have sophisticated equipment which diagnoses such hazards." Carson withdrew a printout from his pocket and unfolded it. "These two images represent the brains of two of my people. One was exposed to adarite, while the other was not. Can you see the difference?"

Both leaders examined the picture, looking unconvinced. Elizabeth couldn't fault them for their resistance to the concept. They had no frame of reference for the data they were seeing and had only the word of some offworlders to demonstrate the danger.

"The Falnori have not been so afflicted." Cestan put the printout aside. "We are in need, but we have health. You believe that to be a consequence of not working in the mines?"

"Not entirely. There's an additional wrinkle."

The doctor paused for a moment before Elizabeth interceded. They'd given enough variations of this speech in the past that she barely had to think about how to tailor it for her current audience. "Governor, the Falnori are descended from the offspring of the Ancients. As such, many of them possess an ability, as you call it, to use Ancient tools. That hereditary ability is marked by a physical trait we call a gene."

"This gene also appears to make the brain resistant to the effects of adarite," Carson continued. "I'd wager that all your warriors are gene carriers, just due to natural selection. Because of the cognitive effects, those without the gene would never become proficient with an adarite whip."

The governor's heightened interest came as little surprise. "Should your theory be correct," he said thoughtfully, lacing his fingers together on the table, "it would imply that the Falnori are better suited to handle adarite than the Nistra."

Galven didn't bother to hide his disdain. "A fortunate

possibility indeed for the Falnori."

"Gentlemen, I see solutions here." Elizabeth could see apprehension stiffening the minister's spine and worried that her proposal would do nothing to lessen it. "A job swap of some type may be feasible. If Falnori gene carriers took over the mining duties, we could improve the overall health of the Nistra dramatically—"

"And now the true goal is brought to light." Galven's eyes glittered. "You mean to steal our livelihood by whatever means necessary," he accused Cestan. "The raids were not sufficient, so now you conspire with these offworlders to manufacture a reason to take the mines from us."

"Now wait just a minute," Carson objected. "The damage caused by adarite exposure is very real. I could demonstrate it for you if I wanted to risk the neurological fitness of everyone present. Since I'm not willing to do that, I'd ask that you let me examine some of your miners to provide evidence."

"I should trust you?"

"Yes, you should." Elizabeth leaned forward. "What would we have to gain from feeding you a lie? Even if the adarite was harmless and my people could use it, we have no reason to favor trade with the Falnori over trade with the Nistra."

"The absence of an obvious reason does not mean there is no possible reason," remarked Galven, sitting back in his chair with an air of tranquility that was plainly false.

"We can help you re-center your economy," she persisted. "You don't have to be slaves to this ore—any of you. It's been the source of far too much conflict over the centuries, and it will continue to poison your relations with each other for as long as you let it."

"Don't be foolish, Galven." Cestan's expression, receptive only moments earlier, was beginning to close down. "You stand in the path of progress."

"I stand for the rights of all Nistra. And I will stand in *your* path should you attempt to take the mines by force."

Damn. Until this point there had been no overt mention of violence. Elizabeth had hoped to avoid it for a while longer. "No one is suggesting the use of force here," she tried, but the Falnori leader quickly ran over her attempt at pacification.

"Neither am I ruling it out. My people will no longer remain idle as our places of honor are defiled and our allies attacked."

"Save the propaganda for your war-hungry public. Perhaps it will comfort them when their children march off to enact an invasion."

Human interaction was the same irrespective of galaxy, it seemed. Elizabeth had recognized the gradual shift in the leaders' posturing, from outrage to resolve, even as it occurred. For all her training, so far she'd been helpless to sway them from their intractable anger. There could be little doubt now that armies were being readied, and she had no idea what would happen if the two sides met on a battlefield.

By nightfall, the hunting party had amassed a considerable bounty. More than any previous hunt had accomplished, if Dantir's triumphant chatter was to be believed. Ronon's tracking abilities were razor-sharp from years of necessity, but he had to admit that these hunters were skilled as well. Each time someone located a paledon, he or she would give a silent signal: right arm extended straight ahead, then bent to tap the forehead. If the animal was in a group, bows and spears were put to use; if alone, Ronon's gun became the weapon of choice, as its effect was louder yet cleaner.

The efficient strategy had netted them almost twenty paledon, which seemed to be as many as ten people could carry. Once they had reached their load capacity, Ilar had directed them to make camp in the foothills of the nearby mountains and transport their game to the village in the morning.

Dantir proved to be adept at building fires, and a circle formed to share a meal and trade tales. The stories felt more fanciful than historical, similar to the fairy tales sometimes referenced by the Earth team. The hunters' earlier suspicion had given way to frank curiosity and openness. Ronon devoured a chunk of tough meat and listened to Teyla recount a legend from her youth, a fable about a young man who showed kindness to an old woman and received great wisdom in return.

He continued to sit near the dying flames after most of the hunters had found places to bed down. Watching the tendrils of smoke weave through the canopy of trees, he tried to remember when he'd started to relax around these people. Trust didn't come naturally to him, at least not anymore; there had been instances in the past of easily-won faith causing harm, either to him or to those he had trusted. It had taken great effort to make himself feel comfortable on Atlantis, let alone consider it his home. Yet, in the span of mere hours on this planet, he'd accepted a place among the hunters, maybe because they'd been so willing to accept him.

Finding a way to use the gate was tomorrow's matter. Tonight they had the bond of a hunting circle.

Ilar sat down beside him, having returned from inspecting the results of the day's hunt. "We are in your debt," she told him warmly. "Your weapon results in a neat kill. Good skins are always in demand for clothing, especially before winter."

"Seems like the least we could do, since you let us join your group." Ronon glanced behind her to where Dantir had finally surrendered to sleep.

Ilar's smile grew fond as she followed his gaze to her son. "All we know of other worlds comes from stories such as the ones told tonight. You must forgive his eagerness. He has never seen anyone like you."

"It doesn't bother me." And it didn't. "You really didn't know what the ring was for? No one's ever come through it before?"

She tucked her legs up underneath her and folded her hands in her lap. "As I said, we do not have many records. If other visitors have come, their stories have been lost."

"What about the raiders—the marauders?" Although he could see her face darken even in the flickering light, he pushed onward. "They came through when we did. For all you know, they may use it all the time."

The hunter hesitated. "We may not be speaking of the same marauders. The rogues who rob our villages come from distant lands on this world. They believe themselves the children of the Ancestors, superior to us and possessed of the right to do whatever they please. We fight them on the occasions when we discover them in the act, but they rarely make the same mistake twice." Her contempt was evident as she prodded the fire with more force than necessary. "The Wraith take lives, and the marauders try to take everything else."

Watching her, Ronon attempted to reconcile the conflict inherent in what little he knew of her people. "You didn't have to trust us," he said. "In your place, I wouldn't have trusted us."

Ilar turned to face him, her features sharpened by the flames. "Our lives are not easy," she replied. "We are aware of this, but we cannot let it shape us or sway our choices. Simple though we may be, we cling to our honor."

He admired her viewpoint, and wasn't sure how to say so. "I can tell."

With another smile, she reached for a folded blanket at the end of her bedroll. "A spare, brought in case Dantir found a way to ruin his. Since he did not, you should take it."

"Thanks. I'll give it to my friend—she could use it more than I could." It occurred to him that Teyla had not lingered near the fire, and he twisted around to scan the area. Locating her, a solitary figure standing next to a massive tree trunk and staring off into the distance, he climbed to his feet. "Excuse me."

By the time he approached, Teyla had summoned a serene expression. Their hosts might have believed it. Ronon didn't. "You all right?"

"Of course. Weary from the hunt, perhaps." Her fingers brushed across her temple before she accepted the blanket he held out to her. "Thank you."

"Thank Ilar."

Teyla nodded. "These are good people. We were fortunate to find them."

"Yeah, we were." He folded his arms. "So why are you over here while they're over there?"

She returned her gaze to the forest and the mountains beyond. "They are good people," she continued quietly, "who know nothing of the Stargate."

The implication was clear. "You're afraid no one on this planet will be able to help us, and we'll be stuck here."

Her eyes flicked to him. "And you are not?"

"I am." Not in the same way, though. That much he could tell just by watching her.

Seeming to understand his unspoken question, she said, "I have never faced such a separation from my people before. There have been times when death appeared likely, of course, but…I truly fear a lifetime spent without them." She held the blanket tight to her chest, looking deeply troubled. "For Athosians, home is defined more by personal bonds than by location. We survived the cullings of our world and the challenges of coming to Lantea because we depended on each other. Even though I now live apart from my people for much of the time, I continue to draw strength from them. The possibility that Athosians will be born, and die, and I will not even know…The loss is unimaginable."

He could think of nothing to say. His experiences had been so vastly different. After a moment, Teyla must have realized that, because she dropped her gaze to the ground in obvious contrition. "Ronon, forgive me. I didn't mean to suggest that this would be easier for you because you were alone for so long."

"I know. But it probably would be." In truth, he envied her, just as he envied the Earth-born Atlanteans, who often took for granted how lucky they were simply to be together. He suspected that Teyla, having lived her life under the shadow of the Wraith, understood him better than anyone.

"It's not going to matter, anyway," he said, out of impulse more than confidence. He wasn't at all used to giving comfort. Still, he reached out and closed a hand around her shoulder, and she lifted her eyes to meet his. "We'll find a dialing device, or Sheppard and McKay will find us. Don't give up yet."

She managed a small, tolerant smile. "I have not."

Of course she hadn't, and in hindsight he felt a bit embarrassed for implying it. Fatigue was beginning to weigh him down, though, so he just squeezed her shoulder and tipped his head toward the last glowing embers of the fire. Acquiescing, she selected a flat piece of unoccupied ground and unfolded the blanket. He found his own space not far away and settled in for the night.

At first light, Ronon found himself less rested than he would have liked. He pushed himself up on one elbow, blinking to clear both his vision and his scattered thoughts. It took a moment for him to recall his surroundings and the events that had led him there, and he grimaced. Sleeping outside had been a common occurrence not so long ago. A year on Atlantis had made him soft.

Dantir instantly appeared in front of him, somehow looking worn-out and enthusiastic at the same time. "If we set out soon, we will be home well before supper," he urged. "Will you show my friends how you hide the blades in your hair? They will not believe it if I tell them. We could even win a wager on it."

Tired or not, Ronon had to grin at the young man. As he started to respond, a blast sliced through the still morning air.

Instinctively, he threw himself flat. Before he could draw his gun, Dantir was sprawled limply on the ground, and bolts of energy rained down on the hunting party.

"Marauders!" someone hissed. Dantir didn't move. Surging with fury, Ronon tracked the source of the shots, forced to squint into the dawn light, and aimed his weapon at the silhouettes crouched near a tree. He took down only two before a blast caught him in the back.

As a gray veil smothered his senses, he spared some anger for himself, for letting down his guard.

# CHAPTER ELEVEN

Nothing ever failed quietly on Atlantis. Radek Zelenka had come to this conclusion quite early in the expedition. Inevitably, experiments went one of three ways: brilliant success, marginal success, or catastrophe.

Rodney's head poked out from behind the lab bench, and he peered with suspicion at the still-sparking components of what might have been a small-scale Ancient weapon utilizing extreme heat. Alternatively, it might have been a curling iron. For all they knew, it might have been a *waffle* iron. "Right," he said brusquely. "Anybody missing any limbs? No? Moving on, then, to a rapid explanation of what the *hell* just happened."

Radek fixed a murderous glare on Kendall. At almost the same moment, Miko murmured something behind her hand that sounded like 'miscalculation.'

"Hold on!" Kendall protested. "You're already pinning this on me? What about—"

"Save it." Rodney cut him off with a dismissive wave. "Exactly how bad are we talking here?"

"Do you measure 'bad' in wasted effort or broken equipment?" Radek grumbled.

"Never mind. As much as I appreciate being asked to witness this delightful fiasco, I'm going back to some productive research. Call me when you fix your theories and/or your test rig."

Atlantis's chief of science stalked out of the lab, leaving the others to survey the damage. Radek sighed and opened a tool drawer. The heat emanating from the unidentified gadget had warped the test stand's casing, and he'd need to clamp the entire apparatus in order to work it back into place.

The directed energy team had been eager to begin studies of the adarite sample, developing numerous potential experiments in the span of a single day. When adarite investigation as a whole had proved unwise, the scientists had quickly turned to other pursuits. Each of them had experienced research setbacks in the past. They were professionals, and they would not spend time licking their wounds.

Kendall had proposed a battery of tests on a cylindrical object they'd once located in one of the city's storage areas. Not understanding its purpose, they'd initially put it aside, but Kendall believed that it might operate on a similar principle to the adarite whips. It appeared that he'd been approximately half correct. Immense heat, yes; easily directed, no.

While the dejected engineer downloaded the data from the failed test, Miko drifted back to her own workstation. Her spare time had been devoted to scouring the Ancient database. There were extensive records on the battle for P7L-418, containing multiple subcategories beyond the main files that had previously been translated, and Miko had expressed to Radek a belief that some further information about the research conducted on that planet must be contained within.

No one seemed willing to believe that such an efficient power source could be completely unavailable to them. Too much was at stake. If not adarite specifically, then *some* aspect of the Ancients' weapons technology ought to provide them at least a head start.

"Message from Linguistics," Miko announced, raising her voice just enough to carry across the lab. It was entirely possible that the Japanese scientist did not in fact know how to shout. "Salazar made a refinement to the database translation program."

Radek kept his focus on the C-clamp he'd been cranking into position. Tweaks to their Ancient translation algorithm weren't uncommon. There were limits to what a computer program could do, and Ancient, like most languages, had numerous subtleties and logical exceptions. "Did he provide a software patch?"

"He did. I will apply it to the 418 records." She bent over her computer again.

For a few minutes, the only sounds in the lab were the metallic taps of Radek's hammer and the repetitive keystrokes of Kendall and Miko. Though the silence was not atypical, today it felt bleaker than usual. Expedition morale tended to ebb and flow with often-changing circumstances, and lately it had been slipping lower. Researchers were frustrated at making little progress, the Marines continued to lose comrades, and the constant low-level danger of a Wraith attack was now partnered with the equally-worrying threat of a replicator incursion.

"*Wakarimasen*," murmured Miko, causing Radek to glance up from his tools. "This does not make sense."

"What is it?"

"The reference to 418's orbital gate was affected by the translation patch."

Radek set aside his work and walked over to stand at her shoulder. "We read earlier that the gate was damaged in the battle. Is that incorrect?"

"No, it was indeed damaged. However, there are more supplemental records linked to this location than I realized. Also…" She pointed to a symbol on the screen. "I have not seen that before. Have you?"

He had, though it took him a few seconds to recall where. Just once, nearly two years ago. If it represented what he thought it did—

"Upload the amended file to the city network," he instructed her, already heading for the door. "Colonel Sheppard needs to know about this. Immediately."

Disorientation lingered long after Teyla regained consciousness. When she opened her eyes to find herself lying on unfamiliar ground, she could not identify her last memory. Firing on the raiders outside the Hall? No—there had been something after that. The hunting party. She felt blurry and vague as she struggled to sit up.

The skewed, half-hidden Stargate was once again within her view, perplexing her. Hadn't they traveled a great distance from the gate?

A few feet away, Ronon dragged himself to one knee. Swaying a bit, he glowered at something behind her. "You," he snarled.

"Don't take it personally. You were a surprise to us as well."

She had heard that voice before. Slowly, because her body seemed reluctant to obey her wishes, she shifted to look.

The lead raider stood over her, holding both his gun and Ronon's. Hers had been appropriated by one of the other raiders beside him. The ship that had provided their escape from P7L-418 sat a short distance away. Their tailored, eclectic clothing and impressive array of personal weapons, likely procured by preying on people like Ilar's, turned her stomach.

"The hunters," said Ronon. "What did you do to them?"

"Stunned them and left them be. There's no money to be made from peladon skins." The leader shrugged, displaying a toothy smile. "You're much more interesting."

Teyla climbed to her feet, unwilling to show weakness in front of these criminals. "We have nothing of value to you."

"Maybe, maybe not." His gaze swept over her, and she fought not to react. "You're not from this world."

Ronon snorted. "You should know. We were dumped here because of you."

The leader cocked his head, as if the remark was unexpected. After a moment, he lowered his weapon. His companions did not do the same. "I'm Sekal. My men and I are in the trading business."

"Stealing, you mean."

"The two are often related, I'll admit. Some prices are more reasonable than others." Sekal appeared unbothered, examining Ronon's gun with a critical eye. "Although we typically operate in this system and its neighbors, we're always looking for new planets to visit—new opportunities, if you will. You may have little of value now, but we saw the equipment your friends carried. I think an arrangement can be made."

Still trying to shake off the effects of the stun, Teyla attempted to grasp his meaning. What did he want from them? "How do you suggest we contact our friends?" she questioned, acid in her tone. "Even if we wanted to make an 'arrangement' with you, we cannot dial the gate."

"Not a problem." Sekal used the gun to gesture at one of his men, who hefted an unwieldy pack on his shoulder. "We bring our own device for that purpose. Makes this gate rather convenient."

"And if we refuse?"

"We would be very…disappointed." There was no need for him to elaborate. His weapons performed the task for him.

Muddled though her thoughts were, she had no intention of allowing this gang any access to Atlantis. Before she could say so, Ronon spoke up.

"You'll get us off this planet if we show you the address of someplace worth going?"

Teyla whirled toward her teammate. Surely he wasn't suggesting—?

Sekal's smile became predatory. "Exactly the deal I had in mind."

"Wait. My friend and I need to confer." She went over to Ronon, ignoring the armed men who surrounded them. If they chose to shoot, they would lose their new 'trading' opportunity.

When Ronon bent to place his head close to hers, she whispered urgently in his ear. "You intend to choose another address, I hope?"

"They've got numbers and weapons on us. If we gate to some unoccupied planet, they'll suspect a trick right away."

On that aspect, his reasoning was sound. It did nothing to soothe her unease. What would happen if they allowed

Sekal's group into Atlantis? There were security procedures; she was certain of that, but she could not make
herself recall them. Her head felt as though a band of steel
had tightened around it.

"We can't," she pleaded, lacking any other argument.

"This is our only chance to get through the gate at all,"
Ronon countered.

"At the risk of endangering our home?"

His eyes slightly unfocused, he stepped back from her
and raised his voice. "Fair trade. We get passage off this
planet. You get a richer place to plunder."

"A place richer than this back-end planet would not be
difficult to find." Sekal crossed his arms. "I expect you to
do far better."

As Teyla submitted a silent prayer for forgiveness,
Ronon smirked. "Wait until you see where we're going."

The scrambling of various personnel to get out of his
path barely registered in Rodney's peripheral vision. He
had one clear goal in mind as he strode down the corridor:
the removal of a certain lieutenant colonel's head from his
rear end.

He had a perfect argument mentally rehearsed, starting
with an attention-grabbing entrance to the control room.
Unfortunately, Sheppard derailed it by not in fact *being*
in the control room. Swearing under his breath, Rodney
caught sight of him sitting in one of the guest chairs in
Elizabeth's office, a laptop computer balanced on his
knees.

*The things I do for the good of this expedition.* Barging
into the office, Rodney declared, "I can't believe you."

Sheppard paused but didn't look up. "Funny. Usually

it's a woman saying that to me."

For a moment, Rodney's indignation was sidetracked by the ergonomic inadequacy of the other man's working conditions. "Why aren't you using the desk?"

"It's not my desk."

"I hardly think you'd be disciplined for usurping the power of a desk, Colonel. Is it still Colonel, or did that end with the oh-so-dramatic surrender of your wings? And who seriously *does* that?"

The laptop was set aside, and Sheppard rose from his chair with a carefully enforced calm. "Good news travels fast," he observed dryly.

"Apparently not fast enough. I had to hear through the geology department grapevine, of all things, that you're resigning." Rodney crossed his arms. "Just like that, huh? For some reason, I thought that irritating fall-on-your-sword predilection of yours might be reserved for instances of saving the city. What a disappointment to be proved wrong."

"This *is* about the city," Sheppard replied, sounding entirely too composed for a man tossing his life out the window. Almost as if he'd rehearsed *his* argument, too. "If I can't do the job—"

"Of course you can do the job. The job, to be militarily coarse, quite often sucks. That is by no measure your fault." It was inconceivable to Rodney that he actually had to explain this. "Do you honestly believe that Caldwell or anyone else could do what you do here? No one could have kept every single member of the expedition alive over the past two-plus years. The fact that you think *you* somehow should have been able to pull it off surpasses even my level of arrogance."

"Rodney—"

But he was hitting his stride and unwilling to let up. "Yes, I got mad about the adarite and about what happened on 418. I get mad when friends die. Would you like a hug?"

Sheppard's eyes narrowed. *Finally, a reaction.* "Don't flatter yourself. You didn't push me into anything. All you did was identify the reality of the situation. I'm making this call because I think it's the best move for everyone."

"Then you're being a coward, and that's uncharacteristic for you. I've never seen you run from anything real. Don't run from this."

Subtlety had never been listed among Rodney's numerous attributes. He'd gone on the offensive because it seemed like the best available tactic, and now he waited to see if the Colonel would acknowledge his superior judgment or deck him.

Bafflingly, Sheppard did neither. He stood in front of Rodney and met his friend's challenging stare without so much as a blink. "You done, Sigmund?" he asked coolly.

Since Rodney had fully expected that strategy to work, he didn't have a lot of ammunition in reserve. "Hardly."

He got a reprieve when their coms signaled. "Colonel, Rodney," Radek's voice hailed them. "Are either of you on the command level?"

The city's military advisor—until further notice—tapped his earpiece. "Yeah, Rodney and I are having a fun little chat up here. You need something, Radek?"

"New information. Possibly very important." Radek sounded out of breath. "Please stay where you are. I will be there shortly."

"Will do."

Fortunately, Rodney rarely needed much in the way of time to regroup. "Tell me something," he demanded once Sheppard had cut the radio connection. "What will you do? When you get back to Earth and you don't have any of this"—he waved haphazardly at the gate-room beyond the office's glass walls—"to get up for?"

That simple question accomplished more than all his earlier attacks. Sheppard's eyes flicked away, though not before a flash of warring emotions could be seen. He turned to retrieve his computer and answered in a low, weary voice. "I don't know."

As unlikely as it seemed, the idea of no longer being able to trade insults or debate inane movies with Sheppard was distressing. The concept of going on missions without him was alarming. And the very thought of being the last remaining member of the prime off-world team wrenched Rodney's insides.

He couldn't say any of that. Instead, he lifted his chin and spoke in a clipped tone. "Well, we'll all be up the same creek, then, won't we?"

The ensuing silence stretched for a few seconds, finally broken by the activation of the gate. As wavering blue light played over them, Rodney followed Sheppard across the walkway to the control room, where the technician quietly affirmed that the radio was active.

Sheppard leaned forward, bracing his hands on a console. "What have you got for us, Lieutenant?"

"Sir, we've completed orbits along eight different longitudinal lines," reported the pilot of Jumper Three. Rodney couldn't put a name or a face to the solemn voice. "The computer says the sensors have mapped the entire planet, from minimum to maximum altitude at which a gate-sized object could remain in orbit, but we've got nothing."

"What do you mean, nothing?" Rodney demanded. "You can't find the gate?"

"Scans show no sign of either a Stargate or any subcutaneous transmitters," the lieutenant replied. "We already ran the jumper diagnostics. Everything's working."

"If everything was working, we'd know where to find Ronon and Teyla." Sheppard pushed off the console and restlessly circled the room. "Are you sure you swept the whole search area? You must have had to divert around wreckage a few times."

"Yes, sir, but the sensor range is large enough to cover the main debris fields from a safe distance." Though the young officer's voice was composed, it was obvious he didn't like giving his boss bad news. "We've done everything we can, sir. I don't think there's anything out here to find."

That was patently absurd. According to the database records, 418's space gate had been damaged in the battle, not obliterated. Complete destruction of a massive naquadah ring would be no mean feat.

Aware that Sheppard had turned an expectant gaze on him, Rodney offered the only theory he could come up with on short notice. "It's possible the gate is surrounded by a high concentration of wreckage containing some component material that masks the naquadah from the sensors' view."

The Colonel's brow furrowed. "What, like there's a bunch of adarite up in orbit, messing with the sensors?"

Rodney spread his hands wide. "I don't see any reason

why that would be the case. I just don't have any better explanation at this point. Give me a half-second to think, would you?"

Sheppard glanced down at the gate; a common habit for those speaking to someone on the other end of the wormhole. "Lieutenant, we're going to work on a sensor modification for you. In the meantime, do one more orbit."

"Which orbit do you want repeated, sir?"

"Surprise me. Stand by."

"Aye, sir. Jumper Three out."

As the event horizon snapped shut, Rodney rounded on Sheppard. "A sensor modification? For an unknown material identification issue that may or may not exist?"

"You just said—"

"I didn't say it was probable," Rodney maintained, "only that it was possible. It can't be adarite up there, or the sensor diagnostic wouldn't have reported everything as functional. I honestly have no idea why they can't find the gate."

Sheppard raked a frustrated hand through his hair. "All right, plan B. Have you been able to convince the dialing computer to open a wormhole to that gate instead of the ground gate when we dial 418's address?"

"I've isolated the necessary procedure. I haven't had any reason to enact it yet, since we're still using the ground gate at the moment." Rodney might have elaborated further had he not heard rapid footsteps approaching behind him.

"Excuse the interruption." Radek appeared in the control room doorway, looking slightly winded. "I think you will want to see this."

Rodney was starting to wonder if whiplash was in his future. "Now what?"

"Refinements to the database translation algorithm." Radek commandeered a computer terminal and called up a file, fingers moving swiftly over the keys. "Miko applied the new software patch from the linguistics team to the record of the battle for P7L-418. The original program ignored a symbol in the description of the planet's space gate. Here."

Finally, a chance for some answers. Rodney leaned in to study the screen. "That symbol shows up in reference to the orbital defense platform we found two years ago at the edge of this star system. What does it mean in the context of a Stargate?"

"Miko is running the algorithm on the rest of the related records now. It will take time, but..." Radek's hesitation stood out in sharp contrast to his earlier haste.

"What?" Rodney's patience was a rather limited resource. "If you're about to say that there isn't a gate in orbit after all, Jumper Three's already a step ahead of you."

"I am saying," Radek answered soberly, "that the second gate is indeed in orbit—housed within a defense platform."

Sheppard frowned. "A gate on a *space station*?"

They'd never come across such a thing before, but why not? It was a reasonable explanation for why the recovery team had been unable to detect the gate's presence. A surrounding structure would hide the gate from unwanted visitors, and—

When the implications of this new knowledge worked their way into Rodney's mind, the resulting influx of hope and dread nearly took his legs out from under him. "What if the station is still intact?" he forced himself to ask.

The color fled from Sheppard's features. Clearly he was coming to the same conclusion Rodney had already formed: if the station still existed amid the debris orbiting P7L-418, and if by some fluke of fortune it was still sealed with a breathable atmosphere... "Teyla and Ronon," he breathed. "God."

He spun toward the nearest tech. "Get a MALP ready *now*. Rodney, work your magic with the dialing computer. We need that space gate." Slapping at his com, he continued, "Contingency team with medical escort to the gate-room ASAP. We've got a potential rescue situation."

The tech scurried off to comply with her orders. Sliding into her chair at the dialing console, Rodney fought back a crushing sense of remorse. If he hadn't stopped Sheppard from charging off on an immediate rescue mission, they might have saved hours, even days their stranded teammates couldn't afford to lose.

Braced for a condemnation, Rodney was surprised when no criticism was forthcoming. Risking a sideways glance, he found Sheppard's gaze burning into the dormant gate. The Colonel was still insistent on shouldering most of the blame himself, no doubt. His decision, his responsibility—all that nonsense. Damn it.

"You know what?" Sheppard said suddenly, an edge of desperation creeping into his voice. "Screw the MALP. Dial the gate. Let's see if we can get 'em on the radio while we're assembling our response team."

"A few more seconds, please. This isn't quite like reprogramming your speed-dial back home." As Rodney worked through the override procedure, he tried not to see the grisly possibilities in his mind's eye. They might find Ronon and Teyla, but the odds of finding them alive and well, cooling their heels in a damaged yet perfectly airtight space station, were almost as slim now as they had ever been.

Before he could begin to input the address for 418, the gate lit up of its own accord. He sat back, caught off-guard. "Unscheduled off-world activation."

"Shield up," Sheppard ordered. The shimmer of the force field snapped into place at almost the same moment as the event horizon. "It's too early to be Elizabeth checking in, isn't it?"

"Yes." Rodney watched the screen that would show him any transmitted access codes. "No IDC yet. If it was Jumper Three, we'd know it by now."

Seconds passed. The rippling pool remained stubbornly silent.

"This is wasting time." Sheppard clenched a fist at his side. "We need to be dialing 418's space gate—a matter of minutes may make the difference for Ronon and Teyla."

"There's nothing we can do to close the connection from this end." Rodney studied the computer for any sign of a transmission. "If there aren't enough particles of sufficient mass coming through, the gate will shut down on its own before long. If there *is* something coming through, our old acquaintance, the thirty-eight-minute clause, comes into effect."

Seemingly grasping at straws, Sheppard activated his com. "Hey, if anyone can hear me out there, this is *not* freaking funny. State your business or let us have our damned gate back!"

Nothing.

Rodney watched the undulating blue surface and did his best to resist the urge to yell at someone.

The leader of the raiders—Ronon hadn't caught his name—jerked his head toward the guy with the pack. Odd that the scrawniest one among them carried the load. Maybe he was their version of McKay, brought along for his brains.

Little Guy shuffled forward and lowered his pack to the ground. Carefully he lifted out an awkward tangle of metal, conduits, and crystals. The contraption had familiar symbol buttons, but it looked as though it had been cobbled together from spare parts.

"That's your dialer?" Ronon eyed it with distrust.

He'd heard the leader give a name, hadn't he? Something with an S. Maybe. S-Man bristled. "It functions. In your position, I'd be grateful for that."

"It functions only because you pay me to keep it that way," groused Little Guy. "In spite of your increasing demands on both it and me."

Definitely their version of McKay.

Sinking to one knee, Ronon studied the dialing device. Teyla crouched beside him, her displeasure evident. They didn't have any better options. The dialer obviously worked well enough, or these guys wouldn't be there.

Of course, there was another problem, one that had slipped his mind until now. "We can't take the ship," Ronon stated. "It'll attract too much attention in the city."

S-Man clearly wasn't happy with that idea. "What kind

of defenses should we expect?"

"Nothing to speak of." Ronon mentally pushed off the ache forming behind his eyes. He had to make this sound good, and sounding good wasn't his strong suit even when he *didn't* feel like his head had been run through a grinder. "The people in the city are scientists, surrounded by more Ancestor technology than they can use—more than you could ever hope to sell. That ship isn't of the Ancestors, and they'll notice it a lot faster than they'll notice your guns."

"So you say." S-Man scrutinized Ronon for a few seconds, likely waiting to see if the other man would flinch. There was a reason, though, that the Marines had stopped inviting Ronon to their poker games. Staring was far easier than talking.

In the end, avarice probably influenced the decision more than anything he'd said. S-Man turned to two of his cronies. "Stay here with the dialer. Wait for us to go through, then take the ship back and wait for us."

Ronon wondered where 'back' was.

He reached for the first symbol and paused. Little Guy remained uncomfortably close, watching his every move. "Back off," Ronon growled.

Startled, the man skittered sideways before recovering his self-control and placing both hands on his hips. "I'm supposed to trust you not to sabotage the dialer?"

"What purpose would that serve?" Teyla asked, her temper quicker than usual.

Ronon glanced up at S-Man. "Showing you the address wasn't part of the agreement," he maintained. "You only get one trip. One's all you'll need to make this worth your while. If you don't trust us, don't follow us through the gate."

"Sekal," complained Little Guy. Right. *Sekal*. That was it.

After a moment of consideration, Sekal told his underling, "You're paranoid. Let 'em dial."

Satisfied that none of the raiders had a good line of sight to the symbols, Ronon entered the address for Atlantis. The pitiful dialer flickered and whirred, and the gate came to life. He watched the initial outburst of the wormhole vaporize the few stubborn blades of grass that had attempted to grow in the danger zone directly in front of the oddly-angled ring.

Two of the raiders immediately started toward the event horizon. "Wait," called Ronon. Maybe he'd forgotten to explain this part. "We have to send a code first. The gate's shielded on the other end."

Teyla's hand went to her GDO, or rather where her GDO should have been. Bastard raiders must have taken it after they'd stunned everyone. Fortunately, they must not have been quite as excited about searching Ronon. He reached into his coat and withdrew the small item.

"Get on with it," Little Guy said impatiently.

*Be glad to.* Ronon was exhausted and achy and wanted to be back on Atlantis more strongly than ever. He started to tap in the code, only to have his wrist grabbed by Teyla. Bewildered, he went to speak, but she leaned in and whispered urgently, "That is not correct."

"Sure it is," he muttered back. "It's the…the transponder code."

The word 'transponder' meant nothing to either of them. It was, however, the term Sheppard had used to describe this particular set of ciphers—and the only term unlikely to arouse suspicion among the raiders.

*"On Earth, aircraft use transponder codes to iden-*
*tify themselves to controllers on the ground or to other*
*aircraft. There are certain numbers that are only used in*
*emergency situations. If you squawk 7500 instead of your*
*assigned code, it means your craft's been hijacked; 7600*
*means you've lost communications; 7700 is a general*
*mayday call. These IDCs will be our version of the seven-*
*thousand series."*

Most of the Marines called them dummy codes,
because in essence they were false. The dummy codes
were common to all off-world teams. As with the transponder numbers, there were three separate codes. The
first was used only in connection with a radio call and
told Atlantis that the conversation was being monitored
by 'unfriendlies.' The remaining two related to the gate
shield and required no radio call: one signified a request
to lower the shield, the other a request to keep it active.

Ronon had no wish to be pulverized, so he planned
to tell Atlantis to drop the shield. But Teyla was shaking
her head as she studied the set of numbers he'd begun to
send.

"That is the wrong shield code." She took the GDO
from his hand and changed the numbers.

"I know which one is which," he insisted. Tired though
he might be, he'd committed the codes to memory long
ago.

"Then it is your intent to leave the shield in place?"

"No! I'm getting it shut down." Ronon reached for the
small transmitter. Once he'd seized it back, his certainty
wavered. Could he have mistakenly swapped the codes?
It was becoming harder and harder to think straight, and

he just couldn't be sure.

Teyla captured his gaze. Her eyes looked clouded, almost fevered. "I am no less capable of error than you," she said. "Especially now. I am having difficulty...seeing the situation accurately."

"Me too," he admitted, scrubbing at his face in an attempt to restore some energy and clarity of thought.

"Even so, I believe this code is right. I ask for your trust."

"What's going on?" the lead raider demanded. "You send the code yet, or what?"

It felt like only a momentary hesitation. Apparently it was enough to raise an alarm with the raiders, because two of them moved toward Teyla and seized her arms. She struggled for a brief time before a third raider aimed a weapon at her head.

"Stop stalling," the leader warned. "I've got no reason other than a business deal to keep you alive."

Ronon's glance shifted between his teammate and the transmitter in his hand. He had no clues to go on, no way to assure himself that either code was correct. All he knew was that Teyla had asked for his trust, and that was the one thing for which she should never have to ask.

He pressed the button to submit her code. "It's done," he said matter-of-factly. "Let's go."

The men detaining Teyla released her arms and shoved her forward. "You two first," instructed the leader.

Ronon raised an eyebrow and put up a token protest. "You think we'd risk dialing empty space on the chance that we'd get a shot at pushing all of you through?"

The leader shrugged. "A pioneering spirit may be admirable, but it can also be quite the health risk. We're not going anywhere you're not willing to go first."

It was best that way, for a number of reasons. In any case, if Ronon had guessed wrong on the code, they wouldn't even have time to comprehend the mistake before their lives were snuffed out.

Together, Ronon and Teyla approached the gate, canted toward them as if daring them to enter. Exchanging a final, wordless glance, they climbed through the event horizon.

# CHAPTER TWELVE

Only a few seconds had passed since the gate had activated, and already John wondered if it might be possible to manually cut power to the system. This waiting game was going nowhere, and it only intensified his frustration over his teammates' uncertain status. *If you'd just sent the damned MALP right at the start...*

"Receiving IDC," Rodney announced suddenly.

Without realizing it, John had drifted to the railing. Now he turned back toward the dialing console. "We don't have anyone off-world other than Elizabeth's group and the Jumper Three team." Except Teyla and Ronon—but that wasn't a thought he could voice.

Rodney's face went slack as he looked up from the screen. "It's a dummy code."

John was at the computer in three strides. He identified the number set instantly. "Everybody out of the control room *now*. Stand by for incoming unknowns!" he warned the security team pouring into the gate-room. Training alone must have driven his reaction, because instinct was shouting *What the hell?*

The control room cleared briskly. As soon as the Marines had taken up their defensive positions, John reached down to lower the shield.

He watched the energy field wink out and waited. Again.

Abruptly, two figures tumbled through the gate. When John recognized them, some small piece of his soul was renewed.

Ronon and Teyla rolled to the side, out of the security team's line of fire. The Satedan leaned up on one elbow. "Six behind us. Stun 'em all!"

"Do it!" John yelled the order down to the Marines.

The next arrivals lost their footing as well, giving the Marines a prime opportunity to target them. His sidearm in his hand out of sheer habit, John made himself hang back and let his people work.

Stun blasts lit up the gate-room. By the time the wormhole finally shut down, six men lay in front of the gate, some sprawled on top of each other. "Secure, sir," Sergeant Young called, directing his team to restrain each intruder.

Ronon picked himself up from the floor and offered a hand to Teyla. John closed his eyes for a moment, the sight of his friends alive and whole almost too much to take in. He'd do whatever was required of him from here on out—gladly—but right now he just needed half a second.

"Incredible," murmured Rodney.

Opening his eyes, John turned to see the chief science officer rising from a crouch behind a console. He shot Rodney a critical look. "Huh. I thought I heard someone say to clear the control room. In fact, I'm pretty sure that was me."

Rodney could go from zero to defensive faster than any human in existence. "What? Ducking is *like* clearing."

Shaking his head, John hurried out of the control room and down the stairs as fast as he could manage without tripping over his boots.

Both Teyla and Ronon looked battered and a bit dazed, but there was no hiding their relief. John could relate. He opened his mouth before his brain could come up with anything to say, and so he stood there gawking like an idiot until rallying with "God, where *were* you guys?"

"Stranded on a planet with no dialing device," replied Teyla, mustering a weak smile. "You can imagine our thankfulness for arriving safely here."

"I think there's enough gratitude to go around." All of a sudden he found himself touching his forehead to hers in the customary Athosian manner. If her grip on his banged-up arm was a little too strong, he couldn't have cared less.

Ronon's priorities were still in order; he'd stepped over a couple of unconscious intruders in order to retrieve his gun from one of them.

Rodney joined the group then, having taken the stairs with more caution than John had, and peered down at the new prisoners. "Those are the raiders—"

"From P7L-418. Yes." Teyla tossed the men a look of contempt. The effect was muted by the dark circles under her eyes.

"Okay. Interesting." Processing that, Rodney frowned. "Did you say *planet*? You weren't on the orbital station?"

"Station?" Re-holstering his weapon, Ronon stared blankly back at him.

"We, uh, thought you'd gotten bounced through 418's space gate." It felt silly now, with the two of them standing there relatively unscathed, but John's throat tightened all the same. "That's why we didn't send a MALP or anything after you. We thought…"

He was saved from finishing the sentence by Teyla's hand on his wrist. "The planet's gate was angled. That is why we stumbled on our arrival here. A MALP likely would have fallen on its side, broken or at least immobile."

Not even ten minutes home after a mission from hell, and already she was trying to reassure him. John appreciated the effort, but it didn't soften the recriminations in his mind.

"Can we stay on topic, please?" Rodney's hands seemed to fly in six different directions at once. "I saw the transit data—you were sent to the orbital gate, which we now know is enclosed in a structure. How did you *not* end up there?"

"How should we know?" Ronon's gaze kept darting from the raiders to the gate and back, as if still trying to put some pieces together in his head. "The gate was stuck between two rock faces, with wreckage all around." Dragging out that recollection seemed to be difficult for him. "Maybe it was damaged."

The pinched expression Rodney tended to get while solving the mysteries of the universe swiftly cleared. "The battle," he realized. "The records said the orbital gate was damaged in the battle. The station was knocked around so badly that its orbit destabilized, and the whole thing plummeted through the planet's atmosphere!"

"Most things get pretty well toasted when that happens," John contributed.

"Not naquadah. It's about as heat-resistant as a material gets. The Stargate would remain intact wherever it fell, while everything around it would have disintegrated on reentry." Rodney's voice warmed in utter amazement.

"It never occurred to me to have the recovery team scan the *surface* when they went orbital to search for your bod—ah, transmitters. You two were on 418 all along."

Teyla looked like she didn't quite comprehend how that could be true. "The hunters who befriended us," she said to Ronon, uncertain.

"Hunters?" John got a flash of memory from the negotiations—something Galven had said. "Could they have been Nistra?"

Rodney sobered quickly at that. "Were you in the mountains?"

It should have been a simple question, but Teyla seemed to have trouble forming an answer. "Mostly the foothills," she said finally.

"Ah. That would explain why you're both a little…" Rodney fluttered his fingers in a vague gesture that might have implied a mental disorder. Ronon sent him a withering glare.

A moment later, John caught up to Rodney's reasoning, and everything clicked. "Take our guests down to the holding cells," he instructed Sergeant Young before turning to the rest of his team. "Let's pay a visit to the infirmary."

Amazing how fast the mood of the city could change. Word of Ronon and Teyla's near-miraculous return had spread so efficiently and elatedly that making an announcement would have been redundant. Nevertheless, John had taken great pleasure in dialing 418—the *original* 418 gate—and informing Elizabeth that their people were home. From the tone of her response, he got the feeling that only diplomatic etiquette had prevented her from hugging the hell out of the nearest person.

She did, however, report that the treaty talks were starting to collapse. Minister Galven hadn't warmed up to the idea of relinquishing control of the mines, and so far they'd failed to convince him that adarite was in fact harmful. Governor Cestan, in turn, seemed to be interpreting Galven's unyielding resistance as a provocation. Both had threatened to post guards around the Hall, and access to the gate had somehow sprung up as an additional point of contention. Elizabeth expressed a belief that she could keep the two leaders at the negotiating table for another day or so. The more John and Rodney could learn about the second gate and the raiders, she told them, the better chance she'd have of staving off a war.

John was more than willing to oblige.

He found Ronon in the mess hall, the first place the Satedan had gone after leaving the infirmary. The medical scans had shown evidence of exposure to a high concentration of adarite, confirming that Teyla and Ronon had indeed been in the mining region of P7L-418. Within an hour, both had displayed marked improvement on basic memory tests and had been turned loose.

When Teyla had requested a brief trip over to the mainland to reunite with her people, she'd looked surprised that John had assigned someone else to fly her there. He hadn't explained that it would be a while before he could look any of the Athosians in the eye after having written off their leader's life. Instead, he'd told her that he was needed for another task. It hadn't even been a lie.

Grabbing a sandwich off the lunch line, John spotted Ronon at a corner table. He ambled over, not surprised to see a stack of emptied plates on the tray. "Hey," he

greeted, spinning the nearest chair a half-turn and strad-
dling it backward. "How's your head?"

"Better." Ronon swallowed a bite of some kind of
mystery meat before continuing. "Still not too clear on a
lot of what happened on the planet."

"The docs said some of those memories won't ever
show up, because they're not really anywhere in your
head to find." John draped his arms over the back of the
chair, his posture far more casual than his next question.
"Want to go chat with our guests and maybe fill in a few
blanks?"

The fork stopped midway to Ronon's mouth as an
expression of malevolent interest came into his eyes.
Without a word he rose from the table and picked up his
tray. John shoved his still-wrapped sandwich into a jacket
pocket, and the pair headed for the detention area.

The six raiders had been given separate cells, not for
their comfort but to preclude any of them from conspir-
ing to escape. At the entry corridor, John nodded to the
Marines on guard duty and asked Ronon, "Did these guys
have a ringleader?"

In response, Ronon walked down the hall, looking
into each doorway until he found who he was looking
for. When he did, he stalked inside, prompting John to
lengthen his stride to catch up.

It had been a while since the city's holding cells had
gotten any use. Their current occupants didn't look like
the physical type, so the force fields hadn't been turned
on. Of course, that could change pretty rapidly if the need
arose. The lead raider sat slouched against one side of his
cell, greasy reddish hair falling into his eyes. He glanced
up at Ronon with grudging admiration. "I have to admit,

you played this well."

Ronon stood in front of the bars, arms folded, saying nothing.

"You want to be the good cop or the bad cop?" John asked his teammate. The look of skepticism he received in reply spoke volumes. He heaved a slightly exaggerated sigh. "Man, I'm *always* the good cop."

When it came to Earth references, Ronon had benefited greatly from Atlantis's movie nights. "Who says we need a good cop?"

"It's more for the entertainment factor than anything else." John strolled around the perimeter of the cell and addressed the raider. "We haven't met. I'm Lieutenant Colonel John Sheppard. You folks have been causing me and my friends trouble on a bunch of different levels lately. You got a name?" The lack of response didn't faze him. "It's no problem if you don't—I've made something of a hobby out of hanging names on the residents of these cells. I'm thinking about going back to 'Steve,' since the original Steve didn't last too long."

"Sekal," the man muttered, shooting a dark glance at Ronon. "As I'm sure your companion has told you."

"Oh, don't worry about him. Ronon's a big softie. Although you did kind of blow your shot at making a decent first *or* second impression on him." John dug the sandwich out of his pocket and took a bite, making Sekal wait and watch. Food hadn't been on the agenda for the prisoners just yet. "Sekal, you're obviously a businessman, so I'll offer you a business deal. Information in exchange for the release of yourself and your men. The deal is contingent on me liking what I hear. If I don't, you'll find a way to make amends, or Ronon will probably get cranky."

Looking from John to a glowering Ronon and back, Sekal lifted his chin. "Ask your questions."

"All right, first question. Who the hell are you jokers?"

Either Sekal was worried enough about his welfare to talk, or he just didn't care about hiding anything. Might have been a combination of the two. "We are of the Cadre."

"The Cadre? I was hoping for some kind of cool pirate-type name. What's the Cadre?"

"We are part of a trade organization that operates in shadow on a number of worlds. We're salvagers, if you prefer. Artifacts of the Ancestors are usually the most lucrative items, but whatever is desired can be procured for the right price."

"Black market. Imagine my surprise. How many people are in this Cadre?"

"More than I personally know." The raider's eyebrow lifted. "Certainly more than you have locked up here."

John walked around to the front of the cell. He needed to see the man's face when he asked this next question. "Are you allied in any way with the Nistra or the Falnori?"

Sekal scoffed. "Those simpletons? We have free rein of their planet. What profit would there be in an alliance?"

The response seemed candid enough. A glance at Ronon told John that their thoughts ran along the same lines. Like they'd suspected, the Falnori and Nistra had built a major aspect of their conflict on baseless assumptions.

"How long have you been stealing from that planet?" John asked.

"Off and on for some years. The ruins near their main gate are a rich source of artifacts. Our first visit alone netted us enough to buy our ship."

"That reminds me." John cocked his head toward Ronon. "Nice work getting them to leave that behind."

Ronon smirked. Looking sullen, Sekal slouched further.

"You're not taking just artifacts, though," pressed John. "You've branched out into swiping adarite from the miners."

"The ore?" Sekal shrugged. "A market for it developed after we sold some devices that run on the stuff."

"Uh huh. Would it surprise you if I said that adarite has dangerous effects?" Watching for a reaction, John took another bite of his sandwich before continuing. "Exposure to it messes with minds in a big way. After a while you'd be pretty much incapacitated, and you wouldn't even know why."

The raider's reply was indifferent. "We never hold onto the ore for long. Once payment's been received, I don't know or care what anyone does with it."

*Nice.* "That's a beautiful sentiment. Really. I'm all choked up." John did another slow lap around the outside of the cell, forcing Sekal to twist around to keep him in view. "How did you find the second gate on the planet?"

"We stumbled upon it some time ago during a visit but found that it had no dialing device. Fortunately, some of our business associates in another system were able to aid us in procuring something suitable for the purpose." Sekal smiled, clearly trying to hold onto a semblance of leverage through attitude alone. "Once we confirmed the manner in which two gates operate under the same address, we could use our device to override the planet's main dialer. The additional gate became a great asset. The miners certainly haven't figured out our methods. I don't think many of them have even recognized the fact that there's a large ring under all the plant growth in those ruins."

"They're pretty aware of being robbed blind," John pointed out, dropping the wry humor from his tone. His patience had limits, and Ronon's posture suggested that this was getting old even faster for him. "Do you have any idea what kind of rift you've opened up on that planet? The Falnori are convinced that it's the Nistra who've been raiding them, and vice versa. They're about to go to war over *your* actions."

Seeing that his captors were getting rattled, Sekal seemed to gain confidence. "We're not responsible," he replied airily, "for the misconceptions of the foolish."

With a growl, Ronon slammed both hands into the bars separating him from the prisoner. When he reached for the cell's locking mechanism, John had to intercede, hurrying over to grab his teammate's shoulder. "Hey! No beat-downs. Even if he is scum."

"They're not foolish," Ronon snarled at Sekal, who'd managed to fold himself into a compact package in a corner of the cell. "They're kind and honorable people. Unlike yours—loyal to nothing except your own fortunes."

If nothing else, John had to give the raider credit for guts. Recovering somewhat, Sekal remarked, "We've found it to be the most beneficial ideology around."

"Where are you based?" Ronon demanded. "What planet?"

Sekal stretched his legs out in front of him and regarded them coolly. In place of an answer, he said, "I could be persuaded to convince the rest of the Cadre to leave your friends the Nistra and Falnori alone. I have little doubt that this city of yours contains enough wealth to pay the fee."

John had seen *The Godfather* plenty of times and recognized a protection racket when he saw one. After pretending to consider the offer for approximately half a second, he turned to Ronon. "I changed my mind. Have fun."

The gasp from inside as he unlocked the cell shouldn't have been satisfying, but it was.

Before Ronon could advance, a voice from the corridor halted them. "Ronon, Colonel." Teyla entered the room, taking in the cowering Sekal and her teammates with raised eyebrows.

"You're back," John greeted her. "Ronon was in the process of scaring the crap out of this guy. Right, buddy?"

Ronon paused, stepped back from the cell's entrance, and relocked the door. "Right."

"I approve. He deserves that and more." Teyla's gaze remained steady. "Since he may still prove useful later, though, I wanted to make sure that someone was here to fill the role of the 'good cop.'"

John thought about objecting to her implication. He decided against it when he couldn't be sure at what point he would have stopped Ronon from attacking this time around. "All right, we've got things to discuss. Let's go up to the briefing room." Facing the raider, who was now officially intimidated, he said, "Remember, your deal depends on me liking what you have to say. So far, I don't. We'll try again later. Enjoy your day."

On the way to the briefing room, he called Rodney, who managed to get there before the rest of them. The scientist was scribbling restlessly on a datapad when they entered. "So we need a plan regarding 418," John stated without preamble, sitting down in his usual chair. "The raiders are an independent third party, but somehow I don't think either Cestan or Galven will suddenly decide to believe us if we tell them that. They've spent far too long building up a hatred for each other to let it go so easily."

"Since the adarite influence is so widespread among the Nistra, their collective knowledge may be as weak as their individual memories," Teyla said. "And the Stargate within their territory was very obscured by foliage overgrowth. We should find out if Minister Galven is even aware of its existence."

"More than that." Ronon paced along one wall of the room. "We need to find a way to keep the Cadre from using that gate."

At the comment, Rodney glanced up from his datapad with a wary expression. "This is starting to feel suspiciously like one of those moments wherein I'm asked to do something that treads the fine line of sanity. For instance, manufacturing a gate shield out of thin air."

Now that he mentioned it, a gate shield sounded like a pretty good idea. John looked at him at the same time the others did, and Rodney recoiled under their scrutiny. "Did everyone miss the derision attached to that statement?"

Teyla didn't hesitate before speaking. "Ronon and I are indebted to the Nistra. The hunting circle did not have to take us in, yet they did."

"We could have been raiders, for all they knew. They trusted us when we said we weren't." Ronon stopped his aimless walking and leaned forward over a chair. "I don't remember much, but I remember that."

"Then let's take care of their problem by removing the gate entirely." Rodney waggled the datapad in his hand. "I did the distance calculation. Once the *Daedalus* returns, it could get to 418 in a couple of days. We can remove the second gate to use as part of our bridge back to the Milky Way."

"Elizabeth said that Galven and Cestan were arguing about gate access, though," John reminded him. "If we can make the second gate functional, they'd have two gates for two societies, and that'd solve that problem."

"While that's a laudable goal, it's not something we can achieve in a reasonable time frame." Rodney blew out a frustrated breath. "None of the gates we've harvested so far for the galactic bridge project have had operational DHDs; that's one of the reasons why they were good candidates for harvesting. *If* I could scrounge up enough spare parts to put together a DHD and a shield control for the the Nistra—and by no means should you take that as a promise that such a thing is possible—it would take weeks. From what we're hearing about the negotiations, the Falnori and Nistra are going to be killing each other long before that."

John realized he was drumming restless fingers on

the tabletop and stilled his hand. Looking at Teyla and Ronon, he asked, "Are you sure there was absolutely nothing in that wreckage that could have been the remains of a DHD?"

"I am sure of very little from our visit," Teyla replied honestly. "We searched the area, but we did not have specialized equipment."

"We could take a jumper through that gate, scan the area with its sensors, and use the onboard dialer to get back." John turned toward Rodney. "Couldn't we?"

"Yes, no, and yes." Rodney rolled his eyes. "The energy emitted from adarite disrupts Ancient sensors, remember? Based on our limited testing, it doesn't affect the power sources used by other Ancient technology, such as the jumper's propulsion system. If you gave me a couple of hours to bend Jumper One's dialing computer to my will, I could force a DHD override and make sure we can arrive via the Nistra gate the way the Cadre did, but we'd have to land and use Earth-built equipment to perform any kind of search."

"Assuming we find something down there, repairing a broken DHD or shield control would be easier than building new ones, right?"

"Wouldn't you expect that to depend largely on the condition of the pieces we find?" Abruptly, Rodney stood up, giving them his real answer. "If we're going to investigate the possibility, we'd better get moving."

"I'll go with you for backup. Since we might be hanging around some adarite deposits, we need to keep this an ATA-only crew." John rose as well. "Teyla, dial 418's main gate while we're prepping the jumper and tell Elizabeth what we're up to. With any luck she can stall Cestan and Galven for a little while. We'll be back in a couple of hours."

He had Jumper One preflighted and all set to go by the time Rodney lugged his scanners aboard. The scientist plopped down in the copilot's seat with a grunt. "Although I complain about Ancient equipment on a regular basis, let me state here and now that their designs are nearly always lighter and more compact than ours."

"Noted." John closed the hatch and powered up the craft. "Control, Jumper One is ready to depart."

"Acknowledged," came the gate tech's response. "Safe trip, Colonel."

As the jumper descended into the gate-room, John got the unnerving sense that Rodney was watching him a little too closely. He glanced over at his friend and immediately deduced the reason. "Don't start," he warned.

As expected, Rodney ignored him. "So how does that brilliant resignation of yours look now?"

Just what he wanted to talk about; he didn't even want to *think* about it. Sure, Ronon and Teyla were safe, and that meant a hell of a lot, but… "Nothing that's happened today changes the lousy decisions I've made lately." Which now had to include the decision to leave his teammates for dead—probably the worst choice of them all.

"In my experience," Rodney blandly observed, "the military in general, and the SGC in particular, is often willing to accept a focus on results over methods. Sometimes I think it's even encouraged."

John sighed. "Let's just get through this, all right?"

The jumper slid through the event horizon, and the wormhole gave him the last word.

# CHAPTER THIRTEEN

In spite of his teammates' assurances that the Nistra generally left the second gate alone, Rodney planned to keep an eye out for suspicious activity throughout his stay on the planet. He was all for trying to head off a war, but he had no desire to be assaulted by a whip, arrow, bullet, or anything else in the process. *Especially* not another damned arrow. Besides, he had no guarantee that other members of this Cadre group wouldn't show up just to make life miserable.

Sheppard cloaked the jumper upon arrival and performed a low-altitude pass over the surrounding wreckage to gain some visual references. The contrast between the rocky slopes here and the thriving Falnori farmlands nearer the Hall was striking. Short of someone actually mentioning one group or the other by name, there would have been no way for Teyla and Ronon to recognize this place as P7L-418.

Rodney had a more immediate concern, however. "Oh, no."

"You know, someday you're going to have your very own fable," Sheppard commented from the pilot's seat. "The Boy Who Cried 'Oh, No.' Or, more accurately, The Boy Who Cried 'We're So Screwed.'"

"You're rarely as amusing as you think you are. And what makes you so sure I didn't just notice an urgent problem, like something about to blow up?"

"No abject terror in your voice. So what's the issue?"

"The sheer size of the debris field." Rodney waved at the long trail of wreckage beyond the jumper's windshield. "The station must have impacted the atmosphere at a fairly shallow angle and disintegrated, scattering fragments across miles of the planet's surface. Remember how long it took to recover even a majority of the pieces of the space shuttle that broke up over Texas? And that effort involved hundreds of people."

"So," the Colonel summed up with his usual eloquence, "needle in a haystack?"

"An entire *field* of haystacks," Rodney corrected unhappily. "We can't possibly find every last scrap of that station, let alone examine it all."

"We'll just have to make a few WAGs, then."

Although Rodney had worked for the U.S. military for years, there were elements of its acronym-laden lexicon that had escaped him. Such omissions weren't wholly accidental on his part. "I don't want to know how WAG translates into standard English, do I?"

"Wild-Ass Guess." With a grin so brief it barely blinked across his face, Sheppard attempted to access the head-up display, only to watch it flicker twice and then display wildly inaccurate data. "Huh. It was worth a try. I'm pretty sure we're not traveling at twice the speed of sound right now, though." Shutting off the HUD, he brought the jumper around in a lazy U-turn. "Looks like the most concentrated area of wreckage is around the gate."

"And that would be the most logical place to find a DHD, in any case." Rodney started to look for a suitable landing site when a warning flashed on the control panel.

Sheppard slapped at it. "Well, crap."

And he had the nerve to snark Rodney for saying 'Oh, no.' Hypocrite. "What?" Rodney demanded. "Something dangerous? Some of us don't read voices as well as you claim to do."

"We just lost our cloak," Sheppard reported. "Guess the sensors aren't the only system affected by proximity to adarite. I'm gonna set us down under those trees, give the jumper whatever cover we can manage."

Rodney was under no illusions; any Nistra who stumbled on the ship would assuredly draw the conclusion that it belonged to a raiding group.

As it turned out, the drooping evergreen branches obscured the jumper rather nicely. Sheppard located camouflage netting in the storage compartment and dragged it over the hull, just to be on the safe side. Not for the first time—although he'd be damned if he'd admit it—Rodney appreciated the officer's instincts. A two-person mission might not be his idea of a fun outing, but in this case the other person was Sheppard, and he trusted Sheppard above anyone else to watch his back when it mattered.

And that, plain and simple, was the reason Sheppard needed to track down Elizabeth once all this blew over and ask for his stupid letter back.

"Got your gear?" the Colonel asked, fastening his vest. They'd brought stun weapons in place of P-90s, which seemed reasonable given the low probability of running into anyone to whom they might need to do permanent harm. All the same, it made Rodney feel a little exposed.

"Yes. Let's get this statistically improbable show on the road."

When he'd warned his team that Earth-built technology would be his only tool in this search, he hadn't been strictly truthful. 'Earth-built' and 'non-Ancient' were not fully interchangeable terms. The Asgard, for instance, had a portable device that acted as a more accurate version of an X-ray fluorescence scan, identifying a sample's component materials almost instantaneously. During a recent *Daedalus* visit, Rodney had badgered Hermiod into leaving one of the units on Atlantis, contending that the ship's inbuilt diagnostics made it redundant to keep such a unit onboard. The SGC hadn't been pleased—something about circumventing the requisition process. In any case, they hadn't tried to fire him, so he'd claimed victory.

The scanner could be programmed to search for particular materials or combinations thereof. He'd calibrated it with the constituents of the naquadah alloy that powered Atlantis's dialing computer, minus those substances which would have combusted under the heat of reentry through the atmosphere. Now he was faced with the rather daunting task of determining where to start.

"On the plus side, we've already got a grid laid out to keep us from losing track of where we've looked." Sheppard crouched to study one of the many branches stuck into the hard ground at relatively constant intervals.

Rodney made a mental note. He wasn't the type to heap praise on people for exhibiting common sense, but Teyla and/or Ronon deserved credit for devising the marking scheme.

The duo moved methodically over the debris field, disturbing as little as possible in the course of their search. On occasion a muted crunch under Rodney's boot would elicit a wince, and a few fragments crumbled into ash at the slightest touch. He told himself that anything truly critical to their cause would have been constructed more sturdily. Sometimes these situations called for a little judicious self-delusion.

He also tried valiantly to ignore the literal and figurative weight of the Stargate looming over them. The ring couldn't possibly be stable in its current cockeyed position, no matter what the physics said.

They'd been sweeping the scanner's beam over wide swaths of ground for the better part of an hour when the unit signaled a hit. "Hmm. Not exactly the right material makeup, but close enough to check out. Under here." Rodney beckoned Sheppard over to a heap of deformed metal. "Help me lift this piece."

The piece in question probably had been a structural support, long and unwieldy. After a couple of fruitless attempts, Sheppard got his shoulder under one end and managed to shift it far enough for Rodney to get one arm awkwardly into the piled wreckage and drag a briefcase-sized chunk of *something* out.

Wiping away sweat with his sleeve, the Colonel plunked himself down next to the beam he'd displaced. "What've you got?"

"Chiefly, a strained back."

"Yeah, yeah." Sheppard peered at their find as Rodney brushed dirt and char off the casing. The surface was badly scratched and even gouged in a number of places—

*Hold on.* Those marks were too uniform to be accidental damage. Rodney scrubbed harder at the burn residue, eventually resorting to the use of his shirttail. When he'd at last gotten the casing as clean as it would ever be, he got out his flashlight and examined the indentations. *Aha.*

Familiarity.

"Doesn't look like part of a DHD," observed Sheppard.

"It isn't. But it might do us some good anyway. See those three larger slots across the end?" Rodney played the light beam across the object's surface. "They match up with the connecting hardware of the download device we use to do maintenance on the jumpers. I think this might be some kind of flight data recorder."

"From the space station?"

"Of course from the space station. If we can get an idea from the records contained in here about what really happened to the station, it'll likely be more productive than fishing around in this junk."

With a shrug, Sheppard climbed to his feet. "All right. Guess we'll head back and plug this thing into Atlantis."

After her latest check-in, Elizabeth felt her first flicker of hope in quite some time. "Gentlemen," she called, stepping down from the stairwell. "I have some information that may help us make progress."

Neither Cestan nor Galven looked terribly impressed by the announcement. Still, they gave her their attention. "Recently, access to the Stargate has emerged as a point of contention," she began. "Minister Galven, there is an Ancient ruin in the foothills of your territory. It once was a station that orbited this planet, and it crashed to the ground hundreds of years ago. Are you familiar with it?"

"I have heard of such a thing," the minister answered, "though we were not aware it fell from the sky. It is little more than rubble, so it has not been of much interest to us."

"You may change your mind about that. The ruin contains another Stargate." Elizabeth had to smile at both leaders' evident surprise. "It doesn't have a dialing device, but my people are already working to rectify that. Once it's functional, there will be no need for the Nistra to share the Hall gate, since you'll have one of your own."

Although Galven might have been caught off-guard, his expression quickly became unreadable. "If this is the case," he said, "and I will need to verify that it is, I am not fully prepared to concede the Hall gate. The Hall itself is to remain neutral, and that may be difficult to maintain with the Falnori controlling the nearby gate."

"We can discuss that," Elizabeth allowed. "There is a more important aspect of the second gate, however. Because it's somewhat hidden and mostly unknown to your people, it's open to use by others—like the raiders. That gate is what gave them the means to terrorize both the Falnori and the Nistra. My people have captured some of them. They're called the Cadre, and they come from off-world."

She waited to gauge their reactions. Cestan sat back in his chair, adjusting his cuffs. "So it is as I have said before. The Nistra declare themselves to be victims of these raiders, and by labeling us as the aggressors they have free rein to act against us without cause."

Galven opened his mouth to counter as one of his messengers appeared on the stairs. He motioned to the young man, who hurried over to deliver his report quietly and urgently.

"The leader of the Cadre told us that his group isn't allied with either of your peoples," said Elizabeth. "It's an independent—"

"Without cause, you claim, Governor?" Galven sprang to his feet, leveling a blazing glare on Cestan. "Word has just reached me that a Nistra hunting party was attacked this very day by your Cadre!"

"*My* Cadre?" Cestan echoed, casting an incredulous glance at Elizabeth. "Do you see how they persist in this delusion?"

"There were dozens of them, with weapons that burn," insisted the minister. "This time they came to do violence on my people without even the façade of stealing goods."

Elizabeth had a fairly good idea she knew what incident Galven was referring to, and she suspected that the tale had been embellished along the way. "Minister, two of my people were there. That's not exactly how they saw it."

She realized her miscalculation when Galven turned his frigid gaze on her. "Do not presume to tell me what happens on my land, Doctor."

"I apologize," she said immediately. "I overstepped my bounds. Please don't allow that to distract you from the issue at hand: the Cadre is an off-world threat taking advantage of the gate in your territory. We should focus on resolving that, and I'm telling you that we *can* resolve it."

"It does not matter what the raiders call themselves, only that more blood has been shed." The news of the latest attack had seemingly forged Galven's resolve in steel. "This will not stand. If the Stargate is being used to invade our land, we will defend it. But we also are prepared to finish what the Falnori have begun."

As he turned to his messenger, Cestan beckoned for

one of his own. Feeling Carson and Lorne's eyes on her,
Elizabeth reached for the bottle of water she'd brought
and wished fleetingly that it held something stronger.
Troops on both sides would soon receive marching
orders, she was sure. Time was now a much more limited
resource, and she was running out of ideas.

As it turned out, hooking up the download device in
the Jumper Bay to the Ancient version of a 'black box,' as
the Colonel insisted on calling it, wasn't the complicated
part of the task. The complicated part was sifting through
the massive quantities of data the recorder promptly spat
out. The system status reports alone, taken at eight-hour
intervals over a span of decades, would have crashed
Rodney's laptop in seconds. Eventually they resorted to
rigging up a buffer program that would only allow the
information Radek specified to pass from the maintenance terminal to the laptop.

"Can't we start at the last recorded data and work backward?"

The lieutenant in charge of jumper maintenance no
doubt thought he was being helpful. For that reason
alone, Rodney refrained from snapping at him. "We can,
and in fact we *have*. Unfortunately, and some might say
predictably, the last recorded data is a series of null sets
broken up by the occasional gibberish. The unit obviously
continued to function long after the station it was meant to
monitor was destroyed."

"We're working on the first set of meaningful data
now," supplied Radek, sitting cross-legged on the floor
while the laptop cranked through the translation algorithm a few lines at a time. Every twenty seconds or so

he leaned forward to tap a few keys. "This set appears to contain information on emergency procedures."

The doors slid open, and Sheppard joined them in the bay. "Hate to rush you guys," he began, "but Dr. Weir just checked in from 418. Things are falling apart over there. Nobody bought her description of the Cadre, for one thing. Galven got word that a Nistra hunting party had been attacked—probably the one the Cadre hit in order to get Ronon and Teyla—and he didn't take it too well."

The maintenance lieutenant must have been a new-comer, because he'd leapt to his feet at his commander's approach. When Sheppard noticed, a few seconds later, he waved distractedly at the young man to relax and leaned back against the extended engine pod of Jumper Three. "Sounds like he's getting a lot of rumors and static from his people. Regardless, he doesn't like the idea of a gate in his territory that he can't control, and he still seems convinced that the raiders are in league with the Falnori. And Elizabeth's not sure what Cestan's up to, except that his posturing is starting to get more serious. So anything you can give us would be useful sooner rather than later."

Of course. Because they'd been on such a loose sched-ule thus far, and he'd missed the pressure. "We're dig-ging into the recorded emergency procedures right now." Rodney left the black box and scooted over to look at Radek's screen. The schematic that appeared took him a few seconds to parse. Once the scale of the diagram became clear, he gave a low whistle. "Okay, I need to rethink my estimation of the wreckage on 418. This sta-tion must have been quite a bit larger than I anticipated."

"How large?" Sheppard wanted to know. "Are we talking 'That's no moon, it's a space station' large?"

Rodney grimaced; he'd really left the door wide open for that one. "Not hardly. Orbital mechanics alone would preclude that. Larger than the *Daedalus*, though."

"Sure didn't get that sense from the area around the gate." Sheppard frowned. "There was a lot of debris, but not *that* much. And I didn't see any huge craters or anything."

"What you saw may have been only one segment of the station." Radek pointed to the lines of text scrolling rapidly across the screen of the maintenance terminal.

After half a decade on the Stargate program, Rodney was no longer impressed by much in the way of technology. When something *did* impress him, he gave credit where due. "Huh."

"Well said." Sheppard craned his neck to look, his eyes nearly crossing at the frantic pace of the text.

In the interest of expediency, Rodney described it to him instead. "The station consisted of three segments, each with its own dedicated operations and life support systems. In a contingency situation, for instance an attack, the segments could be detached and maneuvered into different orbits."

"Split up to present multiple smaller targets, or even send noncombatants out of harm's way. Makes sense."

"Especially if you're trying to protect the gate." Rodney traced a line on the schematic with his finger. "See where the structure closes off and disengages? The gate's in one segment, and the control console for the dialer and shield are in another. That's why the database labeled the station gate as inoperative. The dialer simply wasn't available to be connected to the gate for use."

"Wait a minute. The dialer's on a different segment?" The Colonel cautiously glanced back and forth between the two scientists, as if he doubted he'd gotten the message right. "And we think only the gate segment crashed on the surface?"

"Only the gate segment crashed in the area we investigated," Rodney corrected. No reason to get carried away with unwarranted optimism. "If the station's geosynchronous orbit was destabilized, the other segments could have crashed centuries later on the other side of the planet."

"Or they could have been part of the space junk we spotted in orbit on our first trip to 418," countered Sheppard. "Question is, how can we find out?"

Radek lifted his head. "Miko's database project. We can search the battle records for specific references to the station."

"Now we're talking. Get Miko on it ASAP. Lieutenant, prep Jumper One with three spacesuits and whatever tools these two want." At Rodney and Radek's twin stares, Sheppard offered a wry smile. "I can dodge floating junk to get you there, but finding and removing the dialing computer is all up to you."

Although Rodney wasn't terribly enthused about repeating his one and only experience in a space suit, he understood. No matter what Miko found in the database, nothing could guarantee that the required station segment would have a stable, breathable environment after ten thousand years of drifting. *If* they even managed to locate it.

Sheppard, though, seemed to be taking a favorable search result for granted, striding toward the stairway to the control room. Rodney called after him. "What makes you so sure we'll be able to find the segment we need intact, let alone the dialing computer?"

"Sometimes what looks like confidence is actually a lack of options." The Colonel's pace slowed as he spoke, but he didn't turn back. "If we don't give Elizabeth something, Galven and Cestan are going to order their people to start killing each other. Certain or not, I'm going to go tell her to promise the Nistra a gate shield."

Elizabeth sat alone, both literally and figuratively, at the negotiating table. The past few hours had seen progressively less debate, polite or otherwise. Instead, Cestan and Galven had retreated to opposite sides of the room and formed tight huddles with their advisor-bodyguards. Every so often one of the lackeys would leave or return to the Hall, evidently performing messenger duties.

It would have been the height of naïveté to ignore the likelihood that troops were assembling in both territories. Still, Elizabeth wasn't packing it in just yet. Lieutenant Cadman had just come down the stairs and was reporting quietly to Lorne. The Major listened for a minute before dismissing the Marine and crossing the room to approach the table. From his place against the back wall, Carson leaned in to hear the latest update.

"Ma'am, Colonel Sheppard says Drs. McKay and Zelenka have a lead on the second gate's dialing computer and shield controls. They think it's still on a section of a station in orbit, and they're going up to retrieve it now. They plan to take it directly to the second gate for installation. The Colonel suggests you assure Minister

Galven that they'll have the gate secured within a day and invite him to travel back to the gate to witness it."

"And if they aren't able to get the apparatus they need?" Carson asked quietly.

Lorne kept his voice low and his gaze on Elizabeth. "According to Lieutenant Cadman," he answered, his features utterly inscrutable, "Colonel Sheppard promised to come up with a Plan B and asked that we convey his limitless faith in your ability to bluff."

The situation wasn't amusing in any rational way, yet Elizabeth found herself smirking ruefully. Nobody could pull off a truly deadpan delivery like Lorne. "All right, if that's the extent of what we've got to work with, we might as well get started." She cleared her throat. "Excuse me, Minister."

Though the talks had all but disintegrated and trust was hardly the order of the day, the leaders continued to conduct themselves with the decorum befitting their positions. Small favors. Galven broke off his conversation when addressed and gave her his full attention. "Dr. Weir?"

"I've just received word from my people. They've located a device to dial and operate the shield on the Stargate within your territory." At that, Cestan started listening as well. Elizabeth went on. "It will take a few hours to deliver the device and get it working. As soon as that's completed, you'll have total control of the gate. We'll supply you with code devices to operate the shield so that only people you choose will be able to come through."

The older man looked interested, if unconvinced. "We appreciate the effort. However, closing off the gate will only prevent raids by off-worlders. It cannot stop the raids originating from *this* world."

"Minister, I assure you that the Cadre is very much an off-world threat, one that has nothing to do with the Falnori. All this will become clear when the adarite raids stop after the shield control is installed. I'm simply asking you to give us the time to demonstrate that."

"And in the meantime?"

*Try not to start any battles.* "If nothing else," Elizabeth replied, "you'll have a functional gate all to yourself. If you'd like, you can find more trading partners without needing to use the gate here."

She'd assumed that to be a reasonable concept. Apparently she'd assumed wrong. Galven's face darkened. "You propose that we surrender this land to the Falnori? What of the Hall?"

Before she could deny any such intent, Cestan edged in with a demand of his own. "Do the raids on my people mean nothing? Why should their gate be protected and not ours?"

"*Your* gate?" Galven spat. "I think not."

The Falnori governor allowed his manners to slip. "You hardly use this one. Now you want two?"

"We'll come up with a shield for the gate here as well," Elizabeth hurried to say. She had no idea whether or not it was possible to fashion a gate shield from scratch, but if it needed to be done Rodney and Radek would find a way to make it happen. "Until then we can continue to guard this gate. How long will we need to go without a raid before you're convinced that no one on this planet is involved?"

She never got an answer. Before either man could speak, Cadman appeared on the stairs again. Her stiff-backed posture conveyed a warning more clearly than her words. "Ma'am, we've got some kind of standoff topside."

Only the combined experiences of two-plus years in the Pegasus Galaxy allowed her to take that statement in stride. Even so, the three seconds she took to process it gave Lorne enough of a head start to beat her to the stairwell and up to the Hall's entrance—where he thrust out a hand to halt her.

"Better stay back, Doctor."

"You're not armed either, Major," she pointed out.

"That's true, ma'am, but I think we both know what our respective roles are supposed to be here."

The Falnori and Nistra representatives had followed her up the stairs to investigate. Elizabeth compromised by staying with Carson, a few steps behind Lorne and Cadman, as they climbed the hill toward the gate.

"I need a sit-rep, Lieutenant," the Major said quietly.

"About twenty people showed up out of the eastern edge of the forest," Cadman reported. "They must have come in covertly, split up into pairs, and circled around. They put at least two guys on each of ours before demanding our weapons and sending me off to get you. Nobody's made a move yet—everyone's waiting for someone else to be first."

"What about *their* weapons?"

"Mostly bows and arrows. We could take 'em, sir, but it'd be ugly."

Hearing Galven and Cestan's footfalls behind her, Elizabeth wondered whose soldiers these were—and whether or not they were acting under orders.

The situation at the top of the hill appeared just as

Cadman had described. Having spread out to cover the area around the gate, the Marines had been herded together by a ragged yet focused squad. The four Falnori who had taken part in the sentry duty now knelt on the ground, disarmed. That effectively answered her question.

Although one side wielded P-90s and the other bows, neither showed any sign of backing down.

One soldier glanced over at the newcomers and bobbed his head in acknowledgment. "We serve, Minister."

If Elizabeth had been asked to guess which group would take the first step toward escalating the conflict, she probably would have said the Nistra. Still, a surge of indignation propelled her toward Galven. "Do you really expect to solve anything like this?" she accused. "Through control of the gate?"

"Control of the talks," Galven corrected matter-of-factly. "It is in our interests to complete a new treaty. However, the long-held Falnori view of the Nistra as an inferior people must end. I will no longer negotiate from a position of weakness."

"Galven, you finally have defied all justifications," seethed Cestan. "Peace at the point of a spear is no peace at all."

"My hunters are here to guard the Stargate and this gathering, nothing more. We have no reason to bring bloodshed into an open and sincere proceeding." His emphasis made clear his doubt that the negotiations could truly be described as such.

"And we're meant to take your intent on faith? What will you ask next? Our full harvest?"

Elizabeth battled to maintain some shred of authority. "Minister, we had an agreement for my people to stand guard as an impartial force."

Galven's eyebrows lifted. "Please forgive me, Doctor, if your claims of neutrality no longer reassure me."

And then two of the bows were aimed at her and Carson, sending a ripple of renewed tension through the Marines. A corporal took aim at the hunter pair. "Ma'am, just say the word," the young man stated, his tone deadly earnest.

For a few seconds, the air was silent, and Elizabeth's heartbeat thudded in her ears. It wasn't fear, at least not directly; she knew that the hunters threatening her would be the first to fall if she told the Marines to open fire. Once that happened, however, they'd be set on an irreversible course. The Nistra would see enemies in the Falnori and Lanteans alike, and the casualties on this hill would be only the first.

"Lower your weapons," she said at last.

Bewildered, the Marines looked to Major Lorne for guidance. "You heard the order," Lorne barked, mostly concealing his skepticism. "Be advised that she said *lower*, not *drop*."

Cestan watched the Marines stand down and whirled on Elizabeth. "How can you appease him?" he demanded, betrayal written across his face. "My people…"

Time for some tough love. Mind racing to stay a step ahead, Elizabeth addressed both leaders in a cool voice. "If you're certain this dispute can't be resolved without force, that's your choice. I'm willing to continue mediating up to a point. What I am *not* willing to do is risk my people. With your permission, Minister, I'd like to send these Marines home."

No doubt Galven interpreted that as a victory. Sweeping out a magnanimous hand, he agreed. "You are free to do so."

Lorne leaned in and spoke urgently. "Ma'am, if you're suggesting that we stay here unarmed—"

"Not you, Major. You need to go get Sekal out of his cell, throw him in a jumper, and drag him down here. And bring every last bauble he and his gang had with them, in case any of it's recognizable to either the minister or the governor. If anybody can prove to these two models of intractability that neither group is deliberately antagonizing the other with the raids, it's him."

The Major's eyes narrowed. "All due respect, but if the rest of the team is heading home, you're going to need backup now more than ever. Dr. Beckett can go round up the prisoner instead of me. Right, Doc?"

Carson looked as though he wanted to protest her plan to stay behind. He must have thought better of it, because he blinked rapidly and nodded. "Aye, suppose I can. But I think a few of these Marines had better take the return trip with Sekal."

"I'd recommend it. As quickly as possible." Elizabeth gripped his hands for a brief moment, attempting to convey some kind of reassurance.

She may not have entirely succeeded. Carson's gaze pierced her and he murmured, "I do hope you know what you're doing."

*As much as I ever do in this galaxy.* She alone had made the choice to press on with this Sisyphean task, and she'd be the one to live with the consequences. Stepping back, she told Cadman, "Dial the gate."

The lieutenant marched past a half-dozen hunters, seemingly taking the most direct route to the DHD on purpose so as to prove that the Nistra hadn't won anything. When the gate activated, Elizabeth watched Carson and the Marines troop through and tried not to feel desperately isolated.

Donning her confidence like a cloak, she faced the governor and minister as the wormhole shut down. "This changes nothing about the talks," she informed them. "Control of the gate is not to be used as leverage in any discussion. Keep in mind that my people hold the key to shielding either gate. The first time an ultimatum is issued here—about adarite or raids or anything at all—I'm gone, and no one gets a gate shield."

The presence of the Nistra hunters allowed Galven the freedom to be more accommodating. "Your position is reasonable and understood," he said. "Shall we—"

A sharp *crack,* like the sound of lightning, tore through the air, followed shortly by a cry—and then chaos.

Elizabeth hit the ground on her side, pain blossoming where her hip struck the hard-packed dirt. It took a half-second for her to realize that Lorne had yanked her down, and another half-second to realize that she should be grateful for his instinctive action. Scattered, random flashes illuminated the area around them, and arrows hissed past overhead.

"I think Cestan's team just showed up to play," Lorne said into her ear, struggling to be heard over the shouts of the hunters. "We need to get out of here."

She raised her head to look for the gate. Between it and them lay forty yards and far too many combatants.

Each leader had been swallowed up by a protective cluster of fighters almost immediately. Adarite whips sizzled all around, creating a light show that would have been breathtaking if it hadn't been grisly at the same time. "The Hall," she told him. "We can wait this out in there."

The Major's eyes scanned the newly christened battlefield for the safest route down the hill. No doubt he'd noticed, as she had, that both sides fought in relatively small numbers so far. This wasn't the start of a carefully planned campaign by either group. Rather, it seemed more like a first skirmish between scouting parties. They would have to hope that an opportunity to reach the gate would present itself later, before Atlantis was forced to send a rescue team into the fray.

"Stay as low to the ground as you can until we open up a safe distance," Lorne directed, pointing toward the clearest path. "I'll be right behind you."

Sucking in a breath, Elizabeth began to crawl forward on her forearms, the way she'd seen the Marines do in training. Before long she had to shut her eyes against the long grasses that scratched her face. She wasn't covering ground as fast as she would have liked; Lorne surely could have outdistanced her in seconds. He didn't, of course, instead keeping his body between her and the majority of the fighters.

As the ground started to slope away under her, hope crept into her thoughts. Once they were partway down the hill, the odds of being followed or struck by a stray weapon would diminish.

She'd just gotten brave enough to get up on all fours when she heard a soft moan nearby. One of the Falnori whip-warriors lay in a heap a few feet away, an arrow driven through her thigh. Elizabeth paused, glancing back at Lorne and the first-aid supplies she knew were stored in his vest.

"Helping her might be interpreted as taking sides," he warned under his breath. "Which would be a dangerous thing for us to do."

The warrior looked near to Elizabeth's age, and had she not been wounded she might have carried herself in a similar manner. Her gaze displayed acceptance; she looked as if she knew that the off-worlders would be taking a risk to aid her, and she would understand if they chose not to do so.

It was the most rational viewpoint Elizabeth had seen from anyone on this world in days. She shuffled awkwardly on her hands and knees toward the woman. "Grab her other arm," she told the Major, who moved to comply. Together they dragged the warrior down the hill until they felt safe to stand and pull her arms across their shoulders.

By the time they reached the Hall, Elizabeth's lungs burned with exertion, the sun was inching toward the horizon, and the battle sounded distant. The trio stumbled only a few steps inside the entrance before stopping, unable to negotiate over the rubble on the floor. Trained in basic field medicine, Lorne did his best to make the warrior comfortable and slow the bleeding, although he elected not to remove the arrow from her leg.

"It'll just bleed more if I do. Somebody who knows a lot more than me will have to stitch you up," he told her apologetically, handing over a couple of pills and his canteen. "Take these. They're painkillers." She accepted them with a strained smile.

Exhausted though she was, Elizabeth couldn't resist remarking to Lorne, "Bet you're rethinking your choice to stay here and send Beckett home."

"No, ma'am. I'll take this little paradise any day over the ass-kicking the Colonel would deliver if I left civilians alone and unarmed off-world."

"Thank you." The soft comment came from the woman they'd propped against an overturned bench. "I would not have lasted long had I remained on the battle-field."

"Don't thank us yet. We may not be able to get out of here for some time." Elizabeth sat with her back to the wall and drew her knees up to her chest. "I'm Dr. Weir, by the way, and this is Major Lorne."

"I am Merise. I was one of the first to encounter your people near the gate, days ago."

The name struck a familiar chord. "Teyla mentioned you. She admired your fighting abilities."

"We owe you much for being willing to help us reach for peace." Merise cast her gaze down at the rough projectile embedded in her leg. "Even if it is beyond our grasp. We remain honored by the attempt."

*In other words, thanks for playing, and we have some lovely parting gifts for you.* Just 'trying' had never been good enough for Elizabeth. Still, she had to wonder if she'd been foolish to keep pushing when all signs had pointed to failure. Had she been hopelessly arrogant to believe she could halt a tide that had been building for centuries? Or had it been a blind, desperate play to regain some shred of the rigidly moral life she'd left behind on Earth?

Forcing herself to focus on the immediate situation,

she looked at the Falnori woman. "I'm assuming, based on your quick reaction to the Nistra seizing the gate, that your own army isn't far away."

"It is near," admitted Merise. "My group rode ahead. We did not come to provoke a battle, however. We merely planned to patrol the western woods, as we often do. When we saw that the gate had been overrun, we were in place to act."

"Can't really fault you for that," Lorne said. "But now that the fighting's started, we're going to have to treat this like a war, because that's what it's turned into."

On that cheerful thought, Elizabeth leaned her head back on the wall and closed her eyes.

She must have dozed for a while, since the daylight was all but gone when she opened her eyes again. The Major seemed to be exploring the ruined outer building of the Hall. Across the room, the beam of his flashlight played over broken equipment. "Looking for anything that might be useful as a weapon," he explained quietly, glancing at Merise, who also had fallen asleep. "Just in case."

"That will not be necessary."

Elizabeth pushed herself to her feet as Cestan entered the building. His only damage appeared to be to his robes, which were rumpled and smudged with dirt. Two of his warriors immediately went to assist Merise. "The battle's over?" Elizabeth asked.

The governor's nod was grave. "The first of many, I fear. We suffered few losses, but the gate remains under Nistra control."

"How did you…?"

Intuiting her question, Cestan gave a tired smile.

"There are not many places you could have fled. Especially since Kellec witnessed you taking Merise with you. We are thankful for that."

"I'm relieved you didn't assume malicious intent on our part." Elizabeth let her focus drift toward a splintered window frame and the area beyond it. "The gate's inaccessible, you said?"

"I'm afraid so. I'd like to offer you a place in my army's command post, just on the other side of the woods. You will need protection for the night."

So much for not taking sides. They had no other viable options, though. Grateful for the invitation, Elizabeth nonetheless needed to hear the inevitable confirmed. "And when morning comes?"

There was a bleak, resigned ache in the governor's voice. "Then the conflict which has been expected for generations will finally arrive, and may the Ancestors help us all."

# CHAPTER FOURTEEN

Radek's first view of P7L-418 came at twilight, as Jumper One emerged from the Nistra gate. Had the landscape not been marred by the wreckage of the station segment, he might have thought it pretty, in an austere sort of way. Of course, amid those picturesque mountains lay enough adarite to make him forget his own name, so he wasn't disappointed to watch them grow smaller outside the jumper's windscreen.

Their ascent into planetary orbit took them over both Nistra and Falnori territory, giving them an overhead view of the continent for the first time. A scattering of small lakes demonstrated where the Falnori got the water to irrigate their crops; clusters of rugged stone dwellings set snugly into the foothills must have been the Nistra villages. In between lay a sort of no-man's land of rolling plains and woods. Radek spotted the planet's main gate amid that patchwork and squinted, trying vainly to identify the small figures standing nearby.

"Check that out." Colonel Sheppard put the jumper into a shallow bank, allowing them a better look at the area. Tiny pinpricks of light, dozens of them, were gathered together under the encroaching darkness.

"They're closer to Nistra territory, though not by much." Rodney frowned, not comprehending. "Another settlement?"

"Don't think so." Sheppard called up the HUD. Apparently they'd now gained enough distance from the adarite deposits in the mountains for the sensors to work properly. "Lots of life signs, but no structures. It's a troop encampment. They're stopping for the night."

"From there they'll be able to march to the gate hill by mid-morning." Rodney sat hunched over in the right seat, his elbows resting on the console. "Is there another group out there on the Falnori side?"

In answer, Sheppard ran a sensor sweep to the south. "Sure enough," he confirmed. "Their group's smaller. They'll probably be better fighters, though, since their brains aren't scrambled."

Rodney sighed. "Well, *that's* a warm, fuzzy feeling. These people are determined to fight no matter what."

Radek spoke up from his seat behind them. "Then we should work quickly, I believe."

As Jumper One continued to climb, the lanterns and campfires that dotted the ground shrank into nothingness, soon replaced by starlight from above. Before long, the proximity alarm flashed, surprising no one. "That would be the space junk we've heard so much about." The Colonel shut off the alarm and engaged the jumper's shield. "Hold onto something, all right? If I have to make some sudden moves and the inertial dampeners can't quite keep up, I'd rather not have to peel anybody off the bulkheads."

"Another wonderful thought." Rodney watched with an expression of obvious trepidation at what lay ahead of them.

The jumper approached the labyrinth of wreckage. Radek found the view bizarrely fascinating. A derelict fighter was suspended in a bizarre *pas de deux* with a Wraith Dart, the two craft passing each other so slowly that the motion was almost imperceptible. Farther away, a larger ship floated in an orbit that would have looked perfectly normal if not for the great gash that had torn the ship open from bow to stern.

"Heads up," called Sheppard, abruptly dropping the jumper's nose as a piece of unidentifiable metal sailed past. It continued on its path until impacting another Dart, altering the course of both objects.

Radek shook his head, amazed. In a way, it looked almost as if the battle of so many centuries ago had never ended.

"So the black box specified an orbit for the station, right?" Sheppard verified. "You're not just guessing at a distance above the planet?"

"We recovered a specific orbital height from the emergency procedures, yes." Although Rodney's reply sounded calm and characteristically pedantic, his fingers were wrapped tightly around the armrests. "Unfortunately, as you may have noticed, everything up here is quite effectively demonstrating Newton's laws of motion. Any of this junk could have gotten knocked into the station segment and affected its position sometime in the last ten thousand years. Just get us into orbit and I'll find it on the sensors."

More than once Radek had had cause to appreciate the Ancients' style of computer design. Their technology was highly compatible; it nearly always recognized its own. As long as there was at least a minimal level of power left in the station, it would emit a signal that would light up on the jumper's sensors.

The Colonel navigated smoothly through an array of Darts. Radek had never quite gotten used to seeing things tilt outside the jumper without feeling an associated physiological shift.

"This is a damned minefield," Rodney muttered, ducking his head to study the sensor screen.

"Relax, Rodney," Sheppard advised. "I'd rather fly through this than dodge rocket-propelled grenades. And, unlike any of my rides on Earth, the jumper has a shield."

"Up until we have to dock with the station, sure. At that point, we'll have to shut the shield down, and the whole contraption will be little more than a glorified tin can."

"Let's wait and worry about that if and when we have to, all right?"

As it happened, they didn't have to wait long before Rodney's concern moved from the theoretical to the practical. "Got something," he reported. "Turn right thirty degrees."

Sheppard complied, bringing into view an industrial-looking construct in an orbit slightly higher than the jumper's. "I take it that's what we're looking for?"

"That's it."

The station, thankfully, appeared to have sustained little damage in the millennia following the battle. There were some dents, and one side bore the telltale scorch marks left by a laser cannon, but the jumper dock was unharmed. God only knew how, since there were plenty of stray engine pods and bits of Dart nacelles drifting nearby.

Radek pretended not to notice the Wraith cruiser looming behind the station. Lifeless or not, it was an unsettling sight.

"May I suggest leaving the shield in place until the last

possible moment?" asked Rodney, eying the debris surrounding them.

"Can do." Sheppard turned the jumper cleanly and used the HUD to keep track of their alignment. When only inches separated the back hatch from the dock, he slid his hand across the control panel, and the shield blinked out of existence. A not-quite-gentle *thud* reverberated through the craft, followed by the whisper of an airlock sealing shut. The Colonel twisted in his seat to face his passengers. "Over to you, guys."

Radek leaned over to examine the screen that reported outside conditions. "The interior of the station is not pressurized," he read. "We will have to wear the suits."

One corner of Sheppard's mouth quirked upward. "Stylin'."

Half an hour, four bruised shins, and two dozen multilingual curses later, the trio was sufficiently outfitted. Spacious though the jumper's interior was, it had not been designed to accommodate the expedition's bulky spacesuits—or the clumsy flailing of three people attempting to climb into said suits.

"Maybe the Ancients had a more compact version," theorized Rodney, huffing a little as he tightened the seal around his boot.

Sheppard reached toward his earpiece and made an irritated noise when he inadvertently smacked his glove against his helmet. "The less time we have to spend in these, the better. Let's move out."

Upon lowering the hatch, Radek found himself buoyed, and he couldn't repress a small yelp of surprise. Zero gravity was certainly a new experience. Almost immediately, however, a panel on the wall of the dock flashed, and a hiss could be heard even through their helmets. His boots sank back toward the deck, and he bounced lightly.

Reacting quickly, Rodney used the wall of the jumper to push off, propelling himself toward the panel. "The station must have sensed our arrival. It's trying to restore pressure and oxygen for us."

"Hospitable," remarked the Colonel, keeping one hand on each of the tool cases they'd brought along as they settled back to the floor. "Why do I get the feeling it's not exactly working?"

Radek swallowed hard. The rapid sensations of rising and falling hadn't done much for his equilibrium. A shudder ran through the station, muted because of the lack of gravity. He grabbed onto the edge of the jumper nonetheless.

"Because there isn't enough power," Rodney replied, still studying the panel. The combination of the radio and helmet gave his voice a nasal overtone. "If I'm reading this correctly, the station's got about two percent of its reserve left, and apparently it just tried to draw more than that for the environmental system. That little jolt may have been a bit like our attempt at operating the transporter in the Hall—the equivalent of blowing a fuse."

"*Now* you're okay with simplified explanations. So we're going to be bouncing around in half a G the whole time we're here?" Sheppard asked.

"It's all we've got, Colonel. Take it or leave it."

"I'll take it. As you're always reminding me, your equipment's heavy."

The cases were indeed pleasantly easy to move in the semi-gravity environment. Radek carried one down the sterile gray corridor, acclimatizing himself to the added spring in his step. The repeating geometric pattern on the walls looked to be more decorative than descriptive, so they relied on the map they had recovered from the black box. Rodney called it up on his datapad and held it out in front of him while he led them through the winding corridors. A left, another left, then a right. Through it all their surroundings never seemed to change.

"Sometimes," Sheppard commented as they walked, "I wonder if the Ancients are playing a practical joke on us, what with all the weird crap we get into. Then we end up in a rat maze like this, and I *know* they're screwing with us."

Radek found that viewpoint difficult to dispute.

"The control room for this segment is just up here," Rodney said brusquely, lengthening his already bounding stride to reach an access ladder. Rather than beginning to climb, he stood at the foot of the ladder and waited for Sheppard to bring up the rear. "Why don't you go up first, and we'll hand the tool cases up to you?"

It was hard to tell through the helmets, but Radek suspected the Colonel was watching his teammate with mock surprise. "Don't tell me you're creeped out by the ghost station, Rodney."

"Nice work, Colonel Horror-Movie Cliché. You're just *asking* for a mummified Ancient to fall out of a broom closet on you. Climb, will you?"

Dutifully, Sheppard climbed, his oversized boots fumbling slightly on the rungs, and opened the hatch above him. Radek held both tool cases and handed one at a time up through the gap. His own climb was even less graceful. At last Sheppard reached down and hauled him up by his arms, resulting in a slow-motion tumble to the deck on the higher level.

Radek's head banged against the inside of his helmet. He gritted his teeth and pulled himself upright. The control room resembled a ship's bridge, with a long window dominating one side. The adjoining wall consisted of a huge docking port: an oversized, sealed-off version of the one they'd used for the jumper. This had to be the junction point for the missing gate segment of the station. Had he been present ten thousand years ago, he would have seen a Stargate standing here instead of a bulkhead.

"Aha." Sheppard approached a familiar-looking console in the center of the room. "Come on, Rodney, shake a leg," he urged. "Looks like the dialing computer's going to have to come out of here in pieces."

Another console had caught Radek's attention, glowing with a single line of text in red. He had yet to encounter a form of technology where red did not mean something undesirable. "Rodney!"

"Keep your pressurized pants on," Rodney grumbled, hoisting himself up onto the deck.

"You must translate this." Radek tugged him over to the console almost before he'd gained his footing.

After only a moment, Rodney paled behind his transparent visor. "It's a proximity alarm. We must be close to some of the wreckage."

"No *kidding*."

That statement of dismayed awe came from Sheppard, who stood stock-still at the window. Both Radek and Rodney crossed the room to join him—and Radek felt his stomach lurch in a manner that had nothing to do with the reduced gravity.

The Wraith cruiser he had seen earlier from a distance was no longer quite so distant. Situated below them from this angle, it grew slowly but steadily in the window.

"Are we *that* unlucky?" the Colonel asked bleakly. "These things have been up here for ten thousand years, and they choose today to collide?"

"We must have exerted enough force when we docked to alter the orbit," Rodney breathed, hurrying back over to the console with a demented pseudo-skipping gait. "Even if the station has some kind of a stabilizing system, there can't be enough power left to run it. Objects in motion will continue that motion until acted upon by an outside force, remember?"

Sheppard's expression turned dark. "That Newton was a real son of a bitch."

"How long until impact?" Radek asked.

Rodney checked the readout. "Assuming we don't cause any further alterations to the orbit—eighty-one minutes."

"Okay, it took us about fifteen to get here from the jumper. Give it a little cushion because we'll be carrying a whole bunch of parts…" Chewing on his lower lip, Sheppard looked at the scientists. "Let's see how much of the dialer we can disassemble in fifty minutes."

Radek closed his eyes. It was confirmed: he worked with madmen. Murmuring a short prayer, he opened one of the tool cases and slapped a screwdriver into the Colonel's glove. "Three will accomplish more than two. Just do not touch anything unless or until you are told."

Teyla went quickly to the gate-room as soon as she heard the activation announcement. When she arrived,

Ronon was already there, watching the Marines file out of the event horizon. To her surprise, Carson was the last to emerge before the gate shut down.

Ronon's gaze sharpened. "Where's Dr. Weir?"

"She and Major Lorne stayed behind. I'm meant to send Sekal back with the Marines to aid in proving the Cadre's existence to the Falnori and Nistra leaders." The doctor spread his hands in a helpless gesture. "I can't imagine how Dr. Weir thinks she can avoid a war at this point. A Nistra group came in and took control of the gate not long ago."

"A Nistra group?"

"Aye, working for Minister Galven. He called them hunters—said they'd allow him to negotiate from a position of strength." Carson sighed. "If you call that negotiation."

Exchanging a look with Ronon, Teyla saw her concern reflected in his eyes. Since the miners' greater exposure to adarite weakened them, it made sense that hunters would compose the majority of the Nistra force. And that meant… "Ilar," she said quietly.

Ronon's response was grim. "And Dantir."

A silent understanding reached, they moved as one toward the main-level doors and the weapons lockers just beyond. "Wait a minute," protested Carson, trailing behind them. "What do you two think you're doing? Where's Colonel Sheppard?"

"He took McKay and Zelenka to the station orbiting 418 to get a dialer and shield for the Nistra gate." Ronon strapped his sword to his back.

"So the Colonel just had to go along, did he?"

"He is the most skilled pilot, and they have a time constraint. We believe shielding the Nistra gate from raids may help to head off the conflict." Teyla tucked a stun pistol into her belt along with her staffs.

"Then they'd bloody well hurry up." Carson stared at them both with bewildered eyes. "And that didn't answer my first question."

"Elizabeth has been appealing to the leaders," explained Teyla. "No one has tried to tell the people themselves about the raiders' off-world origins. They are marching off to battle under the belief that they'll be defending their homes."

"We got to know one of the hunting parties." Ronon did a cursory knife check. Teyla had seen him make the motions a hundred times and still was not certain where he kept them all. "They're pretty open-minded. Maybe we can convince them of the truth, and they can convince others before the fighting begins."

Carson grabbed his arm. "Lad, I don't mean to be a spoilsport, but did you not hear me say that the gate is no longer under our control? Noble as your intentions are, is this really worth the risk of getting shot on sight?"

It was a fair question. Teyla glanced at Ronon. The choice was clear in her mind, but she would not decide for him.

"We owe them," Ronon said simply. With that, he turned to go back into the gate-room.

Teyla followed, tapping her radio to alert the control room. "Please dial the main gate on P7L-418."

"Everyone's gone batty around here," the doctor sputtered as the lights began to chase each other around the gate. "Hold on! Does this mean *I'm* meant to be supervising the city?"

"Have fun," Ronon called over his shoulder.

When they stepped out of the gate on 418, all that was visible through the wavering torchlight was the expected swarm of bows and spears. "We come as friends," Teyla said, extending her right arm and then touching her forehead. Catching on, Ronon quickly did the same.

The demonstration of their hunting signal gave the Nistra soldiers pause. "Where did you learn this?" one demanded.

"From the hunting party of Ilar," Ronon answered. "They gave us aid when we were in need. We'd like to return their kindness."

One of the hunters stepped forward. Teyla recognized him as a member of Ilar's group—Temal. "Teyla, Ronon," he greeted them with surprise and relief. "We feared you had been killed by the marauders."

"They tried. We outwitted them." Ronon gave a smirk.

"We have information about your adversary," continued Teyla. Not a lie, but perhaps not the complete truth, either. "Can you tell us where your forces are assembling so that we may deliver it?"

"They make camp for the night in the Beila Plains." Temal pointed toward the northeast. "I will take you there. You will need a mount to reach them before dawn. We can spare one for you, can we not?" He looked to the apparent leader of the guard detail, who nodded, seemingly won over by the promise of enemy secrets.

Partway down the hill grazed a small herd of creatures like the one that had pulled their cart to the Falnori capital. Had that first visit only been a few days ago? Teyla felt unaccountably aged. "Thank you," she told the leader. "We will make sure it is returned to your people."

Neither she nor Ronon was an experienced rider, certainly not on this type of animal. Ronon took the reins, and they both kept a tight grip on the saddle. Temal climbed onto another mount and led them off toward the plains. It was a bumpy, if not wholly unpleasant, journey, complicated somewhat by the darkness.

At last they came upon a field speckled with peladon-hide tents and campfires. So many people, all preparing to fight and die for little more than a mistake.

"I say we avoid the headquarters." Ronon dismounted the animal and nodded toward the larger, sturdier tent visible above the others. "We know Galven's already made up his mind."

At that, Temal looked at them curiously but said nothing.

"I agree." Teyla placed a hand on Ronon's shoulder in order to climb down as well. "Beyond that, I am not sure where to start."

A group of hunters solved the dilemma for them, walking up to them with frank curiosity. Teyla repeated the hand signal and the explanation she'd given at the gate. When Temal questioned them about a group leader named Ilar, the hunters shook their heads but suggested a group five tents away who 'knows everyone.' The process repeated three more times before a young voice from behind shouted, "Ronon! Teyla!"

As they turned, Dantir ran toward them, a wide grin causing his face to glow. "You're alive! We thought—"

"We're not so easily beaten." Ronon caught the boy's shoulders before a collision could occur. "How did you know we were here?"

"Word spread quickly. You don't really blend in."

Looking around at some of the hunters and other soldiers who had gathered, Teyla noted that most of them were closer to her height than to Ronon's. "Where is your hunting party? We must speak to your mother."

"Come." Dantir led them down a row of tents.

At their approach, Ilar rose quickly from the fire she tended. "The Ancestors smile on you," she exclaimed. "We believed you dead by the hand of the Falnori."

The rest of the party swarmed around them, offering sincere greetings. "That is why we have come." Teyla settled beside the fire and motioned for the others to return as well. "We have learned the identity of the marauders who plague your people. They are not Falnori."

Ilar's expression blanked, as if uncertain of what she'd heard. "But they are. They have stolen from us for many seasons—"

"*Someone* has been stealing from you," Ronon interrupted. "After they took us, we managed to trap some of them on our world. They're called the Cadre, and they steal from societies on lots of planets. They use the ring, the same one we came through, to sneak into your territory. They've been doing it to the Falnori, too."

Surprise and confusion were displayed openly on Dantir's face. Hesitant, he asked, "Can that be true?"

"No, it cannot." One of the older men of the party spoke, his voice more resigned than angry. "Our histories may not be well-preserved, but all who have encountered the Falnori know how they view us—as an inferior race, unworthy of being treated as equals."

"No. They merely believe that *you* have been raiding

*them*." Teyla leaned forward. "It has been so long since you've interacted with them in any meaningful way that you do not recognize them, or they you. The Cadre has set you against each other."

"And has this Cadre refused us food, weakened us?" Temal demanded.

How could they explain this? "The weakness many of your people suffer is due to the ore you mine. Think about the most afflicted among you. They are miners, are they not?"

No one responded. Teyla began to hope that she had reached them. "This whole war is based on one misconception after another," she persisted. "Our people are bringing a shield for the ring on your lands, and it will stop the marauders from coming. There is no need to fight."

Ilar laid a gentle hand on her arm, looking both wistful and sympathetic. "I wish I could believe as you do. You are young and have not lived among us. Sadly, there are some aspects of our existence that we cannot change. The hostility of the Falnori is one such constant. We have been called to defend our people, and we shall."

Though disappointed, Teyla could not blame these people for their views. What proof could she offer that might outweigh the beliefs of so many years? Had she really expected to convince an entire society to lay down their arms based solely on her word?

"Then we'll stay with you," Ronon said suddenly, catching her unawares.

Ilar's expression suggested that she had not expected that, either. "You are welcome, of course. But this is not your cause."

"We have to get back to the ring by the Hall, anyway." Ronon's gaze betrayed his true thoughts, however. Teyla followed it to where Dantir sat and felt the weight of hopelessness settle in her chest. The weapon at the boy's belt was crudely made. Still, she had seen and used the Falnori version enough to recognize it as an adarite whip.

Rodney desperately wanted to be able to wipe the sweat off his forehead. The clear plastic faceshield that prevented him from doing so seemed like a unique form of torture. On the plus side, they'd confirmed that the station gate did indeed have a shield and that its control mechanisms were contained in the dialing console. If he could get the dialer down to the planet and get it functioning, the crashed gate would be protected from the Cadre. However...

He glanced up from his work and immediately regretted the action. "I realize we're not quite where we want to be in terms of progress, but that Wraith cruiser is getting awfully big in the window."

"Think positive, Rodney." Sheppard supported the keyboard section of the console while Radek loosened the brackets holding it to the base. "How much time do we have left?"

"Of the fifty-minute estimate? Fourteen minutes."

The keyboard came free, and the Colonel staggered backward to prevent it and him from hitting the deck. "The base is attached quite solidly to the floor," Radek observed. "I believe we will need to take only the components from inside and construct an alternate casing for them later."

"All right. We can empty one of the tool kits and transport the parts in that container."

"I'm way ahead of you on the emptying part." Sheppard surveyed the hand tools strewn across the floor.

If removing each crystal and translucent circuit board was a painfully slow process, arranging them all in the tool kit so that they would be protected in transit was excruciating. In the background, Rodney's traitorous brain kept up a veritable feedback loop of anxiety. With what force would the station strike the cruiser? Would the structure crumple on impact, or would it hold its shape long enough for the venting of the remaining oxygen to knock them into some other piece of junk? Maybe out of orbit entirely? Into the planet's atmosphere?

At long last he set the final piece in place and closed the case. "Okay, time to move, and I do mean *now*. That keyboard section will fit through the hatch, won't it?"

"Guess we'll find out." Sheppard handed the light yet ungainly keyboard to Radek and shimmied down the ladder. The Czech tipped the piece up on its end and cautiously maneuvered it through the hatch into Sheppard's arms. "See? Nothing to it. Somebody get down here to catch the tool case."

Radek jerked his head backwards. Startled, Rodney jumped away. "What the hell was that?"

"My hair is falling in my face," Radek replied, miserably tapping his helmet. "It itches. I thought I could shake it back."

"Guys, time limit?" Sheppard reminded them, as if Rodney could have forgotten. Radek trudged down the ladder, and Rodney handed him one case and then the other before climbing down himself.

Sheppard was already halfway down the corridor by the time Rodney's boots hit the deck and he reached out to take one of the tool cases from Radek. The transition was made awkward when Rodney tried to grip the handle too close to where Radek held it, and their unwieldy gloves collided. The case slipped; Rodney juggled it, stumbling back against the ladder, where he felt the fabric of his suit catch on an edge. He waited a beat, breath frozen in his throat, and soon heard a terrifying *hiss*.

"My suit!" he yelled, scrabbling to find the leak. His sleeve—somewhere on the left sleeve… Both cases fell to the deck as Radek seized Rodney's arm and bunched the torn fabric tightly in his glove. "That won't be airtight," said Rodney, even as the hissing sound grew softer. "We need to seal it."

Having jogged back to them, Sheppard set the dialing keyboard carefully on the deck and crouched by the tool cases. "Tell me what to do, Radek."

"Second drawer," Radek replied. "Duct tape."

"*Duct tape?*" The higher pitch of Rodney's voice must have been due to the onset of hypoxia. "Are you serious? The pressure difference would overcome the adhesive, unless you were planning on essentially mummifying me in duct tape, in which case we'll run out of time before—"

"Time is the issue, Rodney." Radek's grip on his sleeve tightened as the Colonel unwound a length of tape and cut it with a blade from the case. "It only needs to hold for a few minutes. We will move quickly."

"You can say that again!" Rodney concentrated on slowing his respiration down to a manageable rate. His suit was losing oxygen through that tear, and asphyxiation was high on his list of worst ways to die.

Radek took the tape from Sheppard, careful not to tangle it between their gloved fingers. He released his hold on Rodney's suit and slapped the makeshift patch into place in one fluid motion. Feeling perspiration gather along his hairline, Rodney pressed his right hand down over the tape. The telltale sound of escaping air seemed to have stopped—or had it merely exceeded his hearing range?

Either way, he wasn't interested in waiting around to find out. As Radek retrieved one tool case, abandoning the other, and Sheppard once again picked up the dialer components that were the goal of this lamentable mission, Rodney bolted down the hallway.

While the infuriatingly similar corridors didn't make the route any more familiar, determination and a healthy sense of self-preservation worked wonders. Each inhalation seemed to require more effort than the last; Rodney couldn't tell whether that was a function of decreased oxygen availability or his lack of running proficiency. His vision began to tunnel—but at the end of that tunnel lay the welcoming hatch of Jumper One.

No sooner had they piled inside than Radek smacked his hand down on the hatch control. When the jumper had sealed and pressurized itself, all three men tore off their helmets.

Even Sheppard was breathing hard, which somehow made Rodney feel a bit better. "Rodney, you okay?"

"Ask again later," Rodney moaned, drinking in the cool, plentiful air. "Thank God."

"Yes, yes, now we can inhale each other's sweat rather

than just our own," grumbled Radek. "Will you help stow the gear or will you stand there?"

The problem with Radek was that, on rare occasions, he had moments of seeming a little too much like Rodney. It was disconcerting.

While they secured their newly-acquired dialing computer, or at least the important parts of one, Sheppard headed for the cockpit, yanking off his gloves along the way, and wedged his spacesuited body into the pilot's seat to begin the startup sequence. Rodney followed when his task was complete and attempted to squeeze his own suit into the right seat. Nothing doing. He shot the Colonel a preemptive glare. "I don't want to hear a single joke about donuts."

"I can barely breathe, if that makes you feel any better," Sheppard replied tersely, fingers skipping over the controls. "I don't have time to take this stupid suit off. You do."

"Ah. Quite right." Rodney stepped back into the main compartment, and he and Radek reenacted the initial fumbling spacesuit debacle in reverse. When he was finally free of the wretched thing, he lurched back to his seat and cursed in sheer astonishment at the cruiser now dominating the windscreen.

"Yeah." Sheppard's voice sounded as casual as ever, even as his motions became increasingly harried. "Got a brainteaser for you guys."

"What is it?" Radek asked, settling into his seat behind them. Rodney said nothing, filled with a sudden and terrible sense that he already knew what was wrong.

Sheppard twisted as far around as the bulky suit would let him. "I can't disengage the jumper from the dock."

# CHAPTER FIFTEEN

Elizabeth felt the clinging dampness in the air almost before she fully awoke. As she became aware of the heavy canvas tent above her, and the bedroll beneath her, she was struck by a sharp, visceral memory of a camping trip to Vermont. She'd been eleven years old, and her father had dragged her out of a sound sleep to watch the sunrise over the mountains. She'd been enthralled by the colors, the whole world so still and yet more alive than she'd ever imagined. Dad had chuckled at her slack-faced wonder and remarked that everyday problems seemed insignificant next to such a view.

Waking up on another world, in the midst of an army marching to battle, it was Elizabeth who seemed insignificant.

Diplomacy required its participants to see through the eyes of others, to find the issues that mattered most to each side and approach them on a level accessible to all parties. She'd done her best—perhaps more than might have been advisable—to bridge the gap between the Falnori and Nistra, but the actions of the Cadre had not created the cultural divide, merely inflamed it. As for the effects of the adarite, only a direct comparison test would provide the kind of empirical evidence that might convince Galven, and it was simply too late for that now.

"Dr. Weir?"

She pushed herself up to a sitting position and tugged her fingers through sleep-tangled hair. "Morning,

Major."

Lorne folded back one of the tent flaps and crouched to look through the opening. "Thought you'd want to know," he began. "Governor Cestan sent a warrior regiment ahead last night. They had numbers this time, and the scouts just reported back that they were able to take the gate hill."

"I suppose I should be pleased to hear that." Elizabeth rolled her shoulders to work out some of the kinks caused by sleeping on the ground. "They've been gracious hosts."

"They're also more likely than the Nistra to let us use the gate at this point." Reaching into his jacket, the Major withdrew a cloth-wrapped bundle. "Some bread. It's pretty good."

She accepted the bundle with a smile of thanks. "I'd like to think that exposing the Cadre for what they are and shielding the gates on this planet would do a lot to improve the state of affairs. I'm just not sure how we'll manage to accomplish either one in the middle of a battle."

"If you want my opinion, ma'am…"

That was one aspect of military protocol she'd never quite gotten used to. With the exception of John, sometimes they needed a little encouragement to speak their minds. "Of course I do."

Lorne met her gaze squarely. "I think we should bail out of here ASAP, before the fighting around the gate really gets going. We can come back through the other gate in a cloaked jumper to reassess the situation." The longtime Stargate program veteran spoke pragmatically, something she'd always appreciated. "The circumstances have changed since Dr. Beckett left and the Colonel went hunting for a DHD. If we stay here and wait for an opportunity to talk either side down, we'll be taking a big personal risk, and I'm not supposed to let you do that."

He was right, of course, and she didn't dispute a word. What he didn't say—but must have been thinking—was that they were at risk simply by being here.

"Fair enough," she said, gathering her bedroll. "Let's go see if Cestan has a moment to listen to a request."

When she emerged from the borrowed tent, she found the encampment surprisingly active. Although the sun hadn't yet broken free of the horizon, tents were being packed up and fires doused.

Walking through the camp, Lorne a half-step behind, she could see the distinction between the whip-warriors and the larger population of infantry soldiers. The soldiers, mostly men, were strapping thick leather armor over their torsos and affixing swords or crossbows to their backs. Some moved with a sense of vigor, others with apprehension. The warriors, by contrast, wore lighter garments—presumably for agility—and displayed little emotion. Nevertheless, it was clear that all were prepared for what lay ahead.

She found the interaction between the different groups striking in its normalcy. Warriors and soldiers conversed and assisted each other with no apparent class disparity. If she had needed reassurance that the Falnori didn't believe gene-bearers to be inherently superior to others—which ought to include the Nistra—that example told her volumes.

Cestan stood in the center of a small group of advisors while aides disassembled the large tent behind him.

The robes he'd worn throughout the treaty negotiations had been replaced by more practical clothing: the tunic and pants worn by the warriors and the leather breastplate worn by the soldiers. The group disbanded shortly before the governor caught sight of his off-world guests.

"Day's greetings," he said at Elizabeth's approach. "I apologize for the haste, but we must move quickly. When Galven learns that his hunters at the gate have been over-powered, he will accelerate the bulk of his force. We must reach the gate and bolster our unit there before the Nistra can mount an offensive."

"I understand," Elizabeth replied. "In fact, Major Lorne and I would like to make use of the gate before that happens, if possible."

Cestan's lips thinned. "That may be difficult," he admitted. "The Nistra have the advantages of numbers and time—we believe they began their march hours before their strike group took the gate from your guards."

"If your force is smaller, you should be able to cover more ground," Lorne pointed out.

"That is true, and fortunately we have a shorter distance to traverse as well. Once in the forest, our army will divide itself and close in on the gate from multiple sides. If you travel with my western division, which will have the shortest path, you may be able to reach the gate without interference."

'Interference'—what an innocuous euphemism. Elizabeth nodded. "Thank you. I'm sure our needs aren't at the top of your priority list right now."

The Falnori leader surprised her by reaching out to briefly place a hand on her shoulder. "Your efforts here deserve better than this," he said, conveying sincere regret. "I am truly sorry."

She quashed a flare of irrational resentment. On Earth, she had been dismissed more than once by foreign leaders, generally older men who didn't see her as an equal, and she had an instinctual defensive reaction to the concept. Cestan hadn't shown her that same condescension, so it would be unfair of her to interpret his attitude as the typical 'poor girl; you tried your best.' Still, the comment helped to renew her determination. "Governor, I recognize the difficult situation you're in, and I won't try to talk you into laying down your arms when it's clear the Nistra won't do likewise. I *will* ask you, though, to please bear in mind that my people are continuing to explore alternatives. If I can bring you proof that the raiders are not Nistra and protect the gates from their attacks, will you consider a ceasefire?"

"If you can achieve those aims, and convince Galven besides, you will have my support as well as my admiration." The note of cynical reservation in Cestan's voice came as no great shock.

"Unfortunately, Minister Galven has as much reason to be skeptical as you, if not more. I've asked him to give up control of his biggest commodity." A sudden thought occurred to Elizabeth. "You accepted our claim that adarite is harmful to those without the gene—the ability. Did you do so because your people would benefit if the Nistra relinquished the mines? Or do you believe what we've said?"

"In truth, I do believe it," responded Cestan. His gaze became distant. "You see, as a child I was fascinated by the craftsmen who fashioned the adarite whips. I had hopes of learning the trade myself and was apprenticed to one of the capital's finest masters. I struggled for a long year to improve my skills, never to succeed. The master would repeat his lessons, and I would still be unable to put them into practice. Many of us failed at the craft. Although the ability has never measured one's station in life, some of us came to believe that one might be born to a…purpose of sorts." A hint of a smile crossed his features. "From what you have said, it is possible that we were not wholly wrong."

"Maybe that's true," she allowed. "Maybe you were meant instead to lead your people to a new understanding, and a lasting peace."

It was a bold remark, the wisdom of which she reconsidered almost immediately. To her relief, he seemed to take no offense. "I would like nothing more than for that to be true."

His chief warrior—Kellec, she'd been told at some point—interrupted to inform them that the columns were prepared to depart. Elizabeth and Lorne were escorted to join the division that would proceed to the gate by way of the western woods.

The hike was no different from its mirror image the night before: just over an hour long and conducted under partial daylight. Elizabeth fended off a chill that had little to do with the temperature and everything to do with her utter ignorance about what they would find ahead of them.

Relief nearly overwhelmed her when the hill appeared beyond the trees and only Falnori warriors could be seen in the vicinity. They'd succeeded in outpacing the Nistra army. For better or worse, the more Falnori troops that arrived, the more difficult it would be for anyone to take the hill from them. For now, at least, they had the gate. Trading a smile with Lorne, she climbed the slope alongside the commander of the incoming warriors and moved decisively toward the DHD.

She didn't identify the sudden rush of wind past her face as the flight of an arrow until the projectile had driven itself into the shoulder of the warrior to her left.

This time she threw herself to the ground even before Lorne could pull her down. The Major grabbed her anyway and hustled her down the south side of the hill, away from the handful of arrows that followed.

"Low-tech version of snipers," Lorne summed up, breathing heavily. "They're not shooting at the other warriors up there standing guard, just us. Guess some of the Nistra stuck around to make sure no one could use the gate."

Elizabeth leaned back against the incline and did her best to keep her fear from gaining any foothold. If they couldn't escape through the gate, all her earlier attempts to stay neutral had been for nothing. They were about to be in the middle of this war whether they liked it or not.

Word spread quickly through the Nistra ranks about the Falnori's pre-dawn strike on the hill. The news served to stoke already high-running emotions. Some of the hunters wanted to charge ahead and retake the hill right away. They were talked down by their comrades, and the entire group picked up its pace.

Ronon didn't bother to guess at his and Teyla's chances of making it to the gate. The hill area was shaping up to be the central battlefield of this conflict. They'd have to do the best they could to stay on the edge of the fighting and wait for Sheppard and McKay to come back in a jumper.

And their teammates *would* come back. Ronon had never expected such loyalty from his adopted people, had never felt he had the right, but their actions on Sateda not long ago had made their convictions plain.

He and Teyla could, of course, leave the group completely, try to find their way to the second gate, and wait for a pickup. Neither of them had entertained that option for long. For one thing, finding that gate would mean venturing close to the ore-rich mountains, and Ronon had no wish to cloud his mind like that ever again.

Just as important, at least in his view, were the hunters who had taken him in—twice now. Maybe that didn't obligate him to fight alongside them, but it did mean that he couldn't abandon them and still be able to sleep at night.

He walked next to Dantir for the better part of two hours before finally speaking up. "Where'd you get that?" he asked, tipping his head toward the whip on the boy's belt.

As much as Dantir obviously wanted to act the part of a battle-ready soldier, the question drew a glimmer of youthful pride out of him. "These have not been used for many years. They are an honor given only to the hunters, and I am now a hunter."

Ronon had noticed the whips hanging from many of the hunters' belts. He could see rough, uneven threads of adarite running along their falls and recalled the Falnori woman's description of the skill required to craft a good-quality whip. If these people had no one with the gene, it was almost certain that their whips were poor imitations.

Just as the whip-warriors were the select corps of the Falnori army, it seemed the hunters were attempting to fill the elite role for the Nistra. The rest of the crowd mostly carried picks and blunt tools—miners, Ronon assumed, likely to be passable soldiers at best thanks to their work. The hunters would be better, having spent less time in direct contact with adarite.

The Falnori warriors, though, were practiced with whips and unaffected by the adarite. If the hunters went into battle with inferior weapons that they couldn't skillfully use, the result would be very lopsided—and it would only get worse for the Nistra once the adarite began to affect them.

"A real honor," he echoed. "Can I give you some advice? When you use that thing, don't use the power. Just leave it off."

If he'd been looking to dim the boy's admiration, that had probably done it. Dantir stopped for a beat to stare at him. Almost immediately he started walking again, hurt quickly hardening into defensiveness. "I'm old enough to hunt, and I'm old enough to fight."

"No, you're not." The Satedan military had accepted young men, but not this young. Ronon matched his stride without difficulty. "Even so, this has nothing to do with age. The whips are dangerous."

"They're meant to be. They're weapons."

"What Ronon means," said Teyla, joining them, "is that the adarite inside the whip can make people ill. It influences the wielder as well as the victim."

"We've felt it," Ronon asserted. "It's not fun. You start to become unsure about what's happening around you. It's…confusing. In a combat situation it could be deadly."

Shaking his head, Dantir continued on, his steps certain. "If that were true, the whips would not be so esteemed. And the Falnori would not go to such lengths to get adarite for their own."

"The Falnori are different—at least some of them are. It's because of the Ancestors…" Ronon scrubbed a hand over his face as he searched for a better strategy. Telling them that the Falnori possessed an ability they lacked would only offend them. "Look, you're good with your bow. Stick to what you know, and keep your head down."

He could feel Teyla watching him for some time after that. Maybe his frustration was showing too much, or maybe she just understood him too well by now. He wasn't like her, equally good with words and actions. When he glanced over at her, though, her expression was more commiserating than pitying. She didn't have any better ideas to persuade these people, apparently.

If actions were all he had at his disposal, he would act. And if he couldn't stop this senseless conflict, he would at least protect one of its innocents.

The Nistra army approached the hill head-on, rather than sending some of its number through the forests on either side. Ronon wasn't sure it was the wisest plan, but he could see how the types of troops they employed might be better suited to open-field tactics. At the least, it would be easier for the leaders to keep their masses of untrained soldiers together this way.

Speaking of leaders…

He moved closer to Ilar and asked, "Is there a field commander? Someone to tell us what to do?"

"We all understand the goal. Reclaim the hill, and defeat the aggressors." The hunter gazed at the Stargate in the distance, assessing it. "So this is what the ring is meant to be," she mused. "I think I expected something more impressive."

"It's pretty impressive when you step into it and end up on another world." Ronon eased his hand toward his holster. A low buzz of voices hummed all around them: miners and hunters alike preparing themselves for what was to come.

Although little could be seen of the Falnori army, it was a certainty that a great number lay in wait just beyond the start of the trees, which formed a three-sided pocket around the gate. Even if they avoided the area surrounding the Hall of Tribute, directly behind the hill from Ronon's position, the Falnori could easily move personnel in from both the east and west sides of the hill, creating a strong line of defense. Could they be flushed out preemptively without sending too many Nistra into that pocket?

A wordless cry from someone half a mile down the line drew his attention to a handful of Nistra who didn't seem interested in a nuanced plan. The small group charged toward the hill, followed shortly by the surrounding ranks, all shouting with a fervor that betrayed their inexperience.

In moments, Ronon's suspicions were confirmed, as two units of Falnori warriors and soldiers poured out of the forest on either side of the hill to meet them.

Swearing under his breath, he looked at Teyla and found her just as dismayed.

"The Nistra have numbers," she said quietly, almost

too low to be heard through the growing roar of battle. "But still they will be slaughtered."

Still more Falnori appeared over the crest of the hill with bows, aiming at the Nistra front lines. Some of them were picked off by arrows from elsewhere—had the hunters who'd been run off the gate earlier taken up positions in the trees? Regardless, those who held the hill held the high-ground advantage, and at present both belonged to the Falnori.

"We can try to even the odds a little." He drew his gun and fired a few stun bolts into the approaching line of Falnori warriors. Looking reluctant, Teyla did the same. It was only slightly more effective than trying to collect a rainstorm in a bucket, but they couldn't just stand there.

The skill Ronon had admired from the whip-warriors in practice was even more extraordinary in actual conflict. Although the majority of the Falnori force consisted of common soldiers wielding swords or bows, the field was dotted with searing, sizzling threads of light. Any Nistra who came close to the incline was cut down without hesitation or mercy. The lucky ones lost only a hand, the heat of the whip sealing such wounds instantly; the less fortunate took a blow to the torso and were nearly vaporized.

One small point of hope: Dantir had taken Ronon's advice to heart and stayed back, using his bow rather than diving into the close-quarters fight. Ronon kept an eye on the area directly surrounding the boy, stunning any Falnori swordsman who came near.

It wasn't long, however, before the clash spread to envelop them as well, and he had to worry about defending himself as much as Dantir. After dodging the upward swing of a sword, he shifted his gun to his left hand and drew his own blade with his right. Killing a Falnori would bring him no satisfaction, but he would be of no use to anyone if he became another of the nameless dead.

From one side he heard the *hiss-crack* of a whip only a few paces away, and he moved as best he could through the throng to distance himself from the energy discharge. The last thing he needed at a time like this was to lose focus.

Teyla had one of her staffs in her hand, which Ronon thought brave of her, as it wasn't his idea of a deadly weapon. Then again, she moved as though the staff was an extension of her body, easily deflecting the sword of an oncoming assailant and laying him out flat with a blast from her stun pistol.

The first wave of the Nistra attack didn't appear to be gaining any traction. The hill remained solidly under Falnori control as the ground at its base was beginning to clutter with fallen soldiers. "We should fall back and regroup," Ronon shouted over the din. It was hardly a useful observation, because they had no authority or ability to enact a mass retreat. Teyla glanced back and nodded helplessly, taking aim at another warrior to prevent him from activating his whip again.

Before long, though, the main thrust of the Nistra army seemed to falter, the central group that had pushed toward the hill now beginning to withdraw. The Falnori looked content to let them go, at least for the moment, since few attempted to follow. Those who did were quickly targeted by hunters, giving the rest of the Nistra the opportunity to close their ranks in a position very near to where they'd started.

Ronon scanned the lines. Injured soldiers leaned on

comrades or slumped in the grass while their wounds were tended by mostly unskilled hands. Others huddled in groups to relate their experiences in the fight. The vigor that had punctuated the early assault had evaporated, leaving utter confusion in its wake.

He trailed Dantir through the crowd until they found Ilar sitting on a rock, struggling to bind her own bleeding shoulder. A step behind them, Teyla hurried forward and took over for her.

"Where are your commanders?" Ronon asked again. "Shouldn't someone be leading this army?"

When she raised her eyes to him, the vagueness there made him suspect that she had already been strongly affected by the adarite. "We have no leader but Minister Galven, and this place is too dangerous for someone of his importance."

"Is there no one to provide guidance on your strategy and objectives, then?" Teyla secured the bandage.

"Objectives…" Ilar seemed to need all her concentration to answer. "Our objective is to drive the Falnori back and retake the hill."

So she'd said before. Ronon stifled the urge to pound his fist against something. These people knew nothing of battle tactics. They were little better than a gigantic mob, not even organized enough to divide into regiments.

Unbelievably, though, the atmosphere of chaos around them was shifting, becoming more determined. The casualties were being transferred to the rear as others readied their weapons.

*Ancestors help them—they're going to try again.*

When Ilar attempted to get to her feet, Ronon went to assist, sliding an arm under her shoulders. He took the opportunity to stealthily detach the whip from her belt and toss it behind the rock. Even if her shoulder wouldn't allow her much use of her bow, the dagger she carried would serve her better. In fact, being unarmed would serve her better than that cursed whip.

"Ronon," murmured Teyla urgently, drawing his attention. Dantir clearly hadn't lost his zeal; he'd joined one of the front-line groups as it moved back out into the fray.

Biting back a vicious epithet, Ronon pushed through the swarm of soldiers heading onto the battlefield. If he lost track of Dantir now, he'd never find him again. The boy's dirty blond head bobbed in the crowd, still driving forward, even as the Falnori fortified their line in front of the hill.

Tendrils of energy crackled in the air, becoming a constant hum in the background. Ronon ducked a hail of arrows and continued his pursuit of Dantir. Seizing his arm, Teyla yanked him out of the path of an incoming whip. He whirled to stun the aggressor, only to be struck by a stumbling Nistra soldier. Knocked off-balance, Ronon watched the soldier crumple, one leg missing from the mid-thigh down.

The scene was madness, pure and simple. He couldn't control it, guide it, or even slow its inevitable descent into a massacre. All he could do was save one well-meaning kid…

…who'd just lashed out at someone in front of him with a fitfully sparking whip.

Ronon dove forward to finally close the distance between himself and Dantir. The boy had managed to use the whip correctly, at least. By the looks of him, though, he'd been using it for some time now, and the effects were making themselves known. He blinked at a body lying on the ground a few feet away, then stared at the hill with only the barest hint of comprehension.

A Falnori soldier stalked toward him with sword raised, likely thinking he'd found easy prey. Unhesitating, Ronon lunged, grabbing two handfuls of the man's thick leather vest and hauling him backward. The soldier recovered quickly, lashing out with a foot that caught Ronon behind the knee. They both tumbled to the ground.

Someone stepped on Ronon's arm, causing him to lose his grip on his weapon. The gun slid free and was quickly lost from sight in the anarchy of pounding feet. When the soldier rolled to his knees and swung his sword in Dantir's direction, Ronon reacted on instinct and drew one of his knives. He flung it upward, catching the soldier in the neck, just above his protective vest.

As the soldier crashed to the ground, Teyla stunned a group of nearby fighters and used the brief lull to duck low and search the immediate area. At last she came up with the lost gun and tossed it to Ronon.

"Thanks," he said, catching his breath. Dantir looked at him, glassy-eyed, and he tugged the whip from the boy's slack hand. "I *told* you not to use this!"

"We have drawn too much attention," Teyla warned, pointing to their left. Ronon followed her gaze and noticed the tight knot of warriors carving a path through the crowd with their whips. Where everyone else appeared to be adhering to a basic north-south range of movement, this squad looked to be focused on a specific area—the one occupied by the off-worlders in their midst.

Thinking quickly, Ronon shoved Dantir toward Teyla. "Take him and head for the rear. I'll go a different way. They'll have to split up or choose one of us to follow."

Surely Teyla knew that he would be the easier one to track, standing so much taller than the Nistra. Although her indecision showed in her expression, she replied with a sharp, decisive nod. "Good luck."

Then she was gone, vanishing into the crowd with Dantir. She wouldn't be able to stun anyone now without giving away her position, but Ronon had faith that she would find other advantages if needed.

He stooped low and moved through the fighting, trying to evade the relentless warriors. But they gained ground faster than he could, narrowing the gap until he finally was forced to take the offensive.

Only two warriors fell under his spray of stun blasts before an unpowered whip snaked out to rip the gun from his hands. Another coiled around his wrists, instantly binding them. A rough jerk on the whip pitched him forward, and he landed hard on his knees.

"I would not struggle if I were you," said a cold, familiar voice. "All I need do is tighten my grip. Your hands will be severed, your arms withered and useless."

Ronon had been planning to knock over the person in front of him and tear loose the handle of the whip that ensnared him, but that warning made him reconsider. When he looked up, Cestan's chief warrior stood over him.

"This is a grave disappointment," Kellec continued, his weathered features stony. "Now we see what our trust is worth to your people." He turned to his associates. "We will bring him. The governor needs to know the true nature of these so-called friends."

"We're not trying to take sides." It was a weak statement, particularly now, but Ronon didn't have much else to offer. "All I wanted to do was protect one kid until someone could make you people see reason and stop this pointless battle."

"I can't say I admire your method of maintaining neutrality." Kellec pulled on the whip, and Ronon staggered to his feet to avoid falling face-first in the dirt. "You have spilled Falnori blood, which makes you either a common enemy or a traitor. Which label you receive matters only in the sense that it may influence the likelihood of your execution."

# CHAPTER SIXTEEN

"Excuse me?" Rodney's voice jumped into a distinct alto range. "What do you mean, it won't disengage?"

"I mean, I'm giving the jumper every possible version of a 'let go' command, and nothing's happening." John scanned his readouts, feeling suddenly blind. Jumpers didn't do this kind of thing. They didn't make you run checklists to chase glitches the way Earth aircraft did—they helpfully told you what was wrong and what to do about it. Just not today, for some reason. "Everything looks to be working. I don't get it."

"Running a diagnostic." Rodney scowled at the instrument panel as if it had done him a personal injustice. "You're right. No malfunctions."

"Then it must be the station," Radek deduced, rising to stand between the two forward chairs. "The dock is holding us in place."

"Why the hell would it do that?" The drifting Wraith cruiser filled the windscreen completely now, close enough that John could see charred pockmarks scattered all over its hull. He wondered vaguely if the missing third segment of the station had contained weapons.

"Power, or the lack thereof." Rodney bent over the sensor console. "When we docked, the station tried to follow some type of arrival protocol and turn itself on for us."

"And we popped the circuit-breaker because there wasn't enough juice. I remember." It had only been a couple of hours ago, after all. "So the docking clamps were on that circuit?"

"So to speak. I'm reading zero power in the docking and airlock systems." Although Rodney's voice wavered a little, he seemed to have gotten his fear firmly under control. If they had time later, John would be happy to talk him through a full-blown freak-out. 'Later' being the operative word. "The clamps must lock by default when power is lost. Probably to avoid jettisoning an open, unsuspecting craft by accident."

John gritted his teeth. The best-laid damn plans... "That's a very nice emergency procedure for any situation except *this* one."

"The Lagrange Point satellite didn't do that," Radek pointed out, brow furrowing.

It took John a moment to identify the reference. Seemingly half a lifetime had passed since the Wraith siege on Atlantis in the first year of the expedition. Fortunately, Rodney's memory was nothing if not comprehensive. "The Lagrange Point satellite didn't have any power at all when we arrived, so it had no means to enact any emergency procedures. To borrow a phrase, it's the difference between 'dead' and 'mostly dead.'"

"We'll need to transfer power to the dock from here," Radek advised. "Rapidly."

"You don't say," muttered Rodney, already manipulating the HUD to display a schematic of the jumper's power distribution system. Radek immediately pointed to an area around the engine pods and mumbled something under his breath in Czech.

As much as John disliked sounding stupid, he had to ask. "Can we do that?"

Neither scientist looked up from his work. Rodney answered curtly, "Ask us again in a few minutes."

That left John with nothing to do but watch their slow, steady progress toward the cruiser, reinforcing the knowledge that they didn't *have* a few minutes. Rodney's estimates of time were typically overblown when it came to must-have breakthroughs, though. Barely ninety seconds later, Radek ducked behind the pilot's seat. The spacesuit restricted John from pivoting to watch him, but it sounded like he was removing an access panel. "Guys, you want to give me some play-by-play while you're working?"

"The engine pods draw the majority of the jumper's power," Rodney replied absently. "They're also conveniently located near the docking clamps. We're going to send a surge through the pods, just enough to reinitialize the docking system and make it think it's got sufficient power to drop out of emergency lockdown mode."

That made some sense, except for one detail. "The engine pods are retracted right now. Won't we just be zapping ourselves?"

Rodney looked a little startled to hear him make that connection, but he quickly couched his surprise in sarcasm. "Yes, Colonel, A-plus for observation skills. The power surge likely won't transmit through the hull of the jumper—it's shielded to disperse electrical energy. We'll have to extend the pods just a fraction in order to break the hull seal, initiate the surge, then immediately retract the pods again and use the maneuvering thrusters to break free from the dock."

And then take some very fast evasive action to avoid flying smack into the cruiser. John repeated the order of operations in his head. "I'm guessing all this will have to be accomplished in a matter of seconds?"

"Right again. For that reason, let's not waste any time considering the odds of this whole scheme failing miserably. Are we ready?"

"One moment," said Radek, still fiddling with something behind John's seat. "Need to be sure that the correct circuits are left open so that the power surge will not in fact be directed into the jumper's propulsion system."

John pictured a car revving its engine while stuck in neutral. Meanwhile, there was still that pesky cruiser. He waited about five seconds before asking, "How about now?"

It was a good bet that Radek was currently glaring at the back of his head. "Ready. I will reconnect the engines as soon as the surge is discharged. Rodney?"

"All right." Getting out of the spacesuit hadn't stopped Rodney from sweating. "Everybody be prepared to do *exactly* what I say the very second I say it."

"Aren't we always?" John did his best to look innocent.

Rodney's glare, on the other hand, he didn't have to imagine. He could see it just fine. "Give me ten percent extension on the engine pods."

Obediently, John pushed two fingers across the propulsion console and winced at the scraping sound produced when the pods contacted the docking clamps. *Sorry, baby,* he told his jumper silently. *I'll make it up to you.*

"Engines offline," Radek reported.

Inhaling deeply, Rodney placed his hand on the power modulation control and shut his eyes. "Surging in three—two—one—mark!"

The jolt that ran through the craft might have knocked

John to the floor if his suit hadn't been tightly wedged between the panel and the chair. Rodney hung on to his seat's armrests for dear life. "Radek, *now*."

Radek, luckily, was already on the floor. "Engines back online!"

"Colonel, pull in the pods and *go!*"

"On it." The console's glow was just about the sweetest thing John had ever seen. He retracted the engine pods, tapped the maneuvering thrusters to push them free of the dock, and fired up the engines for real.

The distance between the station and the cruiser was shrinking fast. John wrenched the jumper's nose up just in time to skim along the edge of the derelict ship. After a quick scan of the vicinity, he swung his craft around and aimed at the most direct path to empty space, running the engines close to redline.

He didn't see the colossal impact they'd narrowly avoided, since the jumper was racing away from it with all available speed. The HUD, however, showed it to them in an abridged, antiseptic form. One blue wireframe image struck a much larger, red wire-frame image; there was a sharp, bright light; and then the blue one vanished from the screen.

An unexpected clatter against the jumper's hull, like hail on a roof, made John start. "The station," Rodney said in a hushed voice, sounding like he didn't quite believe they were safe. "Or what's left of it, rather."

Radek got up to stand between their seats again. "Next time," he remarked with patently false composure, "shall we cut it a bit closer? I do so enjoy the panic and the flailing."

Adrenaline giveth, and adrenaline taketh away.

Suddenly bone-weary, John waved a hand at Rodney. "You have the controls. Let's head for the second gate and see if Elizabeth's magically found a way to limit the body count down there." With effort, he pushed himself out of the seat. "Radek, get this blasted suit the hell *off* me."

The Falnori command post seemed relatively calm, all things considered. One warrior after another cycled through, delivering a report on his or her unit's status and losses to Cestan before heading back to said unit. Elizabeth watched from a polite distance, listening as best she could without looking like she intended to eavesdrop.

From what she heard, the Falnori could afford to keep their cool. They were winning. The Nistra army had mounted a frontal assault on the hill and been beaten back, only to regroup and make another attempt at the exact same strategy with no better results. They appeared to be withdrawing again, and it wasn't clear if they would change tactics or try their luck a third time.

"Hastings," observed Major Lorne from beside her.

Elizabeth turned toward him, questioning. "I'm sorry?"

"The Nistra are setting this up a little bit like the Battle of Hastings. You know, 1066?"

Her knowledge of British history had limits. "William the Conqueror, right?"

Lorne nodded. "Yes, ma'am. The English formed a shield wall on a ridgeline, and the Normans tried to break it by advancing and quickly retreating, drawing some of the English out in pursuit. They went back and forth several times and progressively weakened the English line."

Putting aside the seriousness of the situation for a moment, Elizabeth sent him a bemused smile. "I've learned something new about you, Major."

"I'm in the profession of arms, ma'am. It's good business to know what's worked in the past and what hasn't. Even a thousand years ago in another galaxy." Lorne allowed himself a faint smile in reply before continuing. "Thing is, in this case, it's not working. Not many of the Falnori are being lured away from their lines to follow the retreat, so the Nistra are losing a lot more of their force than the Falnori are. I don't know why they keep trying it."

She clasped her hands, having no answer. "Maybe they just can't think of any other way."

The more she thought about that concept, the more sense it made. Regardless of the good-natured barbs the Atlantis scientists often tossed at the Marines, military strategy required brainpower. The Nistra army consisted of soldiers who worked the mines, their mental faculties altered in God-only-knew-what manner, and hunters who were attempting to use the adarite whips for the first time, undoubtedly becoming affected as well. It was little wonder that they seemed unable to put together a considered, adaptable strategy.

She'd been immersed in the routines of the planet for long enough that the abrupt crackle of her radio made her jump. "Dr. Weir, Major Lorne, please respond."

The Major scanned the area and steered her by the arm, away from any curious Falnori, before activating his radio. "This is Lorne. Dr. Weir's with me."

"Alderman here, sir. We've just come through the second gate in Jumper Two. We have the Cadre leader Sekal with us as per orders. Where do you want us?"

Lorne glanced at Elizabeth for confirmation, and she nodded. "We're about two klicks south of the primary gate, with the rear echelon of the Falnori army. Lock onto our subcutaneous transmitters, and we'll find you an LZ. Come in cloaked—if either side sees a ship right now, we'll be in for even more chaos."

"Aye, sir."

None of the Falnori equivalent of staff officers seemed to be paying much attention to them, so it wasn't hard to slip away. They were close to the edge of the forest, which restricted potential flight paths somewhat, but Elizabeth had faith in their pilots' skills. Lorne selected an area near a recess in the trees and alerted Jumper Two. Within a few minutes, a familiar hum reached her ears. A slight breeze rippled the neighboring branches, and a patch of grass lay flat in the shape of a jumper footprint.

Out of thin air, the hatch opened, revealing four Marines and a handcuffed prisoner. Elizabeth eyed the group. "I take it Carson decided to stay behind?"

The corner of Sergeant Alderman's mouth twitched. "Ma'am, Dr. Beckett sends his regrets and says that, quote, 'somebody has to mind the blooming city.'"

"I suppose that's reasonable," she allowed, her own smile quickly damped by the sight of Sekal. The Cadre ringleader was well-dressed, if disheveled, and looked almost bored. Although Elizabeth generally tried to avoid making snap judgments, she immediately got the impression that he was accustomed to finding the easiest path through everything in life. He returned her scrutiny for a moment before his gaze slid off to the side.

She wasn't sure quite what she had expected from

him. More defiance, maybe, instead of this…apathy. In the distance, the sounds of the reignited battle could be heard, and her ire flared. "Do you hear that?" she asked him. "Did you see the armies when you flew over? Your actions, more than anything else, triggered this conflict. You must be very proud."

Sekal shifted the cuffs on his wrists. "Your Colonel Sheppard offered me a deal," he said in response.

Days ago, Elizabeth might have played this differently. Now, she wasn't inclined to give even an inch. "Colonel Sheppard may not be mine or a colonel for much longer, so I don't care what kind of deal he offered you." She pretended not to notice the glances exchanged by the Marines; there would be time for explanations later if necessary. "However, I'll make you a new offer. Tell these people the truth about who you are and where you come from, and I'll do my best to keep their leaders from killing you."

The flinch produced by that threat was perversely satisfying. She turned her back on him and faced Lorne. "Let's go. We can start by convincing Governor Cestan and figure the rest out from there."

Once Alderman had secured Jumper Two's hatch, the group started toward the Falnori command post. Along the way, one of the Marines passed Lorne a sidearm, and Elizabeth could almost feel some of the Major's unease bleed away when he tucked the weapon into his holster.

"Hope you didn't have any trouble finding us," she commented to Alderman as they walked.

"No, ma'am," replied the sergeant. "The other transmitter signals were pretty clearly separated. It wasn't tough to figure out which were you two."

They were nearing the command post, which looked more crowded and animated than it had only minutes ago. It took Elizabeth a moment to process what she'd just heard. Other signals? "Colonel Sheppard and Dr. McKay were planning to track down the second gate's dialer and set up its shield controls. But they shouldn't have split up."

Alderman shook his head. "I don't think it was them, ma'am. There was no signal from another jumper, just the individual transmitters. One was in the middle of the Nistra army. The other was headed this way. We figured they were Teyla and—"

She drew up short, cutting him off in mid-sentence. Kellec had just come into view, dragging a captive in much the same manner as they'd brought Sekal. Even from a hundred yards away, the prisoner wasn't difficult to identify.

"Ronon," Alderman finished lamely.

After an aborted attempt at working out the situation from the information currently available to her, Elizabeth realized that she had no chance of divining what the hell was going on. She squeezed her eyes shut for a few seconds, feeling a familiar headache begin to build. "There are days," she told a puzzled Lorne, "when I dearly wish I'd told the President of the United States to take this job and shove it."

Head held high, she marched into the command post, knowing the others would follow and lend weight to her authority. "What's the meaning of this, Governor?" she accused. "This man is one of my people—"

"A fact of which I'm well aware, Doctor." Cestan barely looked up at her approach, the brunt of his anger directed at Ronon. "My chief warrior tells me that your man stood with the enemy, even going so far as to kill several of our soldiers alongside his Nistra brethren."

Before Elizabeth could insist on an explanation from Ronon, the Satedan spoke up. "All but one of them were only stunned, and I would have stunned the last one if I'd had a choice." He focused on her, his dark eyes penetrating. "All I wanted to do was save one kid," he said quietly. "That's all."

She believed him, certainly, and she was gratified to know that her opinion mattered to him. But her testimony might not be enough to free him. "You came back to try to convince the Nistra to break off the attack?" she guessed.

Ronon nodded. "But we couldn't show them any proof, and they're too mixed up by the adarite to see reason."

"So you decided to join them instead?" Kellec broke in, incensed. "We hosted you, showed you our weapons and told you of our customs. And you would make war on us?"

"Could you stand by and watch children die?" Ronon demanded. "Because that was my only other choice!"

"Governor, please." Elizabeth turned her most penitent expression on the Falnori leader. "I don't expect you to forget that this incident occurred. I'd like to ask that you view it as a regrettable exception to the relationship between our peoples."

Cestan regarded her without speaking for a moment, and for the first time she felt that he could be truly dangerous.

".You must understand," he replied, his voice severe,

"how that could be difficult for us. Your man's actions are considered treason. If you do not allow me to condemn him, I am left to wonder how much trust I can place in you."

"Then let me show you something that might help you make your decision." Elizabeth held a hand out to the Marines, who prodded their own prisoner forward. "Governor Cestan, meet Sekal, head of the Cadre."

The Falnori leader circled Sekal, sizing him up. The thief met his probing gaze with only mild interest. "So I'm meant to believe that you lead the band of raiders that has plagued us for so long?" he inquired. Sekal gave no reply.

"I understand that you don't have any way of recognizing him. Maybe you'd recognize some of his work." Elizabeth took the pack offered by one of the Marines and emptied its contents onto the ground. "We confiscated these items from him and the other Cadre members in our custody."

Bending to examine the trinkets, mostly jewelry and small Ancient gadgets of unknown origin, Kellec reached out to claim a wide, silvery wristband. "I have seen this," he announced. "The Hall once held many of them."

Cestan stood in front of Sekal, not allowing him to look away. "You stole from the Hall?"

When Sekal remained silent, Alderman provided encouragement by tapping his P-90 against the man's back.

"We've been many places on your world," Sekal answered at last.

"Including the mining villages of the Nistra?"

"Their ore fetches a good price in some markets."

The Falnori governor raised his eyebrows, betraying no emotion beyond curiosity. "And you have no association with the Nistra, or with these people?" He indicated the Marines with a gesture.

For once, a hint of derision found its way into Sekal's reply. "These people ambushed my men and gave us no means to bargain for release. The Nistra are addled fools. You ask if I associate with them? I laugh."

Elizabeth watched Cestan's bearing, hoping for some clue as to his state of mind. Even after all this, it still came down to trusting the word of others: Sekal's, Ronon's, hers.

On impulse, she decided to lay her cards on the table. "I'm sure you're thinking that we could have staged this. We could be in league with this Cadre, for all you know. But ask yourself this: what would be the benefit to us? Why turn your people against the Nistra, or ally ourselves with one side over the other? Wouldn't the Cadre have been better off if everything had stayed as it was before we arrived, when they could steal from both sides with impunity?"

Whether Cestan had no answer to that or simply wanted to hear her out, she didn't know. She blazed ahead. "History is a compilation of events and experiences, nothing more. It's viewed by each person through a different lens, based on the knowledge and perspective of that person. Your view of the Nistra has been shaped by everything that has happened between your people and theirs over thousands of years. It would make sense for them to be the aggressors here. But isn't it possible that something *else* might be at work?"

She was still forming her next argument when another

voice joined in.

"The Nistra have done the same thing," Ronon said. "Because of the way your two peoples split and started to drift apart, they believe you think you're superior to them. They probably don't even realize that not all of you have the Ancestor ability, because they've spent centuries convincing themselves that you make judgments of worth based on lineage. That's why they believe you abandoned the treaty and are stealing adarite from them. They assume you think you're entitled."

Buoyed by his contribution, Elizabeth shot him a quick look of thanks. To borrow one of John's expressions, it was time to throw for the end zone. She faced Cestan directly, holding his gaze. "You and the Nistra were once a unified community. Wouldn't you like to show them how wrong they are about you? Wouldn't your world be better if you had access to all the adarite you need, and you could stop looking over your shoulder for raiders? Wouldn't it be the will of the Ancestors to see their descendants coexisting and thriving on the world they fought so hard to protect?" Her nails dug into her palm as she tightened a desperate fist. "You can make all those things happen if you'd just step back and listen to each other!"

There was a long pause, during which she replayed in her mind everything she'd just said, wondering if she could have done better, done more.

At last, Cestan turned sharply away. "Enough," he said. "This ends now."

Elizabeth closed her eyes, utterly drained, and said a silent prayer.

"Where are we going?" Dantir struggled weakly to

extricate himself from Teyla's grip. "Let me go! Why will you not let me fight?"

"You can do more for your people by helping me," Teyla told him shortly, guiding him through the mayhem of the battle. It was a challenge to keep a firm hand on the boy's arm while keeping her stun pistol at the ready, but she'd managed that and found an opportunity to 'lose' Dantir's whip besides. She'd steered them away from the front lines and now searched with some urgency for Galven's headquarters. If the minister was not willing to believe the Lanteans' claims about the effects of adarite, she would show him direct evidence.

"Where is Ronon?" asked Dantir suddenly, twisting around to look for his hero. "He was here—?"

"Yes, he was," Teyla replied, summoning her frayed patience. They had seen the warriors closing in on Ronon as they'd fled. That was more than enough for her to sur-mise what had happened to him—and what might hap-pen to him now. "Do you recall how he protected you?" She received a nod. "What do you recall after that?"

After a moment's thought, Dantir gaped at her, bewil-dered and clearly scared. "I don't know," he confessed. "It's blurry, like a dream. Why is it blurry?"

"That is because you began to use the whip, as Ronon told you not to do. It took your memory from you. Do you see at last why the whips are dangerous?"

She realized upon seeing the misery in his eyes that she had spoken too harshly, letting her own anxiety bleed through. He was little more than a child, after all, and this was not his fault.

"I am sorry," she said, softening her tone. "You are not to blame, and you need not fear what happened. It is over now. Nothing will be blurry again so long as you avoid the whips and the ore used to make them."

From then on, she loosened her hold on his arm, and he did not try to run.

They reached the rear of the formation, such as it was, and were confronted by a scene almost as terrible as the battle itself. All around lay the wounded: some pierced by arrows, others laid open by blades, still more bearing the awful burns of the whips. The air was choked with pain-filled moans. Overwhelmed medics, likely those miners considered too small or weak to fight, attempted to tend the injured with what little knowledge and supplies they had. Dazed soldiers stared at nothing, as if struggling to comprehend what had happened to them.

Teyla increased her pace, wanting to spare Dantir the sight as best she could. The young man remained silent, and she knew he had already learned far too much this day.

The Nistra didn't appear to have a command post in the traditional sense. Galven was sequestered inside a tight ring of hunters, one of whom blocked Teyla's path with a bow across her body.

"No one disturbs the minister," he said gruffly.

"Everything that has occurred today should disturb the minister," she fired back. "I come with an explanation and a plan. Each moment we delay costs another life. This one is on your head."

She took advantage of his hesitation and pushed past with Dantir. "Minister Galven!"

The Nistra leader glanced over at her but quickly returned his attention to the soldier reporting to him. Undeterred, she walked up and placed herself squarely within his sight. "Minister, I am Teyla Emmagan. We met at the beginning of the treaty talks."

"I remember you, warrior Emmagan." Although she might have imagined it, there were more lines visible around Galven's eyes and mouth than before, and he moved more slowly, as if aged by defeat. "But I have no time for the fanciful claims of your people when my own are being so savagely beaten."

"I know, Minister. I have been among your people today. I have seen how they struggle bravely to achieve the impossible."

"It should not *be* impossible." Galven's frustration boiled close to the surface. "We have the strength of numbers—"

"And yet your forces cannot focus on the smaller objectives necessary for a successful campaign, only the larger goal." Teyla chose her words with care, as she would get no other chance at this. At the same time, neither could she afford to be subtle. "There is a reason for that: the adarite. Dr. Weir tried to explain how it hinders the mind. Will you listen if the story is told by one of your own?"

The minister's gaze fell on Dantir, who shrank back, no doubt intimidated by the leader of his people. "You have something to say?"

"It's all right," Teyla assured the young man. "Tell him what you remember of the battle."

Dantir twisted the tail of his shirt between his fingers. "I wanted to use my whip," he began tentatively. "Ronon and Teyla told me not to. They used their light weapons to fell many Falnori—"

With a sharp hand, Galven cut him off. "You fight

alongside us?" he asked Teyla, looking rather taken aback by the idea.

"Not to pass judgment on the Falnori, but to protect our benefactors," Teyla answered. "When Ronon and I were in need, your hunters aided us. We could not stand by while they destroyed themselves. Please allow Dantir to finish. This is most important."

At her urging, Dantir spoke up again, his head sinking to his chest in shame. "I wanted to believe Ronon, but I had been given an honored whip, and I had to try it. I don't remember triggering it. I remember nothing more until after Teyla pulled me away."

"The adarite took his memory, as it has done to all your people—slowly for the miners, more suddenly for the hunters today." The urgency Teyla felt began to slip through into her tone, and she did not stifle it. "Dantir does not remember that my friend was dragged away before his eyes. Ronon protected him and was taken by the Falnori because of it. Do you still doubt our sincerity?"

Galven's shock had only increased as she continued to speak. After a moment, he asked quietly, "You have risked yourselves for our people?"

He seemed in awe, more affected by their actions than by anything she'd said about the adarite. In a jolt of comprehension, she realized that they had been addressing the issue the wrong way. The Nistra had split from the Falnori chiefly because of their failure to protect one and all from the Wraith attack. The hunters, excepting Dantir, had fully trusted her and Ronon only after they had shared in the work to be done. These people understood and valued deeds over words. By standing with them in battle, she and Ronon had earned respect. She intended to use whatever influence she had gained as best she could.

"I have, Minister," she replied. "And Ronon has done more. He sacrificed himself to allow Dantir and me to escape, and he may have paid for it with his life. He acted, as I do, because we believe this war need not continue. Your people rage against an enemy which has not wronged you in the manner you think. They fight to defend a commodity, not knowing that it harms them. They are not yet lost, but they desperately need someone to guide them."

She held the older man's gaze securely. "They are good people who will follow if they are led. *Lead* them."

For some time, Galven stared back at her, and the silence scraped away at her resolve.

At last, he swiveled to address one of his guards. "Bring the flag of conference."

Teyla thanked whatever Ancestors might be listening and waited to see what message would be sent to the Falnori. To her surprise, the minister did not assign a representative to carry a proposal to the other side. Instead, he took the flag from his assistant, apparently intending to make the journey himself.

"Are you certain…" she began, only to trail off upon seeing the set of his features.

"You asked me to lead, warrior Emmagan," he said simply.

That moment, more than any before it, showed her that he was indeed deserving of his post.

"Then you will need bodyguards. One with no need of a whip will be helpful." She turned to Dantir. "Stay here," she instructed him, leaving no room for argument.

If Ronon had been killed, as she feared, she would not let his last effort fail now.

With a purposeful stride, Galven started forward, and Teyla prepared to follow him into the heart of the battle.

# CHAPTER SEVENTEEN

When Cestan walked out of the command post, heading for the hill, and ordered that the prisoners be brought along, Ronon once again had no idea whether or not he was about to die. The odds of him being publicly killed as an example had been waxing and waning for some time. He considered the factors involved in making an escape attempt. Could he tear the whip that bound him out of Kellec's hands before the warrior could turn it on? Was the likelihood of his execution great enough to be worth the risk of losing his hands?

Then Weir fell into step beside Cestan, and Ronon banished any thoughts of trying to escape. He would not risk her safety or that of the military team in order to save himself. In any case, the situation was too tenuous to be disturbed further. He would have to take his chances and stay alert for any change.

"I grant that your allegations may be true, Dr. Weir," said the governor, focused not on her but on the Stargate ahead. "Before I address them, however, there is a matter left undone. I cannot ask my people to believe a group of off-worlders if I allow one to go free after taking up arms against us. Treasonous acts have been committed, and punishment must be delivered."

Ronon had lived under a death sentence for seven years, and so—though it took effort—he didn't flinch at this one. To her credit, neither did Weir. Instead, she immediately took three long steps to outpace Cestan and planted herself in his path.

"That's not acceptable to me, Governor," she said firmly. "At the very least, I request that you delay the execution until after a lasting ceasefire is struck. We can discuss the level of punishment at that time. I'm confident that our assistance here will be significant enough to partially mitigate Ronon's offense."

"*If* a lasting ceasefire is struck," Cestan corrected. "I do not share your certainty that Minister Galven will see reason. And I will agree to let you present your case and the raider to him only if you allow my warriors to deliver this one's punishment." A dark gaze, tinted by disdain rather than fury, fixed on Ronon even as he continued to speak to Weir. "He made his choice. If you sincerely want to broker peace on this world, you will stand aside."

Weir stepped away from Cestan to stand in front of Ronon. Although her composure never wavered, her eyes betrayed her conflict. He didn't envy her the terrible quandary she faced. Lives were being lost now, in this moment, and her only chance at bringing it all to a halt was to sacrifice his. Countless unknowns on one side, weighed against one friend on the other.

He knew what the right decision was, and he suspected she did as well. It obviously tore at her soul to contemplate such a thing, so if he could do anything to make it easier for her, he was willing.

"He's right," he said quietly. "I made my choice."

"Ronon," Weir murmured, looking utterly lost. "I can't..."

Barely noticing that she hadn't finished the sentence, Ronon spotted a flash of color from the corner of his eye, making its way across the battlefield on the Nistra side.

He struggled for a second to identify it. When he succeeded, a swell of relief overtook him. This was a true, honest opportunity—for all of them.

"You can," he reassured her. "Just for a while."

"For a *while*? How does that—"

"Ma'am, Governor," Lorne interrupted, apparently every bit as observant as Ronon and looking in the same direction. "Look down there."

As everyone turned to survey the battlefield below, Ronon watched Cestan. The Falnori leader's expression shifted from suspicion to shock and back. "A flag of conference," he said, half to himself.

Lorne drew a small set of field glasses from his vest and peered down at the combatants parting to make way for the banner. The fighting hadn't ceased, but it had slowed. "It's Minister Galven," he stated. "And he's not alone." The Major handed the viewing device to Weir. As soon as she lifted it, the worry fell away from her face.

"It could be a ploy," Kellec pointed out.

"It isn't," declared Weir.

Cestan narrowed his eyes. "How can you be sure?"

She turned to him with a smile born of confidence and poise. "Because I would trust my life to the woman walking beside him."

Her response told Ronon everything he needed to know. *Thank you, Teyla.*

"Ma'am, you could call her," suggested Lorne, tapping his radio.

That hadn't occurred to Ronon, and it didn't seem to have occurred to Weir, either. She hurried to detach her own radio from her jacket. "Teyla, can you hear me?"

A snap of static quickly yielded to a familiar voice. "I

am here, Elizabeth. I have provided some further information to Minister Galven. He is willing to discuss the possibility of a truce. Will Governor Cestan consider a proposal?"

"They should offer surrender, not truce," scoffed Kellec.

The governor waved him silent. "Can you guarantee that the flag of conference will be respected?" he asked Weir.

"I can't," she admitted. "I can, however, offer you the protection of these men." She nodded at the Marines. "Galven took a substantial risk to approach you himself in this manner. I'd consider that a gesture of goodwill."

It seemed obvious that Cestan was less than completely convinced. But certainty wasn't required right now—just an open mind.

"Bring our flag," he ordered a nearby warrior. As the woman hurried off to comply, he turned to Weir. "If the Nistra have plotted to deceive, your man Ronon will not be the only one to suffer punishment."

Weir accepted those terms more readily than Ronon would have; he didn't trust that some overeager Nistra wouldn't take unilateral action. Yet she merely lifted her radio. "We're coming, Teyla. Tell Minister Galven that we especially look forward to introducing him to Sekal, the leader of the Cadre."

After a pause, the response arrived. "I believe that would be very beneficial to all."

"We're on our way."

The flag was obtained and raised on its staff, and at Weir's urging the two Marines not directly guarding Sekal moved to flank Cestan. Kellec tugged Ronon forward with his whip.

The Falnori stationed on the hilltop gaped at the unexpected procession, but they quickly moved aside in deference to their leader. As the flag moved down the slope toward the battlefield, Ronon scanned the masses of soldiers until he could identify Teyla near the Nistra flag. His eyesight was strong, and he could see her face brighten when she located him in return. He tried to look reassuring, even if he couldn't offer much comfort. Good news: he was still alive, a fact which she'd been given good reason to doubt. Bad news: he was still a prisoner.

Ranks continued to part for them, allowing them passage. Most of the fighting in the vicinity had stopped, combatants edging back toward their respective lines in light of the new development. Cestan's group had almost reached the foot of the hill when a raised bow caught Ronon's attention. He'd spent enough time hunting with the people who made and used those bows to recognize that it was not Falnori.

In an instant, the situation was clear. Just as he'd feared, a Nistra hunter was bearing down on Cestan from behind a group of unwitting Falnori soldiers, ready to become a hero by felling the enemy leader...and in so doing he would destroy any chance this world had of finding peace.

Ronon's instincts had always served him well. When the bow was drawn back to loose its arrow, there was no hesitation—he lunged forward and placed himself in its path.

Sergeant Alderman's shout of warning came too late. Before Elizabeth knew what was happening, Ronon was on the ground at Cestan's feet, an arrow embedded in his shoulder, and a group of Falnori soldiers had seized the arms of a defiant Nistra hunter in the crowd.

The would-be assassin quickly found himself in danger of being mauled by the enraged soldiers. They swarmed around him, fists tangling and shouts mingling until Cestan, in a powerfully resonant voice, commanded: "Stop!"

His order produced immediate results. The soldiers went silent, keeping hold of the hunter's arms but no longer dispensing their own justice. Cestan, for his part, stared openly down at the off-worlder sprawled in the grass.

All at once Elizabeth's brain snapped back into real time, and she knelt to help Ronon sit up. The whip that had bound his wrists now lay loosely beside him. She pulled the last slackened loops free. "Are you all right?"

Normally that would be a silly question to ask someone with a projectile sticking out from under his collarbone, but this was Ronon, after all.

The Satedan grunted. "Had plenty worse." He reached up to remove it, and she instinctively swatted his hand away.

"Carson will lay into both of us if I let you pull that out." Elizabeth took the field dressing Lorne offered and made a haphazard effort to stop the sluggish bleeding.

A repetitive *brush-brush* of motion in the grass grew louder before Teyla burst through the circle that had formed around them. The Nistra flag of conference wasn't far behind. "What has happened?" she demanded, flushed from running. "We saw…"

"One of the hunters made an attempt on the governor's

life," Kellec informed her, stooping to reclaim his whip from where it had fallen.

Cestan's nod was vague, as if he'd gone elsewhere to assemble his thoughts. "And the off-worlder moved to protect me."

Amazed, the chief warrior made no move to restrain Ronon again. "You're fortunate that I didn't activate my whip on instinct."

"Yeah, I am," Ronon agreed. He answered the unspoken question as well. "Didn't see another way."

Galven and the rest of his entourage showed up then, visibly caught off-guard by the turn of events. The minister fumbled for a few seconds before stating to Cestan, in lieu of a greeting, "I expect you'll accuse me of having orchestrated this."

For Elizabeth, still crouched next to Ronon, the first glimpse of light at the end of this tunnel appeared when the governor shook his head. "Not this time, Minister." His gaze never left Ronon. "You knew you were to face grave punishment," he said quietly. "Yet you risked your life for the one who planned to execute you."

Elizabeth felt the scrutiny of the surrounding Falnori fall on them. The soldiers, seeing the entirety of the situation, now looked at least as incredulous as their leader.

Only Ronon seemed unfazed. "Guess I did."

Cestan might have suspected the answer, but he asked the question anyway. "Why?"

"If I hadn't, a leader would be dead and no truce would be possible. Your people would have gone on killing each other, and they wouldn't have stopped until long after anyone could remember why the war even started."

"It is as I told you, Minister." Teyla addressed Galven,

whose surprise was fading remarkably quickly into comprehension. "When our convictions are strongly held, we
are willing to take extraordinary steps to further them.
You have seen our actions on both sides of this conflict.
Would we do these things if we wished to favor one over
the other? Would we risk our lives if we were less than
absolutely certain that both are deserving of peace and
prosperity?"

As Teyla crossed the open space to join her teammate,
Elizabeth watched Cestan's expression and realized what
the Athosian must have deduced some time ago in order
to bring Galven to this point. Once again she found herself admiring Teyla's gift for insight.

"You're more alike than you know," she told Galven
and Cestan, giving the bandage to Teyla and rising.
"We're here, standing under the flags of conference
instead of doing battle, because you both allowed us to
demonstrate our intentions on a personal level, through
the actions of individuals. Now we have the opportunity
to take another step. We have the raiders who inflamed
the tensions in custody. We have the means to open up
the second Stargate on this planet for use and shield both
gates from any further attacks." She delivered that last
part smoothly, without adding the *I hope* that dangled in
her mind; they hadn't heard from John or Rodney.

"There are adversaries in this galaxy against whom
we have to stand firm," she maintained. "You know of
the Wraith, and you know that they eventually will come
again. That makes it even more important for us to stop
fighting wars that don't need to be fought. Let's step back
and examine what we've discovered here so that we can
go forward with a real understanding of each other and

our common goals. We can *end* this."

For a moment, the two leaders regarded each other without speaking. Just when Elizabeth began to consider asking Teyla to try, Galven spoke up, only a trace of an accusation in his tone. "Can the Falnori view the Nistra as equals, despite the fact that we do not share the birthright of the Ancestors?"

"We can," answered Cestan, "else my people would not have chosen me to lead them. Like many, I do not possess the ability." He gave the other man only a moment to react to that disclosure before turning the tables. "Can the Nistra accept the loss of the mines?"

"If it is the wisest course, and if we are compensated with the establishment of a new industry, I believe we can adapt."

With that, the ember of hope Elizabeth had harbored for so long finally flared to life. "Gentlemen, may I suggest that you send your armies home so that we can freely discuss details?"

For all her experience in diplomacy, she had never before been so close, quite literally, to organized combat. The cessation of hostilities was fascinating to witness. Much like the start of the talks, there was no grand, formal act. Cestan sent his warriors out to spread the word along the Falnori lines, and Galven returned to the Nistra side, each pledging to approach the Hall of Tribute in a day's time. Perhaps inspired by Ronon's selfless act, Cestan permitted Galven to take the would-be Nistra assassin back to be dealt with by his own people. It was decided that the Cadre prisoner would stay with the Lanteans for now, although both the Falnori and Nistra had some rather understandable questions for him.

On his feet again, the arrow sticking almost comically out of his bandaged shoulder, Ronon eyed Kellec with some distrust. "Rest easy," Cestan reassured him with a smile. "Unless you feel you have not done enough to annul your earlier deeds?"

The Satedan relaxed, even submitting to take a couple of pain tablets from one of the Marines' kits. While he badgered the sergeant to break the end off the arrow—"so I don't take out someone's eye"—the remainder of the Atlantis team watched the armies slowly start to withdraw toward their respective territories, gathering their wounded and dead as they went.

"No offense, ma'am," offered Lorne, "but if you'd told me this morning that we'd be seeing *this* by day's end…"

"I know what you mean, Major."

Elizabeth was about to take her leave of Cestan when she again remembered her radio. "Jumper One, come in," she requested.

John's prompt response came as a distinct relief. "Jumper One here. We're headed for the second gate with the dialer."

"That's good to hear. As it turns out, we've managed to relax your deadline. Hope you didn't rush too much."

"Nahhh…"

"*Rush?*" Rodney's voice overrode John's on the frequency. "Thank you ever so much for your belated generosity, Elizabeth, but we had a rather stringent self-imposed deadline with which to contend. It involved not getting ourselves crushed in an orbiting demolition derby!"

A few mumbled words could be heard in the background. Elizabeth understood just enough Czech to recognize that theirs promised to be an interesting mission report. "Glad to hear you're in one piece, then," Elizabeth told Rodney calmly, knowing full well that it would yank his chain. "We've got a couple of projects now; the dialer and shield controls on the second gate count as one, and we also need to develop a shield or iris for the first gate. How long do you estimate something like that to take?"

"Depends. How many engineers can I threaten with bodily harm?"

"Rodney."

His sigh was audible over the radio. "A couple of days, probably."

"All right. We'll guard the gate until then, in case any more Cadre types decide to drop in." She spoke to her people but also to Cestan, who nodded his thanks.

"Say, Elizabeth," remarked John with exaggerated casualness, "did we miss anything? Because it looks from up here like the Falnori and Nistra armies are packing up and bailing out."

She smiled. "Seeing is believing, gentlemen. We're heading for home. Keep us apprised on your progress with the dialer installation."

"Will do. We may have to send back to base for supplies, since the Dynamic Duo here will need to build a new housing for the controls."

"Which will be a veritable cakewalk in comparison to what we went through to procure the controls in the first place," Rodney griped. "We'll be in touch, Elizabeth."

The end of his transmission coincided with a shout from Alderman. In the time it took Elizabeth to spin toward his voice, everything tilted yet again.

Sekal smirked, one arm around Sergeant Denfield's throat. With his other hand he jabbed a handgun into the sergeant's ribs, the now-useless cuffs hanging from his wrist. "A word of advice," he offered genially to the other Marines now aiming their weapons at him. "Search your prisoners with a bit more care."

"Ma'am, I'm sorry," Denfield gasped out before the arm around his neck constricted in warning.

"Bastard grabbed Denfield's sidearm out of his holster," Lorne reported, his gaze trained down the barrel of his own weapon. "How the hell he picked the cuffs I have no idea."

"They're not the most ingenious confinement device in the galaxy." Sekal, unsurprisingly, looked rather satisfied with himself.

Damn it, they couldn't have come this far only to be shown up by a petty criminal. Elizabeth cursed herself for letting their collective guard down and raised her hands to halt Kellec and his comrades from advancing on the man. Even if their whip strikes were laser-accurate, they couldn't take the chance that Sekal might have just enough time to pull the trigger.

"Congratulations," she said coolly. "You've succeeded in making us look foolish. Now what do you want?"

"I want my men out of your jail. But since prisoner exchanges are often overcomplicated and precarious, I'll settle for one of your ships."

*Not a chance.* It hardly shocked her to learn that he was willing to let his associates rot in order to save his own neck. "You won't be able to fly it, since the jumpers respond only to a specific genetic marker."

The detail didn't seem to bother Sekal. "Then I'll

take a pilot as well. I saw that one"—he jerked his head toward Corporal Vincent—"fly us here. He'll do."

"No, you want me." Lorne stepped forward, lowering his gun. "I outrank him and I'm a better pilot."

Elizabeth closed her eyes. Apparently Atlantis had more than its share of overly altruistic military officers.

Sekal must have considered the ransom for a major to be higher than that for a sergeant. The transfer was conducted efficiently, the raider's weapon hovering close enough to Lorne's temple to preclude any opportunity to jump him.

"Your utter lack of honor is sadly familiar." Cestan folded his arms, radiating contempt.

Lifting his eyebrows, Sekal said, "Where's the honor in being dragged around like a captured beast? Why should I trust that I won't be locked up indefinitely or worse? I see no reason to let any of you determine my fate."

Although hostage situations weren't Elizabeth's forte, she knew enough about reading people to identify Sekal as the goal-oriented type. He wouldn't hurt Lorne without provocation, but if it would further his plan he wouldn't hesitate.

"Hang in there, Major," she offered lamely.

"Hanging in, ma'am." Lorne's wry smile was belied by the insistent gaze he fixed on her. "Lousy time to lose contact with Colonel Sheppard on the radio, huh?"

Feeling the hard plastic in her hand, she quickly grasped his meaning. Unfortunately, so did Sekal. "Throw it away," he demanded. "All of you. No need to get all devious or heroic."

So much for that. There was another way to make this

work, though. Elizabeth nodded and bent to place the radio on the ground. As she did so, she surreptitiously slid her thumb over the leftmost switch and hoped she'd gotten the right one.

"All right, Sekal. You win."

The transmission caught John off-guard. He sat up straighter in his seat. "What was that?"

Radek leaned forward, frowning. "It sounded like—"

"We'll let you gate to whatever address you want," Elizabeth's cautious voice continued, "provided you let the Major go before you step through."

"No deal," came the response. "I want the ship, and he's going to fly it."

John put two and two together and came up with a big problem.

"What the hell—?" Rodney reached out to toggle the radio and yelped when John seized his wrist. "Seriously, what the *hell*?"

"They're on vox," John explained shortly. "Somebody's keyed their radio open, the way you did during that first raider ambush, so we can hear everything that's going on. Things like that don't happen by accident. If you call them now, that son of a bitch Sekal is going to know we're on to him."

He double-checked Jumper One's cloak and adjusted his heading, aiming for the dot on the HUD that symbolized Jumper Two.

"Everybody can walk away from this," the raider was saying. "I'll even send your man back through the gate when I'm done. I'm sure I can find somebody to crack whatever Ancestor locks that ship has."

"Good luck with that," John muttered. The odds of getting a jumper to respond to a non-ATA pilot were about as strong as the odds of finding a Wraith dancing the tango in the Atlantis mess hall. Even so, he didn't want to lose another jumper out of the city's limited fleet—and he definitely wasn't going to trust Sekal to let Lorne go.

"We were supposed to be done with all the tense stuff for a while." Rodney flopped back in his chair, rolling a kink out of his neck. "There are only so many miracles I can pull off in one day."

"Then tag Radek in. Better yet, both of you put your heads together and brainstorm a way to take Sekal down without risking Lorne."

Jumper One closed in on the team's position, and John put the invisible craft into a hover fifty feet above Jumper Two and the small crowd gathered near the edge of the trees. *All right, what do we have to work with?* Sekal had an arm around Lorne's neck and a Beretta jammed into his ribs. Standing a conciliatory distance away were Elizabeth, Cestan, a handful of Marines and Falnori, as well as—Ronon and Teyla?

John used the viewscreen's magnification and spotted an arrow stuck through Ronon's shoulder. The big guy didn't look too bothered, which was about par for the course. After he'd wasted a few seconds trying to figure out what exactly had transpired to set up this situation, John gave up. With the enhanced view, he scanned the holsters of the Marines, found an empty one, and made a mental note to tear Denfield a new one later. There was no excuse for losing a weapon.

"It takes a few minutes to power up the jumper," he heard Elizabeth say as Alderman ineffectually pushed some buttons on the remote. "If you try to enter too soon, it'll give you a jolt. Security feature."

He had to give them both credit for an effective stall tactic. Sekal looked impatient, but not suspicious. *So far,* John amended. They couldn't keep it up indefinitely.

Landing wouldn't do any good—he'd lose the advantage of surprise and end up in the same position as Elizabeth and the others. How to knock Sekal out from above, then? Jumpers weren't equipped with anti-personnel weapons; a mini-drone, needless to say, would be overkill in the extreme.

"Guys, I could use some ideas." He turned to check on the scientists. Rodney and Radek had slid out of their seats to rummage through the contents of the rear storage areas. "You find a tractor beam or anything back there? Maybe an Asgard transporter, and, while you're at it, an Asgard to operate it?"

"We have a simpler strategy in mind. You'll like it." Rodney sat back on his heels in the rear compartment. "Put the jumper exactly where you want it and I'll take over flying—er, hovering—duties. Then just lean out through the back hatch and shoot the guy."

John was a damned good shot, if he said so himself—and a damned good shot 'for a freaking zoomie,' by the grudging admission of more than a few Marines. Still, he wasn't wild about the plan. "As soon as we open the hatch, the interior of the jumper will be visible. Somebody's bound to see us and react enough to tip Sekal off."

"Only if we open it fully," Radek pointed out. "The hatch control is not difficult to manipulate. If we can command a partial opening, just large enough for you to get an arm through, we would, for the most part, preserve the cloak."

"An arm *and* a sightline. I'm not aiming a gun anywhere near my own man without a solid sightline." John couldn't shake the memory of a few paralyzing seconds in the storm-lit gate-room two years ago: looking down the barrel of his P-90 at Kolya and Elizabeth, a matter of inches separating success and tragedy. He hadn't hesitated then, but of course he hadn't had much of a choice.

"I am thinking that a gun may not be the ideal instrument for this." Reaching into the weapons locker under the bench, Radek came up with a taser in one hand and a slightly mad gleam in his eyes.

John returned the Czech's grin. "Radek, I like the way you think."

Although Teyla had faith that her teammates would be able to resolve the standoff with Sekal, she was not sure what form that resolution would take. She was startled, then, when the raider jerked and went rigid with an unintelligible yell.

His reflexes clearly primed, Lorne wrenched free as Sekal tumbled to the ground in convulsions. Teyla followed the pair of slender wires now embedded in Sekal's back up to their source. Suspended only five feet over their heads was a familiar Earth weapon, gripped by an equally familiar, if disembodied, arm.

Seemingly out of nowhere, John Sheppard's head and shoulders appeared. He squeezed the taser's trigger again, and Sekal twitched once more before finally going limp.

The nearby Falnori warriors gaped at the sight of a man's torso floating in midair. Of the Lanteans, no one looked more relieved than Sergeant Denfield, who stepped over Sekal's prone body to retrieve his sidearm.

John offered a wave with the taser. "Somebody call for the cavalry?"

"We certainly did," Elizabeth called up to him, relief evident in her features. "Nicely done, Colonel."

Rodney's grousing could be heard from within the cloaked jumper. "Now *this* had better be the end of the excitement for a good long while. At the very least, I'm owed a long, hot shower and a sandwich the size of my *head*."

Teyla exchanged a smile with Ronon, who'd finally allowed some of the weariness he surely felt to show. At long last, all of them could afford to think about the future.

# CHAPTER EIGHTEEN

Outside the Hall, Elizabeth knelt to inhale the scent of the flowers that grew along one pockmarked stone wall. The very idea of having this moment of serenity, taken at the end of a full day of negotiations, would have been unimaginable just forty-eight hours earlier. She still marveled at the difference in tone between the previous talks and today's.

The decisions being made by Governor Cestan and Minister Galven were groundbreaking, to say the least. In short, the Nistra and Falnori would be trading roles and sizable expanses of territory. Where the informal border once ran east-west through the plains, it would now angle more north-south, so that the richest adarite veins would fall under the jurisdiction of the Falnori, and many of the Nistra would move into more fertile growing lands. The Nistra miners would train the gene-bearing Falnori in the techniques of adarite extraction, and in turn the Falnori would teach the miners about the best farming methods to support their community.

Atlantis had dedicated no small amount of effort to assisting in the transition. Currently, four jumpers were on the planet, already shuttling people to the areas where new settlements would be developed, and a team of scientists and engineers had begun work on a shield for the gate on the hill, now considered to be the south gate. Unlike the north gate, which had started its life as part of an orbital station, the south gate did not have a shield built into its systems. Fortunately, many of the expedition's engineers were conversant in all things Stargate-related, including the iris designed for the gate at the SGC. Although the two gates would not be able to function simultaneously, setting up a schedule of operation had been a relatively smooth process, to the relief of all concerned.

The sun had just begun to sink below the trees when she noticed a figure walking down the slope toward her. Elizabeth recognized the stride even before the unkempt hair became visible enough to be a dead giveaway. "How goes it, Colonel?"

"Radek thinks his team will be able to finish the iris tomorrow," John reported, slowing to a stop beside her. "They were able to salvage a lot of scrap material from the station segment that crashed with the north gate in order to manufacture the panels. Now it's just a matter of getting the panels in place and hooking up the control system."

She doubted it was quite as simple as that. "So far there haven't been any major disturbances among the displaced villages," she said, standing up. "A few disagreements and reluctant citizens, but hardly enough to be a problem. Both the Falnori and Nistra seem to be extremely adaptable when given a reason to be. It's amazing how quickly they came around to our way of thinking once we'd proven ourselves in their view."

"So if we'd just risked life and limb at the beginning of all this, we could have saved ourselves some trouble?" John cocked an eyebrow.

Again, not so simple, and this time Elizabeth suspected he knew it as well as she did. "I think they needed to see that we were truly on their side—both their sides, so to speak. Maybe getting involved in the battle was the only way to accomplish that. I don't know." Although she didn't like to think of violence as being necessary under any conditions, she was beginning to realize the limitations of applying Earth-based principles to Pegasus events. Her single-minded determination to mend this society's rifts had ended in an armistice, but it easily could have ended in disaster. She would not overreach that way again.

"This isn't going to be an overnight fix," she continued. "Many of these people will be setting up new homes, and there's a lot of infrastructure to rebuild."

"Well, we can help them with some start-up supplies, at least. Seems like it ought to get easier as they go."

A question in his gaze, John tipped his head in the direction of the gate. Elizabeth nodded, and they began a comfortable stroll up the incline.

"I think they'll settle in quickly," she agreed. "Galven has allowed Carson's staff to monitor a few of the miners over the next week to see how their neurological function changes as the adarite influence fades. If they're lucky, a lot of the effects will be reversible."

"Here's hoping."

He didn't raise the issue of the weapons research again, nor had she expected him to. Rodney had studied enough records from the Hall for them to agree with the Ancients' decision to abandon the concept. It was frustrating, but it was reality. The Ancient scientists had devoted a massive amount of manpower and resources to the study of adarite within a short time. Becoming increasingly desperate for technological methods to slow the advance of the Wraith, they had built up the ground facility and the associated orbital station in mere weeks, determined to maintain control of the planet against any level of Wraith assault. In that, at least, they had succeeded.

The discovery of adarite's harmful effects had not been made until the scientists took on humans to assist in their research. Then, like the expedition, they had reached a point when they became unwilling to subject themselves and their assistants to further exposure. As a consequence, there was little data on the long-term effects, irrespective of the presence of the ATA gene.

Elizabeth had raised that issue with Galven and Cestan, and she hadn't objected when they'd made clear their intentions to continue mining, at least for the near future. Already their societies had changed dramatically as a result of recent events. She wasn't in a position to dictate to them what risks they could and couldn't assume. They were aware of the potential hazard and would have to make their own decisions as to how to monitor it.

She changed the subject. "I trust you found a suitable planet for our friends from the Cadre?"

At her inquiry, the Colonel couldn't hold back a smirk. "Sure did. It's a quaint little out-of-the-way place with a scenic view of pretty much nothing." He gave a small shrug. "Probably won't take them all that long to find a way to limp home, wherever that is, but at least 418 is one planet they won't be able to bully anymore. If they're dumb enough to try coming back after the warning we gave them about the gate shields…well, I doubt too many people will miss them."

That concept shouldn't have given Elizabeth as much satisfaction as it did. It wasn't terribly moral to imagine someone's molecules slamming into a technological brick wall, criminal or not.

In all likelihood, the Cadre would be up to their old tricks in no time, and she wasn't naïve enough to believe that they were the only scavengers and miscreants prowling around. Still, Atlantis didn't have the resources or the mandate to police the Pegasus Galaxy. All her people could do was try to stamp out trouble where they found it. They had enough problems to handle already, with the constant Wraith threat lurking in the background and now the replicators joining in.

Of course, she had another, more pressing issue to address at the moment, and she had every intention of resolving it before the sun set. "John, before we head back…"

He must have heard something cautious in her tone, because he stopped walking only a step after she did. Taking the initiative, she withdrew his resignation letter from inside her jacket. "I'd like to talk about this."

She knew him too well to expect much of a perceptible reaction. Even so, it gave her hope to see a flicker of regret cross his face. "Did you read it?" he asked neutrally.

"I did." It had hurt, seeing the anguish between the carefully chosen lines, but she'd owed it to him. "And I understand why you felt you had to write it, so I won't trivialize your reasons or ask you to forget about them. But I also understand how you got to that point, even more so now that I can see how strongly I fixated on brokering this peace treaty. I was sure we were doing the right thing for these people, and I wanted so badly to achieve something unquestionably good for a change, that I lost sight of what was happening around me. I made a mistake, just as you did. We're human; we make those sometimes. So I'm asking you…" She held the envelope, slightly creased, out to him. "…to change your mind."

His gaze remained locked on hers for a few seconds, and she was struck by a semi-rational fear that he wouldn't comply. Then, slowly and deliberately, he took the letter from her and pulled a small lighter from his pocket.

The paper was consumed in less than a minute. John held it by one corner, the brief, bright flare sharpening his features. When the flame neared his hand, he let it fall to the ground and extinguished it with the heel of his boot.

Relieved beyond measure, Elizabeth dug into her jacket again and came up with the other item he'd surrendered to her. "I believe these belong to you, then."

She pressed the silver wings into his palm, and he tightened his fingers around hers for a moment, letting the gesture convey everything he couldn't put into words.

"Thank you," he said simply.

"You're welcome."

They resumed walking, and within moments the Stargate loomed over them, surrounded by the iris implementation team packing up their equipment for the night. Elizabeth glanced over at her military commander again, this time with less certainty. "John, if you ever want to talk—about what that letter said or about anything else—you know where to find me."

He nodded and offered a too-ready flash of a smile, and she knew he wouldn't take her up on the offer. He never did, despite how closely they worked together. Although he'd always listen on the occasions when she absolutely had to get something off her chest, he was clearly more comfortable when such conversations were a one-way street. If asked, he evaded, saying that she had enough on her plate without adding anyone's personal hang-ups.

She understood that underneath John's casual demeanor lay a fiercely private man. As much as it disappointed her to know that he was keeping her at arm's length, she wasn't concerned, because she knew that there were others who could and would get to him—whether he liked it or not.

"You really think it's a good idea to go running with a bad shoulder?"

Ronon started to shrug, then thought better of it. He was tired of sitting around, and the arrow hadn't done a great deal of damage. Besides, he had goals for today. From a certain point of view, this was one of them. "Doesn't hurt that much."

"Yeah, yeah, just a flesh wound and all that." Sheppard didn't look convinced. "I'll go with you, but the odds are good that Carson's going to yell, and at that point you're on your own."

Giving a minor concession to his tightly-bound shoulder, Ronon set a sedate pace, one that his team leader had no trouble matching. He made up for it by taking a longer route than usual. The pair wound through much of the occupied portion of the city, jogging past corridor after corridor of laboratory space and down into the more secluded sections that housed the armory and some of the military training rooms.

They ended up on the skywalk that arced high above one of the central atrium areas. Ronon slowed to a walk for a few steps before leaning his good arm on the railing. Beckett probably had been right about not jarring the shoulder, but it didn't ache enough to mention. Taking a long drink of his water bottle, Sheppard braced his forearms on the railing as well and looked out at the activity below.

A squad of Marines emerged from the transporter nearest the shooting range. From their voices and expressions, it was obvious even from a distance that they'd won a competition with one of the other squads. Across the atrium, two blue-shirted scientists walked briskly, in the middle of a heated debate. Early sunlight spilled in through high-set windows and painted angular patterns on the floor, broken only by occasional footsteps.

"Another day, another dollar," Sheppard commented to himself before raising his water bottle again.

Ronon went for the head-on approach. "Would it have been hard? Leaving this behind?"

In mid-drink, Sheppard stopped and glanced over at him. His expression was guarded as he lowered the bottle. "You heard," he said unnecessarily.

"It wasn't much of a secret." A lot of the enlisted had been worried about who might come in to take their commanding officer's place. The rumors had mostly died down by the time Ronon had gotten back from 418 and out of Beckett's clutches, but he'd heard them anyway, and he wanted an explanation. "You really were going to give up and walk away?"

"Try not to take it personally." Sheppard's voice gained a defensive edge. "I wasn't ditching you, seeing as I had cause to think you were dead at the time."

"Is that the reason you did it?" Ronon wanted to

know.

"It's not the whole reason, but yeah."

"What's the whole reason?"

The Colonel seemed to realize that he wouldn't get out of the conversation easily. His shoulders slumped a little. "I thought that you and Teyla were dead because I'd been so fixated on finding us a shiny new weapon that I let our guard down. The whole fiasco started with me." Leaning forward on the railing again, he cast a sideways glance at his teammate. "Not to wander off-topic or anything, but I don't really get why you're not pissed about that."

Starting to shrug, Ronon once more had to stop himself. Force of habit. "You made a judgment call. The raiders messed it up. I don't expect you to be able to predict the future." He took a drink of his own water. "Plus, I'm not dead."

"Through some weird stroke of luck, no, you're not." Sheppard shook his head, his gaze hard. "That doesn't change the fact that I chose wrong, and I've chosen wrong before. It didn't start on this expedition, but I've had to make a hell of a lot more tough decisions here, and I'm not sure how long I can keep making them when the wrong ones cost good people's lives."

Sometimes Ronon managed to forget that, even though they ate meals and watched football together, even though they relied on each other's instincts without hesitation, he and John Sheppard weren't really peers. The other man had been in his military a lot longer and bore scars from a galaxy Ronon had never seen. Still, although Ronon didn't have the same burden of rank, he'd had experiences the Earth expedition couldn't imagine, and he was sure he knew more of conflict than almost any Marine who'd ever stepped through the gate.

"That's what command is," he said bluntly. "Losses are a part of war—any kind of war."

Sheppard spun toward him, his eyes flashing with pain masked as outrage. "You think I don't know that?"

Ronon had never seen that kind of emotion from his team leader before. It didn't deter him. "I think we both know it too well. But you need to give everyone else around here some credit for understanding it, too."

Some of Sheppard's anger-fueled energy dissipated, and he returned to staring out at the sun-streaked atrium.

"It's not that I think other people blame me," he said after a long silence. "Even *I* don't always blame me. It's just…" He let his head hang down over his bent arms. "The Asurans are going to keep hitting us, and sooner or later they're going to come for Atlantis. There's no getting around that. Maybe Colonel Carter and the rest of the SGC will have figured out a better disrupter weapon by then, but that's in no way a guarantee. Someday we're going to be minding our own business and those *things* are just going to show up, in a cityship or in a nanovirus or in some way we haven't even thought of yet. Hell, maybe the Wraith will beat them to it, for all I know."

"We'll fight them."

"Yeah, we will." The Colonel scrubbed a tired hand over his face. "But people will keep dying, no matter what I do."

There wasn't much Ronon could do to counter that statement. He thought for a few moments, watching the stretched light beams on the floor waver with the passing of a cloud. Finally he decided to go with the only reassurance that came to mind.

"When I joined the Satedan military," he began, "my whole recruit class thought our first field commander could do no wrong. He knew so much, and he never hesitated to act when needed. We would have followed him anywhere.

"One day we were assigned to sweep an area for Wraith monitoring devices, and someone triggered a trap. Ten of us were caught away from the rest of the division with Darts inbound. We could have tried to dig in and take cover where we were, or we could have tried to cover the distance back to the main fortified position before the Darts arrived. The commander ordered us to head for the fortification. Only six of us made it.

"He had to make a choice, and half my squad paid for it. After that, we knew he wasn't perfect. But we didn't admire him any less. We followed him because he made smart decisions, but also because he had the courage to make decisions even when he couldn't be sure of the outcome—and even when he knew the outcome would be terrible. It was a difficult duty and we respected him for doing it well."

Ronon drained the last of his water before speaking again. "Now I follow you, and I've never been sorry for it. You can't ask the ones you've lost, but I bet none of your men here regret it, either."

Without waiting for a response, he turned and headed down the sloped walkway, leaving Sheppard alone to think. He didn't know whether or not he'd done anything to help, but he'd said everything he had to say.

*Lieutenant Colonel Sheppard,*
*I've thought about writing this letter a number of times*

*over the past year. Had I managed to force myself to do it at any of those times, it would have looked quite a bit different than this. I guess I could have written one at each of the so-called five stages of grief, although it took me a while to accept that grief was what I felt. After all, Aiden wasn't dead.*

*We watched the news religiously for the first two or three months, sure we'd eventually hear something about him. We couldn't understand why no one ever mentioned his name. Hadn't he paid the same price as the other servicemen who'd been lost? I remembered what you'd said about how highly classified his assignment had been, but the injustice of it all still bothered me terribly.*

*When you sent his belongings home, I was furious with you. I was certain you'd given up on him after you'd promised to do everything you could to keep looking. After a few more months with no word, though, I started to realize that 'missing in action' wasn't the hope we'd thought it was. I still can't fully believe that he's dead—that would be betraying him, somehow—but I'm beginning to accept that he won't be walking through the door tomorrow, or the next day, and I can leave the house without worrying that the phone will ring with urgent news.*

*I spent a lot of time placing blame at first. I had plenty to go around. I blamed the government and the military, and of course you know I blamed you. Right to your face I accused you of abusing Aiden's faith in your leadership. I've come to believe it was shortsighted to say that without any understanding of the events that led to Aiden's loss. It wasn't fair to you, but mostly it wasn't fair to Aiden, because it belittled his judgment. And I realized*

*that he was the one I'd really been trying to blame. I was*
*angry at him for leaving us, for hurting his grandparents,*
*without any explanation of how or why.*

*I don't ever want to feel like that anymore. I love my*
*cousin, and I'm proud of him, no matter where he is. I*
*have to believe that what he chose to fight for—what all*
*of you choose to fight for—is right, even if I can't always*
*see the reasons. Aiden lived for the Marine Corps and*
*for the people he served with. He trusted you, and so I*
*do, too.*

*I'm not completely sure what I'm trying to say to you,*
*Colonel, but I want you to know that I'm not angry any-*
*more. With the help of caring friends, I've found a kind of*
*peace. I hope you've been able to do the same.*

After he'd read the letter straight through for the third
time, John sat back against the steps of the southwest
pier. His fingers reflexively tightened as an ocean breeze
threatened to tug the paper out of his hand. Lara Ford was
a strong person. Stronger than him, in some ways.

The bright-faced lieutenant with the goofy grin and
the penchant for assigning lame nicknames had been a
part of John's team for a year. He'd manned Atlantis's
defenses after the Wraith had overrun the city. Even once
the enzyme had taken hold and he'd barely resembled
the Aiden Ford they'd known, his last act in John's sight
had been to risk himself to save his former team. He
deserved to be remembered. So did Harper, and Travis,
and Markham, and all the others. John just wasn't sure
how to accomplish that without going a little bit nuts in
the process.

He'd heard and understood what Ronon had said earlier. Even the act of telling the story had meant something to him, because he knew he'd just heard more complete sentences from the Satedan than anyone had in months. He'd gotten the message, but he couldn't quite bring himself to fully accept it. Not yet.

The telltale *snick* of the door sounded behind him. He waited, not turning to look. Today was a down day for his team, and anyone who wanted his attention badly enough to find him out here could damn well hike his or her ass a few more yards.

A gentle hand dropped onto his shoulder, and Teyla gracefully took a seat on the step above his. "You and Chewie tag-teaming me today?" he asked, keeping his voice light.

"You were missed at lunch," she responded. Teyla never pushed; that was one of the many things John liked about her. Without a word he held the letter out to her.

"I do not read your language well when it is written by hand." By her expression, though, he could see that she recognized the name at the bottom of the page. "This will take some time."

"I'll wait," he said simply.

While she read, he watched the waves, unchanging and inevitable, bumping against the feet of the city. After a few minutes, she raised her head and handed the letter back. "*Have* you found peace?"

He was pretty sure she already knew the answer to that. Otherwise they wouldn't be out here. "It's not that simple."

"The act is not. The question, however, is."

Exhaling a long breath, he pulled one knee up to his chest. "Not completely. I don't know how. I think maybe

I'm afraid of being *too* okay with the losses. I mean, if a Marine dies and I just pick up and move on, what does that make me?"

Her approving look suggested that his honesty was welcome. "When we traveled on the *Daedalus* to Sateda, I told you that your people's dedication to each other impressed me. I should have said more. I should have told you that such dedication is one of the traits I admire most about your expedition and, even more, about you."

Caught off-guard by the praise, John couldn't figure out how to reply. Teyla might have counted on that reaction, because she pressed on. "The Athosian people have suffered great losses, both before and during my time as their leader. In spite of that, we have managed to move forward. But I believe that the day I accept a loss without pain will be the day I am no longer fit to lead."

She returned her hand to his shoulder and spoke with an earnestness that he couldn't help but believe. "Like everything else, John, it is a balance. As we have faith in you to keep that balance, you must have faith in yourself."

A knot of tension in his stomach seemed to ease at her words. He looked up at her with a faint smile, hoping she'd see the gratitude there. "I'm working on it."

"Work on it between meals," put in a deep voice. "You missed beef stew at lunch."

John started, whipping his head around to find Ronon leaning against the wall by the door. "God! Warn a guy, would you?" The big man only smirked. "Have you been there the whole time?"

Pushing himself off the wall, Ronon nodded at Teyla. "She's better at this stuff than me."

Yet he'd come along for the ride anyway. The knot loosened a little further. "I don't know," John commented truthfully, climbing to his feet. "You weren't half bad."

When the door *snicked* open again, it revealed an impatient scientist. "Are we done dealing with the identity crisis or whatever now? I need the Colonel in the lab."

John folded his arms, choosing to let Rodney's brash question roll off. "For what?"

"What do I ever need out of you in the lab? Your gene." Rodney heaved a put-upon sigh. "As much as it pains me to say this aloud yet again, you have significantly better control with ATA-enabled equipment than I do, especially when I'm trying to operate it and take readings simultaneously. So come be a good little guinea pig for an hour. You'll still have plenty of the day left to be philosophical."

Although John had a suspicion that this was Rodney's unique way of trying to help, he played along. "Yeah? What's in it for me?"

"Funny you should ask." With a waggle of eyebrows—Rodney could not pull off a devious look to save his life—he produced a plastic baggie containing one of Mrs. Beckett's prized scones. "All yours for a single measly hour of your time."

"How the hell did you pry that away from Carson?"

Rodney waved dismissively. "It's for the furtherance of science. If he knew, he'd be honored to contribute."

That only confirmed Rodney's motives. In deference to the man's hard-earned reputation as a self-absorbed pain in the ass, John thanked him the best way he could: by not thanking him. "Don't expect me to share this," he informed Rodney, plucking the bag out of his hand.

"Please. Like I didn't steal one for myself while I was at it?"

*With the help of caring friends*, Lara had said.

Maybe it could be that simple after all. At the least, it was enough to see him through to tomorrow.

John tucked the letter into his jacket and let his teammates lead him back inside.

# ABOUT THE AUTHOR

Elizabeth Christensen owns a T-shirt that says "Actually, I AM a rocket scientist." In her defense, it was a gift from her parents. A civilian engineer at Wright-Patterson Air Force Base, she endures daily the burden of being a University of Michigan alum in the heart of Ohio State territory. She is a native of the Detroit area and misses her hometown hockey team. Alongside her husband, she flies a 1979 Grumman Tiger airplane with a terrific engine and a paint job only a mother could love.

Beth's previous Stargate Atlantis novels are *The Chosen* and *Exogenesis*, both co-authored with Sonny Whitelaw.

• For more information, visit www.elizabethchristensen.com

# STARGATE
## SG·1™

# STARGATE
# ATLANTIS™

**Original novels based on
the hit TV shows,
STARGATE SG-1 and
STARGATE ATLANTIS**

**AVAILABLE NOW**

**For more information, visit
www.stargatenovels.com**

# SNEAK PREVIEW

## STARGATE SG-I: RELATIVITY

### by James Swallow

Daniel reached the top of the stairs and looked up. And up. *And up.* He felt his head swim a little and his balance fluttered. A firm hand pressed into his shoulder and he glanced back to see Teal'c providing the support. "Thanks," he said lamely. "That last step is a doozy."

To be honest, Jackson hadn't really known what to expect. He'd been inside lots of big spaceships before, and one set of corridors looked pretty much like another, right? Granted, the mix-and-match tunnels-and-technology look of the *Wanderer*'s passageways was something new, but this space, this *atrium*… For a moment, it took his breath away. Daniel had imagined they would come out in some sort of room, maybe like a reception chamber or a hall for audiences. He had not expected to find himself standing in the middle of what looked like parkland, having emerged from the side of a shallow hill. For long moments his brain registered a kind of disconnect. The scenery was one of sparse grasses and low, wide trees. The first Earth-like analogy that sprang to mind was the African veldt, a savannah that went off to the horizon – or at least, it would have if there had actually *been* a horizon. Jackson swallowed hard and let his eyes follow the line of the landscape, over the gentle, rolling hills, finding roads and regular, oval lakes, the patchwork of what looked like farmland and clusters of buildings that were bright white stone in the even daylight.

But where the view should have gone to the vanishing point, the land did something very different. It folded up and away, and Daniel tried not to get dizzy as he walked his gaze up it, around and along until he saw the curvature coming together miles over his head. "Whoa."

Suddenly, like one of those weird optical illusion pictures, the sight *popped* in his brain and Jackson's sense of perception caught up to what it was he was actually seeing. "On the inside," he said to himself. "It's inside out. An inside out planet."

"Is that what it is?" said O'Neill. "Oh good. That makes a lot more sense than trees stuck to the ceiling."

Suj, still smiling in faint amusement, held her hands palms up in front of her. "Imagine a map, flat on a table. Then take it and fold it into a tube." She put her hands together. "We are inside that tube, standing on the map. Look up," and she pointed into the air, "and you see the rest of the map arching overhead." Suj inclined her head. "Do not the Tau'ri have similar colonies in their star system?"

"Only in theory," admitted Carter. "I'm familiar with the concept, though." Sam glanced at Daniel and the others. "Back in the Sixties, a scientist called Gerard O'Neill posited the idea of building a huge cylinder in space, or hollowing out an asteroid and setting it to spin along the longest axis." She made a turning motion with her fingers. "The centrifugal force created on the inside surface of the cylinder mimics Earth-normal gravity…" Her voice tailed off. "Never thought I'd ever see one, though."

"O'Neill, huh?" said Jack. "Cool." He gave Suj a look. "No relation, in case you were wondering."

"It's incredible," Daniel took in the scope of the construction. He made out the forms of thin steel towers rising up from the surface like the spokes on a wheel, to meet at a series of spheres along the midline of the massive open chamber. "What are those?"

"The effect of gravity lessens the closer you get to the center of the *Wanderer*," explained Suj. "At the hub there is no effect at all. We maintain artificial solar generators up there to create the illusion of a night and day cycle."

"It's a hell of a lot of real estate to keep in a can," noted Jack.

"The *Wanderer* has been the heart of the Pack since the day of the first escape," said Suj, a little defensively. "Please, if you'll walk with me."

They followed a path down to the nearest of the townships, which lay clustered around the base of one of the steel towers. Close up, Daniel saw that the buildings had an organic feel to them, as if they were made of coral. He wondered if they were grown rather than assembled.

The locals matched the look of Suj and the Pack from the planet. Clothing, technology and the people themselves were an eclectic mixture. This was a magpie culture, he reasoned, tribes of people who had lost their worlds and their identities in the wake of Goa'uld oppression, and then come together to forge a new whole from the fragments. Jackson felt the same rush of excitement as he had on the planet with the stone orbs, the promise of studying something strange and undiscovered; and these were living, breathing people with a vital, ongoing culture, not simply the memorials of a civilization long dead.

In the central square of the township they came upon Vix and Ryn, along with a handful of other men and women who all wore patient and vigilant expressions.

"Hey," said Jack, giving them a jaunty wave. "Nice digs you have here. Love what you've done with the place."

Vix accepted the greeting with a nod. "O'Neill." He turned to his companions. "These are the Tau'ri of Earth. I have brought them to parley."

Ryn said nothing, but an older, dark-skinned man in a heavy tunic and robes stepped closer. "Not what we expected, Vix. Not what we expected at all. Where is the salvage our scouts spoke of?"

"Yeah, about that," offered the colonel. "If I can field that one, I'm thinking that your folks and ours were led on a wild goose chase in that regard."

"There are only war machines down there," explained Vix. "Guardians, I suspect, placed there to protect the stone monoliths. Our sweeps detected nothing that we could use."

The other man frowned. "Our needs-"

"Are known to me," finished Vix bluntly. "Do not question that. This is why I have brought these people to our home. They talk of trade."

"Words cost little," grumbled Ryn.

"Damn right they do," O'Neill broke in. "So, what do you say we see if there's something more tangible we can chat about?" He spread his hands. "We're not the snakeheads, kids. We're here to, uh…" Jack glanced at Sam. "Carter, what was that phrase?"

"Make in-roads, sir," she replied, pulling up the expression from a dull briefing document from the International Oversight Advisory that all of them had been forced to read. The world governments who knew about the Stargate were forever applying pressure for concrete rewards from the program.

"In-roads, right." Jack nodded sagely, and Daniel was struck by the fact that he gave a good impression of knowing what he was doing. "You guys saved our butts back on that pool-table planet. Helluva good way to make new friends."

For the first time, Vix cracked something like a smile. He was warming to them. "You and I will talk, Colonel." He beckoned him closer. "I have chambers where there is food and refreshment.'

Ryn sniffed. "Where you can create secret deals with the Tau'ri to strengthen your own position?"

The other man's outburst made the moment turn awkward. "I will seek only what is best for the Pack," said Vix, at length.

"Then there will be no impediment to my presence as well," retorted the other pilot, darting a look at Suj.

"Ryn is correct," said the historian. "The codes of conduct allow it. One of the Pack for each visitor. But this means O'Neill must have a companion as well."

"Oh, I getcha." Jack nodded. "Teal'c? Come with. We can get a snack."

"What about us, sir?" said Sam.

"Make nice," replied the colonel. "But don't wander too far."

As they departed, the dark-skinned man gave Sam a small bow. "Forgive me, I am remiss. I am Koe, and the Pack's welfare is my remit. Perhaps you and your associate would join me while our leaders talk? I would be pleased to show you some of the *Wanderer*."

"If it pleases you, healer," Suj broke in. "Might I speak with Doctor Jackson? It appears we have some common interests."

The two members of the Pack exchanged glances and Daniel saw a subtle communication pass between them. "Of course," said Koe.

Sam gave him a nod as they parted company and tapped the radio on her gear vest; the message was clear. *Stay in touch – just in case.* Daniel nodded back, and for a moment he felt a slight tinge of disappointment. They'd barely met these people and already they had defaulted to the assumption that the Pack were untrustworthy. It made Jackson feel glum; but then SG-1 had learned through bitter experience that seemingly-friendly faces were often far from it. *The Shavadai, the Eurondans, the Aschen, the Bedrosians... We've had more of our fair share of knives hidden behind smiles.* He sighed and gave Suj a weak grin. *For once,* he hoped, *it would be nice to find the reverse was true.*

# STARGATE SG-1: RELATIVITY

# AVAILABLE OCTOBER 2007

For more information,
visit **www.stargatenovels.com**

# STARGATE ATLANTIS: ENTANGLEMENT

**by Martha Wells**
Price: £6.99 UK | $7.95 US
ISBN-10: 1-905586-03-5
ISBN-13: 978-1-905586-03-5

When Dr. Rodney McKay unlocks an Ancient mystery on a distant moon, he discovers a terrifying threat to the Pegasus galaxy.

Determined to disable the device before it's discovered by the Wraith, Colonel John Sheppard and his team navigate the treacherous ruins of an Ancient outpost. But attempts to destroy the technology are complicated by the arrival of a stranger — a stranger who can't be trusted, a stranger who needs the Ancient device to return home. Cut off from backup, under attack from the Wraith, and with the future of the universe hanging in the balance, Sheppard's team must put aside their doubts and step into the unknown.

However, when your mortal enemy is your only ally, betrayal is just a heartbeat away…

*Series number: SGA-6*

Global disaster threatens the Atlantis homeworld

STARGATE
ATLANTIS

EXOGENESIS
Sonny Whitelaw & Elizabeth Christensen

Based on the hit television series created by
Brad Wright and Robert C. Cooper

Series number: SGA-5

# STARGATE ATLANTIS: EXOGENESIS

**by Sonny Whitelaw &
Elizabeth Christensen**
Price: £6.99 UK | $7.95 US
ISBN-10: 1-905586-02-7
ISBN-13: 978-1-905586-02-8

When Dr. Carson Beckett disturbs the rest of two long-dead Ancients, he unleashes devastating consequences of global proportions.

With the very existence of Lantea at risk, Colonel John Sheppard leads his team on a desperate search for the long lost Ancient device that could save Atlantis. While Teyla Emmagan and Dr. Elizabeth Weir battle the ecological meltdown consuming their world, Colonel Sheppard, Dr. Rodney McKay and Dr. Zelenka travel to a world created by the Ancients themselves. There they discover a human experiment that could mean their salvation...

But the truth is never as simple as it seems, and the team's prejudices lead them to make a fatal error — an error that could slaughter thousands, including their own Dr. McKay.

# STARGATE ATLANTIS: HALCYON

**by James Swallow**
Price: £6.99 UK | $7.95 US
ISBN-10: 1-905586-01-9
ISBN-13: 978-1-905586-01-1

In their ongoing quest for new allies, Atlantis's flagship team travel to Halcyon, a grim industrial world where the Wraith are no longer feared—they are hunted.

Horrified by the brutality of Halcyon's warlike people, Lieutenant Colonel John Sheppard soon becomes caught in the political machinations of Halcyon's aristocracy. In a feudal society where strength means power, he realizes the nobles will stop at nothing to ensure victory over their rivals. Meanwhile, Dr. Rodney McKay enlists the aid of the ruler's daughter to investigate a powerful Ancient structure, but McKay's scientific brilliance has aroused the interest of the planet's most powerful man—a man with a problem he desperately needs McKay to solve.

As Halcyon plunges into a catastrophe of its own making the team must join forces with the warlords—or die at the hands of their bitterest enemy…

# STARGATE ATLANTIS: THE CHOSEN

*A little knowledge is a dangerous thing*

STARGATE ATLANTIS

THE CHOSEN

Sonny Whitelaw & Elizabeth Christensen

Based on the hit television series created by Brad Wright and Robert C. Cooper

Series number: SGA-3

by **Sonny Whitelaw &
Elizabeth Christensen**
Price: £6.99 UK | $7.95 US
ISBN-10: 0-9547343-8-6
ISBN-13: 978-0-9547343-8-1

With Ancient technology scattered across the Pegasus galaxy, the Atlantis team is not surprised to find it in use on a world once defended by Dalera, an Ancient who was cast out of her society for falling in love with a human.

But in the millennia since Dalera's departure much has changed. Her strict rules have been broken, leaving her people open to Wraith attack. Only a few of the Chosen remain to operate Ancient technology vital to their defense and tensions are running high. Revolution simmers close to the surface.

When Major Sheppard and Rodney McKay are revealed as members of the Chosen, Daleran society convulses into chaos. Wanting to help resolve the crisis and yet refusing to prop up an autocratic regime, Sheppard is forced to act when Teyla and Lieutenant Ford are taken hostage by the rebels…

# STARGATE ATLANTIS: RELIQUARY

**by Martha Wells**
Price: £6.99 UK | $7.95 US
ISBN-10: 0-9547343-7-8
ISBN-13: 978-0-9547343-7-4

Series number: SGA-2

While exploring the unused sections of the Ancient city of Atlantis, Major John Sheppard and Dr. Rodney McKay stumble on a recording device that reveals a mysterious new Stargate address. Believing that the address may lead them to a vast repository of Ancient knowledge, the team embarks on a mission to this uncharted world.

There they discover a ruined city, full of whispered secrets and dark shadows. As tempers fray and trust breaks down, the team uncovers the truth at the heart of the city. A truth that spells their destruction.

With half their people compromised, it falls to Major John Sheppard and Dr. Rodney McKay to risk everything in a deadly game of bluff with the enemy. To fail would mean the fall of Atlantis itself — and, for Sheppard, the annihilation of his very humanity...

**Order your copy directly from the publisher today by going to www.stargatenovels.com or send a check or money order made payable to "Fandemonium" to:**

<u>USA orders:</u> $10.82 ($7.95 + $2.87 P&P). Send payment to: Fandemonium Books, PO Box 2178, Decatur, GA 30031-2178.

<u>UK orders:</u> £8.30 (£6.99 + £1.31 P&P). <u>Rest of the World orders:</u> £9.70 (£6.99 + £2.71 P&P). Send payment to: Fandemonium Books, PO Box 795A, Surbiton KT5 8YB, United Kingdom.

Or check your local bookshop – available on special order if they are out of stock (quote the ISBN number listed above).

A novelization of the pilot

STARGATE
ATLANTIS

RISING
Sally Malcolm

Based on the hit television series developed by
Brad Wright and Robert C. Cooper

Series number: SGA-1

# STARGATE ATLANTIS: RISING

**by Sally Malcolm**
Price: £6.99 UK | $7.95 US
ISBN-10: 0-9547343-5-1
ISBN-13: 978-0-9547343-5-0

Following the discovery of an Ancient outpost buried deep in the Antarctic ice sheet, Stargate Command sends a new team of explorers through the Stargate to the distant Pegasus galaxy.

Emerging in an abandoned Ancient city, the team quickly confirms that they have found the Lost City of Atlantis. But, submerged beneath the sea on an alien planet, the city is in danger of catastrophic flooding unless it is raised to the surface. Things go from bad to worse when the team must confront a new enemy known as the Wraith who are bent on destroying Atlantis.

Stargate Atlantis is the exciting new spin-off of the hit TV show, Stargate SG-1. Based on the script of the pilot episode, Rising is a must-read for all fans and includes deleted scenes and dialog not seen on TV—with photos from the pilot episode.

# STARGATE SG-1: RELATIVITY

**by James Swallow**
Price: $7.95 US | $9.95 Canada |
£6.99 UK
ISBN-10: 1-905586-07-8
ISBN-13: 978-1-905586-07-3

Stargate Command's attempts to sign a treaty with the Pack, a race of gypsy space travellers, is jeopardised by a series of attacks from an unknown enemy. While searching for the perpetrators, Jack begins to suspect that the Pack are concealing a dangerous secret.

# STARGATE SG-1: ROSWELL

## by Sonny Whitelaw & Jennifer Fallon

Price: $7.95 US | $9.95 Canada |
£6.99 UK
ISBN-10: 1-905586-04-3
ISBN-13: 978-1-905586-04-2

When a Stargate malfunction throws Colonel Cameron Mitchell, Dr. Daniel Jackson, and Colonel Sam Carter back in time, they only have minutes to live.

But their rescue, by an unlikely duo — General Jack O'Neill and Vala Mal Doran — is only the beginning of their problems. Ordered to rescue an Asgard also marooned in 1947, SG-1 find themselves at the mercy of history. While Jack, Daniel, Sam and Teal'c become embroiled in the Roswell aliens conspiracy, Cam and Vala are stranded in another timeline, desperately searching for a way home.

As the effects of their interference ripple through time, the consequences for the future are catastrophic. Trapped in the past, SG-1 can only watch as their world is overrun by a terrible invader…

# STARGATE SG-1: ALLIANCES

**by Karen Miller**
Price: $7.95 US | $9.95 Canada |
£6.99 UK
ISBN-10: 1-905586-00-0
ISBN-13: 978-1-905586-00-4

All SG-1 wanted was technology to
save Earth from the Goa'uld ... but
the mission to Euronda was a terrible failure. Now the dogs of Wash-
ington are baying for Jack O'Neill's
blood—and Senator Robert Kinsey
is leading the pack.

When Jacob Carter asks General Hammond for SG-1's par-
ticipation in mission for the Tok'ra, it seems like the answer to
O'Neill's dilemma. The secretive Tok'ra are running out of hosts.
Jacob believes he's found the answer—but it means O'Neill and
his team must risk their lives infiltrating a Goa'uld slave breeding
farm to recruit humans willing to join the Tok'ra.

It's a risky proposition ... especially since the fallout from
Euronda has strained the team's bond almost to breaking. If they
can't find a way to put their differences behind them, they might
not make it home alive ...

Their darkest hour may be their last

STARGATE
SG·1.

SURVIVAL OF
THE FITTEST
Sabine C. Bauer

Based on the hit television series developed by
Brad Wright and Jonathan Glassner

Series number: SG1-7

# STARGATE SG-1: SURVIVAL OF THE FITTEST

### by Sabine C. Bauer

Price: $7.95 US | $9.95 Canada |
£6.99 UK
ISBN-10: 0-9547343-9-4
ISBN-13: 978-0-9547343-9-8

Colonel Frank Simmons has never been a friend to SG-1. Working for the shadowy government organisation, the NID, he has hatched a horrifying plan to create an army as devastatingly effective as that of any Goa'uld.

And he will stop at nothing to fulfil his ruthless ambition, even if that means forfeiting the life of the SGC's Chief Medical Officer, Dr. Janet Fraiser. But Simmons underestimates the bond between Stargate Command's officers. When Fraiser, Major Samantha Carter and Teal'c disappear, Colonel Jack O'Neill and Dr. Daniel Jackson are forced to put aside personal differences to follow their trail into a world of savagery and death.

In this complex story of revenge, sacrifice and betrayal, SG-1 must endure their greatest ordeal…

**Order your copy directly from the publisher today by going to www.stargatenovels.com or send a check or money order made payable to "Fandemonium" to:**

**USA orders:** $10.82 ($7.95 + $2.87 P&P). Send payment to: Fandemonium Books, PO Box 2178, Decatur, GA 30031-2178.

**UK orders:** £8.30 (£6.99 + £1.31 P&P). **Rest of the World orders:** £9.70 (£6.99 + £2.71 P&P). Send payment to: Fandemonium Books, PO Box 795A, Surbiton KT5 8YB, United Kingdom.

Or check your local bookshop — available on special order if they are out of stock (quote the ISBN number listed above).

# STARGATE SG-1: SIREN SONG

**Holly Scott and Jaimie Duncan**
Price: $7.95 US | $9.95 Canada |
£6.99 UK
ISBN-10: 0-9547343-6-X
ISBN-13: 978-0-9547343-6-7

Bounty-hunter, Aris Boch, once more has his sights on SG-1. But this time Boch isn't interested in trading them for cash. He needs the unique talents of Dr. Daniel Jackson — and he'll do anything to get them.

Taken to Boch's ravaged home-world, Atropos, Colonel Jack O'Neill and his team are handed over to insane Goa'uld, Sebek. Obsessed with opening a mysterious subterranean vault, Sebek demands that Jackson translate the arcane writing on the doors. When Jackson refuses, the Goa'uld resorts to devastating measures to ensure his cooperation.

With the vault exerting a malign influence on all who draw near, Sebek compels Jackson and O'Neill toward a horror that threatens both their sanity and their lives. Meanwhile, Carter and Teal'c struggle to persuade the starving people of Atropos to risk everything they have to save SG-1 — and free their desolate world of the Goa'uld, forever.

**Order your copy directly from the publisher today by going to www.stargatenovels.com or send a check or money order made payable to "Fandemonium"_ to:**

**USA orders: $10.82 ($7.95 + $2.87 P&P). Send payment to:** **Fandemonium Books, PO Box 2178, Decatur, GA 30031-2178.**

**UK orders: £8.30 (£6.99 + £1.31 P&P). Rest of the World orders: £9.70 (£6.99 + £2.71 P&P). Send payment to:** **Fandemonium Books, PO Box 795A, Surbiton KT5 8YB, United Kingdom.**

Or check your local bookshop – available on special order if they are out of stock (quote the ISBN number listed above).

O'Neill faces a nightmare from his past

STARGATE SG·1

A MATTER OF HONOR
Book One
Sally Malcolm
Based on the hit television series developed by
Brad Wright and Jonathan Glassner

Series number: SG1-3

# STARGATE SG-1: A MATTER OF HONOR

**Part one of two parts
by Sally Malcolm**
Price: $7.95 US | $9.95 Canada | £6.99 UK
ISBN-10: 0-9547343-2-7
ISBN-13: 978-0-9547343-2-9

Five years after Major Henry Boyd and his team, SG-10, were trapped on the edge of a black hole, Colonel Jack O'Neill discovers a device that could bring them home.

But it's owned by the Kinahhi, an advanced and paranoid people, besieged by a ruthless foe. Unwilling to share the technology, the Kinahhi are pursuing their own agenda in the negotiations with Earth's diplomatic delegation. Maneuvering through a maze of tyranny, terrorism and deceit, Dr. Daniel Jackson, Major Samantha Carter and Teal'c unravel a startling truth—a revelation that throws the team into chaos and forces O'Neill to face a nightmare he is determined to forget.

Resolved to rescue Boyd, O'Neill marches back into the hell he swore never to revisit. Only this time, he's taking SG-1 with him...

**Order your copy directly from the publisher today by going to www.stargatenovels.com or send a check or money order made payable to "Fandemonium" to:**

**USA orders:** **$10.82 ($7.95 + $2.87 P&P). Send payment to: Fandemonium Books, PO Box 2178, Decatur, GA 30031-2178.**

**UK orders:** **£8.30 (£6.99 + £1.31 P&P). Rest of the World orders:** **£9.70 (£6.99 + £2.71 P&P). Send payment to: Fandemonium Books, PO Box 795A, Surbiton KT5 8YB, United Kingdom.**

Or check your local bookshop – available on special order if they are out of stock (quote the ISBN number listed above).

# STARGATE SG-1: THE COST OF HONOR

**Part two of two parts
by Sally Malcolm**
Price: $7.95 US | $9.95 Canada |
£6.99 UK
ISBN-10: 0-9547343-4-3
ISBN-13: 978-0-9547343-4-3

In the action-packed sequel to *A Matter of Honor*, SG-1 embark on a desperate mission to save SG-10 from the edge of a black hole. But the price of heroism may be more than they can pay...

Returning to Stargate Command, Colonel Jack O'Neill and his team find more has changed in their absence than they had expected. Nonetheless, O'Neill is determined to face the consequences of their unauthorized activities, only to discover the penalty is far worse than anything he could have imagined.

With the fate of Colonel O'Neill and Major Samantha Carter unknown, and the very survival of the SGC threatened, Dr. Daniel Jackson and Teal'c mount a rescue mission to free their team-mates and reclaim the SGC. Yet returning to the Kinahhi homeworld, they learn a startling truth about its ancient foe. And uncover a horrifying secret...

# STARGATE SG-1: SACRIFICE MOON

Terror stalks the team at night

STARGATE SG·1

SACRIFICE MOON
Julie Fortune

Based on the hit television series developed by
Brad Wright and Jonathan Glassner

Series number: SG1-2

**By Julie Fortune**
Price: $7.95 US | $9.95 Canada |
£6.99 UK
ISBN-10: 0-9547343-1-9
ISBN-13: 978-0-9547343-1-2

*Sacrifice Moon* follows the newly commissioned SG-1 on their first mission through the Stargate.

Their destination is Chalcis, a peaceful society at the heart of the Helos Confederacy of planets. But Chalcis harbors a dark secret, one that pitches SG-1 into a world of bloody chaos, betrayal and madness. Battling to escape the living nightmare, Dr. Daniel Jackson and Captain Samantha Carter soon begin to realize that more than their lives are at stake. They are fighting for their very souls.

But while Col Jack O'Neill and Teal'c struggle to keep the team together, Daniel is hatching a desperate plan that will test SG-1's fledgling bonds of trust and friendship to the limit…

# STARGATE SG-1: TRIAL BY FIRE

**By Sabine C. Bauer**
Price: $7.95 US | $9.95 Canada |
£6.99 UK
ISBN-10: 0-9547343-0-0
ISBN-13: 978-0-9547343-0-5

*Trial by Fire* follows the team as they embark on a mission to Tyros, an ancient society teetering on the brink of war.

A pious people, the Tyreans are devoted to the Canaanite deity, Meleq. When their spiritual leader is savagely murdered during a mission of peace, they beg SG-1 for help against their sworn enemies, the Phrygians.

Initially reluctant to get involved, the team has no choice when Colonel Jack O'Neill is abducted. O'Neill soon discovers his only hope of escape is to join the ruthless Phrygians — if he can survive their barbaric initiation rite.

As Major Samantha Carter, Dr. Daniel Jackson and Teal'c race to his rescue, they find themselves embroiled in a war of shifting allegiances, where truth has many shades and nothing is as it seems.

And, unbeknownst to them all, an old enemy is hiding in the shadows…

**Order your copy directly from the publisher today by going to www.stargatenovels.com or send a check or money order made payable to "Fandemonium" to:**

**USA orders:** $10.82 ($7.95 + $2.87 P&P). Send payment to: Fandemonium Books, PO Box 2178, Decatur, GA 30031-2178.

**UK orders:** £8.30 (£6.99 + £1.31 P&P). **Rest of the World orders:** £9.70 (£6.99 + £2.71 P&P). Send payment to: Fandemonium Books, PO Box 795A, Surbiton KT5 8YB, United Kingdom.

Or check your local bookshop – available on special order if they are out of stock (quote the ISBN number listed above).